Mr. Rebound

TAYLOR KOLEBER

CHAMPAGNE BOOK GROUP

Mr. Rebound

Published by Champagne Book Group
2373 NE Evergreen Avenue, Albany OR 97321 U.S.A.

~~~

First Edition 2022

pISBN: 978-1-77155-457-2

Cover Art by Melody Pond

www.champagnebooks.com

Version_1

For my wife, my children, my family—and for you, the reader. I couldn't have done any of this without you.

Chapter One

Tonight was an ice water night.

Garrett Reid never ordered an actual drink until he knew what his contact would be drinking, whereupon he could order to complement. Until then, he would sip on ice water—mineral, if they had it—and wait.

His arena of choice was The Minefield, a ritzy, upscale joint in Manhattan with a terrible name trying to straddle the fences of wine bar, nightclub, and general social hotspot, to varying degrees of success. He enjoyed the vibe, if only because it forced people to know why they wanted to be in The Minefield before they came. The place deterred the casual bar-hopper. Everybody who walked through the double glass doors had a purpose, and he was no exception.

Drying his trembling fingers on the napkin that came with his woefully non-alcoholic drink, he fought to keep his stylus steady as he prepared a new document. The jitters would return when the contact arrived—never mind meeting the client for the first time—but the point remained the same. After years of charming women as Mr. Rebound, he still suffered from nerves.

It was humbling and refreshing, in a way. The jitters kept him from getting too cocky.

A woman hovered by the leather couch opposite him, across the table. She was short, with sharp blue eyes and high cheekbones. Garrett frowned as she hesitated. They exchanged a moment of tentative eye contact like a silent handshake. Straight blonde hair framed only the left side of her head. The right side had been buzzed down to a fine peach fuzz. It was alternative, striking, and highlighted the smooth curve of her neck, tempting the eyes and lips of any man who might dare to venture. It worked for her.

"Are you, uh…" She looked down at the luminescent screen of her phone. Even in the first hopeful words, her London-based accent was unmistakable, protruding through the waves of music and chatter like a buoy.

Garrett stood, buttoned his suit jacket—manners were manners—and offered his hand.

"Garrett Reid," he said, all class. If he was smooth, if he betrayed no sense of nerves, the contact would relax. If the contact relaxed, he did too. Nervousness would only get in the way. "You'd be Penny?"

"Yes!" She seized his hand in both of hers, giving a vigorous shake. She had a hell of a grip. Calluses on her fingertips scraped against his hands. Guitar player. She had an alt-rock feel about her as it was. Her eyes shone, even in the dim light, as creases erupted across an earnest forehead. "It's so good to meet you."

"Likewise." He smiled, released her from the shake, and gestured to the couch opposite him. "Always nice to make a new acquaintance."

She hemmed and hawed over where on the couch she ought to sit, as though he were a foreign dignitary she was terrified of offending. He gestured, and a nervous laugh burst from her as she planted herself across from him. Her gaze swept their surroundings. He simply watched her and fought to stop her paranoia infecting him.

"So," he said. Her gaze darted back to him as he continued. "I understand you're looking to help out a friend."

Again, she nodded. The woman was a crawling hive of bees under the surface. Perhaps she played speed metal. It would explain the energy and calluses on her fingertips.

"Yes." Her movements were tight. Flinching. Her gaze wouldn't stay in one place. "Yeah, um…yeah, I am. Sorry. I've never done anything like this before."

"I should hope not." He kept his smile in place. "I'm kind of a unique market. I don't know how I'd handle competition."

"Right. Right. Sorry." She fiddled with a bulging diamond ring on her left hand.

He spotted the gleam from across the table. No matching band to make it permanent yet. Just engaged, then.

"This just feels…weird, y'know? Like I'm meeting a hooker. Or secretly organizing a hit." She paused, staring at him with wide eyes. "You're not actually a hitman, are you? Because I've read books where—"

"First you call me a prostitute, and now I'm an assassin?" He kept his tone light, playful. The "hooker" claim stung more than the "hitman" claim, but he kept his expression unchanged. It wasn't the first time he'd been called such. It wouldn't be the last. "I never knew I was so busy."

Panic flashed across her face, her throat bobbing, hidden only moments later by a mask of pure British stoicism. "I'm sorry." Diplomatic to a fault. "I never meant to offend. I just—if your services are really what you offer, then I need your help. I mean, Charlotte said you did wonders with her…"

Charlotte. The last girl he'd helped. A D3 release on a standard contract yielding an immediate referral in Penny. Garrett waved away the praise with a modest smile. "I do what I can."

A waiter in a white suit, drawn by the appearance of new customers, turned to the lady first.

Garrett stole a sip of his ice water as she ordered a gin and tonic. He'd halfway expected a vodka martini or a straight-up beer for her.

"Johnnie Walker Black," he said to the waiter. "On the rocks, please." No need to make it neat until he knew whether the contact would yield a serviceable client. Once he did, he might enjoy a deeper glass.

"Fancy." Penny raised her trim eyebrows. "Also, not helping your 'I'm not a hitman' claim." She laughed, a breathless and reflexive burst of sound, before exhaling and settling back into her chair. If she was relaxed, her still-clenched hands told another story.

He gave her the best placating smile he could muster. "You're fine. Don't worry—Charlotte told you the truth. I'm a professional rebound dater…but if you want to go by what I write on my tax returns, then I'm an 'independent temporary recruitment specialist for a home business.' Apparently, spinning it like that brings in a shocking amount of tax-deductible expenses." He scoffed, shaking his head in disbelief. "Accountants are money wizards."

She nodded, grimacing as she accepted her gin and tonic from the waiter. "See, you're lucky. I don't make anywhere near enough to need an accountant. I'm not a homeowner. There's no mortgage attached to this." She gestured to herself before swigging her drink. "I make rent on my honestly-pretty-crappy apartment with my roommate in Hillcrest, and I work full-time at a Starbucks while I intern at a firm for patent and copyright law."

Garrett plucked his scotch from the circular table between them, hesitating with the glass in the air. "One of those places where 'intern' means 'unpaid legal slave labor?'"

Penny snorted in derision and tapped her glass against his in a toast of commiseration. "I see you're familiar with the term." Before she'd taken a decent drink, she lowered the glass from her lips. The "foreplay" of their interaction was ending. "Why are you getting to know *me*? Shouldn't you be asking about my friend, Arianne? The one I need you to rebound-date?"

"Part of the screening process," he said. "Sometimes women will pretend to be the contact when they're the client. I had to make sure you weren't trying to pull one over on me."

Penny nodded again, drawing a tongue over her teeth. "I could see that."

"In addition..." He forced her to wait, drawing long and slow from his scotch. No need to drain the glass yet. He'd only do that when he had a vocal point to make and needed to draw emphasis to the fact. Tiny touches were the most powerful. "I want to make sure you're a good friend to Arianne. You'll have as much a part to play in the healing process as I will."

She tilted her head, shifting the wave of blonde hair and drawing attention to the creamy curve of her neck as she masked herself with a contemplative look.

He wasn't fooled.

"Very well," she said. "What do I need to tell you about her?"

The job had begun.

He plucked his stylus and set his phone flat on the table. It didn't matter if she saw the screen. He wrote in shorthand. "Start with the basics, and we'll move forward from there."

"Her name is Arianne Reynolds, but she prefers to be called Ari. Only family and close friends get to call her by her whole name. It's like a rite of passage."

He scribbled accordingly. "Tell me about the guy. Her last ex."

"Lucas Thompson. The guy's an absolute bastard." Her face was stony, her voice flat.

"Broke up because..." Garrett gestured with his stylus in a swirling motion, as though stirring the air, trying to spur her on.

"Because he couldn't keep it in his pants, and he had to go and cheat on her." Disgust slipped into her voice like a layer of oil on water. She puckered her mouth before sipping at her drink. "They'd only been together for two months—which is a record for Arianne. She doesn't stay with guys for long."

There was the first red flag. There would probably be several more before they were done. Each would have to be addressed in turn. "Why did he cheat on her?"

"Because he's never happy with what's in front of him." She scoffed, beckoning to the white-suited waiter and ordering a refill on her drink to take the edge off her apparent rising anger. "And the girl he cheated with is a horrible human being."

"Do we know who he cheated with?" Knowing the "who" behind the breakup before he went in would, in his experience, improve his chances of a successful rebound by at least forty-five percent—and if the "who" was a close friend or family member, ninety percent.

She was quick to shake her head. "No clue."

He didn't return the gesture. People didn't cheat simply "because." In his experience, both the people involved and those close to them were too biased to peel back the layers and find the core issue. But, Penny had refused to offer up another reason, and so he made a note and moved on. "Why doesn't Ari stay with guys for long?"

Penny paused, licking her lips as she fidgeted.

He'd hit pay dirt.

"It's more to do with Arianne and less to do with the guys. They can't really handle her. That's why she's been cheated on before." A glance down at her nails. Fleeting eye contact at best.

Garrett wrote without looking away. *Penny nervous on subject of cheating? Nervous about Ari?* "Cheated on... apart from Lucas?"

"He was the third one." Penny quaffed from her drink before she shrugged a little too nonchalantly for Garrett's liking. "It's happened before. It'll probably happen again. Whatever, right?"

He kept his expression neutral. Three times cuckolded was a hell of a red flag from the get-go—as was her sudden casual shift.

"So, guys can't 'handle' her. Is she temperamental?" A neutral word he often used in place of "freaking nuts."

Penny made an "ehhh" sort of sound, waggling one hand as though balancing a scale. "A bit? It's not like she's off her rocker. She likes a challenge, you know? She's just a lot to handle overall."

He leaned back as the waiter slipped between them, delivering the second drink. "How so?"

"Well, for starters, she's tall." She sipped her new gin and tonic before setting it on the table and lifting her hand as far above her head as she could. "Like... ungodly tall."

"And she keeps dating guys who can't handle her being tall?" He'd heard pettier reasons for relationships to fail—one former client had been dumped for never using the right conjugation of "your" in a text message. It was still petty by anyone's standards, but not unheard of in his profession.

"Well, she says she'd date a taller guy in a heartbeat. We just... haven't been able to find one yet." Penny snickered. "Outside of somehow landing a guy from the NBA."

He cleared his throat. "So, how tall are we talking?"

He was five foot ten, which he considered to be a perfectly respectable height. Daniel Craig was five foot ten. If James Bond could be under six foot, then so could he. Besides, if occasion called, Garrett was more than willing to wear rises in his shoes to put him up to the hallowed ground of six foot even. If Ari was truly "ungodly tall" as Penny claimed, it was enough for him to picture a veritable Amazon who spent more time on the court than anywhere else.

Horrible flashbacks to his last athletic client clawed at the back of his mind. To be fair, she'd been an extreme-sports junkie, but it didn't save him from a nasty ice-climbing accident that broke his leg in two places. It gave him a spectacular scar, and it made for a great conversation piece with future clients, but it didn't mean he wanted another.

"I don't know her exact measurement." Penny raised an eyebrow as she sized him up. "But pretty sure you'd be eye level with, like, her collarbone. Maybe."

He pursed his lips, jotting a note in his phone and praying Penny was exaggerating. It would be a first for him, but it would hardly stop him. It did give Lucas's predicament a tiny bit more understanding—not sympathy, not by a longshot, but understanding. Most guys liked to entertain fantasies of being the protector in the relationship. Those fantasies tended to fizzle when his partner could physically look down on him.

"Athletic?" Garrett spun the stylus between his fingers and fought the urge not to cross them for luck.

"You'd think so, but not really." Penny tossed her head back, downing her drink with a final gulp. "She did cross-country in high school, but she was forced to drop out." She grimaced, gesturing to her chest and holding her cupped hands a shocking distance away.

His eyebrows rose. "You're kidding."

"Welcome to 'Arianne 101.'" Penny sniffed. "She doesn't do basketball or volleyball or netball or any of the 'balls, either."

The way the contact talked about the client often told Garrett as much about his upcoming job as the actual information itself. He remained placid, filing away the acidic undercurrent of her voice in his mind. "What does Ari do for a living?"

"Photography. Weddings, mostly. She owns and operates her own studio in Whitestone." She waved a hand, dismissive. "It's small, but she keeps it going."

Independent business owner. Good to know. He scribbled. "Tell me more about Lucas. What kind of guy was he? Besides being a bastard, I mean."

"Well…" She huffed, shifting her jaw, and wouldn't meet his eyes. "He's a dreamy-looking guy. Bit taller than you. Like…six-one, I think? I'm not sure. He's pretentious, though. Spends tons of time at art galleries and exhibits and literature festivals and all that. He always does this thing where he shows off his knowledge and expects you to be able to keep up, then he constantly takes pride in making you think you aren't as cultured as he is when you can't."

Her face fell. Her gaze swept over the table as though examining the shattered pieces of Lucas's reputation, struggling to find a redeeming quality. "But he's a really sweet guy, once you get to know him. Always knows these new places to eat. Fusion cooking and stuff like that. Very up-to-date."

More shorthand. "He and Ari met…?"

"At a wedding." She nodded. "She was the photographer. He was one of the groomsmen."

Garrett grunted in confirmation as he added secondary notes to a category under his notes. Something was missing. He needed more.

"I need you to give me the full story, here." He turned his best steely gaze onto her. "How did Ari find out Lucas was cheating on her?"

A single moment of hesitation.

Her gaze, involuntary, broke contact and fled to the right.

A frozen moment in her posture.

"He told her." Her hands knotted in her lap. Her throat convulsed as she swallowed. "All him. He—well, to hear Arianne tell it, at least—I wasn't there, of course, but—she said *he* said he'd met somebody else. Apparently, to hear her tell it—as in, to hear her hear *him* tell it, of course—working off secondhand information and all—she was perfect for him, and they'd done it together sober, and that was how he knew he didn't want Arianne anymore. Then they fought, and he dumped her." The words tumbled out in a rush, like survivors crawling over each other to be the first out of a burning building.

Garrett remained still, studying her.

"What?" She feigned an innocent shrug. "It's the truth."

He didn't say anything at first, choosing instead to dart his stylus across the screen of his phone. *Penny lied about Lucas Cheat Story. Why?* "Do we know who Lucas cheated with?"

"No." She shook her head. "There's no way he told Arianne who it was, or she would have gone after her and probably punched her lights out. I know I said she wasn't freaking nuts, but she's not above revenge."

Garrett nodded, wrote a question mark next to a category under "third party," and moved on. "Known allergies?"

"Opiates." Penny lifted the toothpick from her empty drink and tongued an olive into her mouth. "I was there when she had her wisdom teeth out. They put her on hydrocodone, and she nearly had to be hospitalized. Couldn't even keep fluids down. The best she can handle for painkillers is some Tylenol, otherwise she's in for a rough time."

"Are those the only drugs she uses? Nothing else prescription or recreational?" He tightened his grip on his stylus.

Penny frowned. "Can I ask why?"

If anything were going to trip up his chance for a new client, it would be his own inadequacies. When he did speak, he kept his voice borderline apologetic, without judgment or guile. "I'm a professional rebound dater, not a psychiatrist. I'm not qualified to handle medication for mental issues or recovery from illegal drugs."

She made a little "o" with her mouth. "I mean… Arianne did try pot once. She hated how badly it gave her the munchies. She also burned through a roll and a half of film on a vintage camera taking pictures of old fruit in her rubbish bin, so she pretty much hates all drugs now. That's all I know."

He snorted with laughter. "Anything else?"

"She's a carnivore." Penny gave a knowing smile, plump lips parting in mischief. "Take her to a vegan place and she'll probably eat you instead of the food."

He laughed again. Truth be told, even for all the red flags, Ari sounded more and more like a pleasure to be around. At worst, he'd have a new scar to show for his efforts. It wouldn't be the first, or even the fifth.

"How fast would you say she moves in a relationship?" This was key. So often, relationships crashed and burned because people moved at different speeds than their partners. Then came miscommunication, which led to misunderstandings, which led to flames—literally, in the past case of Courtney Hazleroth. He shuddered before focusing once more.

"Depends on the guy." Penny gave a wry grin. "If she thinks he's hot but she doesn't see a future with him, she'll probably try and sleep with him after the second or third date then never call him again."

Amazonian tall, back-breaking rack, and moved fast in bed. He wondered if this was an elaborate prank or if Ari was as exaggerated as Penny made her out to be. "What if she thinks there is a future with him?"

Laughter and cocktails slurred her words. "Then she's going to pounce on him the first night." She shook her head. "And every night she can after that."

Even if Ari was half as sexually voracious as Penny described, Ari seemed to be placing too much emphasis in a relationship on sexual pleasures, likely trying to push down the emotional aftershock that accompanied them. He frowned and wrote, *High sexual activity suggestive of emotional insecurity?"* Maybe correct. Maybe not. Either way, one thing was for certain—if he were going to help her adjust to a life of regular healthy dating, sex would have to be off the table for as long as possible.

It sounded, also, like she was used to hearing guys say "yes" to her... which meant a prescribed dose of "no" would be both productive and volatile.

"Um..." He stared at his phone's glowing screen. "I think that's about all I need to get started. What's the name of her wedding studio?"

Penny paused halfway through wrapping her lips around another olive. "Eternal Bride Photography. I might have her business card here somewhere..."

After a moment of fishing in an oversized leather purse, Penny withdrew an eggshell card with black flowery cursive print and handed it over. Garrett took a photo of both sides and shot the messages through to David Kowalski, his tech guy and man-in-the-chair, for him to start his best cyber-stalking work.

"Perfect." Garrett swilled the last of his scotch on the rocks and stood.

She followed suit. "So, this means you'll do it, right?" A nervous smile tugged at the corners of her mouth; hesitant, even disbelieving, like a desert wanderer regarding a mirage.

He smiled, his voice Zen-like in its calm as he said, "Yes, Penny. I'll do it."

"Oh, thank you." Her body deflated, as though exhaling all at once, only to inhale a manic joy as she scooted to the edge of her seat and fumbled with her purse. "How's this work? Do I sign a contract in blood or something?" She tried to laugh. It came out forced and a touch too loud.

"I mean...I won't stop you, if you really want to, but you could just sign this in ink." With a flourish, he withdrew a folded piece of paper and a silver pen from his jacket pocket. "It agrees you will reimburse me for up to seventy-five percent of all dates with the client—in this case, Arianne Reynolds—depending on the duration and expense, and you'll cover a hundred percent of all uninsured hospital visits incurred during the process of her rebound."

"In addition to a thousand-dollar advance to exclusively secure your services and a four-hundred-dollar deposit for every date until services are completed?" sputtered Penny, aghast as she looked over the contract. "You can't be serious!"

"I'm not made of money." He shook his head. "This is my living. I get you're not rolling in dough either, but these are my terms. You're not under any obligation to agree to them."

Her chest heaved as she seemed to struggle under the weight of the expectations before her. "Anything else?" She pouted.

He pulled a spare copy of the contract from a separate pocket and handed it to her. "I'll let you read the fine print on your own, but I need to point out this bit here with Article C—a non-disclosure agreement. Secrecy is paramount to my success. As soon as my clients find out I'm paid to be there, suddenly all the help I'm giving them makes them feel like a project, not a person. Nobody likes that. It hamstrings my work."

He pointed to the table. "You do not—do *not*—tell Ari I am being paid to help her rebound. Any disclosure as to my career or the nature of my services will place you liable for an upfront payment of all projected costs with a three-hundred percent interest rate. Also, depending on how badly the shit hits the fan from you breaking this NDA, I may just drag you through court and sue your ass off on top of it all."

A scowl darkened her face. Her mouth opened as if to explain exactly what obligations he could fulfill with the business end of a nail gun, only to fall silent a moment later as her gaze dropped.

"Fine." She grabbed the pen and signed in resignation. "You win."

The look on her face said it all. There was no selfish sense of financial preservation motivating her to fill out her credit card information. There wasn't even the noble virtue of altruism.

This was guilt.

Penny lied about Lucas Cheat Story. Penny cheated.

"If it helps…" Garrett spoke without looking up, checking her information on the contract. "On the chance my services do not help Ari, you're entitled to an eighty-percent refund on all deposits and reimbursements."

"And what are the odds of that?" she said flatly.

He spun the silver pen between his fingers with a flourish. Only a bit of pride crept into his voice, but it still crept in, nonetheless. "Given my prior success rate? About six-point-three percent. But your friend will be better and happier than ever, and it'll all be thanks to you."

With careful deliberation, he placed Penny's signed contract back in the same pocket. Experience had dictated he create two versions of a contract based on the interview process—which, in mock business fashion, he dubbed the standard and premium contracts. The standard was given to most contacts who passed the interview process without either hitch or hiccup. The standard was much more forgiving and allowed discussion of the process of rebounding and—most importantly—referrals. The standard was for open-and-shut rebounds which were likely to generate further business.

The premium contracts were for people like Penny. People whose motives were shaded, people whose prospects were shaky or who were withholding information. People who could tarnish his reputation or damage his career. People who would create such a nightmarish shitshow of dating that he would shudder at the thought of them.

People like Courtney Hazleroth.

Premium contracts required sensitivity and delicacy to fulfill. They were, by experience, seventy-five percent less likely to yield a serviceable referral, and so were more expensive.

He smiled at Penny, placing a twenty on the table next to the empty glass.

"Next round is on me." He paused to shake her hand before buttoning his suit coat and heading for the door.

He was on the job.

Chapter Two

In her studio, Arianne Reynolds did her absolute best to humor the twitterpated couple who had booked her for their pre-divorce burning material. Her intern, Zoey, a perpetually happy blonde on the heavier side, with a salon blowout job that gave her hair ridiculous volume, hovered by her elbow and exuded all the charisma Ari couldn't muster if her job depended on it—and the worst part was, it did. Eternal Bride Photography was a small place, part of a strip mall, sandwiched between a bagel shop and an accountant.

Still, Arianne did her absolute best to keep the screaming within the confines of her own head. She couldn't screw up a chance at income. Not if she wanted to keep the fledgling studio's doors open and keep her friends employed.

"We found you guys on Pinterest," said the woman. "We *loved* the shoot you did with that couple in Vermont."

Arianne smiled through her teeth at the woman—the plainly named Suzanne Smith—and tried to hide the twitch in her eye. "I wasn't aware those prints had been lifted from my portfolio, but I suppose I'll have to thank the internet for the free exposure."

"Do you think you could do something similar with ours?" said the man—the un-plainly named Eugene Bucklefuster.

His hands were skinny, nails polished and gleaming as bright as Suzanne's. They'd probably had a mani-pedi as a couple. Her stomach flopped as he gesticulated, eager, and beamed at the love of his life clinging to his forearm.

"We were thinking kind of a 'Gatsby in the countryside' aesthetic—y'know, 'roaring twenties meets the Antebellum' thing." He shimmied, holding out his hands as though she were supposed to be floored by the genius of it.

Arianne pasted on the kind of closed-lipped grimace that spoke more to a dealing with a root canal than encouraging his display.

"I'm not your planner, I'm just the photographer," she reminded him. Eugene laughed too loudly, waving his dainty hands as Suzanne nudged him and giggled about how he was "always so enthusiastic" and "that was what she loved about him."

Zoey piped up by her elbow. "We can guarantee Eternal Bride Photography will capture your dream-come-true however you desire." Sunshine dripped from every word, and her toothy smile was as genuine as Arianne's was not. "Here—if you'd like, I can go over some of our more extensive photo and videographing packages..."

Arianne's heart tugged inside her as her intern/secretary/new best friend led them to a glossy flipbook of their services. The blonde was just so...genuine. Nice. Kind. *Patient*. Honestly, she was half the reason the studio was keeping its chin above water. A financial life preserver in a cream pantsuit.

For better or worse, anyway.

Moments later, the happy couple fiddled with a credit card as Zoey rang them up, and Arianne gave a mental cheer. It even spread to her face as she beamed down at them both. Whatever she felt about displays of cheesy romantic affection right in front of her face, the thrill of a financial infusion helped offset it...mostly.

"We can't wait to see you again," said Eugene.

"We bought the full care package," said his fiancée. "Save-the-Date photos, rehearsal dinner, wedding, videography, everything!"

The woman bounced on the spot and grabbed the side of her fiancé's jaw with one hand, bringing his cheek close for a wild kiss. Eugene nudged her and whispered something Arianne didn't care to hear. Suzanne did the same. Everyone but her—including Zoey—burst out laughing.

Arianne wiped the sweat from her palms down the sides of her frustratingly high-water suit pants. The couple made their way toward the single glass door with the push bar that constituted the entrance/exit to her studio.

"Take care," she said, keeping up appearances. "We're so excited to be part of your special day."

As soon as the glass door closed, the bell dinged in relief. Arianne stared through the Windex streaks to the parking lot outside as her shoulders sank. Wedding photography paid the bills, but it didn't fulfill—and the only reason she'd lowered her standards even *this* far was because doing portraiture at a department store studio would have been like gargling drain cleaner for her. There, standing in the mouth of the best bastard child of artistic compromise she'd ever conceived, she chewed on the same tired idea of letting the stupid studio die.

But, if she did, the void of unemployment and the vise of mounting bills would strangle whatever muse she could pin down before she could do anything about it. It had once, pre-Eternal Bride. She couldn't do it again.

Behind her, Zoey typed at a keyboard and cheered, her triumphant voice saving Arianne from a full-blown melancholy. "One Deluxe Platinum Wedding Package booked for Suzanne and Eugene Bucklefuster."

Arianne snorted with laughter at the names, even as cynicism crept into the tail end of her mirth. How any woman could willingly let herself become a "Bucklefuster" was beyond her comprehension. "Well, at least they'll make good use of the stationary when they're getting div—"

She bit down on the "d" word at Zoey's look. Arianne's bitterness was getting the best of her—as if it hadn't been for weeks. Her shoulders sank. "Sorry. Just..."

"It's all right." The sunny blonde slipped out from behind the desk and gave Arianne a soft side-hug. "You're a great photographer, Ari. Anybody can see that as soon as they see your work. It's just... maybe..."

"I know, I have to work on the whole 'people-pleasing' thing." Her voice was razor-thin, slipping between clenched teeth, immediately accompanied by a sharp pang of guilt.

It was hardly Zoey's fault Arianne was stuck doing the lowest-common-denominator of her passion to pay the bills. It certainly wasn't her fault every saccharine, diabetes-inducing couple that strolled in reminded Arianne of what she'd nearly had—what her fingertips had brushed at with *him*—and yo-yoed her between either wanting to vomit or commit homicide. Nor was it Zoey's fault Arianne had to keep the "everything's wonderful and we're happy to assist you" mask stapled on her face for eight hours a day without screaming.

It was fortunate, at least, that Sierra, her assistant photographer, had to take a sick day today. That meant one day's pay Arianne could devote to keeping the lights on.

"I'm just—I'm glad you're here, Zoey." Fatigue hung on every word as Arianne hugged her intern—and friend—sidelong in return. "You cover my ass in ways I can't even begin to mention. Seriously. Thank you."

Zoey wheezed at Arianne's embrace, coughing out a laugh as she was released. "Don't sell yourself short. You're not *that* much of a bitch." She made a face, as though the swear word sat uncomfortably on her tongue, but it was clear in an instant she'd resorted to try it to put a smile on her employer's face.

Arianne placed a hand atop her chest in mock offense. "*Moi?* Why, perish the thought."

The bell dinged, heralding a blast of spring air as the door swung open.

Arianne pinched the bridge of her nose before she pasted yet another people-pleasing expression on her face. *Keep it together, girl. This is another paying customer. This is a good thing. Just a few more hours.* Her eyebrows rose, however, at the sight of her half-head-shaven, diminutive roommate.

"Oh, good." Penny braced herself on the counter, breathless and British and practically buzzing on the spot. It was like someone had hooked her up to a car battery. "You're still here."

"Well, I do work here, pintsize." Arianne glanced away, as though she could see through the walls of her fledgling studio to the pile of gutted envelopes in her desk drawer. *For the moment, anyway.* "What's up?"

"Close up shop." The words came as a splash of cold water. "You're going out tonight."

Arianne burst out laughing.

"No, seriously." Penny's voice was insistent, almost desperate. "You've got a blind date tonight. I've set everything up, but you need to close up now if you're going to get ready and get there on time."

Arianne's mouth hung open. She blinked furiously, as though a mosquito were pulling fly-bys with her eyelashes. Penny, more than any other person alive, knew how the break-up had gone for her. She'd been there for every evening mood swing. Every hated tear that slid out when Arianne didn't want it to. The revenge-lingerie-shopping-spree. This had to be some kind of prank.

"Funny." Her mirth flattened.

"I'm not joking, Arianne. I've been sitting on this for four days now, and I had to bend over backward to make this work, and you're not messing it up, understood?" Penny crossed her arms and wore a grimace so thin it could have disappeared in the seams of the carpet. "Now, do like all you bloody Americans keep saying and 'suck it up, Buttercup.' This is going to be good for you."

"The hell it is," snapped Arianne. Her heart thumped. Deep breaths. Her hair shifted against her nape as she shook her head in tight, firm denials. "I've had a long day at work already, and it's not over yet. When I get home, I'm not going to turn right back around and doll myself up for some greasy-haired mouth-breather you picked out of a hat. I'm putting on sweats, eating a pint of ice cream, and watching Netflix until

I crash. The answer is 'no.'"

Her throat tightened. The answer was "no." Obviously. It had only been two weeks and three days since she'd had her heart ripped out and eviscerated in front of her. That wasn't even half the time she still needed.

Zoey's tentative voice pricked her ears from behind. "I mean… not that it's any of my business…"

Arianne's eye twitched.

"…but maybe you should try it?"

The suggestion was an emotional mule-kick to her back. Zoey was the sunshine-y saver-of-her-financial-ass, but she was about as confrontational as a guppy. Trying to hide her bobbing throat, Arianne's gaze darted between the now-unified front. "What is this, a mutiny on behalf of my love life?"

Zoey shrugged. "Well, you *have* been super stressed at work."

No shit, Arianne seethed. *I got cheated on and dumped by a guy I actually liked. Let's see you handle it gracefully.*

Zoey pressed onward with the same sort of frustratingly genuine selflessness that charity workers and orphan-adopters must have had. "I can man the phones until closing and swing by after to drop the keys off, if you like? We don't have any appointments for the rest of the afternoon, either so…maybe try it? It could be a good way to relax."

"Clearly, you don't understand the nature of blind dates as they relate to stress." Arianne's voice was flat, dull, but the smile on her intern's face was just so beatific and sympathetic. Not in the "aww, you poor thing" way, but in the "I care about you and want to at least do what I can to make your life a little less shitty" way.

The silence stretched in the lobby, as though the air itself were hanging on the words unspoken.

It wasn't like she owed either of them a thing. But, well…she did have to eat, and the best kind of food was "free." There wasn't anything saying she ever had to see this asshole again—and he *would* be an asshole. She had no doubt. But a one-time date—and hell, a one-night-stand—did have its orgasmic benefits, fleeting as they were. Maybe the final straw was less to do with the idea of spending the rest of the night with a stranger and more to do with the harsh truth that if she had to deal with even one more stupid-in-love couple that evening, she was likely to shriek and throttle them. What had happened to her would happen to them. Every time. Inevitably and unstoppably, and they were utter goddamn *morons* if they thought otherwise. Hell, she'd nearly burst out with a tirade in the same vein at Suzanne and Eugene.

Arianne threw up her hands and huffed a sigh in Penny's

direction. "Fine. I'll go on the stupid fricking date. Give me ten to wrap up some paperwork and I'll meet you at home."

Penny's shoulders relaxed. "You won't regret this, Arianne." She was already about-facing and leaving to the death knell of the brass bell. "I promise you."

"Yeah, yeah," Arianne grumbled.

Silence rang for a moment more before she sighed and strode toward her personal office to start shutting things down and locking up.

"Just try to relax and have a good time?" prompted Zoey, from behind the desk. "And if everything goes horribly wrong, you can blame me."

Arianne snorted. "I already blame you."

~ * ~

Half an hour later, Arianne took barely a moment to close her apartment door behind her before turning and slugging her British roommate in the shoulder.

"Ow!" Penny whined, winding her arm.

"That's for setting me up on a blind date without telling me." Arianne gave her a conciliatory squeeze, regardless. "Where am I meeting this poor guy, anyway?"

She stalked through the hallway and around the corner to the bathroom before she paused. Leaning back around the corner, she narrowed her eyes at Penny, who was still fumbling with her coat by the front door. "It *is* a guy, right? Because I know I joke about it, but I don't swing—"

"For God's sake, Arianne." Penny threw up her hands. "*Yes.* You're meeting *him* at *Le Filou* at eight. Upper West Side, so get a move on if you want to beat traffic."

She scoffed. "French dining in Manhattan? Geez. What's he do for a living?"

"By the end of the night, hopefully you." Her voice was almost cryptically neutral.

Arianne snorted with laughter, tugging open the bathroom door. "He should be so lucky," were the last words she graced Penny with before the door clicked shut.

In the safety of the bathroom, under the white noise of the shower, she heaved a sigh and stared herself down in the mirror. Maybe a night out on somebody else's dime wouldn't be so bad. At the very least, a quality dinner would do her better than whatever microwaveable leftovers she'd been planning on dishing up later that evening. And sure, maybe she'd have to spend it in the company of an asshole, but that was what alcohol was for. A good wine-soaked punch to the brain and a romp in the sheets with someone whose name she'd forget by the morning and maybe, *maybe*, she'd be able to keep on washing the taste of heartbreak out of her mind.

She'd always been quick in the shower. Even if she had to wash her hair *and* shave, she could still leave herself silky smooth and whistle-worthy in a matter of minutes. It was a skill that had come with a high school career of cross country. Considering she stood proud at exactly six-foot-five-and-three-quarters, it was—in her entirely non-humble opinion—a skill worth bragging about. Especially when her pixie-like roommate took twice as long to shave half as much leg.

Hair washed, steam wafting, clean-shaven and dripping, Arianne wrapped herself in a pair of maroon towels and fought not to cave against the pressing doubts in the face of the night ahead. Beads of condensation clung to the mirror and rolled down in fat trails, exposing lines of nervous-cheeked reflection as she swept the bathroom door open with a foot.

"I'm going to need more info than this." She fluffed her hair in the towel, fighting to keep her voice steady as she called through the apartment. This wouldn't be another Lucas. This would be an itch to scratch, nothing more. "You vetted him. He's 'attractive' and 'nice.' Does he have a name?"

"Garrett."

"Strike one. How're his nails?" Arianne's attention pricked at the answer as it came wafting through the door, as if born on a cloud of steam.

Penny voice rang back through the apartment. "They're okay. Little rough, but not like he bites them. Like he works with his hands."

It was their unique codification of the male race, exclusive to Arianne and Penelope—if a guy had perfectly manicured fingernails, he was a jerk. True, it made only the most stretched-out sort of logic, but it had yet to fail them in even a single instance.

"Promising." Arianne wiped the mirror dry with her towel and started on her makeup. Eye shadow, eye liner, mascara. "Makes up for the douchey name."

There was a moment of silence from outside the bathroom. She could feel Penny trying not to seethe at her. It brought a selfish smile to Arianne's face. Penny had set her up on a blind date without even running it past her—when she *knew* it was way, way the hell too soon. She deserved the appropriate amount of shit for it.

"He's an independent consultant." Penny, apparently, was refusing to engage. Arianne knew she was listing attributes as she counted on her fingers. "Looks sharp in a suit. Goatee, but nobody's perfect."

"Hmm. Height?" Arianne carefully applied lip liner, eyeing her reflection.

Penny's voice wavered in a thoughtful tone. "I'm not sure. Six foot? Give or take?"

"Passable." She stuck her head through the bathroom doorway, peering across the living room until she caught Penny's eye. "If he makes it through the night, can I count on you to be away until the small hours of the morning?" In fairness, she wouldn't have picked him for a blind date if he was *un*attractive. Even if he was an asshole, Arianne could make do—because, again, alcohol.

"I want you to give this guy a real chance, Arianne," said Penny flatly. "Don't just break him because you can then call it good."

"Why do you care so much?" She finished the last touch of her lipstick, frowning. This was pushy, even for Penny. "It's one blind date. It's not going to go anywhere."

"Not with that attitude," chided Penny. "And I care so much because I'm your friend. Remember? Friends do the things that piss you off but are good for you. That's what makes them friends."

"Nope." Arianne straightened back up and nodded her satisfaction to the mirror, her gaze losing its suspicious glint. "That's what makes you family. Which is also why I get to piss you off."

She didn't mean to grin the way she did. The more info she got, the more a different sort of plan coalesced in her mind. Just because the night wasn't going to go anywhere didn't mean it had to suck.

Not for *her*.

Without hesitating, she crossed to the closet, only vaguely aware of Penny following behind, and selected the articles of her outfit, laying them out with the sort of sacred care a samurai took with his weapons—even if her items of choice were more equivalent to a nuclear bomb than a katana. Her smile widened.

Penny's voice tightened in panic. "Arianne, no."

"Arianne, yes." She raised her chin, defiant.

Her friend paled. "He's going to look like a bloody child next to you."

"Hey, if he's really all that and a bag of *crisps*," she teased with emphasis on the decidedly British saying, "then he should be plenty capable of handling me at my best and jaw-dropping. Besides, we're going to a fancy restaurant, and that means dressing appropriately fancy." She grunted, sucking in her stomach and easing the dress higher before she sat on her mattress and exposed her bare back to her friend. "Zip me up?"

Penny scoffed but seized the zipper to the dress and tugged it up her back as commanded. "Forget looking like a child. He'll think you're going to eat him instead of dinner."

"Thought that was what you wanted." She smirked.

"*Arianne.*" Any trace of goodwill was gone from Penny's expression by this point.

Arianne seized her phone and stuffed it into her purse, checking the time as she rummaged for her keys. It was better this way. Penny couldn't see her already-fading smile. It was the only sign Arianne'd let herself show of the mute, cold bitterness that had re-closed its gin-trap teeth over her heart.

Blind date or no, whoever this "Garrett" was, he'd do the same thing every other guy did—smooth patter, peek at her cleavage when they thought she wouldn't notice, say she wasn't like all the other girls but then treat her the same as everyone else. Dinner, drinks, drunken taxi make-outs, one-night stand, gone by morning. A melancholy song and dance so worn-through her bones ached under the fatigue of it all.

She almost closed the door and turned back around. Getting dolled up was one thing. Crossing the threshold was the point of no return. She'd be committed to a night out.

But she was also starving, showered, and sexy as shit. Maybe she could get through it by smiling through her teeth.

She just had to keep her cards close to her chest and her drinks stronger than usual.

"Don't wait up." She forced her voice to remain casual.

"Keep me posted, love." Penny waggled her phone in the air. "If you need me to bail you out—and yes, I do mean that in the police station sense—give us a ring. I'll come running."

Arianne nodded twice, swallowed once, and ducked wordlessly underneath the door frame.

Chapter Three

Garrett sipped his water, his gaze trained on the door. There were many guiding principles to the first date. These could be bent if occasion warranted, but they usually held true, such as "always hold it in a public place" or "some sort of social lubricant must be involved, either traditional—such as alcohol—or unorthodox—such as the Hokey-Pokey at a soup kitchen, one time."

Beyond the principles, which could be bent, were the ironclad rules to the first date, which were to be adhered to with the orthodoxy of a romantic monk. Rule three, for example, was that on a first date, especially a *blind* date, the guy was to arrive first. This prevented the woman from panicking, or ditching, or worse—feeling like a desperate loser while she waited for her possible Prince Charming to maybe stand her up.

Therefore, Garrett had arrived at *Le Filou* a full fifteen minutes early, fulfilled their reservation, and waited eighteen minutes so far.

He had done zero research on Ari Reynolds beyond the notes he'd taken from Penny. It was important, in his mind. Their first meeting had to be genuine. If he already knew all about Ari, what she looked like, every blemish and freckle and all seven-hundred-forty-two photos on her various social media accounts… no. Mystery always, *always* trumped history.

Besides, the meet-cute provided the foundation from which they would begin their road to rebound.

He checked his phone once more. Five minutes past. Nothing to worry about quite yet. If she stretched it to a full twenty minutes, then he'd call Penny and confirm Ari had at least left her apartment.

No sooner had he gauged the time than a towering shape drifted through the glass doors and hung by the hostess. He kept himself in check until he caught better sight of the person—a brunette in a sleeveless black dress, stretched tight around her expansive bust, cinched around the neck and ending high on the thighs, exposing shapely legs that gave goddamn telephone poles a run for their money in length.

The hostess tapped on a tablet, walking alongside her like a roadrunner beside a giraffe as they crossed the savannah of fine dining.

Instinctively, Garrett stood. This had to be her. Yet, as she approached, head high, hair back, expression confident, he expected… he wasn't sure. Even standing before her, his natural eye level reached only to her shoulders. His gaze darted down, spying the sharp black pumps before speeding back up her legs—how could any one woman have that much leg?—up, up, into her deep hazel eyes.

He suppressed a laugh.

She'd done it on purpose.

"Hi," he said with a nod and a smile. "Garrett." Out came the hand to shake, polite and non-committal. "You must be—"

"Ari, yeah." Her grip was confident, but delicate. No overbearing attempt to put him "in his place."

She met him measure for measure until he gestured to the table and pulled her chair out for her. It was a simple enough test. If she wasn't much for old chivalric gestures, she'd just scooch herself in.

The look she gave him, all raised eyebrows and half-smiles, spoke more to bemusement than sincere appreciation. He was quick to take his own seat across from her. He'd never had to work around such a sharp size difference before. She had to be exacerbating it on purpose with those high-fashion stilts on her feet. Throwing him off. All he had to do was keep calm and keep the ball in his own court. Penny had warned him not to react.

He was on the job.

"Lovely eyes," he said. Hazel was the best color for a woman's eyes. They changed with the lighting. They could be deep honey-gold, chocolate brown, pale green, or even blue. Not that Ari needed to know his preference. She didn't need any more ammo to throw him off.

She didn't say anything.

Instead, her gaze traced over his facial features, and he felt as much as saw her evaluation. He stayed silent, letting her see whatever she wanted as seconds traced past. It wasn't an awkward pause. It was the calm of sparring partners before the first strike.

"Really?" She quirked a single eyebrow. "That's your opening line? 'Lovely eyes?' Did we leave our fedora and neckbeard at home?"

Garrett gave a Cheshire smile in return.

"So, you're saying you *don't* have lovely eyes?" He shrugged and held up his hands innocently. "Hey, I mean—no judgment here. I'm sure you know better than me. You have to live with them."

"That's not—I don't—*hey*—" she sputtered, but she clamped her lips together. "...well played." Her grin finally slipped out, a toothy number that was more like a shark sizing up a rival than someone expecting an innocent night of fun. "To be fair, you don't look that bad in a suit, so I guess it's not a total wash."

"Thanks?" The ghost of a chuckle clung to the edge of his voice. *At least she speaks her mind.*

"What can I say? You made a good first impression, shitty first lines notwithstanding." She grinned wider, as though she'd thrown a verbal haymaker and waited to see if he'd block or counter.

Garrett wasn't fooled, but he was more than happy to play along. "Likewise, Ari. Your hair, especially, looks amazing. Goes with those lovely eyes. Really helps pull attention away from that whole chin situation you've got going on."

A sharp laugh of a single syllable pulsed from Ari. "I will have you know my chin is one of the five sexiest aspects of my face, thank you," she said.

He leaned back in his chair, acting impressed. "According to whom?"

"Focus groups. I just did a shoot at a college wedding. It's amazing the kind of surveys you can run there." Her eyes, highlighted by eyeshadow the color of envy, dared him to keep up, practically sparking in delight. "They also said your tie would have been better served as a noose."

"This is Egyptian silk," said Garrett, mock-offended. "If this is going to be used for anything apart from its job as stylish neckwear, it's going to be for tying one of my wrists to a headboard."

Something mischievous glittered in her gaze as it flicked down to the hand in question. "Just the one wrist?"

"You don't want the other hand restrained, trust me. It can work magic like you wouldn't believe." Early, true, but if he was right about her, she'd counter as quickly.

Ari perched in her seat as a queen upon her throne. One hand waggled long, slender fingers as though trying to hypnotize him. "I'm a professional photographer. If you want to talk about magic fingers, these can do an awful lot once they get hold of a camera... including make my chin look good." A smile more sincere than cynical blossomed across her face and betrayed the presence of faint dimples.

Garrett drank in the look until it was snatched away. It was a shame. Behind the snark, she really did have a smile to make someone go weak at the knees. If getting Ari to rebound was going to work, he'd have to earn that sincerity more and more.

The challenge and reward were more than motivation enough.

"Any suggestions on what's good here?" She pursed her lips. It was a good sign—she was willing to jump straight into dinner rather than the precursory talking over drinks. She seemed to have enough emotional calluses to run that gauntlet without flinching.

"I heard the mushroom risotto is supposed to be great. I've also heard they do this amazing vegan cheeseburger." To his credit, he delivered both lines with a straight face.

Ari was happy to pull a face on his behalf.

"My thoughts exactly." He laughed.

"How do they even—"

"I have no idea. Something to do with the cheese being made of cashews, or something. I think it's a vegetarian patty, and..." He fumbled for the words before giving up and sighing.

A moment later, a waiter approached their table, exuding non-judgmental welcoming and offering them both wine lists with menus.

Garrett nodded to his date in deference, both in a turn of chivalry and to see what she would order.

She went straight for the wine list, as he suspected, and took only a moment before ordering a hearty Cabernet Sauvignon. One glass. No food yet. He couldn't fault her. His own stomach had turned at the thought of the meatless travesty that dared masquerade as a burger. So, he ordered one glass to match, and the waiter whisked away to serve.

She waited just long enough for him to be out of earshot before leaning forward conspiratorially. A solid inch of cleavage peeked out from the window-like neckline of her dress, as though eager to eavesdrop on what she would say beyond the long chocolate-brown locks that threatened to hide the lightly freckled skin from view.

"Can I be real, for a moment? No judgment? Since—well, we both know what this is, right?" Gone was any trace of earlier snark. Behind her expression was the pain he knew she had. The exposure of an unclosed wound. Still fresh. Still bleeding.

He'd been there.

Garrett leaned forward, closing the distance.

"What is this?" He brought his best poker face to the fore.

"It's a rebound date." She stared him down, her voice flat and matter of fact. "Penny set me up with you. She means well, and I'm sure you totally do too, but I don't want to pretend like this is going to be anything more than what it is."

He had the good manners to fake hiding disappointment. This wasn't the first time a client had held their situation up to the cold lens of reality. Nor would it be the last. It meant she was emotionally honest with herself. That, above all, was a good sign.

"So, you're still kind of getting over someone?" he prompted.

"No 'kind of' about it." Her mouth took the angle of an aged tombstone in the ground. "He cheated, then dumped me for her."

Garrett let the silence stretch a beat, just long enough to show he was digesting the new information and taking care how to respond.

"I'm sorry," he began. Cliché but necessary. Taking the meta angle would work better with a girl as sharp as her. Relationships that had died via cheating were a common occurrence in his line of work, and no matter the context, no matter the person... it always chafed, like a splinter in the soul. Shit like this was half the reason he'd become Mr. Rebound in the first place.

He pressed forward, his voice ringing with necessary empathy. "I won't say 'that sucks,' because that's obvious. But I will say there are no expectations for tonight. Let's just see where it takes us." Not too much empathy, or it'd be insincere. Not too little, or he'd be uncaring. There was a balance to be maintained. How she reacted would tell him if he'd evened the scales.

"See where it takes us," she echoed. A sigh leaked out, like she deflated and escaped all at once; a prisoner who had starved themselves skinny enough to slip out of chains worn so long the imprints of the links would never fade. Still—within that pithy vagary was hope. "Tonight" was the subject of more love and pop songs than could be counted. "Tonight" represented the immediate unknown future—and the future, by definition, meant anything was possible. Even something like a good time.

"I could roll with that," she said.

An electric thrill surged through Garrett at the intoxicating hope dripping into her gaze.

The corners of her mouth twitched. "That said...what do you say we pound a glass of stupid-expensive wine, leave a tip, then get the hell out of here and go somewhere where the burger patties are no smaller than a pound and served with tons of cheese fries?"

He blinked, silent. It wasn't the first time this had happened to him, but it didn't matter. He would abide by the primary rule of all first rebound dates—go with the flow. If it didn't feel organic, there couldn't be a second date.

"Sounds perfect." He sat back with a grin, just in time for a fresh-faced young man in an apron to present the bottle of wine for their approval and expertly uncork and pour. A single glass for each of them, then both waiter and sommelier were dismissed with a polite word and a wave.

He swirled the wine in the glass, letting the tannins mellow or whatever the hell it was wine snobs said wine had to do before it was drunk. Fortunately, it made Ari snort. She must have thought he was being ironic.

"I can taste the burger and fries now." He toasted without drinking, nodding once in respect. "Seriously. Do you know how rare it is I find a girl with an appreciation for real cuisine?"

Judging by the set of Ari's eyebrows, she remained unimpressed. "We aren't that rare, dude. You've probably been searching in the wrong places."

"Well, point is, whatever Dick McDickface was thinking when he cheated on you, it must have been under the influence of drugs." He shook his head.

"I'm pretty sure he was sick of having to go up to kiss me goodnight," she said simply. "Or he couldn't handle a girl who knows what she likes. As if triggering herself, she leaned forward on her elbows, glass of wine untouched. "I mean, look," she began. "I have this theory."

"I love theories." He matched her posture.

Her hands gestured back and forth, emerald nails glittering in the light. "Well, it's simple, and a doozy. Theory is, in every relationship, there can only be one dominant person. One's dominant, one's submissive."

He grinned. "Kinky."

"Not like that, moron." She swatted his arm.

Playful physical contact. Name calling. Good signs. Especially when her gaze shifted to the side and she smirked, just once, just for long enough to let that cheeky side out for a gasp of air. "At least, not *entirely* like that."

"Not entirely." He toasted her with his wine glass. "Good to know there's some wiggle room there."

"Watch it," she said, though her smile didn't diminish. "Point is, there can only be one dominant person in the relationship. The healthiest relationships never have that be a fixed point. They take turns. Sometimes multiple times in a date. Sometimes multiple times in a conversation. But you can't have two dominant people together, or it goes down in flames. Just like how you can't have two submissive people together, or they'd never get anywhere or do anything."

"Interesting." Garrett pursed his lips, daring to sample the wine. In his opinion, the drink mirrored her to a "T"—full-bodied, acidic, with deep notes of black cherry and a subtle undercurrent of vanilla. Her theory, as well, held merit—some merit, at least, even if it seemed to reduce all interactions to a power balance in a manner wholly unsavory to him, but it felt accurate enough on a surface level.

She didn't waste time. "What do you think?"

"I think if one person is spending a majority of their time being the dominant one in a relationship, it means they're not exactly open to compromise," he said. "Nor should compromises have to suck. I mean, the best ones—the fairest compromises—they always piss people off. That's how you know they're solid compromises. But I think if you don't have two people who can bounce off each other, keep each other on their toes in a good way… then you don't have a relationship that'll last."

Ari followed his every motion, mouth twisting as she swished the drink around. "All right, genius. If you had to guess about my last relationship—and don't lie, because I *know* Penny told you about him— what would you say the problem was?" Her finger snapped up, pointing a purple fingernail straight at his chest. "Was I too dominant, or was he?"

"Neither." He held her gaze. "The problem was that he cheated on you."

She held still. When he didn't flinch, she broke into the most delighted smile he'd seen yet and lifted her glass.

"Now that," she positively beamed, "is something I will drink to."

He clinked his glass against hers, letting the crystal ring and the vibrations tingle his fingers. "Here's to new beginnings and leaving behind the kind of idiots who cheat on perfectly good people."

"Who cheat on *anyone*," Ari amended.

"Anyone." He drank.

She drank deeper, exposing the creamy base of her throat as her head tilted back by degrees until she rocked forward with an empty glass and the sharp tinge of fine wine on her breath.

"I thought wine was supposed to be savored." He took his own sweet time finishing his Cabernet. "Isn't that the point of wine?"

"That's the point of wine for connoisseurs." She didn't so much as bat an eyelid. "A connoisseur, I am not. I'm hungry. Besides, my philosophy is that when you find something good, you take as much of it as you can as soon as you can get it…before it's all gone."

He grunted in accord before lifting the glass to his lips and struggling to chug. He could hold his alcohol, true, but it still felt wrong to be downing wine this fast. Wrong on a level of principle, but he'd cope. Placing his glass back on the table, he struggled not to cough against a burning throat and the prickles of tears in the corners of his eyes.

She chuckled and fished in her purse. "C'mon, featherweight. You cover the wine; I'll cover the food. We'll call it even."

"How magnanimous," he wheezed, knowing full well the cost of the two glasses of Cabernet, plus tip, would be more than whatever burger-and-fries-combo from any restaurant she might drag him to. It didn't stop him from dabbing his mouth with the serviette, counting out enough for a twenty percent tip—always tip well, the fourth rule of a first date—and eyed her up and down once more as she towered over him in six-inch pumps. If there was any doubt as to who was supposed to be the dominant one tonight, it was left somewhere around her ankles and the designer-brand shoes she flaunted.

Or maybe it was left by the wide-eyed hostess who gave Ari the half-second silent "holy hell is she real?" up-and-down as the standing six-foot-eleven brunette ducked—literally *ducked*—under the restaurant door frame and out into the cool night air.

Giving the hostess a smile, he plucked his jacket from the coat rack.

This was going to be a first date for the books.

Chapter Four

"Well, you wanted burgers and fries." Garrett glanced up to the current dominant member of their two-person party. "Are we going to wing this, or do you have a restaurant in mind?"

"As a matter of fact, I do." Her heels clicked against the pavement as she strode down the sidewalk. "One of those hole-in-the-wall places. The kind you usually drive by without ever going in. Fantastic burgers." Her breath misted in front of her lips. The tiny precursors of goosebumps spread across her legs and arms.

He unbuttoned his jacket in preparation.

She glanced down at him before patting his arm. "Keep it on." There was more charity in her voice than condescension. "I grew up in Chicago. Autumn has nothing on me. This is prime cross-country weather, here."

"Okay, see, *that,* I could see you doing." He kept his coat unbuttoned regardless. It was a woman's prerogative to change her mind, after all.

Ari gave him a sidelong look, a pep in her voice as well as in her step. "Is that a crack about my height?"

"What? Every cross-country runner I knew was taller than me. At least I didn't say basketball or whatever."

She chuckled, drifting closer to his personal bubble as they walked. Not quite side-to-side, but if she was signaling to link arms with him, she wouldn't have to move much closer. "Cross-country was my first love. I took it up in high school, freshman year. I was already six-foot by then and growing like a fricking weed, so my stride was great. Practice pushed my cardio to the next level, and then I was outpacing seniors like it's not even a thing."

He nodded his approval. "Impressive."

"Yeah." She lifted her chin, seeming to swell with pride. "I was."

"What happened?" Penny had told him, of course, but he held a strict policy of confirming as many facts from the source as possible.

Sure enough, Ari nodded downward. "Tits happened."

He snorted with laughter before looking back to her. She wasn't laughing along. "Wait…you're serious?"

"Seriously serious." She shrugged. "I couldn't find a decent sports bra my size, and the back pain started shaving entire minutes off my time. Dad brought up the idea of having a reduction, but I was afraid of surgery, so I didn't want to. I mean, what kind of father brings up surgery like that to their teenage daughter?"

"One trying to be supportive?" The words were out, meek and bowed under the weight of being the devil's advocate, before he saw the "really?" look on her face. He winced. "Sorry."

She sniffed once. "No, I get it. He just sucked at it."

His mind raced as they turned a corner, their shadows stretching under the streetlight. He had to try a different tack. "I mean, parents can push really hard when their kid has a gift. Look at Olympics parents. They drill their kids like nothing else, y'know?"

A grimace pulled at her plump lips before she softened and relented with a nod. "Yeah, I came to that same conclusion after a while. Dad could've done a better job of bringing it up than just informing me over breakfast he'd gone ahead and booked the consultation for the surgery anyway—"

"Holy shit, Ari." Garrett's jaw fell open.

"That was pretty much my reaction." She gazed away. "I think that was the worst shouting match that had ever happened in our house. Not that it even mattered in the end. Six months into my junior year, I tore my ACL at the start of practice and had to go under the knife anyway. By the time it healed, I'd found my love for photography. That's how I got my college scholarship."

Garrett nodded, absorbing every word of information with the efficacy of a sponge. "Besides, it's not like shaving everything to up your time in a swimming competition. You can let your hair grow back. I don't think it works quite the same way with boobs."

Her eyebrows rose as she tapped the crosswalk signal. "That's the exact example I brought up when my dad talked about it."

"Great minds," he responded simply.

"I'll say." She seemed more at ease as she approached a single door at street level in the never-ending gleaming façade of the skyscrapers that made up Hell's Kitchen. The windows were clean, and a simple red-blue neon sign read "OPEN." She swept the door open by the push bar and allowed Garrett his first face-full of the most divine grilled-beef smells he'd ever encountered.

"Welcome," said Ari, "to Rooster Jim's Bar and Tavern."

"Whatever this is I'm smelling, I will order one to eat and one to take home and preserve for the good of mankind." Garrett swallowed hard. Whatever happened, however the premium contract would be executed, he knew down to his bones he would be coming back until he'd tried every item on the menu.

She strode past him, heels thumping on an old oak plank floor littered with the dust of crushed peanut shells. Barrels of said peanuts were placed at strategic leaning locations. There was one register, one person working it, and past the cashier one person in a greasy apron dinged a bell and placed a plate on the steel counter. Black metal chairs, tables bolted into the floor, booths lining the rim, and classic rock pounding over the speakers to be enjoyed by all four other people in the restaurant. A true hole-in-the-wall grill.

She beamed down at the perky cashier with her hair in a wild bun. "Hey, Lindsey."

"Ari! What's up?" She practically levitated behind the register with the energy she exuded.

Ari held up her fingers. "Two for tonight."

"I'll tell Makoto to start up the Firecracker." Lindsey bounced on the spot, all bright teeth and quirky lapel buttons.

"The 'Firecracker?'" Garrett lifted an eyebrow.

Ari graced him with a smirk and nodded. "I've seen you can handle downing fine wine." She rested her elbows on a wooden banister as she leaned back. "Even if you got a little cough-y. Now I want to see how you handle your spicy food."

He remained unfazed. If Ari was trying to run him through the dietary gauntlet on the first date—a gauntlet she'd run several lesser men through judging by how she and Lindsey were on a familiar basis by name *and* order—she'd need to up her game. A previous client had taken him to a place that served traditional Guatemalan food. Whatever spicy food Rooster Jim's might have to offer, it couldn't do anything worse to him than the jellied cow tongue had. Still, he played along. "You trying to kill my taste buds all in one night?"

"Maybe." She bobbed her head. A challenge. "Is that a problem, small fry?"

He met her gaze. "Maybe. Does this place have small fries?"

She gave a half-shrug in compromise. "Depends how you define it? They're shoestring fries, but they do them *good* here."

He nodded, pursing his lips as he kept up the banter over fries vs. potato wedges vs. waffle-cut while agreeing on the undisputed superiority of the curly-fry over all other forms of potato. She watched him, in turn, and he noted it out of the corner of his eye as she strode toward a booth in the corner.

Her dress and pumps and his suit clashed with the rocker-T-shirt-and-jeans vibe of Rooster Jim's. Try as they might, the few other diners couldn't help but stare, eyebrows raised at the sight before turning back to their business. Under the thump of Zeppelin, he heard comments being made about them both. They were, after all, radically overdressed.

Her eyes glinted in the overhead light as she slid into the booth, scooting along and wincing as the table bucked and shifted.

"Sorry. Knees," she explained, tucking her legs to the side.

He couldn't restrain a chuckle.

She knew. She had known from the get-go Penny was trying to set her up with a rebound date, and Ari was putting him through this entire charade to get him to realize there was no chance, normally or otherwise, that he would have of landing a girl as impressive as her.

Therein lay her weakness.

"We're pretty dressed up for a place like Rooster Jim's." He spun the saltshaker in idle circles in front of him. "But apparently you come here often?"

"I like dressing nicely and coming to normal establishments." Her voice was perfectly innocent, like a dog welcoming home an owner and thinking it didn't see the mess of shredded toilet paper behind it. "I don't have many hipster quirks about me, but this is one of them."

"You have others?"

"Hey, you spend as much time in art school and the photography business as I do, you're bound to pick up a few by osmosis, whether you like it or not."

He laughed, letting his gaze roam over her as he pleased. She didn't flinch, presenting a front as calm and used to being examined as any painting in a museum. He needed more from her—more *of* her—if he was going to figure out how best to get her to rebound from her previous train wreck of a relationship. More of her personality. Her fears. Her hopes.

Maybe most importantly, more of what she wanted.

"So, you shared one of your theories with me." He kept his gaze on her. "Mind if I pick your brain a bit?"

"You're the open book of the two of us." Her honey-brown gaze dropped to the saltshaker, as though the white crystals crusted around the edge might ward off whatever demons he hoped to summon. "I don't open up so easily."

"Maybe I can help." He abandoned the shaker, a little too aware of his own heartbeat. "You said this was a rebound date and everything, right? So, if we're not going to waste each other's time, let's crack this peanut and see what we find."

"Pistachio. Much healthier." Her gaze remained on the saltshaker.

He frowned. "The nut doesn't matter, Ari."

"First time I've heard a guy say that." There was no quip or joy in her voice. Just a statement of fact, spoken more to the saltshaker than to him.

An unrehearsed snort of laughter kicked out of him as he

dropped his head in disbelief. Even as he was enjoying her company, he'd found the first useful nugget—she deflected with humor. Lots of people did, but he didn't think she'd be the type. Maybe it was her inherent sarcasm, but he had her pegged as the type to wall up instead of deflecting.

Apparently not.

"Okay. So, this is still the 'get to know you' portion of the night, isn't it?" His stomach growled. He pushed past it. The 'Firecracker,' or whatever it was, would be along shortly. "Tell me something, Ari. Why do you go on dates?"

She sat back in the booth, her arms crossed. Her gaze, however, fixed on his, like a bull staring down a matador across the arena. Not aggressive, not hesitant. Alert. Ready to react however it needed for survival, whether by fleeing or by goring her opponent.

"I go on dates," she said, her tone flat and rigid, "to find a guy I like and be with him."

"Okay. Good." He nodded. "Is that all?"

"Does there have to be more?" Her gaze darted to the right. Defensive. "Why do *you* go on dates?"

"To find a girl I like." His answer was only the tip of his iceberg. A practiced routine. A spiel. "Not to mention find out what qualities I would admire in a future spouse, what qualities in myself would stop me from being a good husband, and to learn and develop emotionally."

She blinked. Deliberate. Slow. No pulse disturbed the flat line of her mouth. Her nostrils twitched, as though smelling the pre-cooked line he'd fed her and sensing the frozen interior. "Garrett, if I wanted a textbook answer, I'd pick up a shitty self-help book from a recycled bookstore."

With the same deliberation, she leaned forward onto her elbows. The smell of wine on her breath mingled with the liquid courage dominating and soured his empty stomach. A single errant strand of glossy brown hair stretched from her bangs, tickling his forehead. Even in the light tickling touch, it felt soft enough there seemed to be more life in her hair than he had in his entire body. She was close enough to tempt. To taunt. To tease. Her face filled his vision. Close. Too close. Heat coursed through his fingers as his heart kicked up to jackhammer speed.

"Go a level deeper for me." Her eyes narrowed, the envy-colored eyeshadow highlighting them to a bladed degree, searching for a reason to distrust. A reason to shy away from the dagger she must have suspected to be behind the cloak of his non-judgmental affection. "Why do you *really* go on dates? Especially with women you've never really met before?"

He took a breath to try and steady himself, only succeeding in inhaling a waft of her perfume that clouded all judgment. Even through the miasmatic heaven of grilled beef scents that infused the place, her perfume was an undercurrent, separate and distinct and somehow superior to his beleaguered brain than anything else. A full-bodied, bubbly, intoxicating sort of smell, like the love child of a mango and a pheromone musk. Oddly sweet, given her bold personality, but enough to drag his mind off-track. He blinked. Shook himself. *Focus.*

Behind the self-aware line he'd fed her, behind the textbook prose that made so much sense yet sat as stiff as a starched collar on a corpse... why did he go on dates?

Well, he had an answer for that too. The best lies were the repackaged truth, after all, and God knew he couldn't say "because they pay me."

"I go out with women I've never met before because I believe in hope," he managed.

She quirked an eyebrow.

He had to continue. "I believe everything goes on. Nothing is so bad that you can't recover. A broken heart. Broken home. Constant pain. Whatever. I believe hope is an integral part of love, and maybe, if I keep taking shots at it—in the dark, in the light, whatever—maybe, one day, I'll find it." He swallowed against a dry mouth. It wasn't *lying*, per se. The philosophy behind it was true. He'd just never exactly considered the ramifications of it.

A burst of air brushed past her plump pink lips as she scoffed.

"*Bull—shit.*" She drew out the two syllables of condemnation like a cheese wire carving through flesh. "What, do you practice that in the mirror or something?"

His mouth fell open. His head rang with the feeling of metaphysical concussion. She'd—she just—

She snickered. "No, no—let me guess—you read it off a chocolate wrapper. Give me a fricking break. Nobody actually believes that."

He closed his mouth. Nervous sweat slicked his palms. Worse, his heart pounded a mile a minute. The line should have worked. It was poetic, it was classy, it was filled with truth even if it wasn't one hundred percent true for *him*.

He lifted his gaze. "I go on dates because I have a lot to offer to someone, and I want to make someone in my life happy beyond myself." His insides quivered, but beneath the quivering was a feeling of iron. His heart beat slowed. There was a ringing quality to his words, and even if she couldn't hear it, he could feel it.

He never should have said something so personal.

Her lips taunted, a distance away, as the mocking smile fell. Her hazel eyes glossed. Softened.

"See?" Her gaze changed. It was almost rueful. "That wasn't so hard, was it?"

He stayed quiet and let the silence hang around them, a bubble of tension floating in a tussled sea of classic rock and the musky smell of crushed peanut shells. Seconds ebbed by. In each one, she didn't back down. Didn't blink. Met his gaze, measure for measure.

This was all wrong.

"All right, enough of the heavy shit." She sat back and crossed her arms. "Let's get this back on track. Something fun. Where are you from? Where'd you go to school? Mother's maiden name? Street you grew up on?"

The flat-footed feeling washed away as he laughed and became himself once more. "What, are you trying to get to know me or get the security questions to my bank account?"

She smiled, bemused, just in time for a wave of ambient light and heat to jab him in the side of the head.

Blinking, he recoiled, his mouth forming an "o."

"So, when they say 'Firecracker—'"

"They literally mean 'fire,' yeah." She grinned in triumph as Lindsey hefted a rack of kebabs, flames crackling through the grill on which they rested, and dished the dozen delicacies onto his plate. "If you finish the entire thing without a refill on your drink, you get them for free."

Garrett eyed them as he would a cobra on the table. Each was a solid ten inches, stuffed to the gills with beef, various bell peppers, and the wicked black lengths of gustatory hellfire that were ghost peppers.

"Before you even ask," added Ari with glee, "the meat is also soaked in hot sauce."

There was no backing down. She'd already taken him into uncomfortable personal territory and shown him new light and goddammit *that was supposed to be his job*. The fact she was smoking hot only made it worse. Now he was faced with a straightforward, testosterone-fueled challenge. He just had to eat the thing.

This, he could do.

"Well, then." He lifted his watering gaze from the meal to Lindsey, his executioner, before turning them to Ari, his ferrywoman over the spicy River Styx. "When I finish this, and I get them for free, you are going to pay dearly."

"Oh yeah?" Her nose twitched, and she sniffed. She glanced

from Lindsey to grill to food to Garrett, her brow furrowing. "Why do I smell burni—oh my God, you're on *fire*—"

Lindsey yelped and clapped her hands over her mouth.

His jacket sleeve was an un-fabric shade of bright organic yellow and orange and spreading. There wasn't time for questioning. There wasn't time for panic. There was only time for action. His free hand shot out to clutch the perspiring plastic cup of Coke and dumped it all on his sleeve, ice and soda and straw and all. Without even checking to see if the flames were extinguished, he snatched Ari's drink and doubled down. Ice clattered to the wooden floor as he wrenched himself free of the jacket—thankfully, it came off without a hitch—and hurled it aside, slapping at his arm and checking the rest of himself.

A slight plume of gray smoke drifted from the fabric. Beyond that, and the slack jaws from everyone else in the place, the atmosphere had faded to a tense silence. He eased his heart out of his throat, smoothing down his arm again, and again, checking for any kind of burn. It was superficial at best, jacket-ruining at worst. Honestly, two drinks dumped and hurling his jacket to the floor felt silly, in hindsight. As though there was a dignified way to put out a personal clothing fire.

Around the room, the few other patrons held their phones up, wide-eyed, capturing every sordid detail. Nobody said a word until Lindsey whimpered.

"Please don't sue," she begged. "I'm so, so sorry—I need this job so badly, and I swore to my manager this wouldn't happen again, and—"

"Again?" Garrett coughed, trying not to laugh with blatant disbelief. "How many times have you set someone on fire with this thing?"

"I don't know? A few?" She cringed until her head seemed in danger of turtling clear into her body.

Ari rose awkwardly in the booth, straightening the hem of her dress as she planted a placating hand on Lindsey's arm.

"Don't worry, girl. He's not going to sue." Ari's gaze sharpened. "Is he?"

Normally, no, he wouldn't have sued. Nor was he going to criticize Lindsey for any clumsiness (or possible pathological pyromania) on her part. That would be in direct violation of the second rule of the first date—never criticize the girl's friends. But he would be billing the hell out of Penny for the loss of his jacket.

"Of course not," he said. "Accidents happen. Besides, what better way to..." He paused to lift a kebab for emphasis, ghost peppers glistening in the fluorescent light. "*Spice* up our date?"

The pun earned a long beat of disbelief, followed by a snigger of laughter from Lindsey and a deep, pained groan from Ari.

"I'll comp both your meals." The russet-haired waitress backed away, nearly tipping the grill before she caught it with a clatter. "Gift cards, too. A-and pay for the jacket. Just—I am so, so, *so* sorry."

"You're fine." He smoothed his arm down one last time, leaving his ruined jacket in its smoldering bundle on the floor.

She cowered once, nodded twice, and scurried away, mouse-like.

His client, however, looked impressed. "Most guys I know would've lost their shit about being set on fire on a first date."

"Nah." He forced enough of a cocky front to hand-wave the entire experience away as he tugged the first mouthful of kebab from the skewer. "Not the worst thing to happen to me on a first date."

And suddenly, Ari brightened.

"Tell me this is the part of the night where we swap horror stories." She jabbed in his direction with a shoestring fry. "Because, if we are, I *guarantee* you I will win."

"You're on." He coughed hard, fighting the deep throbbing burn consuming his tongue.

She wasn't kidding. The Firecracker was like eating fire. Delicious, well-seasoned, juicy, meaty fire. Better yet, Ari was coming to him on *his* turf for this round. He was a professional rebound dater, for crying out loud.

Running the horror story gauntlet was one of his moves. A smooth and polished arrow in his quiver. None of this getting-caught-off-guard shit again.

Even if it had been kind of nice, in a terrifying way.

"Med student," started Ari. "Felt the need to tell me I was in the oh-point-oh-five percent of women on the planet for my height and literally wanted to make Punnett squares to see how tall our kids would be."

"Veterinarian assistant," countered Garrett. "Took me to a dog park and offered to squeeze a Rottweiler's butt glands. Sprayed it all over my shoes."

"Guy challenged me to a drinking contest. Puked on *my* shoes." She shook her head. "Dumbass had never heard the phrase 'liquor before beer.'"

"Took me back to her apartment, sat me down, and told me the backstories to each of her comic-book-named cats when she knew I was allergic to cats." He grimaced. "I took enough antihistamines that night to choke a bull, and I still couldn't see straight."

She smiled wider. "Got a guy back to the bedroom for a night and found him crouched in my closet sniffing my shoes. Secret foot fetish."

"Ice climbing with an adrenaline junkie girl," said Garrett. It was his *piece de resistance*, his ace in the hole. "The ice screw holding my bolt came out of the wall. Fell twenty feet and broke my leg on a big chunk of frozen rock."

Ari whistled, before settling back with a note of unmistakable finality. "Guy tried to have a three-way with me and his roommate— who was one of my exes who had staged the entire thing to try and get one last fling with me. Tased him and walked out."

Garrett's eyes widened. "Tased who? Your ex? Or his roommate?"

Her voice went as cold as his mouth was hot. "Yes."

He took the time to devour another kebab. The silence stretched on as he struggled not to imagine her coming at him with that black crackling instrument of pants-wetting pain. Worse, he was racking his brain for something to one-up her, and nothing was coming. The ice climbing incident with Yolanda was his go-to for the worst first date. There had to be something worse in his history. There had to be.

If only his mouth wasn't turning into Satan's personal furnace.

Ari sipped at her refilled drink, triumphant. "You know what the problem is with your stories? All the ones you told?"

"Do... tell..." He panted, fanning his mouth, all pretense at smiling gone.

"They're all *good*." The corners of her eyes tightened. "Sure, your shoes got ruined, you spent a night with horrible allergies, and you broke your leg, but those stories are all *good*. If any of those girls had turned out to be 'the one', they're the stories you both would have told your friends for years to come. You guys would have laughed about it, and it would've made you stronger as a couple."

Even through the pain, he could tell there was more to the point she was making. "And...?"

"And none of my stories have that." Sadness finally came through, palpable and true, as much in her gaze as her voice. "All of my best horror stories only happened because the guy was never truthful from the start."

He forced himself to look pensive despite the heat flushing his cheeks and the sweat trickling down his temples and the snot running from his nose as he cleaned the last kebab from its skewer.

"I just really hope you aren't the same." She gave him a smile that held the same hope he'd spoken of not ten minutes earlier. The hope

of the future.
    The hope of happiness.
    Shit.

Chapter Five

This had not been how the night was supposed to go.

Arianne's mind had been racing ahead, unencumbered by the wine she had that night, toward the next step. Everything she'd thought ahead of time had been wrong. He hadn't been an asshole. Sure, she had to dig in and pry a bit to get him to stop trying to be suave and be honest instead, but he'd doubled down on it and, well... it was humbling, the way he'd opened up.

Her heels clicked on the stone stairs that led to her apartment door. She paused, staring the eternal distance down to the handle. He was waiting behind her. Her tongue danced over her lips, just once, before she turned on the spot and gazed to him.

"Garrett." Her lips moved with silent predecessors, trying out a half-dozen different ways of asking, her gaze flickering to her door and back, before she forced out her next words, "come inside."

There was just enough upward inflection in the last syllable to make her wonder if she'd meant it as a question but pushed it out as a statement instead. Heat prickled across her cheeks. Slowly, she ran her hand up the side of his arm, until she cupped the side of his neck. Her fingertips toyed with the edges of his hair. Not greasy. Not a mouth-breather. Flawed, sure, but a quality guy. She smiled against her internal gnawing. *Take what you can take before it's gone.*

"I shouldn't," he began.

"So?" Quick to counter. Maybe too quick. "You said there were no expectations tonight. 'Let's see what happens.'" Something itched in the back of her mind. "How are we going to see what happens if you don't come inside?"

His smile slackened. "Because, Ari, while you enjoy taking all you can before it's gone, I prefer to savor it. Take my time."

It sounded like another cheesy-ass line, except it matched everything else about him so far.

"Are you talking with wine or women?" She crossed her arms. Rueful tingles raced across her fingertips and palm from where her touch left his neck. Maybe he wasn't drunk enough. They'd only had the one glass of Cabernet, back at the French place. She didn't even feel it. He didn't seem to be *that* much of a featherweight, either.

"I have this great *Chateau de Chasselas.*" She sniffed, rolling her eyes under the weight of her own conscience. "Well, my roommate does, but she won't mind." This was for the greater good. She'd leave pantyhose on the doorknob, like she'd joked, and Penny could get over all of it. This *was* giving him a real chance. "We can make it last all night...and so can I."

His gaze darted to Arianne's lips.

With a casual toss of her hair to the side, exposing her neck, she drank in his expression. That half-lidded, murky cloud over his crystal-blue eyes. The small of her back ached, but she hunched over to try and close a portion of the space from their height difference. She was more than close enough to kiss. He wouldn't even need to get on tiptoes.

Sure, she could have just kicked off her heels, but she wasn't going to make it *easy* for him. He should have been chomping at the bit. Should have had his lips and tongue against hers and his hands on her ass already.

The half-lidded look over his eyes disappeared like the golden hour of light. He opened his mouth. "I'm saying no, Ari."

A single laugh kicked out of her before her sense of humor flickered and died.

But the look on his face didn't flinch. Regret was there, sure, but it was sober. Intelligent. Everything it wasn't supposed to be. She searched his eyes, sweat dampening her armpits. Her knees shook, as though they might collapse under her and send her tumbling into some godforsaken abyss.

"My roommate isn't home, if that's what you're worried about?" Her mind raced ahead of her words. Reason. There had to be a reason.

"No, that's not it." He wasn't even looking at her tits. Just keeping eye contact. All that goddamn respectful-ass eye contact that made her feel like she was shrinking before him. "I had an amazing time tonight, Ari...even if I did get set on fire."

She snorted, though it came out as more of a breathless scoff. He did like talking. Maybe if he kept flapping his lips, he'd get out the "why" behind his bullshit "no."

His brows knit together. Sincerity. Honesty. Both good and bad at the same time and clogging her throat. "I know you're still hurting from your last relationship. Like you said—this *was* kind of a rebound date. I'd like to take you out again. There's always time for wine and everything afterward. Just… not tonight. Not on the first date."

Her mouth twitched with the ghosts of words that would never be spoken. Silence pulsed in waves between them as he gave her a soft, regretful smile. Goosebumps erupted across her skin. Finally, his hand alighted on her upper arm, and it was everything she could do to stare down at him as though he'd proved the sky was green.

This wasn't right.

But it felt wrong to call it "wrong."

A burst of hope ripped through her as he rose to his tiptoes. It would have been so easy to just—just *grab* him, and slam him back against her door, and just goddamn *kiss* him—but then he closed the gap…only for every muscle in her body to freeze as his lips pressed to her cheek instead.

A trillion thoughts ripped through her mind.

Don't stop.

Get off me.

Just kiss me for real, you pussy.

Please, don't.

Are you thirteen?

This is everything I want.

You stingy son of a bitch.

He held the moment, letting his lips relax from her cheek by degrees, long, lingering, and chaste.

She couldn't blink. Her eyes were wide. Her voice had crumbled away, her throat dry. Their gazes were held in taut and equal solitude.

"I'll take you out again next Tuesday." There was a calmness in his voice, a humble matter-of-factness that belied any kind of cocky male ego. "Call you tomorrow."

She might have grunted. Made some kind of brain-dead cavewoman sound. The world was upside-down and back to front, and he didn't even look back at her as he descended the steps and crossed onto the sidewalk.

Then he was around the corner and gone like a dream, and she remained. Silent. Sweaty. Shell-shocked.

Alone.

He'd said "no." She'd offered him wine and the unforgettable company of herself and an open bed, and he'd said "no." Her mind was a tornado of auto-cannibalistic thought, ripping apart every interaction they had over the last three hours and laying it bare to the bones. The culprit behind his "no" had to be something she'd missed. He hadn't seemed intimidated by her height—maybe her figure? Because she'd been the one to say "come upstairs" instead of him? Had he already had too much to drink? Because they'd ditched his reservation at *Le Filou* to hit up Rooster Jim's instead? Was his arm burned?

She silently cursed herself. His arm. She should've offered him an ice pack for his arm. It would have been a plenty plausible reason to come inside.

Instead, because of her tripping at the finish line, the potential satisfaction of their evening had waltzed away without so much as a backward glance.

The shellshock withered and crisped as her throat tightened.

Fine, she seethed. Her fingers twitched, as though she could wrap them around his throat. *Be like that. Hope my voicemail keeps you warm at night.*

Her six-inch pumps ground against the concrete of the front doorstep as she spun and tried to shove the door open, only to slam her forehead against the top of the doorframe.

"*Motherf—*" Pain lanced through her head, more insulting than agonizing. She reeled back and clutched her brow. Growling, she yanked the fashionable stilts off her feet and ducked for good measure, stomping barefoot inside her apartment. The door made a satisfying slamming sound behind her.

The tendrils of her sexual frustration clawed at the walls as her head throbbed. Everything came alive to her, from the framed photo of her and Penny beaming at the camera in their apartment to the walls and carpet themselves, all mocking how Arianne dared re-enter so alone. Still, she rested her aching brow against the cool wood of the door, closing her eyes and listening to the insistent thumping of her pulse in her temples.

She'd opened up so much. Maybe not according to him, but anyone who knew her would know she didn't just—

But he *didn't* know her. Penny had given him an overview. Talked up the good points, glossed over the bad. That was the whole point of convincing someone to go on a first date in the first place, let alone a blind date. Smile just so. Be funny, but not *too* funny. Whatever it took to get them into bed, where the two of you could get some satisfaction. Give them something to fawn over and fondle for the night and discard each other with mutual hollow promises come the dawn. Get what you could get while you could get it. Don't let them in. Don't let them weigh you, and measure you, and—inevitably, inexorably, inescapably—find you wanting.

Lucas hadn't found her wanting.

Until he had.

And a few minutes ago, neither had Garrett. To make matters worse, he'd said no because he *liked* her, not lusted after her. Because he wanted a second *date*, not a second orgasm.

Now she had twenty-four hours to decide whether to grant his request.

Tossing her shoes through the open doorway of her bedroom, she didn't much care where they landed. Instead, she struggled behind herself, clawing at her back and twisting her arms into chicken wings until she caught the zipper to her dress and unzipped it far enough to be able to breathe again.

She trudged to the fridge and clutched the bottle of *Chateau de Chasselas.* Hard, long breaths hissed in and out of her as she stared at the flowery script and the label and fought a silent battle with herself. It was a perfectly good bottle. Drinking it could spite Garrett. Show him through some strange, psychic, space-and-time penetrating way what he was missing.

But she also loathed the thought of being the kind of girl who threw a hissy fit and drank herself stupid because a guy she liked wouldn't pound her on a first date.

Groaning, she shoved the bottle back into the fridge and swiped an ice cream sandwich instead, lying to herself that she was hungry. A poor substitute, but at least she wasn't getting plastered. That couldn't be healthy.

"That was the last ice cream sandwich, I hope you know," came her roommate's voice.

She was probably trying to be funny, but her British accent made her sound snide. She paused in the entryway of their bathroom, her sweats proclaiming allegiance to Manchester Utd. and her baggy T-shirt defecting to the Chicago Bears. Her half-blonde waterfall of hair was damp and matted.

Steam clung to the mirror behind her. "I take it the date went well?"

Arianne huffed, her mouth twisting as a traitorous quiver came to her bottom lip. Just one, just brief enough to show before she clamped down on it. "Yup. You picked a real winner, Sherlock." Staring at the fridge, she rose to sit on the kitchen counter and debate whether to eat, drink, or bitch her feelings away. At least, until she caught sight of Penny, who was awkwardly dragging one of the recliners across the carpet. "What are you doing?"

"Coming to sit beside you." She grunted, jerking the furniture forward.

"In the recliner?" Arianne squinted in confusion, glancing down by where her legs dangled off the edge. "Just grab one of the kitchen stools."

"Bugger that." Penny's socks slid on the carpet as she fought for traction against the weight of the massive armchair. "Just because you're sitting on something hard and uncomfy doesn't mean I want to."

Despite herself, Arianne chuckled and relented, quitting kitchen counter for plush leather couch instead. "C'mon, pintsize. You win. What do you want to know?"

Penny sighed in relief, abandoning her attempt to rearrange the furniture as she plopped down next to Arianne. "Well, first of all, I want to know if there's going to be a second date."

"He says," she managed at last. Because of course, *of course* her insightful shit of a roommate would go right for the jugular and want an answer to the hardest question of the lot. Just like she'd know if she lied about it. "Next Tuesday. Apparently."

Penny narrowed her eyes. "You don't sound so sure."

"I'm not." It was the honest truth.

"On your end or his?" A note of concern hung on the end of Penny's words.

Arianne sighed. "Mine."

Tonight was a night to go puking out all her secrets, it seemed. She'd been pried open by Garrett's coaxing words, his easygoing personality, and just when it seemed like there would be a chance to close the wounds she'd opened herself, along came her roommate.

"We hit it off super well." Arianne grimaced. "He's smart, he's witty, he kept up with me, and he rolls with the punches. Knew full well it was a rebound date and I'm hung up on Lucas still, and he was completely okay with it. He wants a second date because he likes me." She shuddered. The concept was horrifying and cathartic and uncomfortable all at the same time, like a conservative going to their first nudist beach.

"Do you like him back?" Penny tilted her head. "It sure seems like it."

Arianne stayed quiet for several moments before pouting. "What's it sound like?"

Truth itself had wormed its greedy fingers into her and through her and wore her like a glove. She slumped against the leather couch, limp and compliant, staring at the ceiling. There wasn't much point in trying to keep it in. Not with Penny. "Yeah, okay? I like him. A lot." Simple. Small words. "I shouldn't. Not this fast. Not after Lucas. But I do. So, I invited him in, and he turned me down."

Penny scoffed once. "Yeah. *He* turned you down."

Arianne remained silent, her gaze locked onto the ceiling.

"Bugger me, you're serious," came Penny's awed voice.

"Yeah. But it wasn't until after he said 'no' that he told me he's taking me out again." The rejection still stung. Worse, she couldn't stop reliving the tingles of his lips on her cheek.

"Told you?" Penny sounded skeptical. "He didn't ask?"

"No." She sighed before the corners of her mouth tugged upward against her will. "But I'm not exactly inclined to complain."

They shared a moment as they laughed together before Penny shifted slightly. "So, he said 'no' to the Great and Powerful Arianne. Didn't want to see the dominatrix behind the curtain?"

Arianne clamped her mouth shut. The truth was, she had an awful lot more lace than leather packed away in her special drawer. Not that she ever would have admitted it. So maybe she enjoyed being a little more submissive in the bedroom. It was nice to be eye level with a man in bed rather than towering over him the entire time. Height difference meant nothing when they were lying down.

Instead, she gave another laugh and shrugged. "Maybe he's just not a fan of *Chateau de Chasselas*."

Penny's eyes widened as she bolted for the fridge. *"You didn't—"*

"Nah." Arianne laughed. "I was going to, but then he said he didn't want to come up, so I ate the last ice cream sandwich instead. Should have offered it to him. He could've put it on his arm."

She stayed quiet, clearly waiting for an explanation.

"He got set on fire at dinner." *He was right. It did "heat" up our date. Spice up? Whatever. It was a shit dad joke anyway.*

Penny snorted. "This one too, huh?"

Arianne rolled her eyes. "Oh, bite me, pintsize." She exhaled, once, before regaling her with the rest of the details of the night's events. Halfway through the recounting, she forced herself to stop. "What?"

Penny had an odd, bemused look that was entirely unlike her. "I have another question."

Arianne remained unfazed. "Shoot."

"Tell me everything you know about Garrett." Penny propped herself up against the couch, turning bodily to face her.

She opened her mouth to comply, but for the second time that night, the words didn't come. Her own eyes widened in horror as she gaped down at Penny, who sat in smug satisfaction. Arianne's throat bobbed as she scrabbled at the coffin lid of her own condemnation.

"Okay—so—I know—I know *some* stuff," she sputtered. "Like...he's hot, and he doesn't actually speak French even though we had reservations at an authentic French restaurant…"

Not technically true, she had to admit. For all she knew, he was fluent and just hadn't articulated it around her. They'd only stared at the wine list then skedaddled. But there had to be more she knew about him. There had to be. "He said he goes on dates because he has tons to offer, and he wants to be happy with somebody apart from himself."

At that, Penny burst out laughing.

Embarrassment burned through Arianne's face from cheekbones to chin

Penny nudged her side, a playful grin bouncing over her features. "So, was he worth taking off early?"

Arianne swore she could hear her wallet screaming from her purse. Just like that, the world had kicked its own axis back on track. Heartbreak and dating and sex or no sex, none of that would change the black and choppy financial waters through which her leaky little lifeboat-studio was paddling.

But it was also a good fricking question.

"Man…" A long, slow breath hissed out from between her teeth as she stared aimlessly outward. "…too soon to tell, I think. Ask again when I get the next utilities bill."

Penny had the good manners to wince. "Well, back to happier topics, then. Did you get anything else out of him? What he's like? Favorite food? Any tattoos?"

She swallowed and remained quiet as her cheeks burned anew.

Penny shook her head. "You talked about yourself the entire time, didn't you?"

"I… ugh, fine. Yes. Yes, I did." She scoffed, as much disgusted at her own behavior as Penny's ability to predict it. "But that's because he kept asking about me. He was interesting. Engaged. A good conversation partner. That's a good thing."

"Oh, of course." Her roommate's eyes practically glittered with mischief. "I set you up with somebody you described as 'engaged.' Those relationships *never* end in disaster."

Arianne pointed a threatening finger at her diminutive roommate. "If you jinx me, bitch, I won't drink that bottle of fancy wine you're saving, I'll dump it down the drain."

"You wouldn't." A defensive outburst hidden behind a nervous laugh.

Arianne bounced her eyebrows, grinning. "Try me."

Penny threw up her hands and rose from the sofa, shaking her head. "I need to get a safe for my alcohol, I swear. A proper liquor cabinet. With a combination lock. And you need to ask him about himself a lot more when you go out with him next Tuesday."

"Oh, so now you're telling me I'm going out with him again too?" Arianne bobbed her head, trying not to grin. "Ballsy."

Penny rounded on her with an intensity that would have made a tyrannosaur back off. "You're bloody well right I am. You're going to go out with him and ask him all about himself and you're going to like it, and I am going to hear all about it when you get home, and it is going to be perfectly good for the both of us. Understood?"

A sinking feeling threatened to pull Arianne's rising good mood kicking and screaming to a shakier, uglier precipice over a darker abyss. "Penny? Did something happen between you and Keith?"

Penny bristled, stalking to the kitchen. The deep popping sound of a bottle opening was answer enough. "We fought. We made up after, but... it was bad." Everything in her movements told the truth—she was clinging tooth and nail to keep everything under a hood. "What gave it away?"

"You're cracking open a bottle of wine and insisting I keep dating the guy you set me up with," she said. "Also, you're...uh... you're not wearing your ring."

"We took it to the jewelers to get resized," Penny insisted. "I've lost weight. Stress."

Arianne rose, silent, before walking over and turning the British girl to face her instead of the glass of dark red she was about to drown herself in.

They stood for minutes, holding each other in silence, before mutually agreeing it was time for bed. Penny wiped her eyes once before padding away to the bedroom and locking the door.

Mute, Arianne twisted the cork back into the bottle and stuck it into the refrigerator. It wasn't perfect, but it would last longer than if it was left out in the open.

Funny how that worked.

Swiping the glass Penny had neglected, Arianne lifted it to her lips and downed the entire thing in one cheek-bulging gulp. Garrett may have preferred to take his time with things, but she saw what she wanted and took her fill. Even if her throat burned and the taste was overwhelming and the strength hit her like a gut punch. That was who she was. For better or worse, she wouldn't compromise.

Besides, she had shit to do. Voicemails to check. Invoices to file. Wedding photos to touch up. Marketing strategies to figure out.

No rest for the wicked.

Chapter Six

With a singed shirt sleeve and rueful thoughts, Garrett wove his way down Flatbush Avenue, meandering into the midst of the quiet suburbia of Mill Basin, Brooklyn, before crawling into home base and parking. Every step up his driveway-for-one that led to the door of his polite bachelor pad was like slogging through molasses.

She hadn't even called out after him. Even a curse word would have satisfied him.

Frozen at the doorway, key in the lock, his mind slipped back into the memory of kissing her cheek. Warm. Smooth. Her skin was a revelation in textures. Human beings didn't have skin that soft. She was a goddess. An angel. Some larger-than-life deity with a broken heart and emaciated hope.

She needed help.

More than that, though... maybe he did. It had been brief—and now, with the benefit of distance and hindsight, he could recognize it— but for a heartbeat, he'd considered it. Darting upward into a kiss to leave her breathless. Chasing her inside and drinking deep from Penny's bottle of *Chateau de Chasselas* and making passionate, unbridled love to that tower of a woman until dawn would rise. Living life according to the Philosophy of Ari.

But he knew—then and now—it wouldn't last.

It would arc high only to come down in flames on re-entry. That was not what he did. That was not what she needed. That was all she'd been getting from guys, and the entire situation needed to be reformed. Above all, reformation did not mean more of the bitter broken same with a different wrapper.

Locking the door behind him was a lonely sigh of relief.

Planting an ice pack on his arm—which felt fine but was more for the sake of soothing anxiety over burns than anything—was better.

His half of the duplex was built for him and his lifestyle—a one-bedroom, one bathroom, lavish-yet-cozy slice of heaven where he could seek refuge from the world. Plenty big for a guy and his ego, plenty spacious for a cute breakfast, but unwieldy for any couple to live there properly. It was a deliberate choice on his part. "Mr. Rebound," by definition, couldn't settle down. No woman would be at ease in a long-term relationship with a guy who was paid to date women for a living.

He grimaced as he crossed the short journey from bathroom to living room, flopped on a plush black couch, and seized the remote. His apartment was sparsely but deliberately decorated. A framed photo of a blonde woman and an older man with a girl and a boy between them. Another photo, with the girl in Peace Corps camo, the boy in graduation robes, and sadness in the woman's eyes. An orchid on the kitchen counter that he was doing his damnedest to keep alive, with partial success. An exercise bar strapped to the doorframe, the grip on the handles well-worn and wrapped with rough tape to toughen his hands and give the illusion of rough work. Best of all, a seventy-inch plasma screen mounted on the wall like the manliest of electronic trophies, proclaiming the virtues of ESPN and baseball highlights. Normally, Garrett would have devoured the statistics, the instant replays, the commentary, but tonight had been the first date of a new rebound contract.

That meant *Field of Dreams*.

His heart came alive as he picked up the movie halfway through. It didn't matter where he started, or finished, or came in. He knew every line. Every facial expression. The music, present where it needed to be and absent in the better places. Acting had been—was still—his passion, but baseball had been his pastime. Nor was there any better baseball movie than *Field of Dreams*. He had a kinship with Ray Kinsella, the humble Iowa corn farmer, commanded by a voice on the wind to build a baseball field in the middle of his crop. He'd never expected to do it. He'd nearly given everything for it. He'd gone out of his way, gone to the end of his hope and his resources, worn everything to the line on a windy promise of '*if you build it, they will come.*'

But, at the end of it all, the promise had come true. He had built it. They had come. The ghosts of the greats. "Shoeless" Joe Jackson, Archibald "Moonlight" Graham, Buck Weaver.

Including, last of all, Ray's estranged, long-deceased father.

The thump at the front door was an unwelcome distraction.

With a sigh, he paused the movie and swept open the door to reveal his visitor—a short, plump brunette with raised eyebrows, denim cutoffs, and a faded Eiffel Tower T-shirt. A large to-go cup with a straw was present in one hand—pure sweet tea with a thick lemon wedge inside. Most people's biology dictated that they were eighty percent water and zero percent tea. Olivia Williams, a born and raised Alabaman who'd taken the trip into "Yankee-land," had taken that as a challenge.

"C'mere, girl. How're you?" He couldn't restrain a grin, even in the lateness of the hour.

She embraced him as only his best friend could. "I'd be better if you'd invite me in. It's fricking freezing out here."

"Then you should've worn better clothing." Still, he immediately ushered her in, all the same. This was basically her second home. She was the non-related sister he actually liked.

The door closed behind her as she moved through his apartment as she had so often before. Past the family photos. Past the framed college diploma. Past the photo of Garrett at age eight in his elementary school production of *Peter Pan*.

The acting bug had bitten him early. He'd loved his first play. He'd hated the role of Hook. The beard had been scratchy, the shirt had been too puffy, and the hook cover had made his hand all sweaty and smell like plastic...but the smiles on people's faces had been a revelation. The crash of the applause for the first time, like a wave against the prow of their plywood Jolly Roger, had changed his life more than his minor in psychology ever had.

Instead, Olivia stood before his majestic television and rolled her eyes hard enough she must have been checking her own brain for damage. "Who is she?"

He blinked, innocent. "What do you mean?"

She gestured to the TV. "You're watching *Field of Dreams* again."

"It's a good movie." He looked back and forth between friend and screen. "What's wrong with *Field of Dreams*?"

"You only do that when you're about to put on your Mr. Rebound mask and go dating someone again." She sipped at her tea, lifting her eyebrows in an irrefutable "I am your best friend, therefore cut to the chase" fashion. "So, who is she?"

"It's not a mask." He stalked past her to flop back onto the couch.

"Dude. You bend yourself out of shape and pretend to be whatever you think she needs, all to help her get over a guy. It's a mask."

It may have been true, but that didn't mean he wouldn't defend his position. "It's like baseball, okay? If you're—"

Olivia groaned. "Oh, Lord, not a baseball analogy, please—"

"If you're up at bat, Olivia," he repeated, narrowing his eyes, "and you get hit by the ball one too many times, you start to flinch. You hold back on your swing because you're too focused on having to dodge a ball. Then you get struck out. It's not that you suck as a batter for flinching. It's that you need to feel safe to swing away." He gestured with his hands, firm in the point he made.

Olivia lifted an eyebrow. "So, the girls you rebound have been hit with too many balls and now they can't handle their wood?"

He covered his face.

She just cackled.

"I didn't mean it like that," he grumbled. "What I mean is, they've had a run of crappy pitchers, and I'm like a batting cage. Change comes from within. I don't teach them anything. I just make it possible by providing the right environment." He tossed the remote onto the couch beside him. "It's therapeutic."

"Maybe for them." She gestured with her drink toward him before stealing another mouthful. "For you, it's unhealthy as sin."

"It doesn't need to be healthy for me. What matters is the girl." His gaze fell, his mind pulled back to the front doorstep. *We could have made it last all night...but it would have been a mistake.*

"Great. So, I'm right. Who's the girl?" She grinned, unrepentant.

Weariness crept into his bones as he sighed, impotent, against the couch. "Her name is Ari. She's a wedding photographer. Happy?"

"Ecstatic." Her Southern accent was thick with sarcasm and good humor. The to-go cup rattled as she sucked air instead of tea. Licking her lips and frowning, she crossed the apartment to the fridge and tugged open the door. She rummaged in the fridge, bottles clinking in audible dissatisfaction. "How many times do I have to tell you? Sweet tea. Get some. All you have in here is micro-brew."

"Not true." He tucked an arm over the back of the couch, pulling himself around to peer after her. "I have two percent. Also some fruit punch."

"Hawaiian?"

"Uh..." He racked his brain. "Berry Blast."

"Ick." She hip-checked the fridge door shut with a clatter. "Who was it that turned you onto that crap? Miranda?"

He grinned at the ghosts of successful clients past. "Erin."

"Whatever. I can't keep track. I'm amazed you can." Olivia's face screwed up, the cogs spinning furiously, before she threw up her hands and tried and rebalance the ratio of tea-to-blood in her body with a glass of water.

"This *is* what I do for a living." He bit back on commenting on any injuries he'd suffered during his years as Mr. Rebound. Mostly physical. He took extreme precautions to prevent any more emotional scars.

His job required it.

Exhaling after chugging the glass, she rounded the counter. There was something different in the way she was approaching him. "Garrett, only a sociopath would call this 'living.'"

He sniffed once, crossing his arms. "Says the girl who kicked this off to begin with."

One way or another, it had all started with her.

They'd met in college and become instant friends. By graduation time, he was a barista with a useless Theatre Arts degree and a string of casual dates that went nowhere. She was a dental hygienist with a loving boyfriend and all signs pointing to a bright shiny ring.

Rising from the couch, he swiped and filled his own glass of water, shaking his head. "Remind me, again—who agreed to the idea that we go out? Hm? After your boyfriend took off and kicked your feelings in the dick?"

"Hon, my feelings do not have a penis." She laughed viciously, and he could have sworn fangs were peeking over her lips. "If anything, they have a supple and extremely ladylike vagina."

Garrett cringed before scrubbing a hand over his face. "C'mon, Olivia. What I do is a good thing. Structured dates, deliberate and purposeful. The girls I help—provided they don't dump me before the contract is up—go on to live happy, healthy romantic lives. It's worked for lots of girls prior." He hugged her around the shoulders. "Case in point."

Her mouth puckered, and her shoulders sagged. "I know," she relented. "I get it. I just worry about you, man. You can't draw from an empty well."

He stared at the screen, still paused on the contemplative face of a young Kevin Costner. "My well doesn't need to be full because I don't draw from it."

The last time he had didn't bear talking about.

He turned the remote over in his hands, sighing. "Now, are you finally going to tell me why you're showing up on my doorstep at—" he glanced at the wall-clock, lifting an eyebrow, "—a quarter to midnight?"

Wordless, Olivia crossed the room and took a seat beside him. Her wedding ring glinted in the light. Garrett had been her Man of Honor. Five years of happy marriage had followed since. Her eyes creased at the corners as she offered up the kind of humble, small smile a person wears when their life is revolving on a very small axis.

"I wanted to let you know—Nathan and I... we're going to start a family."

His eyes widened before he dropped his gaze, laser-like, to focus on her belly. "You're not—"

She laughed and swatted his arm. "No, doofus. But we've made the decision, and we're going to start trying to have ourselves a tiny human. Figure I needed to start tapping into my inherent maternal instincts and all that." She beamed at him, practically bursting with pride. "Besides, this is the kind of news you share in person."

"Man...you are going to be the best tiny-human-nurturer the world has ever seen." His cheeks ached from smiling. "And I bet you guys are going to get pregnant fast."

"Hopefully not *too* fast." She snorted once, shaking her head. "Any extra cushion we can get on our savings is a blessing."

"Amen," he intoned, solemn.

Being Mr. Rebound paid well—not *exorbitantly*, of course, but well enough—but the looming arbiter of bills was always present. "So, after that bombshell, are you going to sit down and watch a forgotten classic with me, or keep criticizing my career and choice in beverages?" He waggled his eyebrows. "You'll need to get used to staying off your feet, O ye tiny-human-nurturer-of-delicate-constitution."

"I'm not pregnant *yet*," she laughed. "Besides, it's late. I'll take off and let you do your ritual thing." She grimaced, but the empathy in her eyes was clear as satin. "Love you."

"Love you too."

She waved as she sauntered toward his door. "Just check in on occasion, okay? And for the love of God, please don't have sex with this one too."

He scoffed in mock offense. "You make it sound like I have sex with *all* of them."

"Close enough." She slid back into her flats with a dismissive wave of her hand.

"Not *remotely*, thank you." He sniffed once, indignant. "It's a judgement call made with extreme care and sobriety, based on situational context and a massive list of variable factors, and it is entirely to do with her emotional recovery and catharsis."

"Uh-huh." Her arms were crossed as she raised a single eyebrow. An enviable talent. "You're still getting paid for it. Dress it up however you want."

Sometimes, there was no winning with her. "Well, at least I'm safe about it."

She gazed to the side, mischief flitting across her features. "It's overrated."

He pointed at her chest. "Uh, you just told me—you and Nathan are trying to start a family. Protection is kind of *against* the point in that case."

"Just saying." She laughed at her own joke as she swept open the door and bid him goodbye. "See you in the hospital when you bust your other leg."

He snorted to himself as the door closed.

True, his leg twinged a little, and his arm tingled, but the phantom pain faded as the movie resumed.

If ever he did settle down, it would need to be someone passionate, and faithful, and wild. Someone understanding, but pragmatic. Someone with life experience but who knew how important the home—and by extension, family—was.

Someone who could see his past as not just a laundry-list of women's names and phone numbers, but the stream of mended hearts underneath it all, and still love him. Someone who never compromised on what was right.

He could dream, anyway.

Chapter Seven

7:38 AM. Phase 1 - Subject - Arianne Reynolds. Projected release time: D6. Method: Levo Nolo Contendere. Recon and recap ASAP.

Barely a minute later, Garrett's phone *blooped* right back. David, his tech guy and man-in-the-chair, prompt as always. *Come on over. Full spread.*

Garrett dressed in a matter of minutes and was out the door with his shirt halfway buttoned. "Full spread" was David-speak for the miracle his wife, Lauren, could perform—not with Excel or some other spreadsheet application, but in the kitchen. She was a chef by trade, perpetually perky and pulling pages from both the Betty Crocker and Paula Dean schools of cooking. According to her, food didn't have to be insanely extravagant. It just had to be mouth-orgasm tasty. If this was going to be anything like last time, he needed to get there before David took the last strips of applewood-smoked bacon.

In the early days of his career as Mr. Rebound, Garrett had struggled enough in keeping himself afloat with his barista paycheck, let alone accommodating the inherent financial strain of constantly paying for dates with random clients. Fortunately, in an airport bar over the Christmas holidays, he had met David.

They'd joined forces a short time later. True, *technically* speaking, David was at the office for CyberTek Industries, where he made an obscene amount of money debugging updates for programs regulating financial coding. But he also worked from home, which allowed "Mr. Rebound, Inc." to have their own Batcave in the making. It was David's idea to start charging for Mr. Rebound's services. Nothing extravagant—a retainer for his services and a stipend to cover the cost of dates, which would be as expensive as necessary and not a penny more.

Traffic passed in a horrible series of red lights and douchebags who didn't use their signals until he was parked on the curb and stumbling through the unlocked front door. The smells of breakfast led him down the hallway like a beckoning finger. There, seated at the table, were two of his favorite people in the world. His partner-in-crime, with his laptop open beside his plate, and his partner's partner, with a spread of waffles, fresh berries, various toppings and condiments, milk, juices, a platter of sausage and one of hash browns spread before them.

Sure enough, one of the plates was empty, bearing its hopeless offerings of a stained paper towel and crusted salt as David devoured the last piece of the bacon with an innocent shrug.

Garrett cursed his luck and every red light that had stopped him before giving David a clap on the shoulder by way of greeting. "Got here as quick as I could. Not quick enough, apparently."

"Relax." Lauren cut in before David could respond and nodded to a cast-iron skillet left on the stove top. "I made extra. Kyle's friend came over this morning, so we made a ton."

Garrett immediately claimed his bacon prize, plopping down across the table from the happily married couple. "You are a goddess."

She snorted, dismissing his compliment like so much hot air. "Uh-huh, uh-huh. Let's see you say that when you're bacon-sober." Her eyes crinkled at the edges, nonetheless.

David dabbed at his lips with a napkin. "No man should have to be bacon-sober, sweetheart. It's the worst kind of prohibition."

"What's wrong with being bacon-sober? Jews don't eat bacon. They're fine." Lauren chuckled.

"Yeah, but—"

"So, David," interjected Garrett, after swallowing a bite of waffle and whipped cream. "Did the advance from our latest client come through?"

David tapped at a laptop. "Yeah. Penny sent through the advance and the deposit for last night's date. It's the weekend, so it'll take a few days before it shows up in the account, but it should be fine."

Satisfied, Garrett chased breakfast with a glass of apple juice and immediately sought a refill. Lauren had a cast-iron rule that the only juice that would pass the threshold of their house would be one hundred percent organic, even if they had to drive twenty miles to a farmer's market for the stuff. Fortunately, internet shopping being what it was, he had gifted her a subscription to a place in Washington that shipped organic apple juice across the country. They'd loved it, and he'd benefited by sampling the wares most times he came over.

He paused, staring into the brass-colored liquid in his mug. Ari would probably appreciate a subscription as well. Or maybe she'd mock him. She'd probably mock him. But then she'd probably also sign up for it with that twinkle in her eyes that said she actually liked it...or so he hoped.

He shook his head once. This was getting out of hand. It had been one date. One first rebound date. There was still so much more to do, and he needed to be focusing on her, not the way she made him feel.

Five dates to go, at any rate.

"Okay." A knowing smile sat on David's face, half-bemused, half-concerned, as he leaned over and pecked Lauren's cheek. "Let me help Lauren clear up the mess, and we'll get straight into outlining a strategy."

Lauren crossed to the kitchen and began carefully wiping out the skillet. "I know you guys have your entrepreneurial home-business thing, but just remember Kyle has his first ortho appointment at noon."

David stood by her side, nodding in response as he seized a towel to dry the dishes. "And then we're going grocery shopping. I'm on it, darling."

They met in a kiss. Garrett watched from his chair as though through a pane of frosted glass. Domestic life suited them. More, it looked *good* on them. Not to mention their Kyle was already four.

Garrett had been Mr. Rebound for years, now. He had changed lives. David's and Lauren's were two more examples. They weren't jewels in his crown. There was no crown. Garrett couldn't demean or quantify them like that. Better by far if nobody paid attention to the man behind the curtain. He was the wizard, guiding people to what they needed while ultimately, in the grand scheme of things, lying his ass off the entire time.

Lying kept things professional.

Plus, with David's help, Garrett had been able to make a living doing this. Not like the financial purgatory-limbo nightmare he'd been living as an out-of-work almost-actor in a coffee shop. Now, he had his own place. A car he actually *owned*. Lying, one way or another, kept food on the table and hearts mended around him. No single woman could be worth giving all that up.

He thanked Lauren quietly for the magnificent breakfast as she cleared away his place. Finally, he followed David down the navy-blue carpeted hallway, past the framed family portraits and wedding shots and crayon doodles from Kyle-aged-one to his home office, where they closed the glass doors and took their respective swivel seats.

"New premium contract..." he muttered, tapping at his laptop while Garrett swiped a marker and moved to the massive whiteboard on the opposite wall. "And...done. Let's make a pathway to rebound for Arianne Reynolds."

"Let's." Garrett scribbled her name at the top. "Projected release time: D6."

It helped to keep all aspects of his job sounding like actual corporate business gibberish. Not only did it deter snoops and sticky-beaks, but it felt like this was a legitimate business venture instead of what might have been the oddest self-created job in history.

"So, six dates." David dragged a cable from a projector to the laptop. On the opposite wall, he brought up an enlarged image of Ari's Facebook page. "You think she really needs that many?"

"Based on an initial assessment, yeah." Garrett stroked his goatee. "At the most, we might need a break-off date after the sixth, but I can't see a reason to go beyond that."

As he spoke, he stretched a timeline across the whiteboard and marked the end of their time together with an "x." Where in the future he'd come face-to-face with that ugly little cross, he couldn't say—but it would come, inevitable and undesirable as it might be.

David grunted, fingers flying across the keyboard. "Long haul, then. How're you going to break it off?"

Garrett guided the marker across the marble-white board like the chisel of a stonecutter across a headstone. "*Levo Nolo Contendere.*"

The rapid-fire *takkatakkatakka* of fingers on keys cut short as David glowered. "Dude. *English.*"

Garrett rolled his eyes. "No-contest-boost. I'll say I took a job in a city with enough of a distance gap to make breaking off realistic—say, six hours' drive-time or something. When the 'break-up' comes, I can let her down easily by boosting her confidence. 'Look, let's be honest, you're completely out of my league anyway, and I don't want to tie you down when you can do so much better—I'll be fine, you go ahead and do you,' that sort of thing. She's feeling like she can take on the world, Penny pays us out, and we move on."

David nodded, scrolling through posted photos of Ari on her Facebook and Instagram feeds as he hunted for a demographic of guys she seemed to be into, as he'd done with clients prior.

Garrett fell silent as he examined his own handwriting. There was so, so, *so* much that could go wrong in the interim, but that was the nature of love and dating. Not the least of which, of course, was the chance Penny would somehow screw everything all to hell and back.

Prescient as ever, David's next question was "What do we know about the contact? Penny... Ansel—Anhelsel—An—Penny What's-Her-Face?"

"Anselheurst." Garrett sighed. "British. Kind of a pop-alt-rock feel. She didn't come outright and say it, but I'm pretty sure she's the reason Ari's prior relationship collapsed."

"Manipulation?" They'd seen plenty of that before.

Garrett shook his head. "Cheating."

David groaned. "Oh, joy. One of *those*."

"She denied it outright, but you could see it in her body language." Garrett tugged his phone from the pocket of his most-relaxed jeans, unlocking the screen with a swipe of his thumb, but still eyeing the shorthand notes he'd taken during his meeting in The Minefield.

The way she'd averted her gaze. The almost pathological insistence that she hadn't done anything. How she hadn't tried to negotiate, or to address any financial strain, or the supposed injustice of having to pay so much for her friend's happiness.

It all added up to Penny cheating with Lucas. "I put her on a premium contract to be safe."

"That's still going to be sticky." David's voice was taut as he blew up her Facebook profile picture like a massive scarlet letter. "Because, unless she's severely behind in updating her account…"

A man, tagged in the photo as Keith, was down on one knee with a black velvet box in one hand. Her hands covered her mouth, and tears were visible in her eyes, even from the distance of the camera. Her relationship status matched their suspicions, listed as "Engaged to Keith McAlhambra."

Garrett's mouth twisted as the apple juice aftertaste soured.

"Well…" He spoke slowly, trying to gauge his words against the incriminating evidence on Penny and their sprawling plans across the whiteboard. "That doesn't have to affect our plans for Ari. Not entirely."

He nodded with each sentence, more convinced of his correct direction as his mind raced for rationale. "Not at all, come to think of it. She knows Lucas cheated, just not with who. For Ari to successfully get over him and move ahead with her own life, she doesn't need to. It wouldn't matter if it was with Penny. The fact remains he cheated, and he was the one to break off the relationship, not Ari. She just needs to come to terms with the fact he was unfaithful."

David frowned. "What about the 'why?'"

"What *about* the 'why?'"

"Hey, I actually listen to all your relationship-analysis crap, you know. I don't just do your accounting and cyberstalking." David scoffed. "You're always going on about the 'why.' A girl needs to know *why* a guy cheated on her before she can really make peace with it. How is Ari Reynolds any different?"

The question silenced him as effectively as the Firecracker he'd had last night.

"She's different because..." He fumbled for a way to fill in the silence. "Uh..."

David narrowed his eyes, the stylus twirling between his fingers. "Tell me everything about Ari. And the first date."

Garrett sighed, unable to stop the corners of his mouth pulling upward. "I don't even know where to begin, man. She's... incredible."

"How so?" Still, he spun the stylus.

Garrett couldn't fight a chuckle at the memory of Ari drawing out "bullshit" at his expense. "She called me out."

"On?"

"On *everything*. I brought my 'A'-grade material, and the only thing she conceded on was that Lucas was trash." He stuffed his phone back into his pocket, marveling at the prior night. "She made me laugh; I made her laugh. She's clever, she's cocky, she's hurt, she's flirtatious. Every move, every trick, every line I brought was dead in the water with her."

He wasn't used to someone challenging him so much—let alone *winning* so often. It did make the selfish victory of the doorstop denial that much more satisfying, even if he'd had one blue-balled night to follow. She was eager for a second date, too, if Penny was telling the truth. Visions of Ari coming at him like a succubus, intent on nothing short of conquering and claiming him as a trophy of her own, danced through his mind.

He snorted. Even her dominance theory was turning out to have more traction than he wanted.

"Okay. But she doesn't know about your job, right?" There was an unmistakable edge in David's voice as the stylus spun to a stop in his grip. "We don't need another Courtney."

Hearing the "C" word was like a bucket of ice water over his crotch. Garrett's mid-morning fantasies of Ari vanished in a blink.

"No." Short and sharp. "One Courtney is more than enough."

"Good." David sifted through Penny's online photos some more before nodding. "I think we have enough material here to go on. What's the plan for the second date?"

Garrett grunted, stroking his goatee as he pondered. "We spent most of the first date talking about her—her life, her romantic history, interests, that stuff. She'll probably want to try and turn the focus onto me this time."

"And that's...bad?"

"Not at all. But it's what she wants, not what she needs." He tapped at his phone, doing a quick search before flashing the screen at his assistant. "Penny told me Tuesday is Ari's day off. I'll take her here.

Keep the focus on her."

David squinted at the screen. "Photography exhibition at the Robert Mann Gallery in the Upper East Side. Bit obvious, isn't it?"

Garrett remained silent. True, it was on the nose, and something of a gamble—taking a photographer to a photography exhibit on their day off—but it would put her in a comfortable, familiar arena.

The silence stretched on before David cleared his throat. "You, uh…you didn't answer my question earlier."

Garrett blinked. "Which one?"

"The one about Ari not needing to know why Lucas cheated."

"Oh." He stared at the line across the board, ending with its small and ugly "x." It felt too representative, in a way. Everybody was an ex waiting to happen, in the great and grand scheme of it all. Even a person who lived happily married for their entire life would wind up single again once their spouse died.

He drew in a breath. "No. You're right. She needs to know. I can't answer that for her…but Penny could."

The silence churned like a bloated stomach.

"Any idea on when you're going to burst that pimple?" David's furious typing clattered against the keys of his keyboard.

Garrett shook his head. "No, but whenever I do, it's going to get ugly." He took quick stock of the time before he nodded to himself. "That should about do us for this morning. Good session."

David frowned. "Why? What time is it?"

"It's a quarter past noon. Kyle's got his thing, remember? Orthopedics?"

David hurriedly saved their work, closing up shop while cursing under his breath. Sure enough, a rap on the glass doors of the home office heralded Lauren, concern on her face.

"Sweetie—"

"Yup. I'm on it. Kyle." The sliding glass door rattled in its base as he opened it and darted through, stealing a quick peck on her cheek. "I'm sorry, hon. We ran long."

Abandoned, Garrett snapped photos of the whiteboard and plan before flipping it back to face the wall. He sighed. David was right. He was always right. That was why he was the eyes and ears, the tech guy. The brain to Garrett's heart. To stop him from tripping over his own stupid overeager emotions.

Still, he had the rest of the day to himself, and idle hands would dent his chances at doing his job to the best of his ability.

Best, then, he familiarized himself with the photography exhibit for their second date.

Chapter Eight

"Oh my *god!* Are you Courtney Hazleroth? @CourtofCourtney on Instagram?" The girl couldn't have been older than fourteen but dressed like she was trying to pass for legal. The look worked for her.

Courtney beamed. "Like, is there any other?"

"Can we grab a selfie together?" The young girl bounced on the balls of her feet, almost ready to explode.

"Uh, of course we can." She huddled close, pursing her lips together just so. The phone's camera flash was inconsequential. She was used to it. Hell, she *bathed* in it.

Courtney watched the starstruck young fan tapping at her phone as she bounced away. Contentment blossomed around her heart before she turned toward her haven and heaven. Selfies with fans were a staple of going out. Influencers had to influence, after all. Besides, it was always nice to be able to do charity work like that. But she wasn't there for fan interactions or shoulder-rubbing. No, this was much, much more important. This was for *love.*

People could say what they wanted about finding inner peace in yoga classes or whatever, but there was nothing—*nothing*—that could bring unfiltered inner peace like a dress boutique. If Starbucks was her home-away-from-home, then this boutique, Ophelia's Boutique, tucked away in the Upper East Side, was her church. The calm fluorescent lighting, the soft carpet, the clean glass, the gleaming chrome racks, the smell of in-store brand-name perfume... then there were the works of art. Milan. Paris. Barcelona. All straight from the runway, all gorgeous. True, their price tags reflected their artistry—as well they ought to. Half the prestige of wearing a gorgeous number was reflected in how much one paid for it. She needed the perfect outfit for tonight.

After all, it wasn't every night when a girl got engaged to the love of her life, was it?

Tapping a perfectly manicured fingernail against her strawberry-pink lips, she perused the racks the way Aphrodite might wander through a garden. The outfit had to be perfect. *Perfect.* Something slinky, but sweet. Something that wouldn't make her look desperate, or like she expected him to pop the question. Something that implied "bride" without dropping the title in his lap.

The fact he wasn't expecting to see her tonight was inconsequential at best. The fact he hadn't seen her for over a year was a little more irritating, but she worked around it. He'd sent her love letters aplenty, and she cherished every single one. They were even sprayed with his cologne.

Okay, so she'd had to write the letters for him. And buy a bottle to spray on them herself.

But so what?

Garrett Reid was the love of her life. He had been from the moment he'd swept in, all handsome blue eyes and white teeth and understanding soul. He was so smart. Cultured. And not just, like, theater-cultured. *Book*-cultured. He'd been the one to take her to her first play, like in the Shakespeare days or whatever. They'd gone on their first date together to see *Wicked*. On Broadway.

So what if she'd never seen a musical before despite living in Manhattan? She'd been able to share that first with him. Or, more accurately, she'd shared half the first with him. There had been an "incident" where they didn't get to see the second act—which was completely unfair, because the stupid lead witch was just being the *worst* to the poor Elph-what's-her-name, and apparently everybody *had* to get all upset because Courtney tried to *do* something about it.

After they'd been walked out by security and cheated from seeing the rest of the show, he'd made it up to her by taking her to see *The Importance of Being Earnest*. It was like *Downton Abbey* if it was a comedy, and—in her opinion—far superior to boring old *Wicked*.

Plus, it had clearly been a sign. Cecily and Algernon had been destined to be together from the start, and they were obviously metaphors for herself and Garrett. She was Cecily, the beautiful, petite, blonde genius from a well-to-do family. He was Algernon, the dashing, roguish man with a good heart beneath his erring, wayward ways. Algernon and Garrett even had their own cute nicknames—Algy and Gare-bear. Most importantly, Algy and Cecily wound up together at the end of the play *and* the book. That meant she and Garrett had to wind up together too. It was only logical.

True, it was taking longer than she would have liked, but nobody said true love came without sacrifice.

Pursing her lips, she selected a tasteful cyan number. That would bring out her eyes, match his own, and it was a restful color that symbolized relaxation. With a nod, she whisked away into the changing room. After all, clothing that looked good on the rack did not always look good on the person.

Peeling away her strategically placed layers on layers, she slid into what she hoped would be her engagement outfit, zipped it up, and smoothed it down. Check side mirror. Check head on. Check other side. Twist. Twirl. Pose. *Slay it, girl.* Chiffon, scoop-neck, trimmed with a fabric belt at the waist to give her a truly heart-stopping hourglass figure and ended tastefully low on the thigh but still above the knee.

All she would have to do now was pair it with the perfect set of shoes, and Garrett, her darling Gare-bear, would be kneeling before her. Ideally. In theory. Once she showed up at his house. Hopefully, she wouldn't have to pick out her own ring as well, but if he had to accompany her to the jewelers to get some ideas then buy it while her back was turned, well…she could live with that.

Taking a very necessary extra moment to admire herself in the full-length mirrors, she huffed. Of course, none of her friends could be bothered showing up to help her shop. They'd all been too busy with some pathetic excuse or other, like "I'm having my album launch party in Pomona Beach" or "what do you mean you can't make it I told you about this weeks ago" or "this is the last time Courtney I swear to God." Honestly. Sometimes, it was like they didn't even care. With a frown souring her good mood, she carefully slipped out of her to-be-engaged number and put her myriad of regular form-fitting clothes back on.

Stepping out of the changing room, she froze. Some pasty white little man was standing in front of her with sweat stains in the armpits of his business shirt and a big manila envelope in his hands.

"C-Courtney Hazleroth?" he stammered.

She gave him a gentle, Instagram-worthy smile. Yet another fan, intimidated by her star power. "Speaking."

He held out the envelope with both hands. Based on past experience, it was probably a love letter. It wouldn't have been her first, or even her thirtieth. The pale shy guys like this one usually couldn't get their words out properly. It was kind of hot, in a sickly beta-male sort of way. Situation-specific hotness. Unlike Garrett, who was hot twenty-four seven.

"For me?" She kept up her sweet smile as she hung her dress on the still-open change room door and took the envelope with both hands. There were sweat marks on the envelope where his fingers had been touching it. *Ew.*

The man gulped. "Y-y-you've been served. W-we're sorry this

took so long to get to you—normally this only takes about two weeks—but, uh…everyone who got your case kind of, um…q-quit…"

"Served?" she said, trying not to frown. Frowning made wrinkles. She tugged at the little tab and tore open the envelope, slipping a sheet of paper into her hand as she read the words of the bold header.

"In the Justice Court… county clerk…" Her eyes widened at the next words. Her voice rang through the entire boutique like a shattering window. "*Cease and desist?*"

She whipped her head up, but the pasty man was already long gone. Instead, other shoppers were doing that thing people always did around her where they stared while trying to look like they weren't staring. Peeking at her. Watching her. Gawking. Trying to hide their phones behind a hand or a clothing rack with a gap for the camera to still see through.

Rage twitched at the edge of her eyes. Maybe it wasn't so bad. Maybe it was a mistake. She glared at the paper as it shook in her hand, scouring over the details. Filed against the party of Courtney Hazleroth, for the protection—the actual *protection*—of…

…of Garrett Reid.

This had to be some kind of mistake.

She closed her eyes, forcing herself to take a slow, deep breath. Ophelia's was a church of fashion. She couldn't go profaning the inner peace she found in here with a bit of a temper tantrum, no matter how justified it may have been in the moment. By the time she'd taken three such breaths, she felt better about the situation. The silly piece of paper was crushed into a ball in her hand. It wouldn't make a difference. If anything, it was just one more excuse to go talking to her Gare-bear.

But it did put a damper on what was supposed to be a celebration for the night.

A tall, slender brunette wearing the muted black pantsuit of an Ophelia's employee glided up to her, wearing a simpering expression. "Is everything all right, miss?"

Courtney chewed her lip for a moment before shaking her head. "Not quite. But I'll be back."

Chapter Nine

Well, that was a colossal bore, thought Garrett, ditching the Robert Mann Gallery in Manhattan after only half an hour. It was barely populated in the afternoon hours, and those few people who were there were the impossibly pretentious perusers who wore turtlenecks and eyeliner without even a semblance of irony. How many ways a photographer could take a photo of a crack in a sidewalk with the blurry image of a leafy stalk emerging was something Garrett had never needed to know. Though, apparently, the answer was "enough to fill a frigging wall."

But lest he be blown away by the artistic ambrosia that was Monochrome Sidewalk Crack, he couldn't possibly have been prepared for the sheer visionary brilliance that was Sepia-Toned Broken Cell phone, or Monochrome Rusty Car, or the veritable *masterpiece* that was the main event of Grayscale Sunlight Through Dirty Broken Window.

As he shut himself in his car and groaned, he did have to admit there was at least one upside. This was good practice. He'd bluffed his way through a full ten minutes of artsy-fartsy conversation with someone who'd seemed at least distantly contented with Garrett's hot air and usage of photography buzzwords like "chiaroscuro" and "depth of field." If he could make it through that without being dismissed as a buffoon on par with a politician, he could make it through a conversation with Ari.

He stared at his phone as his body went through the motions. Jittery nerves. Clammy hands, sweaty palms, fat-feeling fingers. He should have overcome these tremblings a dozen clients before this point. A hundred clients before.

But it made him feel so freaking *alive*.

With a swig of water, he dialed Ari's number and listened to the cold judgment of the dial tone. This was around the time she took her lunch break, according to Penny. Hopefully, Ari's personal cell was still turned on. Calling via her actual number would have been an overstep—

particularly when she never actually told him where she worked. True, the business card from Penny was still sitting pretty in his wallet, but *Ari* didn't know that.

After five rings, her voice filled the line. "Hey."

Shitshitshitshit— "Uh—h-hi—"

"—you know what to do. If it's urgent, call me again." An apathetic "beep" signaled the start of her voicemail.

He hung up.

The silence rang in the car, punctuated by his heaving breaths. He swore he could *hear* himself sweating. An earthquake had seized his insides. The nerves were normal. The strength of them, though—that was not.

He sighed, staring blankly through the windshield. It was fine. Everything was fine. Nothing was wrong. He could just call her tonight, when he knew she'd be off work. This was a completely understandable, easily surmountable obstacle that he'd come across a hundred times in his career.

Unless she shut him down.

Unless she canceled the second date.

His throat closed, tight and clenched—but he couldn't call again. Normally, he would have been bound by the desperation rule of three— namely, a would-be suitor *never* was the one to reach out for contact three times in a row. Three unanswered texts, three missed calls, three emails, three carrier pigeons—whatever combination thereof, a would-be suitor was never to hit that magic number of three. If they did, the stink of desperation would infect their every message afterward.

But there, Ari's voicemail had tightened it to a rule of *two*. "If it's urgent, call me again." A confirmation on a second date wasn't urgent—and "urgent," by nature, meant "time-sensitive." The confirmation wasn't "time-sensitive."

Swallowing, he rubbed a hand over his face. He was fine. Everything was fine. He should have left a voicemail, but it was whatever. Totally whatever. She'd see the missed call. She'd call back.

Shit.

~ * ~

Arianne's office consisted of a simple cubicle of a space with a soundproof door, a nice computer desk, and her own sleek black office phone. Sure, the entire place was small enough she could have stuck her head out her door and called out to either of her employees, but this felt much fancier.

She swiveled in her office chair with the languid motion of a hangman's noose tightening. Arianne stared at her cellphone in both hands as though the slightest movement would cause it to explode.

The screen read "Garrett — Missed Call."

True to his word, he'd called her the next day.

Her wide gaze remained glued to the screen, watching to see if the little icon marking a voice message would flash up. Seconds ticked past in thumping heartbeats as she scrambled to come up with some kind of plan. Some kind of answer.

Was this a call to confirm their date on Tuesday? It *was* her day off. Not that he knew.

Was this to see how she was doing? She wouldn't entirely object.

Did she even want to see him again? Oh, hell yes, she did, as much to enjoy the presence of his company again as to seduce him into a slobbering mess before leaving him out to dry, unfulfilled, as righteous payback.

The question she couldn't answer, however, was a simple one—did she call him back, or wait for him to call again? There was no icon for a voice message yet, which meant he was either leaving her a whopping five-minute voicemail, or nothing at all.

She swallowed once, shook herself twice. This was ridiculous. There was nothing to be gained in getting herself tied up in knots over a guy, no matter how hot. Or how earnest. Or how funny, or how much he could roll with every punch she'd thrown his way, or how he looked at her like—

Goddammit.

She tossed her cell aside. It clattered across her desk as she snatched the proper black business line and tapped a number. She needed a distraction in the form of work, and she needed it now.

"Zoey?" she said into the phone. "Is our three-thirty here yet?"

It was going on four o'clock.

"Oh. Right," said Zoey. "No. They called and canceled."

Arianne groaned. "When?"

"Like…three hours ago?" Her wince was evident in every word.

"And you didn't tell me this because…?"

"You were out to lunch!" Zoey protested, defensive. "I would've told you when you got back, but that's when I went to lunch, and then… I guess I just forgot."

"You just—" Her breath crackled in the earpiece as she sighed through gritted teeth. "Fine. They were our last appointment for the day, right?"

"Let me see…" The sound of a mouse clicking repeatedly, combined with Zoey's mumbling of "hang on… one sec… okay, give me a moment…" was enough to push Arianne over the edge.

She hung up the business phone and stuffed her cell back into her pocket. The office door clicked shut as she stalked past Sierra, her assistant, who took one look at Arianne's expression and fell into step behind her boss.

"Zoey?" she asked.

"Something like that." Arianne glanced back and down at Sierra, Arianne's mouth twisting. Her stride turned to a walk, then to a pondering drift.

"I could use your help too, actually. Come with me." Her voice left it clear there was no choice in the matter.

The look on Sierra's face was one of arriving for a dental appointment, resigned to an unpleasant but necessary experience. She followed through the photography studio and out to the front office, abandoned save for Zoey, clicking furiously as she struggled through tabs and tried to find the proper schedule on the computer screen. Like a teenager caught with porn, she jumped and cringed.

"Ari!" she yelped. "I'm sorry—I was—I tried to find the schedule, but then I opened the budget by accident, and—"

"We need to talk." Arianne dragged a chair over from the waiting area, turning it around to sit backward, resting her elbows on the backrest. Sierra followed suit, sitting like a regular person.

Zoey remained frozen in her office chair with her gaze glued to Arianne. "Am I fired?"

She sniffed. "Technically, you're still an intern, so the term would be 'dismissed,' not 'terminated.'" She waved a hand. "But that's semantics."

She sighed as the foundation of her self-esteem flaked apart. This didn't need to happen. Not really. But the fact remained she couldn't think of another option outside of Penny, and that was no option at all. Not after last night. She had enough on her plate. Arianne hadn't asked any further about the details of the fight with her fiancé, but apparently it had been vicious enough to leave Penny crying. Arianne had heard the unsteady breathing and not-quite-muffled whines from her bedroom before she fell asleep herself.

Therefore, this was her only option.

"Okay, so…I went out on a date last night." Arianne cast her gaze to the moss-green carpet. "And this guy is… I can't even begin to describe him. In a good way, I mean, but just… like… *damn*, man. And he just called back, and I let it go to voicemail, and I have no idea what to do." She scoffed, shaking her head in disbelief at her own predicament as she ran her fingers through her hair and rested her temple in her palm.

"Even if I did call him back, what do I even say?"

Zoey blinked.

"Wait." Sierra leaned in with a frown. "So she's *not* fired—dismissed—whatever?"

"Huh?" Arianne looked from one to the other and back. "No, she isn't fired. She's been here like two weeks. She's going to make mistakes. I'm not that heartless. Besides, she's covered my ass more times than I can count. Especially with kids. You've seen me with kids."

"And teens." Sierra snorted. "My sister is still terrified of you. Hell of a way to take her prom photos, Arianne."

"Oh, bite me." She waved a hand in dismissal. "So, what if I was short with her? She kept squirming."

"Short?" Sierra lifted a thin eyebrow. "You threatened to stuff her corsage down her throat and hang her from the ceiling fan."

"Not to her face, I didn't." It was a basic rule of thumb—never speak bad about a customer in front of them. But it was one of a hundred examples Sierra could have pulled out of her hat. One way or another, her artistic talents weren't cut out for this specific vein of people-pleasing, and she knew it. "Ugh. Whatever."

Zoey let out a slight giggle before venturing to speak. "So... you're not mad?"

Arianne waved a hand. "Nah. People cancel all the time. It's whatever." She rolled her eyes as her wallet silently chided her from her purse. "Well, okay, it's not *whatever*. It's not good. But I've got a shoot in Kentucky later this week, and then one in Oregon—praise be to Katie—so we should be okay to keep the lights on in here for another week."

The "Katie" in question was her older sister, Katie Reynolds, a flight attendant and the silent crux of Eternal Bride Photography staying afloat even half as long as it had. Family of airline employees were able to fly free, which meant that—though her online market struggled for life in general—Arianne was able to offer her services nationwide.

"Sweet." Sierra sniffed and kicked back in her chair, stretching her spindly tan legs before her. "So, tell us about these guy troubles again?"

"Also, are you allowed to talk guy issues in the office?" Zoey looked from assistant to business owner with apprehension. Her earlier failures still weighed on her, plain to see.

Arianne glanced out the glass front door to make sure nobody was walking toward their place. Even the parking lot out front of the strip mall was deserted. "I mean, neither of you are planning on suing for inappropriate workplace behavior or anything, are you?"

Zoey shook her head vigorously.

Sierra shrugged, pursing her lips to hide a teasing smile.

It was enough of a "no" for Arianne.

Arianne dropped her hand from her temple, snickering. "Zoey, girl, loosen up. It's fine. This is workplace camaraderie. Getting to know your coworkers. You've got, what, five weeks left on your capstone for your administrative assistant course? You're going to get hired on as long as you don't assault a customer or burn the place to the ground." *And as long as I can afford to*, she added silently.

Zoey's face blossomed into relaxed contentment. "So, are you going to tell us what's going on? I mean…whatever it is, it's important enough for you to come out of your office, and time's a-ticking. Are you calling him back or what?"

Arianne threw up her hands. "I have no idea, okay? I like him. He's hot. Douchey goatee, but if you picture him without it, he'd probably look like he's in high school."

"Ouch." Sierra pressed her lips tight, hiding a smile.

Zoey cringed. "Yikes."

"Thank you," snapped Arianne, a little defensive on his behalf.

Partly because it reflected her own choice in guys. Partly because she might have, kind of, wanted him to keep the goatee on. Ordinarily, facial hair was a turnoff. It was too easy to imagine microbial bugs crawling around in the whiskers. But when he'd kissed her cheek last night, it had been this sensation of scratchy and smooth, rough and sweet, all mixed together. It was intoxicating. Maybe she'd become a beard girl at this rate.

Small steps, anyway. She'd start with a trim goatee.

She gave Sierra and Zoey the highlights of the prior night, all the parts they needed to know—they laughed at the Firecracker incident until Sierra was crying—but by the end, both of them had come to the same conclusion.

"Call him back." Zoey's voice rang with surprising confidence.

"Wha—now?" Arianne blustered, looking from one friend to the other.

"Right the hell now, girl. We'll coach you." The look on Sierra's face was positively carnivorous, her wicked grin flashing off white teeth that glinted like fangs.

Arianne stared at her in silence for several moments, trying to gauge if this was more enthusiasm toward helping Arianne in her love life or trying to put her in a position to squirm.

Zoey grinned with matching glee. "You'll do great. What's the matter? Don't you trust us?"

Arianne gave her a flat stare, trying to ignore her own nerves as they crept their niggling fingers around her throat. "Would you trust you?"

Sierra slapped Arianne's arm. "It's been like twenty minutes already. Call him."

Her fingers felt fat as she swiped and tapped at her phone's screen. Her palms were sweaty. In fact, her entire body felt like it was about to drip from every inch and leave an Arianne-shaped sweat mark on the chair. If he didn't pick up, well, she could handle it. If he did—her stomach flopped. Even after one date, she was turned around enough she'd deigned to ask her employees for help.

Sure, they were also her friends, but it was the principle of the thing.

"I'll say I was doing a shoot." Biting her lip, she looked from Zoey to Sierra for confirmation.

Zoey nodded.

Sierra gave a thumb's-up.

"Here goes." Arianne tried to keep her voice light. Carefree. Casual. It came out as a squeak.

Five heart-stopping bursts of dial tone. Garrett's voice filled the line. "Hi," he said.

Shitshitshitshit— "Uh—what's up, man?" Her voice was high. Every word ripped out of her with enough cringe factor to make her friends wince.

"This is Garrett Reid. Please leave your name, your number, and the time you called, and I'll get back to you at the earliest opportunity. Take care!" An apathetic "beep" signaled the start of his voicemail.

Arianne slammed her thumb down on the red telephone icon.

Lucas had always made her feel like she was crawling over gravel just to keep his attention. With Garrett... well, it was only one date, but the attention he'd paid her—shit, she'd just say it—the *validation* was like a drug. Better by far to cut herself off before she was an addict. Better to go cold turkey than to crash.

"He didn't pick up." She tried not to sound frantic. "It's fine. Probably. Right?"

"Sure." Sierra said. "Everybody's played 'phone tag' before. Besides, if he didn't pick up, he's probably driving and being responsible by not being on his phone at the same time."

"Or he's crapping his brains out from the Firecracker, and he didn't want to talk to you on the john." Zoey laughed.

Both were plausible. Neither made Arianne feel any better.

Chapter Ten

The bathroom was filled with the sound of a horn section and bass guitar thumping out a driving rhythm. Garrett rubbed a hand towel across the mirror as he eased the steam away from his reflection. Showered, with deodorant and cologne carefully applied, all that remained was to trim the goatee to lasered perfection. Ari was quite possibly the hottest woman he'd ever rebounded. Ergo, he needed to bring his physical A-game.

Today was Tuesday. Their second date was due to kick off in approximately one hour. The gallery was half an hour down the interstate—forty-two minutes with traffic—and he would arrive exactly one minute early. Always better that the man arrives early. Especially after he'd shut her down on her front doorstep. He needed to take that opportunity to abate her gnawing insecurities.

His phone lay on the counter, hooked to a Bluetooth speaker providing him with the belting voice of Billy Joel urging Garrett to "Tell Her About It" as he set about tracing the edges of his goatee with a straight razor. It always made him feel fancier, truth be told. There was something irreplaceable about going old-school like this. He *had* to slow down. He *had* to pay attention to what he was doing.

Garrett paused mid-stroke, taking the lyrics at face value. The very point of his work was to do just what the song said. He *was* for real. He *did* care about the girls he was helping to rebound from past heartbreaks.

He just couldn't let them know he was paid to do it.

"Sorry, Billy." He tapped his phone. "Not helping."

The thumping horns and Billy's insistence on timely honesty was cut off by the next track. Garrett smiled to himself, shifting back to the mirror as he traced across the edge of his upper lip. Besides, Billy Joel was fun to jam out to, but Garrett always been more of a Chicago guy. Some Genesis if he was feeling cheesy. All of it was thanks to the classic tastes of his father, the tinny portable CD player he had on board his boat, and the hours spent—

Garrett froze in horror. His reflection stared back in pale fear. He hadn't been paying attention. He'd been impatient.

A chunk of goatee lay suspended like folic lifeblood on the trembling blade of the razor, severed from his face and leaving a horrible awkward angle to his moustache.

"I can fix this," he uttered, hurriedly taking mental measurements of his facial hair and trying to figure out how in the world he was going to live up to that claim. Maybe taking out the clippers and shaving certain angles into it? Kind of a spiky, avant-garde-ish goatee? Claim it was to help fit into the hipster photography exhibit? He could win points for looking like a goof. Maybe take it down to a soul patch?

He groaned. There was only one choice available to him in the time allotted.

Humming a soulful rendition of "Taps," he went to work.

~ * ~

Only two minutes behind schedule, Garrett Reid stepped out of his front door in a white silk shirt, charcoal blazer, and matching slacks. Enough for a business casual attire. Any tie would have been overkill. Of course, maybe it could have drawn attention away from the naked horror that was his smooth, goatee-free mouth and jaw and the downright boyish face he was now cursed with until it could properly grow back in. His chin already felt cold without it.

His shoes were Oxford, he looked like Yale, his degree was Michigan State, and his hand was on the door of his Mitsubishi Lancer when everything froze. Not a sound was to be heard, save the thumping of blood in his ears and the bony rapping of high heels on asphalt. He knew the sound of that walk. The cold feeling surrounding the ghost of his goatee slid through the skin and bone, muscle and sinew, plunging down into his soul. The faintest traces of hyper-sugary perfume clung to the air like the scent of death from downwind.

She'd found him. She never should have been able to find him.

"Gare-bear?" said the harpy. "That totally *is* you! I'd know that cutie-patootie in those business pants from down the street. Ugh, like— do you know how *hard* I have had to look for you? Hashtag-frustration! Did you really have to move to *Brooklyn* when the Upper East Side is a thing?"

His legs were lead. His hand had melted to the door. He was on the job. She couldn't be here.

"So, we need to, like, have a real talk, okay?" Her voice dripped Starbucks frappuccino and glitter. "I got your little paper-legal-thing in the mail. Like, what even is that about?"

She closed in. He was a terrified rabbit with his back to a boulder. She, the lioness with the spittle dripping from her fangs. He didn't even have his goatee to hide behind. No good could come of this.

Ari was waiting.

He didn't remember getting in the car. He didn't even realize what was going on until Courtney's screech of indignation mingled with the sound of his engine and the scrabbling *rattatatat* of her fake nails on his window. The tires squealed in a proper, unrehearsed, Hollywood-level peel out. His rear-view mirror shone with the reflection of the short, blonde, curveless creature, standing in the road and yelling after him.

Garrett swerved in manic, random turns through side streets and through the back of a grocery store parking lot, desperate to make it to thicker traffic. There was safety in numbers. His free hand thumbed at his phone as fast as it could.

There was a click on the other side. "Garrett?" David's frown was audible in his voice. "What's up? You should be on your way to—"

"*Code C!*" He slammed on his turn signal in a furiously polite flash, merging left, then right again as he slid around a ponderous trailer truck.

David sputtered on the other side. "Wha—how—didn't you send—"

"*Yes, I sent her the cease and desist!*" His voice hit a pitch reserved for rusty gate hinges.

"Then why is she at your house?" The sound of a keyboard clacking echoed through the phone.

"I don't know—she shouldn't even know where I live!" Garrett swallowed, drumming his fingers on the leather of the steering wheel as he skidded to a halt at a red light.

There was no safety in stopping. He was naked. Exposed. Any second now, he'd see her Daddy-bought pink Dodge Charger bearing down on him like the most basic-girl Grim Reaper. Or maybe Barbie's crazy third-wheel cousin. She would chase him down and rip out his throat with her high-pitched giggles and endless Tweets and then wrap his corpse in a faux-mink-fur-shawl before stuffing him and mounting him in her bathroom to take mirror selfies with.

His palms were slick against the steering wheel as he saw a glob of bubble gum-painted car several vehicles back. There was no mistaking it. Not when the distant speck of blonde hair emerged from the side window, bracing a hand on the roof as she hung halfway out and tried to peer up the line of traffic to him. He could almost make out her expression in the side mirror. It was the same lovesick furious look she'd had on their last disastrous date, when she'd pulled the unspeakable trick with the lasagna. He'd never even seen her eat. She had to subsist on nothing but java and the vapid ether of social media.

The light turned green.

He stomped on the gas.

The rest of the traffic was much slower to follow, moving at a wholly more civilized and casual speed. Behind him, the pink Charger struggled to weave between a white post office truck and a ponderous trailer-hauler. The hairs on the nape of his neck still stood at needlepoint. Not enough. Not far away enough. He needed an escape. Not when her Dodge Charger had so much more under the hood than his run-of-the-mill Mitsubishi Lancer. He cut left down a side street and out onto a one-way road parallel to the frontage road. Traffic was the only reason he'd evaded her thus far. He needed more.

He sped onto the bustling haven of Interstate 678.

Four lanes of gorgeous, thick, interweaving vehicles drove at speeds in blatant contradiction to the posted limit down shimmering lanes of concrete. In those rapids, Garrett was free. He was a minnow who had slipped away from the fingers of the fisherwoman and mingled with a school of hundreds. Exits passed, vehicles shifted and changed lanes, and he hid behind the sheer wall of an Amazon semi-trailer for several miles, deliberately matching its speed and ignoring the two times that a hefty topless Jeep flashed its brights in the rear mirror. He was hidden. He was safe.

"You good, man?" David broke the silence from the speaker.

Garrett guided his car back over to the furthest lane, slipping into the off-ramp with no sign of eye-searing pink anywhere.

"I think I'm good," he whispered. He didn't trust his luck, but he wasn't going to jinx himself, either. "I think—I think we're clear. We are a go for second date."

"Roger that." David heaved a crackling sigh of relief through the phone. "Godspeed, soldier."

Garrett steered into a crowded parking garage and chose a random spot in the middle of a gaggle of cars some five floors up. A little earlier, a lot more shaken, and a hundred percent less goatee'd than he'd intended, but the fact remained that he'd made it.

He just had to attend a pretentious photography exhibit with a woman who made her living off the stuff and act like he knew what she was talking about in order to convey enough interest to help her believe guys really could listen when she talked in order to continue to establish his Mr. Rebound-brand arena for her own self-help to take place.

What could go wrong?

~ * ~

She'd lost him. *Again.* How could this keep happening to her?

Courtney gritted her teeth until her pulse throbbed in her temples, and she feared her marble-white veneers would crack. He'd just *run.* Like a scared little hamster. He'd taken his stupid car onto the stupid interstate, and he'd left her behind without even a word. She'd even called him by her special nickname. He was so warm, so loving... he was Garrett, her Gare-bear, and he'd abandoned her again.

Heaving an aggravated sigh, she steered into the nearest Starbucks. It was fine. They would work around it. He was skittish. Shy. It was okay. She hadn't exactly had a lot of luck finding Mr. Right before her Gare-bear had come in and rescued her from the tipsy mess of relationships she'd been drowning in. Nobody committed to her. Nobody listened. Nobody asked, or cared, or even kind of all-that-much seemed to actually, well... *like* her. Nobody but him. He was patient, he was fun, he was kind and attentive. He was everything she could have wanted and *did* want.

Then she'd found out what he did for a living.

Stepping up to the counter, she glared daggers at the girl with the hair extensions and braces who scribbled her order on a notepad. Not even a barista. Just a cashier.

"What do you *mean,* 'we don't have Apple pay yet?'" snapped Courtney. Because she really needed this on top of what had just happened. "Perfect. Yeah—no, no, it's fine. I didn't realize we lived in caveman times or whatever. No, go ahead. Run my card."

Like hell was she leaving a tip.

Arms crossed, current-season Prada heels tapping against the coffee shop vinyl tiling, she watched the shrewish cashier ring up her venti caramel macchiato with two-thirds skim and the double-glazed cran-apple scone. Courtney deserved a cheat day after the way she was treated. In fact, she was even magnanimous enough to smile through closed lips at the disaster running her card before stalking back to her faithful pink stallion.

This was just a rough patch. Gare-bear struggled with being loyal to her, was all. That wasn't something she had been expecting, sure, but it also wasn't the worst thing to find in a guy. At least he wasn't selling crystal meth out of his college dorm, or worse—poor. If he needed to go working out his issues in the arms of other women, well, okay. She could understand. She didn't have to approve, but she could understand.

She paused to position her coffee cup by her lips and quirk her eyebrow to the exact angle, snapping and hashtagging and posting her photo. After all, she had followers to satiate. Courtney Hazleroth was a hot commodity, desirable to hundreds of thousands of followers. People *wanted* her, goddammit.

So why did her Gare-bear keep running?

Scarfing a bite of her scone and taking care not to smear her lip gloss, she thrust the Dodge Charger into gear. Streets faded as she munched and sipped and fumed. She was following her heart. Every Disney movie and inspiring Pinterest quote said that was the point of life. She dreamed of him. They were destined to be together. If he couldn't see that yet, she'd have to open his eyes.

Her best bet was to confront the girl who had started him down this whole course in the first place.

The sucky part about the suburbs was that there was never any valet parking. Like she wanted to park her first-class stallion next to the grungy pick-up truck or the stupid navy-blue soccer mom van, but there was no choice.

Pouting, she guided the car to a gentle stop by the curb. Maybe they'd get a glimpse of fine living when they saw her. This was a good thing. It'd inspire them. She adjusted one of the several straps on her shoulder and approached the front door. Off-white paint and actual dirt on it. Plucking the brass knocker between two manicured nails, she slammed it against the door until it opened to reveal the whore who had first corrupted her Gare-bear.

"Courtney?" In mismatched T-shirt and leggings, Olivia blinked back at her like she was an alien. Had it really been that long since Olivia had seen someone who didn't look like a total mess? "Uh—what are you doing here?"

She crept outside, taking care to close the door behind her. That was plenty fine by Courtney's standards. The inside smelled, and if Olivia was anything to measure by, the decor would be somewhere between want-to-be-HOA-lady and off-brand-IKEA clashing. Classless at best, dingy at worst.

Courtney blew a blonde lock out of her view and stared Olivia up and down. "I'm looking for Garrett," she said. "I know you know where he is."

Olivia blinked. "I—what?" Her gaze slid over Courtney's shoulder, as if searching for a hidden camera.

Courtney snapped her fingers in front of the housewife. "Eyes down here. I'm looking for Garrett. Where is he?"

"How the hell should I know?" asked the liar. "I haven't talked to him today."

"Oh, but you have been talking to him?" Courtney folded her

arms. "Who's he seeing now? Some other slut who needs a rebound?"

Olivia frowned. "She's not a slut."

"So he *is* seeing someone other than me." Of course he was. The same problematic behavior. She had her work cut out for her.

A ragged sigh burst from the obstacle in the doorway. "Courtney, you two broke—"

"Do *not* say 'broke up.'" She took a calming breath, putting her hands out as if she could freeze time in that very instant and make reality right again by willpower alone. "We're on a break. He's working out some issues, and I respect that. He just needs to know what's acceptable and what isn't."

Olivia stared at her through eyes that resembled slits between dusty blinds. "Broke up," she said. "Over. Finito. Double-punched your ticket to Splitsville. Dumped you like a brick. Your relationship ended."

"We're just on a break!" Panic clutched at her throat. Her chest heaved. "He's my everything, Olivia. He's the best man I've ever been with, and I need to show him that I—that *we* can be perfect! Don't you get that?"

The world around her felt like a painting left in the rain, mottled and dribbled and ruined, leaving only their section of concrete porch and this whore who had ruined Garrett. "We're in *love*. You don't even know what that's like."

Olivia's face could have been carved out of stone. "Well... I'm *married*, so..."

"Oh, please." Courtney waved a hand in dismissal. "That doesn't mean anything anymore. What Gare-bear and I had was *real*."

The liar drew a tongue across her bland, collagen-less lips and drew in a slow breath. Maybe she was trying to inflate herself. Make herself look bigger, like animals that were trying to intimidate others on nature documentaries. It wouldn't work.

Courtney drew herself up to her full height of five-foot-one, silently wishing she'd worn heels. It would have closed the gap between this stupid Amazon five-foot-seven mess-in-leggings with her hair in a bun. Stupid Olivia and her stupid stupidity.

Neither of them moved an inch for several seconds.

"I'm going back inside." Olivia spoke with all the enthusiasm of a doped-up sloth. "He's not here. Go away, Courtney. Leave him alone."

"Not until you tell me who this bitch is!" she yelled at the closing door. There was no response from inside. Her cheeks burned. Dirt be damned. She wrapped her fingers into a fist and pounded. "Let me *in*, Olivia! We belong together!"

A man's voice sounded inside. Not her Gare-bear. Must have

been the lowlife that married the hick housewife. It was muffled, but she could hear the teasing tone through the crack in the door. "Honey? Did you bring home another lesbian?"

"No. It's just Courtney."

"Oh." The teasing tone fell flat. "Should I get the hose?"

"No. It's my fault." A wheezing sound. She might have sighed. Courtney couldn't tell. "I shouldn't have fed her. She'll keep coming around if she thinks there's something for her."

"I'll get the hose," said the man.

There were several seconds of silence that followed. Maybe they really were going to spray her down like some mangy hairball with claws.

"Don't you goddamn dare!" she yelled at the door. "Olivia? Get *back* here!" Courtney slapped at the wood with both hands, shaking loose a layer of fine dust that sent her stumbling back in a coughing fit.

Nothing.

Fuming, Courtney stomped away from their squalid suburban piece of shit and back to her faithful stallion. For as unpleasant as this had been, it had been worth it. She could now officially confirm her Gare-bear had gone sniffing after some other skirt that wasn't hers.

Not this time. She wasn't going to let him destroy himself seeking out love that wasn't theirs. Love that couldn't possibly fulfil him the way she did.

Contorting her face into her most innocent, heartbroken expression, she snapped a photo and thumbed at her phone's keyboard with vindictive speed. It was time to widen her search radius. Maybe call in a few favors from those of her followers who were kind enough to donate money in exchange for a few special photos. They'd already been kind enough to leak his address (even if it had taken them way, *way* the hell too long to find it). Surely, they'd help a girl out with a real-time location. After all, social media was wide-reaching. It would only be a matter of time before she would find the love of her life and give him the honey he craved, and then they'd both be satisfied.

She bit into her cran-apple scone and abandoned the suburbs for richer pastures. "I'm coming, Gare-bear."

Chapter Eleven

Five minutes late to the exhibit, Arianne untangled herself from between driver's seat and steering wheel, trying not to have her internal squirming match her external quite so much. The amount of time she'd taken to preen and prepare herself had been beyond indulgent. Even Marie Antoinette would have lifted an eyebrow.

Garrett hadn't run screaming when she'd stood at seven feet of Reynolds bombshell for their first date. So, for this go-around, she had one and only one goal—get him drooling over her. That wasn't going to happen if he was looking at the photos on the wall. So, instead of her sexy-yet-monstrous six-inch pumps with a cocktail dress, it was a modest pair of black two-inch heels, matching black stockings and shocking hot pink skirt, and a sleek black sweater that clung to her torso and plumped and accentuated exactly what it needed to.

Every head she passed stayed on her and followed her, the guys admiring and the girls in awe and shock. She forced herself not to grin. If she were turning this many heads, Garrett would have to be putty in her hands. Providing, of course, that her winning personality didn't go botching it like she had on her doorstep.

As she swept through the revolving door and into the brisk air-conditioned interior of the exhibit, she cast her gaze about with the hesitant, eager nerves of a mouse seeking a slice of fruit. Her palms were sweating as she glanced from person to person, scouring the lobby as she walked. Maybe he was already inside. Maybe she was early. She darted for her phone to check for missed calls or missed messages.

Nothing.

She exhaled, smoothing her hands on her skirt. Whatever. It wasn't like she hadn't been stood up before. It meant nothing. At least she could still get a good viewing of the exhibit. It wasn't like she—

"Ari?" Garrett's voice sounded over the white noise of the interior. Behind her.

She turned around and burst into a smile as he strode toward her. He was there, even if he'd phrased her name as a question. She wasn't abandoned. Her gaze raked over him, drinking him in, every bit, until she saw the naked youthfulness around his mouth.

"I, uh, see you shaved." She stifled a snort.

He blinked once at her, confused, puppy-like, until he feigned an expression of abject pain. "I know, I know. It's a long story. Really. A full-on epic. Princess, dragon, magic sword, the whole she-bang."

Arianne giggled. She actually *giggled*. Clearing her throat, she jerked a hand out to rub over his upper arm. Solid to the touch. Promising. But it was so early in the date, and she had to get to know him so much better than he already knew her.

Penny had counselled her accordingly. "No, no, keep it off. You look better clean-shaven."

Garrett scoffed, looking to the side. "You're just saying that." He kept looking around, though, glancing in every direction before double-checking behind him, toward the entrance.

Arianne followed his gaze, frowning on the inside. "No, really." She tried to sound sincere. "I mean, sure, you look like you're twenty, but you looked kind of douchey with it on before. Besides, guys looking younger is in vogue right now, so…silver lining?"

He was looking back at the entrance again. "Huh?"

Her smile cracked. "Expecting a third wheel, are we?" she teased. Her voice hitched a touch too tight. "C'mon. You opened Pandora's Box by taking me to a photography exhibit, trust me."

And just like that, she took him by the hand and led him toward the gallery attendant, who nodded in the picture of professionalism— even if his gaze did give her that rapid once-over that people thought she never noticed. Yes, she was a lot of woman to take in. People kept forgetting there were girls in the world taller than six feet.

They faded into a slow shuffle as they passed under a chrome car bumper, twisted and elongated into a multifaceted arch that served as a gateway into the exhibit. His hand was still in her grasp. Electric tingles rioted under her fingertips. He hadn't moved to lace fingers yet, but even the opportunity had her on tenterhooks. *Just hold my hand, dammit.*

She glanced at him, trying to gauge a reaction. He seemed frazzled, lost, his gaze sweeping over her as much as the first set of displayed photos themselves. Sure enough, his gaze locked onto the curved shelf of her breasts for an entire second before moving on to her hot pink skirt, where they darted away as if burned.

Arianne held still, lost in the fray of mixed signals as she watched him watching her and everything else. He was acting like a politician without security, like a man chained to a table with two pills before him and a choice between poison or placebo.

Maybe this was a pity date. Maybe he really couldn't handle dating a girl taller than him. Maybe she'd scared him off and everything from the last date, all his "honesty," had just been better-sounding lies that she'd bought into because she'd been so desperate for a not-Lucas.

Finally, Garrett's gaze met hers with the penetrating, peel-her-apart stare with which she knew he must have had yet never used. This was one of those moments—like at *Le Filou*, like at Rooster Jim's, like on her front doorstep—where she could see his guardrails fall away. Where he was sincere to an unfiltered extent.

Her throat clenched. Even before he spoke, when he looked at her like this, she knew his words could crack her open. *Goddammit.*

"I'm sorry if I seem distracted." His voice was low. "I had a run-in with someone unpleasant from my past, earlier today. It's nothing."

Her insides soured, rage caught in a single snapshot moment. Caught in the paralyzing line of his gaze, before she could so much as twitch, he slid his fingers between hers and squeezed, just once, just affectionate enough. Rough calluses at the base of his fingers rubbed against her smoother, lotion-caressed skin. Strength radiated from him. Her long, slender fingers were slower to react, but they closed around his hand just as surely. She even traced the back of his knuckles with one thumb as a giddy smile tugged at the edges of her hot pink lips.

"So…" Garrett smiled up at her. He couldn't quite let his hand hang due to their nine-inch height difference, but he didn't seem fazed at all. "What do you think of this one?" He gestured toward a photo of a crack in an asphalt sidewalk shot in monochrome. Beneath, the brass plaque read "Belief."

Arianne stared for several seconds. Her mind whirled as she peeled away the layers of pulsing pheromones long enough to examine the photograph. "Derivative, but it's solid stuff," she began. Then, unable to stop herself, the explanation broke out of her like the shoot of a plant that had just burrowed its way through concrete. This was her time to shine.

"He's got great depth of field, and his lines are kind of wonky, but that's totally deliberate. He brings you close enough to see the grains and minor seams in the concrete, and that's supposed to symbolise the compromises and holes people make in their own beliefs—at least, until you get to the crack itself, which is the focus of the photo as a whole. It's obviously representative of a large divide that can't be resolved, and the picture is in black and white, which is usually used as an indicator to focus on the way light is used, but here it's probably supposed to remind the viewer of the black and white way that belief often is. Y'know, 'if it's not like this, then it has to be like that.'" She took a breath. "We can't see into the crack, and there's nothing but darkness within, which would suggest the photographer is trying to say that holding black and white beliefs is hopeless because there will always be compromises and holes in it which can't be mended, but within those holes is nothing but darkness. He's probably trying to make a point about religion or something, which has been done like a billion times. So, yeah." She shrugged. "Derivative."

Garrett stared at her for several seconds in astute silence before a shaky, breathy snicker slipped between lips she desperately wanted to taste. The snicker swelled until he was out-and-out laughing, drawing more than one indignant sniff from musing exhibitgoers around them.

"Man…" He squeezed her hand in a way that made her toes curl inside her stockings. "You were not kidding. Pandora's Box."

"Hey, this is what I make my living doing." A familiar burn swept through her cheeks as she nudged him playfully. "I run a photography studio. I have to know my craft. Most of the symbolism and critiquing stuff you learn in art school is useless, but if you don't know how to evaluate an artistic shot, odds are, you're not going to be able to create one yourself."

He examined the grains of the concrete, frozen in eternal greyscale for all to see. "So is it easier to do what this guy did or harder to do what you do?"

The stretching feeling inside of her, the freedom of cutting loose, withered and died in the heat of his innocent question. "Harder to do what I do." She tried—God, she tried—not to sound bitter. "This guy's doing what he loves."

"Have you tried going for this instead?" He glanced up to her. "Artsy stuff? I mean… nothing on you, but wedding photography doesn't seem like your shtick."

She sniffed. "That's because it isn't. I fricking hate it. 'Sit still, chin up, turn out to me, drop your shoulder; okay, now look at each other, big smiles, goooood,'" she drawled. Saccharine toxicity dripped from every word. "Kid's stuff. But the market for wedding and portrait photographers is good, and it makes good money—which is good, because I have bills to pay, and being a small business owner sounds good on paper, and… well, yeah." She tried not to cringe. That had to be one too many "good"s for him to take that at face value.

"You could try getting published?" He gazed for only a moment at the photo of the sidewalk crack before scanning the milling attendees once more, but his words were directed at her. "Do a coffee-table book-of-photography thing?"

She shook her head. "Wouldn't work. I don't have—look, just—just drop it, okay?"

He nodded once and caressed her hand in his, staying silent. *Blessedly* silent. He didn't ask anything about her own insecurities. Her cowardice. The bitter, oily river in her gut that whispered *you don't have the talent, you know it, you've wasted too much time elsewhere, you're a failure, you'll never succeed* every time she even thought about picking up the camera for herself. He didn't ask. He'd dropped it. Like she'd wanted.

Working against her own feelings, she wore an indulgent smile as they went to the next picture, and she spotted him peering around when he thought she wasn't watching. Then the same for the next picture, and the next. How he was managing to tightrope between engaging in the conversation and being so obviously distracted had her heart threatening to grab rebar and concrete mix and build some proper fortress walls around it. She was right in front of him, the little shit. Anybody who cared to give her half a glance and wasn't perturbed by her height could tell she was *smoking* hot.

Anybody but Garrett, apparently.

"So, where'd you study photography?" He wasn't even looking at her when he'd asked it, craning his neck to peer across the crowds and down the next hallway of pictures.

Arianne stopped in her tracks like a boat run aground. "Art Institute at the University of Chicago," she said flatly. "Why, are you looking for someone else?"

"Huh?" He glanced back up at her.

She dropped his hand. "It's fine. Whatever." Her lips drew together, and her arms crossed. The main photo was before them, an enormous, life-size, grayscale image of sunlight filtering through a broken window. Dirt lay thick on the glass, the shattered edges fat and softened by wind and erosion. Motes of dust gleamed white in the picture.

Garrett, to his credit, didn't try to take her hand back. "So, um—what does it mean when something is found to be 'derivative?'" he asked. "I mean, I know what the definition of the word is, but does it have a different connotation when it comes to photography, or…?"

"It's some term art critics use whenever they don't like a piece but need to sound smarter than just saying 'there's nothing wrong with it but I don't really like it,'" she said. "It's why I dropped out of college. Everything I turned in, every assignment and portfolio, was 'derivative.' If there's any reason I've failed at anything, it's because I'm 'derivative.'"

"Ari—"

"Look, it's whatever. I get it. You're distracted." She huffed. "Whoever it was that you bumped into earlier, you've brought them with you, whether you like it or not."

His mouth puckered, bitter as bile. "You're right. I owe you a hell of an apology." He ran both hands through his hair, a long exhale hissing out from him. "I'm sorry. I'm with you. I promise. I... Can I be honest?"

"It'd be a nice change of pace." She stared down at him with the imposing, distant glare of a judge hearing the pithy case of a beggar representing himself in court. He should have understood. It should have been obvious from a single look at her—she'd gone all out for him. Plus, they were surrounded by the work around which her entire life and passion revolved, and he couldn't even pretend to be interested.

"I don't get photography," said Garrett, tripping into his apology from the starting line. "I was never good at unravelling art the way you can. I thought this would be somewhere you'd enjoy coming, and if I or the 'art'" —he even made the indicting air-quote finger gesture— "have made you feel even the least bit 'derivative,' then I am sorry. It wasn't my intention in the slightest. Nor should I have brought my own issues with this person into our date. It was wrong of me."

Arianne's lips lost their tension. As apologies went, it was on the eloquent side, but if there was any art going on in the entire exhibit, it was the way sincerity dripped from every word he said. There was honest pain in those eyes. He couldn't stand the idea of wasting her time, let alone offending her.

Well, how about that. He was learning to cut the shit.

"Look, um... how about we get out of here?" He jerked his head toward the exit. "It's a gorgeous day outside, and since every picture on the wall in here is clearly 'derivative,'" he said, grinning to her, "let's go somewhere and enjoy the sun. What do you say?"

She licked her lips almost subconsciously. Just because she might have forgiven him for his ignorant *faux pas*—specifically, ignoring her—didn't mean she had to let him off the hook yet. Not when he'd hijacked the very change-of-plans she was going to implement herself. "Answer three questions first."

Garrett nodded in an instant. "Hit me."

"First—do you like the beach?" It almost seemed redundant. Who didn't like the beach?

"Love it." He held her gaze, speaking with the sort of intensity of someone under oath.

She stared right back. "Good. We're going there. Second—who's this person from your past who's got you all paranoid shit-zophrenic?"

He sighed, and a half-shake of his head in sour disbelief told her volumes before he even spoke. "Psycho ex. She has too much stalker in her for her own good. We broke up ages ago, and I made it *extraordinarily* clear, but she still won't let go. Again, I'm sorry."

Arianne puckered her lips, and she followed the same motion of his that had been pissing her off the whole time—scanning the crowd for this mystery woman. It took balls to confess to that. Besides, the stupid rational part of her brain that would never shut up at the worst possible times reminded her that if she'd come face-to-face with Lucas earlier that day, she would be more of a frazzled mess than Garrett was by a mile.

The third question was nearly blurted out as "do I have to worry about her," but then she met his gaze again, and that pale blue gaze slid into her and cupped her heart and whispered to drop the concrete, put the rebar away. Her arms hung at her sides. Her cheeks burned anew.

"I like when you blush, by the way," he added. "It brings out your freckles. It's really cute."

She normally powdered the hell out of her freckles to hide them—a habit Lucas had encouraged, claiming it made her look older and more likely to be "taken seriously." No one had ever complimented them before.

"Third question," she said. "How do you feel about PDA?"

"I'm fine with it, as long as it's not excessive." He blinked up at her. "Why?"

She didn't wait a moment longer. She cupped those clean-shaven cheeks in her hands and pressed her lips to his in a hungry, swift kiss. Fire coursed through her face and fingertips and sent quivers through her entire body.

When she parted at half the speed with which she'd come, letting her lips and the taste of the kiss linger before drawing away, she giggled.

Garrett stared blankly at her mouth, stunned, like his brain had parachuted out the back of his skull. After long, stretched seconds, he blinked once, then twice. Speechless.

She twisted her lips into a predatory smile.

"I, uh," he started. "Beach. I don't have a swimsuit."

"Don't worry." She strutted past him, cutting through the crowd. "I already bought you one."

"Wait—you—what?" His head twitched in a double take, his brows furrowing in confusion.

She laced her fingers with his and tugged him along, feigning innocence. "What's the matter?" she said. Her gaze flicked over him with confidence. With possession. "I sized you up as soon as I met you."

She bit back on uproarious laughter as she stepped out into the sunshine. Besides, it wasn't like he was obligated to wear the suit she bought for him. She wouldn't be offended if he just wore his clothes as he was or even if the swim trunks turned out to be hideous on him.

The only thing that mattered would be how the suit looked discarded in a pile of his clothes on her bedroom floor tonight.

Chapter Twelve

She had literally hijacked his second date, and yet he was completely okay with it.

It wasn't the promise of seeing Ari Reynolds in a swimsuit that stayed his anxiety or frustration in the face of altered plans.

It wasn't the potential of seeing Ari Reynolds in a bikini that had him clambering into the passenger seat of her car.

It wasn't the possibility of seeing Ari Reynolds wearing nothing at all that kept him smiling all the way through the drive to the beach.

Orchard Beach was, thankfully, largely deserted on a Tuesday. Truth be told, the mile-long slice of gorgeousness was a decent piece of relaxation and didn't deserve to be located somewhere like the Bronx. Garrett supposed that just meant a diamond could be found in every rough. Padding through the shifting, uncertain terrain to the rest rooms, he stripped, secured his belongings in one of the electronic pay-to-use changing lockers, then drew up the drawstrings of the gifted swim trunks.

He was hardly self-conscious. He was an actor—or stood on the cusp of it, once upon a time. As such, he went to the gym on occasion but found more pleasure in working out at home, in the privacy of his bachelor pad. His culinary skills had been honed over his time as Mr. Rebound, and he made sure to eat healthy at all personal meals (particularly when he so often ate out with clients). Vigorous exercise compensated for the rest—but deliberately not *too* vigorous.

Prior experience proved that women felt more comfortable dating a guy with a "normal" physique, lest they feel inadequate by comparison. Worse, if he was *too* much of a walking photoshopped Adonis, it could jeopardize his contract—his clients wondered what "a guy who looked like that" was doing with "a girl who looked like her." His job required him to remain bodily-approachable, but still swoon worthy.

In short, he kept himself trim, taut, and exactly a seven-point-two-five out of ten.

There was only the slightest hint of his junk against the mottled black-and-white board shorts, even if they did end high enough on his thighs to peg him for a seventies-era NBA player. If this was what she meant by having "sized him up," there had to be something else at work. Some deliberate ploy to keep him self-conscious. If she'd already *had* a swimsuit for him, then she'd been planning to take him to the beach from the start.

That was supposed to be *his* move.

His thoughts whirled around, trying a hundred ways to figure out how she'd wrested control from him. How she'd *predicted* him. It was imposs—

He stopped considering it the second Ari's pale foot hit the sand and she ducked out of the women's changing room. His gaze was drawn up those smooth legs to the sleek navy-blue swimsuit bottoms that hugged her figure. A blue-white polka-dot ribbon buckled around the hips beneath a surprisingly modest tankini top that nevertheless left several inches of cleavage peeking out. The self-assured smile of a conqueror adorned her face. He couldn't keep his own mind clear enough to imagine the look that her eyes must have held, hidden behind the mirrored aviators she kept on.

Several seconds of awestruck silence slipped between them before she hooked a finger over the side of her sunglasses, dragging them down the bridge of her nose.

"All right, Garrett," she said. "Sunbathe, swim, or walk?"

The entire ensemble and how she wore it threatened to send his train of thought derailing off a bridge and into the chasm of out-and-out fantasizing.

He shook himself. He was on the *job*, dammit. He was there to help her. Not to enjoy her. "All three," he said. "In reverse order."

She bobbed her eyebrows and grinned. He offered his arm, mock-dramatic, as though they were young sophisticates who were mistaking the sunny-yet-near-deserted beach for an exquisite art gallery.

He supposed the comparison wasn't too far off, in retrospect, but then she looped her arm around his and her skin, smooth and fair, pressed against him, and he forgot all about comparisons as they walked along the edge of the tide.

"You look good." Ari's mouth twisted into a sort of shy half-smile, as though she were divulging a secret. "I think I do a pretty good job at picking out swimsuits for guys."

The sound of waves tumbling along the sand formed a peaceful sort of white-noise cocoon around them, the sand firm and wet underfoot.

"Do you do that often?" he asked.

"Nah." She shot him a sidelong glance, the corners of her eyes creasing in delight. "Just because I like you."

Like the snap of a single firecracker vibrating through the air, he sensed her flinching more through intuition than through any physical sensation. He let the words hang, just long enough to see if she would stumble or stammer over them, working to judge their intent. If there was ever a weakness in the English language, it was that the word "like" could carry such damning weight in so many contexts.

Her gaze bore into him, laser-focused, and he waited until the tide washed back in and coated their bare ankles with foam once more. Nothing from her. No retraction.

She was into him, then. This was not a casual, flippant admittance of a preference toward him. She had feelings for him. She'd held his hand, kissed him, and confessed to liking him, all in the space of the first half of the second date. More than anything, the moment of metaphysical glass shattering brought Garrett back from his attraction and planted his mental feet on the ground. She was exactly where he expected her to be—a textbook "Type E," or "moving too fast in a rebound relationship."

Brakes would need to be applied with care with Type E's. If he opened with the phrase "taking it slow"—or, heaven help him, if he made the rookie mistake of using the words "moving too fast"—the chances for a successful rebound would implode, and he would be out eighty percent of the stipend he'd received. She could not slap him on as an eager numbing bandage to the wounds left in her heart by Lucas. Garrett had to sanitize them; wash, and stitch, and then she would heal on her own, with time.

"You're not so bad yourself." He kept his tone light. Her arm shifted against him, threatening to betray a moment of panic.

He squeezed it to his side, as though a gentle embrace, and glanced up at her with a private, winning smile. He did, indeed, like her back. More than he should, which threatened to doom them both if he couldn't get his own feelings back in check.

"So, Ari." He peered at the horizon of blue-on-blue, white caps of waves dotting the bay. "I'm going to take a shot in the dark here and say…you're the eldest child in your family?"

He was lying. She was absolutely the middle child. Even if he hadn't learned that fact from her Facebook page, courtesy of David's research and profiling, she had all the markings of someone who'd grown up with both older and younger siblings.

"Good guess." She shook her head. "Nope. Second of four."

"No kidding?"

"Mmhmm. All girls. We used to joke that we'd be like the six-foot versions of the Bennett sisters. I think that's why Dad actually stopped after four."

Garrett snorted with laughter at the thought of a Mr. Reynolds massaging his temples and sequestering himself in the family study while Ari caused havoc and defied outdated social norms. It took significant effort to peel his fantasies away from picturing her in a corset and dress. A single look at her navy tankini served as more than fuel enough.

"My oldest sister, Katie, is engaged. Younger sister, Joey, is a junior at University of Chicago. Jenny is a senior in high school."

"Katie, Ari, Joey, Jenny." It made sense. Her family seemed to have a thing for nicknames.

"Katherine, Arianne, Josephine, Jennifer." She nodded along with each full name. "If we'd had a fifth sister, Mum says she would have named her 'Ellie,' for Elizabeth."

He blanched. It was instinct, by this point. Five clients in a row named "Elizabeth" a year back had ruined him on ever hearing the name again. Even *Pride and Prejudice* had been tainted, a reality he rued with a passion.

Ari looked at him with something resembling bemusement. "Your crazy-stalker-ex wouldn't happen to be named 'Elizabeth,' would she?"

He huffed out a laugh. "What gave it away?" The lie sat on his tongue like honey.

He couldn't risk Ari knowing the truth about Courtney. Now that a Code C had been called on his current operation, it was certainly within her interest to be aware of her existence—but the unfortunate truth about Courtney was she had a *titanic* presence on every form of social media.

She stubbornly, steadfastly refused to remove the photos of the two of them from her Instagram, let alone her Twitter, Facebook, Snapchat, YouTube, Google...he couldn't keep track.

For some reason he couldn't fathom, she had yet to reveal the details of his career online.

He could only assume it was from shame.

Why, then, she so doggedly kept fighting to "win him back" was, he suspected, one of the great unknowable mysteries of the universe.

"So, tell me about your family," he prompted. "How did Katie meet her fiancé?"

"On a plane."

He noted the change in Ari's expression as they left footprints in the sand behind them, and she opened up to him. Now he knew how she looked when she spoke with pride in someone else.

"Katie's a flight attendant. She met her fiancé on a flight from Portland to Miami. He's..." Ari laughed and shook her head. "Katie has tried to explain his job to me like half a dozen times, but I'll never understand it. Something to do with randomization for optimization for... I don't even know. He does computing. That's about as far as I can get. But he makes bank, and he treats her like a princess."

Ari clamped her mouth shut, clearing her throat as she stumbled over her own words. "But, uh—enough about me or my family. Tell me about you."

"What's to tell?" He added a charming scoff, waving a hand in deflection. "Does Katie have difficulty on an airplane? She has to be tall, right?"

"She makes it work." Ari's mouth wilted toward a frown. "Do you not have a good relationship with your family?"

Garrett grunted, noncommittal, even as his gaze slipped out to the waves in the distance. "Mom's not bad. We don't really talk much. One older sister, Emily. She's overseas, in the Peace Corps. That's us."

"And Dad?" The title hung in the air, punctuated by discordant splashes as they wandered through the surf and mud.

He grunted again, stooping to pluck a flat, smooth brown rock from where it was half-buried in the sand. "Around part-time until I was fifteen," he said.

Gingerly, he brushed away the grains of sand that clung to the rock with his fingers, polishing it on his swim trunks. "He went full-time from there."

"Oh. That's—that's good, isn't it?" She dipped her head, trying to catch his gaze.

With a whip-like snap of his arm, he sent the rock skimming out across the waves, where it skittered twice before a wave engulfed it and dragged it down to the depths. "Full-time deceased."

The silence fell about them, punctuated only by the passionless hunger of the waves against the shore as the shadow of a large pier loomed before them.

"You set me up for that, didn't you?" Suspicion colored her sympathy.

He let out a quiet chuckle. "Guilty. But seriously, it's fine. You get so much sympathy from people, you develop kind of this gallows humor about the whole thing. Besides, it was over a decade ago. I've grown up and moved on without him. It's fine."

"Still, that's kind of morbid, isn't it?" She stepped in front of him, blocking his path as they stood in the shadow of the pier. From high above them, echoing on the breeze like so many mental ghosts, was the quiet murmur of pedestrian voices.

He paid them no mind. They couldn't be seen from this angle.

Ari hooked her sunglasses through the shoulder strap of her swimsuit.

In her deep hazel gaze was all the sympathy he never wanted and all the concern he found himself yearning for. "I mean, my parents divorced, but that doesn't mean I'd be okay if one of them *died*."

"Look, it's…" He sighed, slowly, and crossed his arms.

It was clear they weren't taking another step down the beach until he'd addressed the matter in a satisfactory manner for her. His mind raced over a hundred upon a hundred different ways he'd explained it in the past, to well-wishers and exes and rebound clients and to those closest to him. Whichever way he brought the matter to a close, it had to be something that would help her, not give him closure that he already had anyway. He did have it too. He'd sworn it to himself years ago. There was no point picking at the scar.

"Dad used to love going out on fishing trips. He had this dinky speedboat, but he treated it like a sixty-foot yacht." His gaze wandered away from Ari, focusing on non-specific spots on the sand, darkened by water. "He used to spend most of his time out there drinking. Sometimes he'd actually come back with fish, and we'd do a fish fry for dinner. Cajun-style, battered, breadcrumbed, sometimes sautéed… Mom's a great cook." A nostalgic chuckle pierced the gloom settling over him. He wouldn't go to pieces in this rendition, but like the saying went—the best way to help oneself was to help others.

The voices up on top of the pier had gone silent.

"Time came, he went out on a trip when I was fifteen and didn't come back. Coast Guard found his boat adrift in the waves with like twenty empty bottles in the cabin. They never found his body, so the official report read that he was 'lost at sea.' We figured he got drunk enough to pass out, then accidentally rolled off the edge and drowned." He shrugged, waiting for seconds to pass before lifting his gaze to hers again. "We got through it. That's what matters."

He gave her a sad little smile. It was her cue, in a sense, to see how she would do with "heavy" subject material. It was only the second date, true, but she had deliberately gone seeking after this. It was the second rule of the second date—if she wants you to open up, give her seventy-five percent. Show her vulnerability without the full overwhelming brutality of an exposed soul.

There was an odd look in her eyes. It took him a moment, but when he realized what it was, it threw him off-guard as though she'd given him a left hook across the jaw.

Envy. She was looking at him in envy, made even more confusing when she stepped forward, arms lifting into a hug.

Her fingertips had barely brushed his sides when an enormous cloud of sand crashed over them, blown on the breeze, and coating them in heavy, thick, gritty dust from head to toe.

His eyes screwed shut. He coughed once, turning his head away from Ari to spit out the granules that had wound up against his lips and on his tongue. A moment later, he frowned, wiping most it from his eyes and shaking it out of his hair. It didn't feel like sand against his skin. Too light, too fine. Dusty. There was a faint burned smell to it. Worse, it wasn't golden yellow, or even an off-cream or brown. It was off-white, if anything.

Then the voices drifted down from the top of the pier, carried on the same wind that had desecrated them. Or rather, that they had unknowingly desecrated.

"Bye, Grandma Perkins."

Garrett froze on the spot. One look at Ari told him she'd heard it too.

Her face screwed up. She had the posture of a terrified doe at the edge of a forest, ready to sprint into comfort and safety and hiding. He seized her wrist as he strained to follow the overhead thumps of footsteps receding from the pier. Every speck of ash on him chafed his skin and burned with the mental condemnation of what it was. They had to wait. If they ran screaming into the ocean, it would destroy whatever funeral the family above were having.

"Wait," he whispered, his voice barely audible over the tantalising lap of the tide on the shore.

Ari's voice was a ghostly croak, eking out of her word by disbelieving word. "I have grandma in my cleavage."

Garrett wasn't quite sure what was sand and what was ash, but he was at least seventy percent sure he had grandma somewhere worse on him.

When he was sure he couldn't even imagine the sounds of anyone left on the pier above, he released her wrist and followed on her heels as they sprinted into the surf and threw themselves in with reckless abandon. The cold ocean water was a miracle, and he lapped it up and spat it out, savoring the sharp salty tang on his tongue as it overpowered the dusty bitterness that was Grandma Perkins.

He dunked his head beneath a wave, pawing furiously at his hair. He clawed at his chest, dug in his nails, shoved under his swim trunks, and scoured every inch therein. He rubbed himself against the muddy sand under the surface. He dunked and re-dunked himself, moving to a new area of water every time. He had no idea what Ari was doing or where she'd gone. All he knew was that he was, by the time he surfaced for a time uncountable, finally mostly kind of clean. From the ash, at least.

He spat again and again, wiping his mouth with the back of a hand he carefully inspected for even a single flake, and waded back toward the shore. Ari stood by the massive barnacled pillar of the pier, looking half-drowned, hugging herself.

"Do we—what do we—like—" A dozen dead sentences sat on her lips.

He frowned before she pointed past him, to the leftover clouds of white and gray, cast upon the sand like the worst kind of human jetsam. Everything that had blown past and hadn't coated them head to toe remained splayed out for the world to see.

"I guess we, uh... we should do a proper burial," he said, fumbling for decorum.

"Yeah," said Ari, in a masterpiece of eloquence.

They shared a single, silent look, before moving as one. They descended to their knees, scooping and pushing together crests of sand, guiding the ashes into a rough pile down by the edge of the tide. A solemn air fell about them as they worked. With each handful of sand and ash they recovered, it reminded him that this had been a person, once upon a time, no different than either of them.

Finally, Ari scooped a small pile of mud over the top, forming a humble mound by the pillar of the pier, while Garrett happened upon a twig of driftwood and gently inserted it as an impoverished marker.

Their work complete, they stood side by side and stared down.

"Do we say anything?" He glanced up to his date and fellow gravedigger.

Ari stared in silence for several more moments before she cleared her throat. "Here lies Grandma Perkins. We're sorry the last people she came into contact with weren't her family. So, um... rest in peace, and go with God? Or something. Maybe you were an atheist. In which case, um... sucks that you're dead?" Her eyes creased at the edges as she looked away. "Eulogies are *not* my strong suit."

He pulled her into a sidelong hug around her upper arms. "I thought it was lovely."

"Liar." Still, she nudged him in a way that bespoke more affection than irritation. "You say something."

Garrett cleared his throat, voice raspy from the ocean water he'd gargled not moments earlier. "Grandma Perkins... whoever you were, you were loved. You found a husband in Grandpa Perkins—probably, I mean—and your kids loved you, and they gave you grandkids, and it sounded like they were all there to see you go, so... I hope you lived a good life. If your family is any sign, I think it's safe to say you did. So... y'know. Bye."

Ari gazed down at him. "That was better than mine."

He snorted in dismissal. "Still wasn't that good."

She glanced back, over her shoulder, in the direction of her car. Her lips pursed for a moment—but only a moment. "I'm close by. My roommate and I have an apartment in Hillcrest, about twenty minutes from here. You can shower off at my place. If you want, I mean. Not to—it's—yeah. If you want."

Her expression shifted like the clouds on the horizon. It was the second time she'd invited him into her lair, and this time with the express purpose of getting him out of his clothes. Unlike her prior attempt, though, her hesitation had risen significantly. Enough that he felt safe to say what he wanted.

"That sounds amazing." His sandy footprints were already trailing away from the spontaneous grave. "Though you may want to throw out the loofah once we're finished. Y'know. Not to speak ill of the dead or anything."

She chuckled, a breathy, relieved sound as she caught up, taking lengthy strides through the sand. "That is the most intimate I've ever been with a dead person."

Garrett just stared at her and waited for her to backpedal.

To her credit, she stared him down and put on her best devil-may-care smile, even if it faltered at the edges. "Yeah, I know what I said. Bite me. You know what I mean."

Arriving at her car, Garrett took care to lay his towel across the passenger seat and did his best not to track sand into the interior. Ari folded herself into the driver's seat, long limbs curling and pretzeling, and Garrett listened to the purr of the car's engine as they left the beach behind.

They spoke in quiet voices, speculating about the unknowns that proximity-to-the-dead always provoked for the space of an afternoon. Grand topics like Life, Death, the Afterlife. Mercy. Justice. Judgment. Even through the softness and the sharing, he couldn't keep his hand on the mental brakes. The way her mind worked was a wonder.

He followed her up the stairs as she slid her keys into the lock and ducked under the door frame, finishing her insistence that there had to be some kind of karmic justice at the end of it all.

"And for those of us who are just kind of in the middle?" he asked, pausing at the welcome mat. His mind raced. Safety was relative. This was a courtesy shower to get the remnants of the pier debacle off him and that was it. It was still early evening. This was the second date. She was a Type E. Sex was *off* the table.

But it was still a monstrous gamble in crossing that threshold.

"Dunno," said Ari, from down the hall. "Mom had some Mormons over one time. They had an explanation for that. I don't remember what it was, but it sounded good. Maybe I'll Google it while you're cleaning dead grandma out of your swim trunks."

Garrett fought a dry heave as he shuffled across the entryway and closed the door behind him. His gaze darted about with the unflinching gaze of a hunter, prying from each detail more and more about Ari Reynolds and what she was like. Photos lined the hallway into the main room, showing her posing with Penny, with other friends, and with girls bearing a strong family resemblance.

"Ari?" He turned on the spot before his ashy date offered him a bubblegum-pink towel.

"Shower's in there. Don't take too long, okay? I think I got more on me than you did." She shuddered.

He nodded, wordless, and stepped past. He made it a single stride before she caught his wrist in one hand.

"Garrett?" She stood close enough to smell the ocean on her. Close enough for his gaze to be drawn to the grains of salt and sand clinging to her skin and down to the cleavage peeking from her navy blue tankini. Her hand slid down his wrist to lace fingers with him, just for a moment. "I'm glad we're not dead." She favored him with a vulnerable half-smile.

He swallowed hard. "Me too, Ari." His voice sounded hollow on his own ears.

She leaned down, her head bowing in an unmistakable "I'm going to kiss you" fashion, only to pause halfway.

Garrett, in turn, recoiled just enough to show that they were sharing the same thought. Despite their mutual attraction, the mental aftertaste of Grandma Perkins was still on their lips. He gave her hand a squeeze and slipped out, locking the bathroom door behind him. His heart threatened to pound through his ribs. The towel was rough and hideous in his hands.

He dropped it to the bathmat. Peeled off the swim trunks. Turned on the shower. The echoing sound of running water helped isolate him, and he gripped the sink, staring himself down in the bathroom mirror.

"Garrett," he whispered to his reflection, locking the man in a cold steel stare. "You cannot have sex with Ari Reynolds. If you do, you will shoot this entire operation in the dick and ruin things for an amazing woman. Do not. Have sex. With her."

Breathing hard, he closed the shower curtain behind him, repeating the last six words as he set about scrubbing himself raw.

Chapter Thirteen

"Arianne Reynolds, you are going to have sex with Garrett Reid, and it is going to be amazing." She stared down her reflection in the vanity mirror in her bedroom. She wet the inside of her lips with her tongue as she pondered on her words. After a moment, she added a mental asterisk to the statement. "Once you are showered and cleaned up."

Her makeup had run from her sudden faceplant into the ocean and her hair had dried in a scraggly, poofy mess that threatened to grow bigger as it frizzed. If she was going to jump his bones before she rode him back to his car at the beach—and prove to herself, and him, and anyone else that she was worth his time—then this would not do. Anything that had touched cremation ash could not be used to seduce a guy.

The drawer with her lingerie yielded to her a feast of variety. Lace and satin, translucent and opaque, ranging from modest and tasteful to decadent and dripping, all folded and color-coordinated. Her gaze searched as much as her fingers, frittering and fluttering through as she struggled to choose.

"Ari?" came Garrett's voice from down the hall.

She flinched, instinctively shoving the drawer halfway shut and nearly smashing her fingers. "Yeah?"

"I kind of realized... I, uh—I don't have anything to wear." A beat of awkward silence. "I left my clothes in the changing room locker. Back at the beach. And my car is back at the gallery."

"Oh." That certainly hadn't occurred to her. Not even a little. Nor did she have to bite back on a saucy suggestion that his problem wasn't a problem at all. Nope. "Hang on. I'll find you something."

She rose, taking care to close her drawer as she went pawing through her other clothes. It was a blessing and sort of a depressing curse that, being the height of the average NBA player, her sweatpants could be loaned to a guy without much hassle. Her gaze raked over the towering pile of laundry in the basket as she frowned. Not that he'd exactly want to wear her pre-used sweats. Not to mention the issue of a shirt. Arianne had rarely been able to cozy up in another guy's oversized hoodie…well, not unless he was a titan of a man.

Her heart seized as her hand settled on a hoodie, almost comfortably sized for her, with the Lakers logo emblazoned on it. She swiped at it—and the all-too-familiar pair of blue jeans underneath—and held them close, giving the hoodie an experimental sniff. It was faint, barely even there—maybe even more psychosomatic than actual scent—but the wisps of cologne set her knees shaking and her hair standing on the back of her neck.

"How do you feel about yoga pants and a tank top?" she called. It was an effort to hide her thumping heart behind a teasing tone.

There was a pause that measured exactly two seconds. "Do you have anything else?"

She snickered, walking toward the crack in the bathroom door where his face was pressed. Clean-shaven, glistening cheeks, and damp messy hair. Hopefully, he couldn't hear her swallowing as she handed him the hoodie and jeans.

"Here. These should do it," she said. "You can leave your swim trunks here. They're probably better off burned."

Garrett cringed at her words.

She couldn't help but laugh. "Now hurry up. I want to get cleaned off too, you know."

Moments later, he stepped out. The jeans were loose, the hoodie draped over him. Sleeves too long. Hood flopped back. She paused in front of the doorway and just… stared. Her head swam from the mixed signals. The blend of old relationship pain and new relationship fears, and everything it represented, rooted her to the spot. She hadn't thrown his clothes out. It'd been easier to pretend he'd be coming back for them. Easier to pretend there would be another confrontation, one where she would naturally say everything she'd come up with in the shower and at three in the morning after the fact; everything that sounded stinging and sassy to where she would emerge the victor of the breakup instead of the crying and shouting and collapsing guilt and furious reactive tasing that had marked the destruction of what they'd had. Instead, she'd just pulled the clothes right out. Given them to the newest guy in her life.

Granted, maybe it was poetic irony that the ashes of her former relationship would now be used to cover the man who had just been covered in literal ashes, but it was hard to appreciate as she stared him down.

He tugged at the waistband of the pants, frowning, before glancing up at her. "These aren't girl clothes."

With the effort of a heroine, she lifted her shoulders into a nonchalant shrug. "Good eye, Sherlock. They're left over from the last guy to be here. It's nothing. He's not exactly coming back to claim them" —*or me, for that matter*— "so you can keep them if you want. Now, scoot."

He obeyed, but his brow still furrowed like he was fumbling at a mystery. "Did these belong to Lucas? Or some other guy?"

She shut the door in his face.

Peeling the tankini off and cranking the shower as hot as it could go, she set about purging every last fleck of ash from her skin. Breathing came as a struggle. A silent whimper clogged her throat as she fought the tsunami of emotion threatening to have her somehow both horny and crying all at once. For one moment, in some small way, Lucas had been standing before her once again. Like they'd never splintered apart.

She whispered several dark curses as she scrubbed herself from head to toe and back again, sniffling a few times as the quiet grief slipped out. *Fine. Whatever.* Lucas could stay with whatever mystery skank had captured both his heart and his dick. Garrett had taken her on two dates, and so far, had yet to make even a single negative comment about Arianne's height or appearance, hadn't belittled her or made her feel less intelligent or less cultured, hadn't tried to cop any kind of feel or accidental boob-brush, and—from the first moment—treated her better than Lucas ever had.

She was going to pin Garrett to the carpet. Him, smelling faintly of the one man she could never let herself have anymore and ever, and they would all be better for it. Herself, Garrett, and even Lucas, in a way.

The shower squeaked off as she dried herself. Her makeup was done to subtle perfection in only a few minutes. Funny how a yawning, abyssal need for physical intimacy could spur a person to be exact.

She sucked her teeth as she stared herself down in the bathroom mirror.

Screw the lingerie.

She spared a second to comb her fingers through her hair before standing straight and tall, thrusting her shoulders back and putting her second-biggest features on display. With a single, calming breath, she swept open the door and strode out into the living room, bare feet leaving the ghosts of damp footprints on the wood as she stood and gazed down at Garrett Reid, sitting on the couch—

And at the wide-eyed, slack-jawed face of her older sister, Katie, who was sitting next to him and averting her gaze. "Um—Arianne?"

"*Shit!*" Arianne shrieked, motoring backward around the corner as she slapped her arms over her chest and privates. As soon as she was out of eyesight, she sprinted for her bedroom. The door slammed hard enough to shake the windows.

"Katie? What the *bitchshit* are you doing here?" she yelled through gritted teeth. She swore her cheeks would combust in a millisecond and burn the flesh from her face. It would serve her right for pulling such a stupid, asinine, *sophomoric* move. "You're supposed to be in *goddamn Toronto*."

A muffled voice poked under her doorway, too obscured to be discernible. Katie, timid as always, and probably rattled by seeing her sister strutting out naked with a guy home.

Arianne scoffed a laugh as she yanked on the same leggings and tank top she'd teased Garrett with earlier. Katie must have knocked on the door in the exact window of time when Arianne was showering, and Garrett must have answered.

Arianne would have to rip him a new one for that.

Later.

Cheeks alive with a mushroom cloud of heat, she stomped back out into the living room and sat in the plush leather recliner across from her unintentional flash-ees. "Why aren't you in Toronto?" She stared at the carpet as though trying to burn a hole through it.

"There was an electrical outage at EWR," mumbled Katie, who was more than used to repeating herself. "Um... sorry. Newark Liberty International Airport. They canceled flights all day, so I thought I'd come and, um... surprise you."

Arianne lifted her gaze by degrees, just enough to take stock of Katie and Garrett in her peripherals. Katie stared sidelong at Garrett, who appeared to be invested, body and soul, in deciphering the artistic merits of a sepia-toned sunrise Arianne had framed on the far wall.

Katie cringed at the look on her younger sister's face, fumbling with her hands in her lap. "I didn't know you'd have company over."

Arianne dug her fingernails into the sheer fabric of her leggings, bunching them in her grip. It was a conscious effort to unclench her teeth. "You could have called."

"I did. Um...five times. I left voicemails." Katie always mumbled, save for her fake-cheery stewardess persona.

Arianne had heard her older sister actually yell only once, when their younger sister Joey tried a skateboarding trick off the roof that broken her leg in two places. Worse, Arianne knew full well why she hadn't received any of the communication. She'd shut her phone off the second she'd left the apartment for this utter disaster of a date. She buried her face in her hands, raking her nails across her scalp in a pithy attempt to find catharsis through pain.

Garrett cleared his throat. "Katie? Could you give me a lift back to my car? It's at the art gallery. Robert Mann. Upper East Side."

Panic ran through Arianne with the cold certainty of a knife sliding flat across her throat. "Garrett," she began, but could only muster a sort of strangled, pleading look.

He met her gaze with that same soul-piercing pale blue stare, the kind that penetrated so much further than she ever let anyone. It was the gaze God would give a person—sympathetic and loving and just judgmental enough to make her feel about as big as a bug. Though, she had to admit, the judgment may have been her own conscience screaming at her.

"It's all right, Ari." He had the kindness to smile, even if it was a few teeth shy of being completely okay. "This was fun. Eventful," he amended with a chuckle. "I'll call you tonight, okay? Just shoot me a text when you and Katie finish catching up."

Arianne was on her feet in a moment. She had to at least own up. This couldn't just be damage control. "Just—can I talk to you outside for a second?" She glared at her sister, her expression hardening like frost. "Alone?"

His smile fading, he nodded.

"I'll be waiting," said Katie, as helpful as she was oblivious.

Outside, Arianne closed the front door and blinked in the early evening sunlight. Maybe this could be the chance to clear the air, especially given what had happened the last time they both stood on her front porch.

She braced herself for another shutdown. "I should ex—"

"You don't have to." He interrupted in a way that had her tongue thick enough to bulge against her tonsils and cut off her breath. His touch was reassuring and terrifying all at once as his fingers laced with hers. "I get it."

She watched him carefully. "You do?"

"Yeah." His expression seemed almost carefree. "We had a disastrous second date. Basically nothing went right, and you're still seriously hung up on Lucas. You said you were, back on our first date. That *was* less than a week ago." Garrett plucked at the incriminating hoodie, frowning. "Plus, I can't imagine I'm stirring up the best feelings in you when I'm literally wearing his leftover clothes."

"It's hard." The admission was weakness she never wanted to show. "He cheated on me. I just...I don't get *why*. I know I shouldn't need to, but it's like—I can't move on until I know. He picked another girl over me. Like I wasn't enough."

Garrett stayed silent, that sympathetic curl at the edge of his lips remaining. Not like Lucas, who always talked over her—but had such interesting things to say. Intelligent things. Artistic things. He always had that look like he was waiting for her to be more, even if she had no idea what.

Not like how Garrett looked at her.

She sighed and shuffled her feet, casting her gaze down as if she were a toddler before her first mall Santa. "Look…it's only the second date, and so far, I've had you set on fire, we've been covered in dead grandma, and I came at you with no clothes on. We might want to chalk this up to a scratch and move on to other people."

His snort of laughter came as a gust of fresh air to both her mind and heart. "Are you kidding? If this is the worst it can get, then it means we can only go up from here."

She pursed her lips, mulling over the possibility. "And if this is just the beginning of the shitstorm that is our future romance?"

"Then it'll be good for both of us." He raised his chin in a defiant sort of way. "Any future relationships will be a cakewalk in comparison."

Arianne laughed. "Romantic endurance training?"

"Something like that." Pure possibility glittered in his eyes. A devil-may-care look. Maybe he was a glutton for punishment. Maybe they both were. Somehow, they were both smiling.

He hadn't released her hand yet, and she had no intention of letting go. Instead, she drew a thumb across the back of his hand, smooth and affectionate, and her gaze darted to his lips. A clear request. He met her gaze, clouded for a moment, before he rose to his tiptoes in his own affectionate gesture to try and close the height gap.

Oh, but he was a keeper, this one.

With a giddy little giggle, she grabbed his face between both hands and planted a passionate kiss on him—and she even snuck in some tongue, electric tingles spreading across her mouth—before separating with as much force as she met. Again, he stared up past her with that dazed look that made her fight the urge to toss her hair with pride.

"Uh—right." He cleared his throat once, descending from whatever cloud in the sky she'd sent him through. "Like I said. I'll call you tonight, and we'll talk some more, okay? And, uh…" He seemed to come to himself, smiling up at her in a way both charming and distant all at once. Maybe he still wasn't quite back down to earth. "How about a third date?"

She didn't hesitate. "You think you can survive a third one?"

A flicker of the devil-may-care look came back. "Only one way to find out."

"I get to plan it, this time." Maybe it was wrong to tease him so much, but it was just so *fun*. "Some kind of extreme mud-run challenge. Barbed wire and explosions. We can't make it too easy, can we?"

Garrett looked like he might pass out, but to his eternal credit, he took her at her word and nodded. "I'll see what I can do."

She rolled her eyes, trying not to let her smile tinge toward straight-up silly. "I'm joking, doofus. Call me tonight. I'll wait up."

Squeezing his hand, long and slow, she finally let him go and committed him to the care of Katie, who loomed over him almost as much as she did at merely an inch shorter than her. It wasn't his fault, but between the twin towers of Katie and Arianne, he looked downright, well...small. It happened to everyone.

The Reynolds girls had pissed off the height fairy something fierce during their adolescences. Arianne had used to joke that she'd not only pissed her off but kidnapped her and held her until the boob fairy came to pay her ransom. Not that she'd ever say something like that to Garrett. He needed to think she was clever, not fifteen.

Katie sidled past her, eyes glued to anything in the street but her, and Arianne's smile shrank as they drove away. True, Katie was always shy, but...something was different here.

Striding back inside, Arianne swiped at her phone, selecting the first voicemail, and pressing "play."

~ * ~

Being on a beach and *not* being in a bikini was just wrong on principle. Even if Courtney felt the teensiest bit bloated from an impromptu cheat day, and if the cran-apple scone had left an odd aftertaste in her mouth, and even if the beach was in the *Bronx*, the fact remained that sun, plus sand, plus Courtney Hazleroth, was supposed to equal bikini selfie. Instead, she was still in the outfit she'd planned for her great and grand reunion with her Gare-bear. Totally inappropriate for the location.

God, nothing was going her way.

She huffed, plucking her heels off and carrying them in two fingers as she padded through the shifting sands. Her phone was clutched tight in her grip. One of her faithful followers, an employee at one of the big credit card companies, had sent her a text. Very tech savvy. Sure, his message had been padded with stuff about "information privacy laws" and "I'm going out on a limb" and "you're worth it, my goddess angel" and all that stuff, but the juicy core at the heart of the message had been what had sent her screeching through the streets in her pink stallion.

An hour ago, Garrett had used his Visa to rent the usage of a beach locker.

She'd already scoured the beach. He was nowhere in sight—well, not unless he was snorkeling or whatever, but he wouldn't do that. Gare-bear hated the water. She knew that. They knew each other. Intimately. That was why they were perfect for each other.

Without hesitation, she planted a hand on the door with the little man-silhouette sign and strode right inside. Locker four-twenty-seven. Just like April twenty-seventh, the day of their first date together. It had to be a sign. Garrett was letting her know he was still thinking of her. Sure, okay, so he'd gone running off through traffic at the sight of her, but that didn't mean anything. He was confused. Turned around by all these other sluts he'd gone sniffing after, thinking he could find his happiness anywhere but her. He knew what he was doing what was wrong.

If anything, choosing this locker number was a cry for help.

The bathroom smelled like ocean and dude. Honestly, not as bad as she was thinking. Kind of a heavy-blanket smell that seemed infused into the grit in the floor as she strode to the locker. She'd need to send her faithful follower something jaw-dropping if this lead panned out. Maybe a photo with something lacy. She'd figure it out later. For now, she needed to get into locker four-twenty-seven.

"Do you freaking mind, man?" said a voice. Deep. Guy's voice.

Courtney glanced over her shoulder to see a towering specimen of deliciousness with a towel tugged tight around his waist, held in place with one fist. Bronze skin. Rippling abs. Thick, corded arms. Shoulders she could drink in. Sandy brown hair and brown eyes. A small sterling silver cross pendant around his neck.

Yum.

Oh. Right.

He stared at her, indignant. She hurriedly painted on a panicked, frenzied look, hitching her breath in her throat and adding a girlish whine as she folded in on herself.

"Please—y-you've got to help me," she begged. "I'm sorry—I know I'm not supposed to be in here, but—m-my nephew—he's diabetic, and his stuff is in the locker a-and I don't know the code. It's an emergency!"

The man-treat's eyes narrowed. "He needs insulin?"

"Yes!" she pleaded. She even slapped the locker door with both hands, as if panic rendered her actions futile. "Please—can you help me... I don't know, break in, or something? He needs his medicine. He's only eight, and he's all pale and sickly, and—"

"Type one or two?"

"Uhh—one?" She blinked.

He nodded, his voice all business. "Did his breath smell sweet? Like fruit?"

"I think so?" She fumbled with the locker, trying to cram her immaculate nails into the gap in the door and pry it open. "Please just—"

"Short of breath? Stomach pains?"

"Yes! All of that!" She struggled to keep her frustration down. Her imaginary nephew was suffering, and this surfer guy was playing twenty questions with her. The man tucked his towel neatly into a knot by his hip and strode across the changing room, heading for a second bank of lockers.

"He's going into ketoacidosis," he said. "It's all right. I've got type one as well. There's insulin in my locker."

Courtney tilted her head, squinting. "Keto-who-da-what-now?"

The man paused, his earthy brown bangs dangling down into his eyes in a way that was intensely hot and also completely beside the point.

"Ketoacidosis," he repeated. "You're taking care of your diabetic nephew without knowing the first thing about his condition?"

The air between them thickened. She exhaled raggedly, pinching the bridge between her eyes. She didn't have *time* for this.

"Ugh... god, *fine*," she huffed. "I don't have a sick nephew. I just need to get into locker four-twenty-seven, okay?"

He narrowed his eyes at her behind his bangs. She shook her head, fuming as she dug out her wallet from her purse. The one surfer dream with muscles, and he had to be Dr. House, M.D, on top of it all. Couldn't be a regular meathead who would bow before her puppy dog eyes and fake nephew story, *nope*. Couldn't have that. Couldn't have *anything* today.

"Two hundred bucks." She held up the cash between two fingers. "Can you make it happen?"

The hot guy sighed before walking toward her.

She held her ground, staring up the rippling muscle. If this had been any other day, she would have done everything in her considerable flirtatious power to have this guy wrapped around her finger and inviting her to ride in the passenger seat of the topless doorless Jeep that she just *knew* he owned. Any other day, and maybe she would have been giggling and imagining licking runny ice cream out of the crevices between his abs.

But this was today, and this was to do with *her goddamn Gare-bear.*

"See, if you'd led with that, instead of trying to play the 'sick fake nephew' card, I would've agreed sooner." He plucked the cash from between her fingers.

Her lips pressed together until they felt like pieces of paper instead of her plump, collagen-enhanced masterpieces. Her hands started to tremble. She turned away. Closed her eyes. *Breathe, Courtney. Breathe.*

After several seconds, a metallic click and rattle echoed in the change room.

"Done." The guy strode back over to the pile of clothes on the wooden bench and swiped them with his other hand. "Now, if you'll excuse me, I'm going to finish getting dressed on the *other* side of the lockers."

She didn't say a word. She only traced the contours of his back with her gaze as he stomped away. Mental dessert for weak moments. Instead, she strode to the locker and stared at its contents. The suit jacket. The white business shirt that she knew was pure silk, even before she touched it. The slacks. The sensible black shoes. Oxfords, not brogues. Garrett had impeccable taste.

Her throat bobbed as she reached in, her fingertips trembling. One did not snatch these things up. One lifted them gently. Cradled them. Eased them off their pedestal like the big golden thingie from the first Indiana Jones movie.

Her eyes slipped shut as she pressed the bundle to her face and inhaled. For a moment—a perfect, transcendent, untouchable moment—it was like she was back in his arms again. The soft brush of his shirt against her face. The cologne, and the way it mingled with his natural scent to leave her weak at the knees and jelly inside. Like everything would be okay, and there, in his embrace, nothing in the world could hurt her.

His pants were heavy. He'd left his phone in the pockets. And his wallet.

His wallet.

She was fishing through in a heartbeat and skipping her own heartbeat a second later as she withdrew a business card.

Eternal Bride Photography.

Gare-bear was looking up wedding photographers.

All the breath rushed out of Courtney. Everything froze. The business card trembled between her fingers.

He really *was* going to propose to her.

A cold sweat erupted over her, head to toe. The dress. She hadn't bought the dress from Ophelia's. He couldn't propose to Courtney while she was in a skirt and blouse. He'd gone to all this trouble—all the cat-and-mouse-ing, all the chases. Pretending to be with other women. All to throw her off what was going to be the biggest surprise of her entire life.

Squealing in delight, she shoved everything back into the locker. Sure, she'd been planning on swiping his clothes so she could have something to hold at night, but that was *before*. This changed *everything*. Instead, she scrambled in her purse for her pink gel pen and heart-shaped sticky-notes and scribbled a happy little note. If this was going to be themed after their first date, that could only mean he'd be meeting her at the Ferris wheel in Luna Park on Coney Island. It was just like her favorite movie, *The Notebook*. He knew that. He'd known all along.

She pressed the sticky note to her lips, pouring every ounce of love that she could muster, from the tips of her toes to her perfect hair, all into the lipstick mark. With a flourish, she pinned it to his wallet and left it on top of the pile of clothes, before sprinting out.

She had some *serious* shopping to do.

"I'm coming, Gare-bear."

Chapter Fourteen

"The Code Courtney has gotten worse." Garrett's voice was hoarse. The sticky note, tainted with lipstick from the Devil Herself, burdened his fingers. It wasn't just what was on it. The feeling of violation that it brought was half the pain.

"Worse?" David's eyes widened behind his square-framed glasses. "Define 'worse.'"

Wordless, Garrett placed the note on the desk as though it would explode and take his hands with it. The hair on the back of his neck stood to unholy attention. He could imagine, all too easily, her shrill voice echoing through the cell phone signals in the air and calling that syrupy nickname from his pocket.

"She left this on my wallet." He swallowed. "Which was with my clothes. *Locked inside a pay-to-use locker.*"

David placed his stylus on the desk with the grim motion of the skeletal Reaper laying his scythe aside in deference to an even higher power. "Do we have a contingency plan for dealing with this?"

"She knows where I live now." Garrett shook his head as though he could rewrite reality and make it not so. "And apparently, she's capable of following me to places without my knowing. Staying at a hotel or over here or at Olivia's isn't going to throw her off for long."

"Any ideas?" Even without having been in the car alongside him during the Code C, David sounded shaky.

Garrett forced his mind out of animal panic and back to the realm of semi-cohesive thought. "I mean... so far, it's only a sticky-note, so I don't think we can exactly get the cops involved over that."

David grunted, non-committal.

"She can't live outside my place twenty-four seven." He stroked the naked areas of his chin where once his goatee had been. In retrospect, it should have been an omen that warned Garrett of the hell coming upon his doorstep. "Even if she wants to go full stalker, she has to sleep and eat sometime. I can change up my schedule at random intervals. Take different routes. It'll be a hassle, but I can handle it."

David grimaced. "I guess, until then… maybe get more accurate with the garden hose or something?"

A silence fell over them as thoughts of the Code C lingered. Garrett folded his arms, staring at the thin red line across the whiteboard that represented Ari's progression toward full recovery from heartbreak.

"On a different note, we really should come up with a good name for this place," he said. "Batman has his Batcave. Superman has his Fortress of Solitude. What does Mr. Rebound have?"

David laughed. "Dead grandma in his underwear."

Garret cringed, his skin crawling in phantom response to the memory. "Dude."

"Oh, come on. That will never not be funny, and you know it." David reclined in his office chair, plucking the stylus back from the desk with an artful twirl as he glanced at the tablet in his hand. "Ari's got a point, though. I mean, so far, you've been set on fire and taken a cremation ash shower. I'm seeing broken bones in your future."

He shook his head, grimacing at the thought. "Well, we've been there before."

David looked like he didn't know whether to laugh or bang his head against the desk.

Garrett kept his arms crossed, staring at the red line with the intensity of a gunslinger sizing up his opponent. "I should mention—she manifested as a Type E about halfway through the date." He glanced back to his assistant.

"'Moving too quickly,'" translated David. "How'd she get there?"

"All the signs were present. Admission of intense feelings on only the second date. Constant physical contact. There was this expectation of future affection and just 'a future' in general. You could see it in her eyes. Not to mention, coming onto me stark naked is kind of a giveaway."

David whistled. "What was that like?"

"Dude. You're *married*." Garrett punched his arm, squinting and frowning in a distinctly "what the hell?" sort of expression.

David rolled his eyes. "Not like that, moron. I meant how did you react?"

"Professionally." He fixed David with a blunt stare. "I'm not going to jeopardize her recovery."

"Mm-hmm," David grunted in affirmation, updating her progress on the spreadsheet.

Garrett, however, stared off into space, letting his mind drift back to the vision of her. Spurred on by the thought, his mind drifted forward, constructing cute fantasies of their phone call that would take place later tonight. He'd be charming; she'd be flirty. They'd talk. Laugh. Tease. Feel the sweet, melted-chocolate-chip feelings of a budding romance.

He blinked as David snapped his fingers. The look on his assistant's face was enough to crumple up the fantasies and stuff them into a back pocket in his brain.

"Garrett. Not a good sign. I said your name twice." He grimaced. "You were thinking about Ari, weren't you?"

Garrett shrugged, his gaze darting away. "Of course. That's why we're here."

"You had a lovesick look on your face—scratch that, you *have* a lovesick look on your face." He reached out to snap his fingers in front of Garrett's face again. "If you're going to do this, I need you to pump the brakes. You have a job to do, 'Mr. Rebound.' You cannot go falling for this girl."

"I'm not." He jerked out of the way of the finger-snap, fighting tooth and nail not to sound defensive. "I'm plotting out the third date."

"The big one," said David. "Uh-huh. Forgive me if I'm a little frosty in the face of this chick. That's what you pay me to be."

Garrett nodded. It was true. The level of social chameleon artistry that he undertook to rebound so many different kinds of women took a toll. More than once, he'd drifted past professionalism and into genuine affection for a client, and that was where David came in. He needed a man to tighten the mask when it started to come loose. Every disguise could fray at the seams. Emotional disguises were the most form-fitting of all—and, to do what he did, every disguise was emotional. It had to be. If it wasn't, if he started drawing from his well, no good would come of it.

"Answer me this," said David. "She already brought up the possibility of the two of you going your separate ways. Why not cut it here and call it a D2 release? How necessary is it for you to keep seeing her all the way up to D6?"

"It's extremely necessary." Garrett uncrossed his arms. No defensive posture. This was for the collective good. "She only said that because she was trying to save face. She'd just tried to seduce me at a time when I *had* to reject her for the sake of a successful rebound—and it happened in front of her *sister*. If I really did leave now, she wouldn't be fully rebounded from Lucas. She has to go out on a high note, not believing that her first re-exposure to the world of dating consists of accidental pyrotechnics and poorly-timed nudity."

"Gotcha." David nodded. Garrett could only hope it was more from the clinical way he'd explained himself than the actual meaning behind his words as his wingman pressed on. "So, do you have any ideas for how to go about the big one?"

"A few things are percolating in the back of my mind." He waved a hand in non-committal fashion. "She's planning it—but I need to have a good talk with her roommate first."

"Penny Ansel-What's-It?" David opened the spreadsheet. "You going to find out why she ruined Ari's former relationship?"

"I'm going to pop the pimple." Garrett exhaled, fighting the creeping dread at the idea. "It's crucial. Until we find out why Penny did what she did, there's no way I can help Ari properly."

"Any idea when you want to do this?"

"Before the third date," Garrett said firmly. "The last time Ari saw me, I was wearing her ex-boyfriend's clothes. I'll do some damage control tonight, but I'd definitely feel a lot more comfortable knowing everything I can about how to help her before we go into the big one."

"Roger that." David heaved a sigh as he leaned back in his chair and spun in a circle, eyeing their progress.

Garrett let his gaze wander from assistant to tablet screen to whiteboard and back, fighting the feelings of dread. Things were already getting hairy. He was falling for Ari harder than he needed, her roommate was the reason she needed a rebound in the first place, and to top it all off, the glittery spectre of Courtney Hazleroth was hovering over his mind and business like a death shroud.

"I think that'll do us for tonight," said Garrett, swallowing. "Next meeting will be after I confront Penny."

David tapped at his tablet with finality before placing it back on the desk. "Done and done. Want to stay for dinner? We're doing lasagn—oh. Right."

Garrett laughed as he left the office. It wasn't his aversion to the dish Courtney had forever ruined that had him bidding a swift farewell to Lauren, nor what pushed him into his car and through the slick rain-washed streets back to his house. Thankfully, there was no bubblegum-pink eye-scar of a Dodge Charger waiting outside to ruin him.

No, what had him moving so quickly, and smiling so widely, was the thought of calling Ari and just being able to talk with her.

Heart beating a delighted cadence, he called her.

~ * ~

The red numbers on his alarm clock were threatening to turn over into a snaking, bloated "2:00 AM" by the time he thumbed the red telephone icon. They'd each apologized for various infractions—some minor, like his answering her apartment door without her permission; some major, like her display of *seductionus interruptus* in the living room.

They'd gone from awkward jokes to awkward laughter, to genuine laughter, to his favorite part of talking with anyone—sharing themselves and the experiences that made up their lives. He'd heard second-hand stories about Katie and her flight attendant skills, and how she was a shy naive flower but a career of smiling through her teeth had given her a vicious poker face. He'd heard stories of Ari, how she'd floundered as a freelance photojournalist before she caved and taken out a loan to open her own studio.

He'd shared stories of David and the time he'd sworn he could take care of a neighbor's Jack Russell terrier, only to come home and find the dog sitting, terrified, on top of the ceiling fan. To this day, they still had no clue what had happened, but hearing Ari laugh about it somehow made the eternal confusion seem worth it.

He'd followed up with a story of how he and an unnamed "friend" had been thrown out of a Broadway performance of *Wicked* after said "friend" had literally started booing Galinda and the way she'd treated Elphaba. Said small blonde manic "friend" had also hurled the balled-up playbill and clocked Galinda in the head—an impressive shot, considering they'd been seated on the mezzanine—and thrown her drink in the security guard's face.

Ari had talked about Lucas.

Garrett had listened.

Finally, they'd bid each other goodnight and hung up.

Minutes ticked past as his palms sweat and he stared at the ceiling, struggling and reflecting on everything he'd said. Everything he'd done. He traced his lips with his tongue as he clambered into bed and stared, forlorn, at the empty space across from him. It was the unfortunate and necessary reality of his work. He could never bring a girl home. At the end of the day, it wasn't the job that made things messy. He did. His stupid, overeager emotions did. The job was the safeguard that kept everything in check.

The glare of his phone screen pierced his tired eyes. Squinting, he found a text from Ari, indicating an attachment to the message. Most likely a meme, or a gif, or some kind of image reaction, he guessed. A cute kitten waving a paw and falling asleep where it stood or something.

It was not.

His jaw gaped as he stared at a photo taken at selfie angle. Her dark hair was messy, voluminous. Her eyes were darker, deep and entrancing, fatigued but in a way all too human that served to make her, in his mind, even more desirable. Her skin was light, pale in the filter, with the spattering of freckles across her cheeks enough to make his knees weak…as was the immense swell of cleavage, bulging against her forearm and slender fingers as she held back a tidal wave of softness.

The caption read "Just reminding you what you had to look forward to before we were interrupted. xox. Goodnight ;P"

The phone fell from his hands as he stared at the ceiling.

Like he was going to get any sleep *now*.

Chapter Fifteen

Laughter bounced off the walls of the interior of Eternal Bride Photography. Zoey doubled over, bracing herself with both arms on the front desk. Sierra was suspended like a marionette halfway from falling as she clutched at the edge of a chair for support and wiped tears from her eyes with the other hand. Arianne flushed with embarrassment.

"And he—" Zoey gasped, gesticulating as though she were trying to speak through three levels of language translation before the words could come out in English. "He just—he grabs you and makes you *wait* until they're gone before you can clean up?"

Arianne shook her head. "I didn't know whether to punch his lights out for making me wait or volunteer him for sainthood for being so goddamn considerate."

"I would've done both," said Sierra. Her knees finally gave out, and she missed the seat as gravity had its way with her, ripping a fresh burst of giggles from her. "I cannot believe it."

"Ari, honey…" Zoey's cheeks were bright red as she fanned herself. "I don't want to jinx you or anything, but I think this might be a sign. Like, at this rate, your third date is going to have both of you arrested for an accidental bomb threat or something."

"Honestly, that might make things easier for everyone," Arianne muttered. In the back of her mind, she could hear Katie's voicemail, apologetic to the point of tears. "There's a reason why I called this team meeting, and it wasn't to do with the shitstorm of a second date I had."

"Aw, really, *linda*?" Sierra pouted. "And here I thought we were just your sounding board for your love life."

Arianne narrowed her eyes.

Sierra beamed, while Zoey squirmed. "So… what's the reason for the meeting?"

Arianne sighed. Her gaze scoured the carpet, the walls, trying to suss out where might be the least conspicuous place to leave a gaping fist-hole in the wall. Yes, she was the owner, operator, and proprietor of Eternal Bride Photography, but Sierra and Zoey weren't just her employees. They were her friends. Even if this hadn't been a professional matter, they deserved to know.

"I got a phone call from Katie." Her voice was low, bitter, like a Chicago winter wind. "The airline changed their policy on family passes. As of two days ago, we can't—well, I mean, *I* can't—fly for free anymore. The fares are still, like, half-off, but I've done the math, and…"

Her nostrils flared as she fumed. God, she hated this taste. The feeling like burned film was being shoved into her mouth, acidic and acrid. Not just failure, but failure *forced* onto her. "Eternal Bride Photography can no longer offer its services nationwide and expect to make a profit. Not unless we hike up our prices by almost double or cut your wages by about seventy-five percent, and those just aren't viable options. It also means that unless we see a sharp increase in local traffic—which also isn't likely, since we're in the off-season right now—we'll be lucky to make it another month before we have to close our doors."

Other women might have cowered before the reality of informing her friends that they were now soon-to-be-unemployed. Arianne stared, her mouth a flat line, her breathing even. It was what it was. The universe shoveled shit onto her plate, and she had to eat it. Sometimes, it splashed out and hit her friends. What mattered was that she could get what good there was to get while it was available—and she had. Running a business with Sierra, bringing in Zoey, had been amazing times, and they weren't *technically* over yet. But what would come after—if anything—didn't bear thinking about.

"*Merda*," muttered Sierra.

Zoey's shoulders slumped.

Arianne grimaced, tapping their shoulders. "Hey. C'mon. We've still got some shoots lined up that'll bring in some income. We're not out of business yet. Just… heading that way. Unless something changes."

Sierra stared at the ceiling and hissed a long breath out between her teeth.

Zoey, however, looked ready to cry.

Arianne swallowed, turning her gaze aside as though she were intruding on a dirty moment. *Great. Just great.* She threw up her hands in futility. "Look, I'm sorry, okay? It's the reality of the situation."

A tiny tremble rippled through Zoey's voice as she mumbled, "Can we go back to laughing about you getting covered in dead grandma?"

Arianne couldn't tell if it was more of a whimper or a restrained laugh, but it was enough to force a wry chuckle out of her. There was a reason Zoey was the Little Miss Sunshine out of everyone in Arianne's life. No matter what, Zoey could make a laugh out of an awkward situation.

"If you want to keep laughing at my shitty luck, sure," Arianne said. "But the story doesn't end at the beach."

"Wait, what?" Sierra latched onto the bait with eager eyes. "You're telling me it gets worse?"

Zoey leaned forward like a junkie facing down the promise of a new fix.

Arianne twisted her tongue against her teeth. They were her friends. But even in the face of potential unemployment, they didn't need to know every tiny naked detail about her huge, naked mistake. She scoffed, abridging her account to sound more PG-13 than the truth.

"So he saw you in your underwear as you were walking out of the shower?" said Zoey.

"Totally by accident?" echoed Sierra.

They shared a single look.

"Yeah, no," said Zoey.

"I don't buy it." Sierra shook her head. "What *really* happened?"

"What *matters* is," said Arianne, speaking loud enough to drown out her friends' scepticism and any scheming machinations they may have been on the verge of planning. "He saw me in a compromising and less-than-fully-clothed position, and the only things I could give him to wear were stuff left over from Lucas." Her throat closed.

Whether she liked it or not—and she was certain she did not—there was still pain saying his name. Garrett was a soothing, cooling balm, at once tingling and exciting, but the fact remained and would forever remain—she had been burned.

Zoey's and Sierra's smiles both shrank into sympathetic grimaces.

"How'd you handle that?" said Zoey.

Arianne sighed, shrugging in a fashion wholly non-committal. "It messed me up. How do you think? I mean, yeah, second date and all, but seeing the guy you like wearing the clothes left over from your cheating ex? Plus, they still kind of smelled like Lucas. Faint cologne smell. You know what I mean."

"How do you know that he smelled like it?" Sierra, this time, frowned in confusion.

"We hugged." It was the truth. Just not all of it.

"I'm so sorry, sweetie." Zoey, empathetic as ever, brushed a hand over Arianne's upper arm.

"It's whatever." She fought the urge to shy away from the comfort. "The point is, I told him I'd plan the third date, and I've got nothing up my sleeve. What the hell do I do?"

She could practically hear the cogs turning in their brains, pondering and reminiscing over every date they had in their respective lives—at least, the ones that had turned out good. She was racking her own brain, sifting through memories pleasant and painful of outings with guys, whether they ended in the bedroom or the passenger seat. Tradition usually dictated the back seat, but a woman who bordered six and a half feet tall was usually too much woman to be crammed into the back of the average sedan. A truck bed, certainly, but pickups were on the rare side in New York.

She frowned, sad and quiet. Through memories of one-night stands, hook-ups, tipsy club dances, and midnight make-outs, her repertoire of actual dates upon which to draw looked woefully small. She didn't entirely like what that said about her.

"Any ideas?" she repeated, suddenly glum.

"I have one." Zoey sat upright so quickly her long blonde hair whipped up and into her face. Spluttering, she wiped the strands free from her eyelashes and mouth, fumbling for composure. "I, uh, met a guy at a park once—"

"So, internet dating," translated Sierra.

Zoey made a face. "Don't judge," she huffed. "Do you know how hard it is to meet a decent guy by…I dunno, wandering around? They don't exactly fall into your lap or anything. Besides, there's plenty of—"

"The date?" interjected Arianne.

Zoey pouted, looking warily between Sierra and Arianne, before relenting. "We went to this arcade and played laser tag. Dry ice and black lights and everything. It was actually a ton of fun."

Arianne was less than convinced. "I'm seeing corndogs, sticky carpet floors, and a bunch of twelve-year-olds. Sounds like a riveting time."

Zoey lifted her eyebrows and something akin to a saucy grin came over her. "Try a place with a bunch of dim lighting, dark corners, and sneaking around. Believe me, actually playing laser tag is only half the fun of going to a laser tag place."

Arianne chewed her tongue, trying to imagine herself announcing to the man who'd taken her to French dining for a first date that she was going to take him to a laser tag arena. Though, to be fair, he'd been happy to ditch his own reservation in favor of Rooster Jim's. She glanced back over to a still-talking Zoey.

"We hit up a session in the early afternoon on a weekday when it's basically deserted, and the attendants running it don't really give a crap as long as you don't break anything or injure yourselves," she said. "It was cute, it was fun… plus, afterward, he took me out to get cotton candy."

"Sounds cheesy as hell," said Sierra, her voice flat.

"Don't write off the cheesy dates just because they're cheesy," said Zoey, rising to the defense. "Cheesy can be good sometimes."

"What ever happened to this guy?" Arianne asked.

Zoey fidgeted and mumbled something about him moving to Canada, and for a single malicious second, Arianne wondered if Zoey had in fact been talking about a childhood birthday party instead of a date as an adult.

Arianne sat back in her chair and mused. A seed of an idea took root in her mind, blossoming as she poured terrifying amounts of mental peat moss onto it. "Y'know, I think she's on the right track."

"Uh-huh. I can totally imagine you in a laser tag vest." Sierra crossed her arms.

Arianne shook her head once. "Paintball."

"After you've had him set on fire and had cremation ashes dumped on you both? I know you were joking about the whole 'bomb threat' thing but taking him somewhere with almost actual guns?" blustered Sierra. "You've got to be kidding."

"I think it'll be great," said Zoey. The two shared a satisfied nod, united under the banner of Team Paintball against Sierra's one-woman anti-paintball crusade. "Guys love the chance to go all paramilitary and show off for girls. Besides, if she caps him right in the sack, think what kind of a story it'll make."

Arianne froze. The world seemed tilted, as though she'd been wearing glasses she never knew about that had been bumped askew on the bridge of her nose. "Sorry?"

Zoey smiled in complete ignorance of the weight of her own words. "Yeah. I mean, setting him on fire? The Grandma Perkins's ashes incident? Those are both amazing stories. Even if you and Garrett don't work out, those are stories you can share over drinks with anybody for years to come. Paintballing seems like it'd be a good chance for another one."

Arianne's breath left her in a quiet laugh. Unwilling, uncontrolled, but not unwelcome, the corners of her mouth lifted as she stared at the floor. For a moment, she felt like somebody had handed her a tremendous bouquet of roses for no reason other than trying her best. "Zoey, you're amazing."

The atmosphere inside of The Minefield differed so fundamentally during the day than at night that the rising of the sun may as well have heralded a shift from a fever dream to a sunlit graveyard. The place was lit up by the cheerful noon, and Garrett sat in slacks and a sports coat, tracing the beads of condensation on his glass of ice water. He wished he'd worn a full-blown HAZMAT suit instead. His phone sat out on the table. His panini lay on a marble white plate, untouched. He kept his mind cold, professional, and unfeeling as a surgeon's scalpel. This wasn't just business. This was messy, ugly, nitty-gritty business.

The glass door to the front swung open, light shining off the half-waterfall of blonde hair on the diminutive British pimple who crept a few steps inside and hesitated, gazing around the battlefield of black chairs and bar stools.

He lifted an arm in a salute as much as a beacon.

Penny wandered over.

He tapped his phone once and turned the screen face-down.

"I got your message," she said, her voice clipped in concern. She slid her purse from her shoulder and hung it on the chair. "Was there a problem with the account? I didn't have time to stop by an ATM before I got here, so if you need me to pay you in cash or something, well—I got the receipt saying the payment had been wired, so—"

"The money isn't the problem," he said. "I need to talk with you about Ari."

Her mouth closed, lips pursing, before she nodded. "Right. Yes. Well, I was hoping I'd get some kind of an update from you, considering I've gone in the hole almost a thousand dollars so far, and—"

"I need to know," he interrupted, staring her down like a priest meeting a vampire at the edge of church property, "why you cheated with Lucas and brought Ari's relationship to an end."

Penny bristled. "Well, if you've dragged me all the way across town simply to throw baseless allegations at me, I'll have to reconsider whether hiring you was worth it," she snapped. "Ever heard of 'buyer's remorse?'"

"If you really thought hiring me wasn't going to be worth it, you never would have done it to begin with," he said, cutting her protests off at the hamstrings. "Furthermore, you can't threaten to tell Ari who I am or what I do, because not only does it break our legally binding NDA, but it brings you down as much as it does me. Most of all, it proves to Ari that she can never trust anybody again unless they're related to her. You're too good of a friend to do that."

The popping had begun.

Penny's face contorted behind a furious shade of crimson. "You played me."

"You played yourself." His voice was flat. "If you want me to be able to do the job you paid me to do, I need to know *everything*. The one thing you don't tell me is the one thing that will gut my chances to help her." He wet his lips with the water, taking his time to let the silence between gulps work its razor wire marionettes into her.

"Now…" He placed the glass back on the table. "Tell me why you and Lucas slept together when both of you were in committed relationships."

"We didn't cheat." An unthinking response. Automatic. "He cheated with me. I didn't cheat. I…lapsed in judgment."

Garrett raised a single eyebrow. "Is that what Keith thinks?"

The pimple spurted.

"How *dare* you," she snarled. "What goes on in my personal life is none of your business. I hired you to improve Arianne's love life, not go sniffing around in mine!"

He scoffed. "One Facebook search is all it took to find out you're engaged, Penelope."

"Don't call me that. It's 'Penny.'" The correction was pithy. Petty.

He didn't so much as blink. "Then answer the question. Does Keith know?"

Her revolting, pus-covered secret oozed across his hands as he coaxed it out. The things he did to help people. To help Ari. To get paid. Sometimes they didn't feel worth it.

"No." She sagged in her chair. "I haven't told him."

He grunted, nodding at her to go on.

Slowly, under his prying gaze, she told him all that happened. The pimple was open, and he worked and poked until nothing came out but clarity.

Garrett remained silent for a long time. "Have you seen him since?"

"No," she said.

He let the silence stretch before he sipped at his water. "Based on projections, Ari should be completely rebounded from Lucas by the end of our sixth date." An errant bead of condensation merged from glass to tabletop. "After that, provided nothing changes, we should be able to conclude our arrangement and go our separate ways."

"I look forward to it," spat Penny. "Anything else? Maybe you want to call me a whore, too? A bad friend?"

"I haven't yet, and I don't intend on it." He lifted his gaze from tabletop to incensed Brit. "If you were as bad as you think you are, you wouldn't have hired me to try to fix your mistakes."

Her gaze darted back and forth, searching him, likely wondering if he'd insulted her or not. His poker face was as effective as a mirror, and he gave her nothing save the tiniest hint of a professional smile.

"You haven't told Ari yet, have you?" he prompted.

"What do you think?" Her voice was acidic enough to sear his heart.

He frowned, making a tiny "hm" sound as he picked up his phone and stylus and scribbled something in a note-taking app. Her face contorted, suspicion now overwhelming her indignation. She was starkly pretty when she scowled, and the accent made it worse, in his opinion. If only she wasn't slimy as kelp on the inside.

"Should I—" she started, before cutting herself off. "No. You know what? I don't need you to tell me what I *should* do. What I need to know is, if I tell her, will that mean I have to pay you longer or not?"

"Tell her what?"

"Tell her that Lucas cheated with me." For a moment, the look in her blue eyes was one of shocking vulnerability.

He stayed quiet. Seconds ticked by. His mind raced. Angle after angle was considered, consulted, attacked, and discarded. In the end, it was a yes or no question.

The tingling ghost of Ari's kiss brushed across his lips, his cheek.

He dried his sweaty palms against his slacks.

"No," he said. "If you tell her you're the reason Lucas dumped her, you won't have to pay me as long as you would have if you stayed silent." He lifted his gaze to Penny, staring at her with an intensity that dared her to call him out, one guilty conscience to another.

She shifted in her chair, taking several deep breaths, before she jerked up and clutched her purse from where it hung. A vein pulsed in the corner of her jaw that wasn't hidden by the mess of golden tresses that splashed over her shoulder. "I think it's best if we don't speak again unless we absolutely have to," said Penny, through clenched teeth.

"I think—"

The rush of wind heralded the swift arrival of her purse, leather and buckles and weight loaded with centrifugal force from where she swung it by the straps. It cuffed him across the side of the head with an awkward, heavy impact, enough to send him twisting in his chair and jolting the table.

"Asshole." She stalked away as though she were leaving a lesser, dirtier creature to wallow in filth and muck.

It didn't seem to occur to her that it was her own muck he was having to wallow in as she shoved open the glass entrance door and strode out into the bright afternoon sunlight.

Rubbing the side of his head, Garrett retrieved his phone from the table and silently tapped it again, ending the lengthy voice recording he'd taken and saving the entire file before messaging it to David. It would be added to the record.

With a sigh, Garrett lifted the cold panini from his plate and took a bite. Not as good as it could have been, but not too shabby at all.

In a nutshell, it would do.

~ * ~

By the time Arianne arrived back at her apartment from work, she was in markedly better spirits about the prospects of both her future and the bottle of wine in one hand. Katie was crashing at her place until the weekend, whereupon she was—apparently—due to go out to Dallas, then from there to Sao Paolo. She'd messaged Arianne to grab a nice bottle of white wine from the store on her way home.

There was a deeper reason that this made her smile. Katie, for all her flight attendant time, was a self-confessed and shyly enthusiastic foodie, and she considered the shining chrome slate of a stocked kitchen with the same passion Arianne held on a new photoshop program and lens set.

In Katie's opinion, all important conversations were to be enjoyed over a meal that had been done to perfection and left those involved too pleased with what went in their mouths to ever be angered or upset by what went in their ears.

Asking Arianne to pick up a bottle of wine meant that a.) Katie was finally ready to talk about what the other four cryptic stammering voicemails she'd left were about—not including the airline policy change for family passes that had taken a shotgun to the kneecaps of Eternal Bride Photography—and b.) Arianne was going to have a spectacular dinner to top it all off.

As she ducked through the front door, her nose twitched, eager for a preview of what would surely leave her drooling. Last she'd heard, Katie had been on an Asian binge. Arianne was seeing a duck soup or mango foie gras or something ridiculously fancy that had taken eleven hours to slow-cook in the husk of a dragon's belly buried in clay pots and danced over by a crane.

The inside of her apartment smelled like…her apartment.

"Katie?" She sniffed harder. Still no smells. "I'm home!"

"Kitchen," came the reply.

Arianne brightened, striding down the hallway of framed photos.

Maybe she couldn't smell anything because it was all still captured in pans or something. Or maybe Katie had started cooking late. That wouldn't be the worst thing.

"So, I got the wine." Arianne glanced at the label to remind herself of the name and year. "Nothing super fancy, since finances are tight this month, but I've got a big wedding I'm shooting in Chicago this week, so that'll bring in some. The drive is going to be a bitch, but them's the breaks, right?"

She was rambling, and she knew it, as she placed the bottle of wine on the dining room table and looked out at the simple settings and places. The food was already served.

Blinking, she looked from plate to Katie and back. "Um," she managed.

Katie fidgeted. "I know. I, uh, don't usually go for this, but, like... I thought it'd kind of fit the theme of what we need to talk about," she mumbled. Her gaze locked onto their dinner instead of her sister.

Arianne frowned, trying to piece together the culinary puzzle before her. "Why are we talking about Burger King?"

"It's, um—it's McDonald's." Katie's gaze refused to leave the burger bun, which—in fairness—didn't look all that bad but was still far from the masterpiece of dining Arianne had been expecting.

"Whatever. It's fast food. Why are we talking about fast food, and why has it taken you three days to open up about it?" She snorted, seating herself without asking and seizing the corkscrew from where it lay on the table beside the bottle. She twisted until the tell-tale *pop* heralded the alcohol she would need to get through the conversation.

Katie's mumble was barely audible over the sound of wine sloshing into Arianne's glass. "I got us fast food because it's easy, and cheap, and, um...that's kind of what I wanted to talk to you about."

The dregs of Arianne's good mood slipped away with the *clunk* of the bottle on the table as she replaced it. Fantastic. This wasn't going to be a talk about whatever was on Katie's mind. No, this would be her shy, engaged, only-ever-kissed-one-man prude of a sister chastising her in the most magnificently passive-aggressive way about Arianne's sexual appetites and her exhibition in front of Garrett. Oh, sure, it would all come from a place of "love," but the overall message would be the same. She had to treat herself better. Her affection needed to be worth more. She couldn't be so *derivative*.

Katie would make a great mom one day, Arianne was sure of it.

"Shouldn't have gotten white wine, then." She grumbled, tossing her head back and downing the first glass of what was sure to be many for the night. "You want to call me cheap and easy to my face and get away with it, Katie? You bring me a goddamn eight pack of cherry wine coolers and put me in a cheerleader's outfit while you chew me out under the bleachers for stealing your boyfriend."

Katie's head tilted in confusion. "You were never a cheerleader, Arianne."

"It's called 'sarcasm,' Katie. Now spill it." Huffing, she poured herself a second glass before swiping at some of the limp fries. "Go on. Get it all out."

Her sister pawed at the tablecloth, her gaze averted. "I—I wasn't saying that about you, really. It's why the wine—because, um, it's kind of classy, too, in a way—"

Arianne jerked her head in a sharp shake, speaking around the fries as she gulped them down. "You are not helping your apology, girl."

"I'm not—look, I—do you know any good photographers?" The tablecloth was twisted into a small tornado between Katie's long, slender fingers.

A rush of air kicked out of Arianne, her jaw slack in disbelief. "*Wow.* Really? Because your own *sister*, who makes her *living* off—"

"I want to try boudoir photos!" Katie clenched her eyes as hard as her fists as she directed her frustration and fury straight down into the double cheeseburger leaving a grease smear on the plate. Her voice bounced off the walls and ceiling and echoed through the entire apartment, ringing in the echoing silence left in its wake.

Arianne just stared, wondering if she could psychically materialize a dunce cap over her own head.

Katie's cheeks heated into a record-breaking blush as she opened her eyes and devoted both hands to twisting and untwisting the tablecloth. "Look, I'm—I want to try it." Her voice was as soft as her yell had been loud. "I don't... I've saved myself for marriage, and so has Orlando, and I-I want him to be able to think of me... y'know... sexually."

"Okay." It was all Arianne could say in response. A simple, barely cognizant, "did you really just say that" sort of utterance as she stared, wide-eyed, at her older sister. Her prude, prim, proper older sister.

"So, I, uh—I know some girls will kind of do, like, boudoir photos. Like, for a pre-wedding kind of thing, and, uh...I thought I'd try it out." She heaved a deep breath, trying to calm herself down as much from the confession as from her actual crime of raising her voice above a polite and friendly tone.

"Okay." Arianne thought she could hear a distant ringing in her ears, like she'd been given a concussion by sheer world-view upheaval.

"So, I was thinking, since you're already my wedding

photographer, but..."

Finally, the suggestion filled in the gap in Arianne's mind that had been blown open by her older sister's words. "Katie..." She cringed. "I'm flattered, but—"

"I know, I know," stammered her older sister, releasing the tablecloth to put her hands in the air in a universal "slow down" gesture. "I was thinking of asking you to take them, but that'd be... y'know, *weird*."

"Definitely weird." Arianne choked on some strange offspring between a scoff and a laugh before she brought the second straight glass of white wine to her lips and drank it dry.

The alcohol churned in her stomach before she opted to pick up one of the two burgers on her plate and tear a bite out of one. Katie had been conscientious enough to get her a second burger. Fast food portions were often smaller than a restaurant, and her sister knew Arianne's appetite far outstripped her own—for which she was grateful.

"So, what did you need my help f—" she started, before her eyes widened. "—oh... *Ohhhh*."

"Outfit... suggestions... yeah." Katie offered up her best in the newest line of nervous giggles as she poked at a limp fry with a fingertip almost as slender. "I've never had the luck with guys that you have. I thought maybe you could give me some advice on what looks good and what doesn't. Y'know, help me figure out what I like or what, um... what... y'know. What guys like."

Arianne took a deep breath, and then another, and another. The bite of burger she chewed felt heavy and thick, like Play-Doh. "Um," she began. This time, it was her turn to play with the tablecloth. "Katie... no offense or anything, but why don't you just talk to Orlando about this?"

Katie blinked, confused. "Huh?"

"Well, I mean, you're my sister. I know we've butted heads every now and then. But, like, Orlando is basically God's gift to guy-dom, to hear you tell it." said Arianne with a frown. "He's always been super understanding, right?"

The smile that lit Katie's face was the stuff fairy tales were made of. Like she'd pulled aside the edge of the curtain that led to Heaven. All because of her fiancé. To light up like that about a guy, one who returned her feelings and committed to stay faithful, to stay loyal, to love and to have and to hold...

"Of course." Her voice was soft. Almost freaking reverent. "I've never had to worry. I love him. He loves me. He accepts me. It's kind of perfect, you know? I can tell him anything."

Well, wasn't that the goddamn Hallmark movie dream. The wine in Arianne's stomach roiled, and she shoved an enormous bite of burger down atop it, speaking with her mouth full to try and keep the quivering longing inside her from growing any bigger. "So, you two are a big lovey-dovey emotional perfect pair." She chomped at the fast food. "You didn't answer my question. You can't tell him about wanting to try boudoir photography because…?"

Katie hesitated. "W-well, a few reasons." Her mouth crooked into a traitorous smile. "First of all, like it or not, I'm a Reynolds."

Arianne nearly snorted a chunk of hamburger out of her nose. Across the four girls of her family, there were two universal truths—they were all over six feet tall, and every last one of them were filled with enough insecurities to destabilize Fort Knox. A parental divorce in their teens and the abject failure of the male race to appreciate women who weren't built like pixies tended to dig emotional thorns into a woman's soul.

"Second," continued Katie, chewing her bottom lip. "I'm good with all the emotional stuff. It's… well, all the—all the 'sexy stuff.' It's new. And it's, well… scary. What if Orlando doesn't like it?"

The gaps between the lines were big enough to hold a photo shoot, and Arianne was reading each bit of it with the ice-cold sobriety of a nun standing before God. Katie wasn't afraid Orlando wouldn't like sex, or boudoir photos, or "sexy stuff." She was afraid he wouldn't like that new side of her. That the validation, the acceptance, the understanding—the love—would stretch only so far. She was afraid of being vulnerable—but in a sexual way.

A way in which Arianne thrived.

Katie's strengths were Arianne's fears, and now Katie's fears were driving her to Arianne.

Her palms left sweat marks against the tablecloth.

"He'll like it." She forced herself to believe it. "He'll like you, Katie. He's a good guy. It takes a lot to—to open up like that to someone. He'll see that."

Arianne had the truth clenched between her teeth and choking her from the inside out. Katie was shy and painfully naïve. But there she was, staring her weakness in the face and doing what she could to get past it. Doing what Arianne had never done. To say nothing of the men she'd dated in the past…and to say everything about why they'd left. Why they'd strayed. Why they'd sought a listening ear in the arms of other women. Why Lucas had strayed. How Garrett might do the same if she didn't get her shit under control.

"Okay, but… you realize you're coming to me for advice on lingerie and sex?" Better by far to change the subject. A girl could only handle so many life-altering revelations in one night. "You're going to open Pandora's Box here. You know that, right?"

Sweat practically erupted from her older sister's pores as Katie blustered and panicked. "L-Look," she stammered, "I don't want to open Pandora's Box, okay? Just... just maybe crack one corner a bit. Sort of get a peek inside. Don't go ripping open everything and throwing me in. I know you."

"Relax. We won't get to the spiked harnesses and ball gags until later tonight." Arianne gave her sister a borderline sinister look.

Katie turned an unhealthy shade of "holy shit" pale.

"By the way..." said Arianne, raising a finger. "Million-dollar idea— 'Pandora's Box' as a lingerie shop name."

"Arianne..." Katie's voice weakened.

"Now, then." Arianne placed the glass of wine back on the table, unfinished. "Let's get you out of those clothes and modeling some of the stuff I've got so you can see how it looks."

"*Arianne.*" Katie's voice hit the exact blend between a terrified yelp and a reflexive snap of elderly sibling authority.

Arianne laughed before waving a hand in a supreme act of mercy. "I'm just screwing around. I'm proud of you, sis."

"Proud of me?" Katie blinked. "For telling you I want to try out taking sexy photos?"

Shaking her head, Arianne finished her dinner and poured the last of the wine into a glass for each of them. "For opening up to me. I, uh... I know I'm difficult to talk to sometimes."

A deep blanket of understanding had rested over her, and the world seemed more defined, as though she could actually see the strings that guided people through their lives and made them what they were— and for once, she could see her own strings the clearest.

Katie managed a weak smile as took her glass delicately between three fingers. "You're my sister. I love you. Of course I was going to come to you."

They toasted, the clink of glass resonating through their bond, and each was reflected in turn. Katie sipped, dainty and deliberate.

Arianne, for once, drank slowly.

Wine was supposed to be savored, after all.

Chapter Sixteen

The third date is better summarized as the big one. A vast majority of women in Western civilization believed they could know whether or not a guy was going to be right for them by the end of the third date. This, along with the first kiss, was the biggest hurdle a man would have to jump if he wanted to find any sort of extended romance with a woman. The third date was the make-or-break. It was, in short, the big one.

If all went to plan, they should be masterstrokes of dating—works of romantic art that would make Casanova himself raise a glass in respect—which was why Garrett was lying on his bed and staring at the ceiling in horror.

Ari was planning the third date instead of him.

He hadn't even thought about it at the time. This was supposed to be a work of emotional cardiothoracic surgery, and he'd given the tools and rule of the operating room to the patient herself. It was easy to write off as an excuse in the face of what had happened—cremation ashes and a naked Ari did not a clear mind make—but this was still a first. He'd never let control of the big one slip out of his hands before.

A sour taste rose in the back of his throat. What, was he going to call her and explain that he needed to be the one to plan their third date because…because why? He had control issues? Because *that* was the way to continue to ingratiate himself with her. No, he had no choice but to brace himself for whatever Ari had planned and try to turn it to his advantage.

He stared at the screen of his phone in his white-knuckled hand.
10:17 AM Good morning! Excited to see you today :) Meet me at my place at noon.
10:18 AM Good morning, beautiful! Excited to see you too! What are we doing for our date?
10:18 AM You'll just have to find out :P Dress for the outdoors.

Heavy clothing, if you can. No skin.

10:19 AM Do I have to worry about ticks or something? Are we going hiking?

10:19 AM I said it was a surprise! Trust me ;) Bring a change of clothes for after too.

He'd racked his brains on potential activities that could require him to keep all his skin covered in eighty-degree weather and require a change of clothes. Somehow, his mind kept locking onto motocross racing. The thought sent chills through his gut. She'd been joking about the mud run under barbed wire, but the suspense was driving his imagination to dangerous places.

So, he laid there, in an athletic long-sleeved top and cargo pants, counting the passage of time in nervous fantasies and slow breaths, until the collar of the tightening deadline pulled him out the door and across town, traffic be damned, to Ari's apartment.

He rapped his knuckles on her door.

Muffled voices sounded on the other side before footsteps approached and the door swung open. His fear mutated to apprehension in a split second. He hadn't even said a word and already he had to improvise.

"Oh," said Penny. "You're here for Arianne."

"Hi, Penny." He forced himself to smile. Ari had to be able to overhear anything they said—and, to her knowledge, he hadn't spoken with Penny since she'd set them up on their first blind date. That was an illusion that would best serve all parties involved. "It's been a while. Seriously, thank you so much for setting me up with Ari. It's been a blast."

"I'm sure." Her gaze was flat, her words clipped and artificially sweet. "You're going somewhere with guns today. Have fun." She stalked away.

Garrett's heart froze. Maybe Courtney had gotten to her. Or to Ari. Maybe the gun thing was a cover.

"Ari," he called, stepping inside and looking around for his mysterious date—or for the blonde menace. "Please tell me I'm not going to get shot today."

Her voice echoed back from behind her bedroom door. "Relax. It's not going to kill you. There's armor to rent at the place."

She strode out of her bedroom in a heavy jacket, tank top, and tight-fitting pants, all blurring together in a melding, mesmerizing display of woodland camo gear. Her dirt brown eyes flicked over his choice of athletic wardrobe as she scoffed. "Man, you're going to be sore by tonight."

~ * ~

"Winchester Park Paintball Arena?" As Garrett read the sign on the complex, he dared to breathe properly for the first time since they'd left.

Paintball. He could work with it. While he was never a fan of a sport with the word "pain" right there in the name, it was hardly ice climbing or pole vaulting. Plus, with no Courtney in sight and no detectable tension between Ari and Penny, the true nature of his profession had to still be in the dark. He was safe. Relatively.

Ari put on her best innocent face, her plump lips drawn into a pout. "What? Did you think I was taking you to an actual gun range? Honestly, Garrett. I'm not going to kill you. I'm just going to shoot you. Probably a lot."

He gave her a long, slow side-eye. "Somehow that notion does not provide me with comfort."

Ari laughed but laced her fingers with his.

Behind the cashier counter, fearsome-looking paintball guns hung on the wall, all sleek design and smooth finish and very, very gun-looking. Now that the suspense was out of the way, this was something he could work with. Paintball. Team sports. Chances to team up and be cute, chances to battle head-to-head and be even cuter. The principles of the activity were well within his repertoire.

"Just don't be too scared," she said. Her grin was nothing short of diabolical as she ruffled his hair. "I promise I'll let you stay in for a whole minute before I take you out."

He nudged her ribs in retaliation. "Then I'll have forty-five seconds to relish your walk of shame after I take you out first."

Her eyebrows snapped up, and she laughed, loud peals of honesty bouncing off the walls as they met with the half-dozen others in the group. There were two instructors to give them the safety explanations, all of which boiled down to basic common sense anyway.

Divided into two teams, Garrett traded saucy looks with Ari as they strapped on their goggles and ear protection. He and his three teammates were given the illustrious and intimidating name of Team Blue; Ari and her cohorts, Team Red, led by an instructor around a corner and away, presumably to the opposite side of the arena.

Garrett hazed out everything besides the gist of the orientation. Last team with a man standing wins. Best of three rounds won the day, then they'd turn them loose and give them a crate of paint-filled water balloons to add to the chaos.

In a moment, Team Blue was ushered out into the blinding sunlight.

Garrett stayed in a crouched run, headlong into the outdoor arena. A wide, flat grassy field stretched before them, dotted with red and blue inflatable blobs the size of trucks to allow for cover in strategic locations. On the far end, a good fifty yards out, he saw glimpses of the villainous Team Red and a tall, curvy girl in camo taking cover behind a red wall.

His heart raced. Heat spread through his body as he sprinted a short distance and planted his shoulder against the springy face of a blue wall.

The game was on.

"Hey, Ari." He flexed his grip around his paintball gun. Giddy adrenaline surged through his veins. "Ready for that walk of shame?"

The pneumatic *punf-punf-punf* of shots rang out from both sides. The blue wall shook against him as a spray of paintballs splattered into the opposite side.

"You really shouldn't call out like that." Ari's voice was gleeful. "You'll give yourself away."

His adrenaline spurted through him in electric bursts. He peered through his goggles. Left. Right. No one in sight.

He dropped to one knee in a low crouch, curling around the side of the blue blob-wall. Aimed with the focus that came from intense, hyperactive concentration. Snatches of movement. Shapes. His gaze suckered onto anything that twitched.

A body sprinted from cover to the left.

He swiveled and pumped the trigger with the burning intensity of a hunter. A stream of merciless blue paintballs streaked through the air and splattered a streak against the leg of a Team Red player, who staggered.

Garrett forced his gaze past. No time to glory in the kill. He had to—

The bubbling thunder of paintballs splattered the wall over his head. He flinched low and shoved himself backward, skidding on his butt and flopping ungainly into safety. Ari's exasperated cry mingled with that of two others.

After a second dash from cover to cover, accompanied by the fierce whistling of paintballs, he chanced a look at the scoreboard. They were tied at three points each. Only he and one other from Team Red were left on the field.

"You still alive, baby?" He adjusted his grip on his gun.

Her voice was triumphant, loaded with the joy that came from tight competition. "Come on over and find out!"

Garrett's breath came in short fast gasps. Heat washed over his body. His goggles were fogging up, but he squinted through them as he darted from cover to cover, from blob to blob, and finally from blue into red territory.

"Ari?" Hunter vs. hunted. Prey vs. predator. He couldn't tell which applied more to him or more to her. He just knew he had to have her. Just because she wasn't much for sports didn't mean she didn't enjoy competition.

"Other side," came the reply, punctuated with a laugh and close enough to send a fresh spurt of adrenaline through him.

His footsteps were light, feeling for all the world like he was treading on broken glass, land mines, and bear traps.

After a spectacular diving somersault, head over heels over paint-streaked grass and righting himself in a military crouch, he peered through foggy goggles down the sleek black barrel of his gun at the statuesque brunette in her camo outfit—

Who was splattered with paint and standing in the sheltered observation area with the rest of those taken out from the game.

"Wha—" managed Garrett before his back exploded in firecrackers that sent him toppling forward with a pained grunt.

The sting seared through him as the other players laughed and cheered in equal measure, and the remaining Team Red member—a wiry, military-enthusiast-looking college kid with shaved sides and a jaw like a brick who'd come in his own white Stormtrooper armor—jogged past him and accepted his victorious high-fives from the rest of the group.

Through the burning pain and the welts Garrett was sure were developing on his back, he couldn't help but laugh. His own amusement mingled with the gleeful cackles of Ari as he trotted over to the observation area.

"How was it?" she said. "Getting pegged for the first time?"

He puckered his lips and stared into the distance with the self-important air reserved for the most pompous of sommeliers. "A sharp, powerful sensation at first, resolving into a deep but not unpleasant ache that permeates through the muscles. Overall, I'd pair it with a nice brie and water crackers."

She snorted and shook her head in disbelief. "You are such a dork." Still, she seemed unable to wipe the fondness from her eyes.

He squeezed her hand, offering her an intimate smile before they parted again for round two. His tongue danced over his lips as she left. Something in his chest tugged after her—a fleeting impulse, an imagined moment. He bit the smile from his face as he jogged back to Team Blue.

Deep at the core of the third date, the entire point thereof, were the emotions that ran between the two invested parties. The activity was good, but it was an interchangeable wrapper over the issue at the core—trust. They had to have fun. Start to trust again. Feel safe in the batting cage he'd established—but they couldn't get too comfortable. They had to leave the big one asking themselves if they really wanted to pursue things with him.

The answer, in order to be a successful rebound, had to be exactly sixty-five percent of a yes.

Round two went in a flash. Garrett was taken out early, but not before he'd scored a spectacularly lucky shot through a narrow gap that pinged Ari on the back of her left shoulder and sent her spinning. They'd joined in the observation area and linked hands, trading jokes and quips about who was better, how one would nail the other next time—totally in the paintball way and not in any way a double entendre, of course—and the bell rang for a third round.

He went to walk away, but Ari tightened her fingers around his hand, pulling him back.

"Garrett." Her smile was gone. In its place was a dangerous look he'd only seen once before—vulnerability. "Do you believe in soulmates?"

He froze under her words. Something specific had to prompt her asking that kind of question. She'd not been one for ethereal, wishy-washy, romantic subjects like soulmates. It was downright sappy by her standards.

Had Penny finally told her that she'd cheated on Lucas?

No. It was impossible. If she had, Ari never would have been so calm back at her apartment. Nor could Penny have broken her NDA, or the big one never would have happened.

Garrett opened his mouth to respond, only to glance over his shoulder. The rest of the brave battalion of Team Blue had left without him. Ari's villainous cohorts on Team Red had left behind their tallest member in kind. He could have fed her any of a dozen ready-baked lines, but her eyes betrayed a discerning mental taste. More to the point, she deserved better than his pre-packaged rebound quips.

"I'll tell you after, when we have time," he said at last.

She nodded, clearly dissatisfied, but she perked up as he blew her a kiss before they returned to the splattered field of battle. The third and final round would decide the winner.

Cold flecks of paint splattered across his cheek like liquid shrapnel. The sound of thunder followed as paintballs smashed into the blobstacle by his head. He yelped, scrambling for cover. Paintballs hissed past him as he dropped into a deep skid, ripping up the grass in his path until he was carried safely behind a wall of bright red. He hadn't been paying the slightest bit of attention to his surroundings. While he wasn't out, yet, he'd lost himself in the belly of the beast with who knew how many players still in. He couldn't count on his teammates to come rescue him. Hell, he didn't know them from Adam, let alone any of their names.

The air tasted of paint and the grassy tang of "outside air." His goggles were slick against his face. He scurried around a red pillar the size of a minivan—

—and stood barrel-to-barrel with his date.

They held each other's gaze, caught in a standoff. Incredulous, fearful half-smiles spread across their faces, caught between laughing and threatening. The first person hit would be out. The second person's shots would not count. Mutually assured destruction was an impossibility. It was merely who could be the most calculating, the most heartless. Who had the guts to squeeze the trigger first.

"So?" Ari stared him down. "Do you have an answer?"

"Huh?" He flinched.

She didn't fire.

"Soulmates." Her voice was firm. "Do you believe in them?"

One long, camouflaged leg extended, and she drifted closer to him with the same fluid grace as a willow frond swaying in the breeze.

He kept his finger on the trigger as she took another step. Too close.

She lowered her paintball gun. "It's a valid question," she said. "Relax. We're the last ones left. We can talk as long as we want."

He immediately checked behind him, expecting a Stormtrooper with a black barrel to add a fresh new series of welts to his back. Nobody. He looked to Ari, who—incredibly—hadn't taken the chance to gun him down while he was distracted.

She was serious.

His eyes narrowed a degree. Just a touch. The last dregs of suspicion pushed him to ask, just to be safe. "What about the rest of the game?"

"Screw the game. This is important." She stalked forward, stooping over until she pressed her heart to his barrel. "Either shoot me or answer me, Garrett."

His mouth flapped. His gaze darted over her. Down to where his barrel pressed into the softness behind her camo jacket. Back up to her unblinking hazel eyes, protected behind the plastic visor.

Finally, he lowered the gun and sighed, flopping back against the red blobstacle.

"Way to pick a complex subject." It was less of an introduction and more of a vocal bluff while he struggled to piece together his feelings on the subject—his *real* feelings.

He thought back to his parents. The way his father had treated his mother. The processional line of guys—not men, but guys—that had come to fill the hole in her heart after they'd lost him. How the would-be's never hung around because there was always the one percent of hope in his father's miraculous return from sea. How they'd smelled that hope from the get-go, and how it had always, always driven them away. Most for the better. Some, as much as he was disgusted to admit, for the worse.

Images of Nathan looking at Olivia as though she were the only thing in the world that mattered drifted across his mind. Memories of David and Lauren, laughing and sharing samples of chocolate cake batter from the same wooden spoon while leaving flour-dusted handprints on scandalous areas of each other's clothes, followed soon after.

He had his answer.

"No." He rested the back of his head against the rubber wall, staring up at the blank slate of the cloudless blue. "Not in the traditional way. I do believe people have the potential to become soulmates when they first meet. They can have a strong predisposition toward it. But I believe a soulmate is something you become for someone, not something you are."

Ari's fingers brushed his cheeks before carefully scooping under and lifting his goggles away from his eyes. He blinked as cool air rushed across his eyelashes, just long enough for his vision to be obscured by her face.

Then her lips descended to his, pausing at that first tingling contact. By degrees, he moved with her, deeper into the kiss which blossomed from her lips throughout his entire body. The slight tilt of her head. The rising feeling, until her immense chest was pressed against him. The stroking of her hands, rising to curl behind his neck and finger through his hair. His arm, snaking around the small of her back. Their thighs moving together. The tiny, almost inaudible whimpers of pleasure.

There was no tongue. This was something too pure, too emotional, for a cheap or titillating French touch.

This was a lover's kiss.

And then she had to ruin it by squeezing the trigger.

Pain ripped across his thigh like a nuclear bomb. His leg spasmed out from under him as his shriek of pain was at first muffled by her mouth, then rang out loud and clear. He half-bounced, half-tumbled down her body, sandwiched between her and the red rubber wall, until he was on the grass and clutching his leg. It wasn't fatal. He probably wasn't even bleeding. It just hurt like a *mother*.

She stepped back to allow him some air, towering over him and grinning with impish innocence. "What?" she said sweetly. "All's fair in love and paintball." She bounced on the balls of her feet before sauntering away, strolling as casually as any tourist toward the observation area.

He gasped for breath, shaking his head as he seized his discarded paintball gun with the same righteous indignation as a vengeful god. Jamming the stock to his shoulder, he peered down the sight, propping himself up with one arm as he took aim square at her perky, camouflage-coated posterior.

Punf-punf.

Ari yelped and jumped, her hands clutching at each cheek, which were now decorated with overlapping splotches of blue paint.

"Revenge!" He laughed as he struggled back up to his feet and limped after her. She stared at the blue on her hands, left over from where she'd checked on her butt wounds, and shook her head in disbelief.

"You capped me in the ass? Seriously?" Her tone was incredulous, but the smile on her face was unabashedly mischievous.

"You shot me point blank," he countered. "And entirely too close to my nuts."

"Okay. Okay. Fair. We'll call it even." She heaved a sigh, content, before grabbing his hand and looping it up over her shoulder. "C'mon, Limpy McGee, let's see if you can at least survive what's next."

~ * ~

After a quick change of clothes and a moment to sequester their paint-splattered gear into plastic grocery bags, they'd made it back to her car—albeit half-supporting each other and limping across the asphalt. Garrett wore a simple blue cotton T-shirt with his dark denim jeans that clung too tight for comfort to his "battle wound." The bruise on his thigh was approximately the size and color of a walloped apple. Ari had opted for a scoop-neck emerald blouse that brought out the golden-brown of her irises and pencil skirt that, from the way she was clearly loathe to take any lengthy strides, clung too tightly to the revenge he'd taken on her ass.

From his place in the passenger seat, he couldn't stop staring. She was stunning. And, for once, she only wore a simple pair of ballet flats instead of any sort of heels. For the first time, he was seeing her at her normal height of six-foot-five, which didn't seem quite as intimidating as the seven-foot goddess he'd met on their first date.

She winced, her breath hissing through her teeth as she eased herself into the driver's seat.

He chuckled, his pride stinging almost as much as his thigh. "How's that karma feel?"

She gave him a sidelong look, one eyebrow rising. "Trust me, Garrett, this isn't what karma feels like," she said. "That's in my purse."

His head tilted to the side, confused for a moment, before Ari made a buzzing noise as a hint.

Suddenly, the dots connected. "Did you name your *taser* 'Karma?'"

"Yeah." She laughed. "I had it inscribed on the side. Karma's always good to me."

He groaned, as much for the pun as for her confession that she'd used it before. Her smooth skin slid against him, lacing her fingers with his, and happy minutes ticked past with the red and green traffic lights as they simply were together.

"I liked what you said about soulmates." Finally, Ari broke the silence.

He sat up. Furrowed his brow. She didn't sound like her usual self. Her voice was too soft. Humbled.

"Like... a lot," she continued. "At first, I asked you—y'know, did the whole 'vulnerable' thing—just to screw with you. I figured you'd try something goofy. Give me a smoldering stare and say 'you make me believe' or some kind of cheesy shit. But I saw how you looked when you talked about it, and... you were being honest with me. You opened up to me."

He didn't dare interrupt.

"I've always thought soulmates was something for people who weren't me," she said. "Then Lucas came along, and he could keep pace with me in every way—art, and sex, and—and everything, and I thought—maybe. Maybe. But then he and some other girl did it sober, and... I don't know. I like your thing better." She fell silent, drumming her fingers on the steering wheel as if impatient with her own confession.

He stayed mute. He had to. This was exactly what she needed to get out. But seeing that side, that softness, stirred something primal in his chest. He kept his jaw locked and his eyes on her.

He was on the job.

"I don't want to believe he and this other girl are soulmates," she continued. "I want to believe it's going to fall apart in ashes and flames and shit, because it's what he deserves for hurting me, but at the same time... if this other girl really *is* his soulmate or whatever..." She grimaced, shaking her head. "Do you see where I'm coming from?" Her grip tightened around his hand, clutching it for support as she steered into the parking lot of a deli.

"It sounds like you're close to getting over him." His smile was teasing, but affectionate. "Careful. That road leads to happiness."

"I wouldn't go that far." She cast her gaze down and ruefully away. "I think I'm to the point where I don't want him back. I wouldn't say I'm over him."

"Doesn't that seem like the same thing? All that's left now is to find something better to fill the gap."

She stayed quiet for several seconds. A warmth spread in his hand as she smoothed her thumb over the back of it. Her eyes were low, her gaze curling over to him with the tentative, earnest movements of a kicked puppy. "I don't know if we're going to 'become' soulmates," she mumbled. "But I look at how much I've changed since I met you, and... I don't want to stop."

Inherent in the last phrase was a question that sent lightning through his chest. On the one hand, she could have meant "I don't want to stop changing." On the other, she could have meant "I don't want to stop seeing you." Maybe she meant neither. Maybe she meant some intoxicating mix of both. Prickles of heat washed through his palms. Warmed the inside of his chest.

The big one was leaning too hard into the sixty-five percent of the "yes." Pushing it too high. He needed to do something stupid. Tap into some touch of testosterone-fueled douchetitude. Something. Anything. She was getting too attached. God, he could see it in the way she looked at him.

In his private moments, when it was a lonely night awake in his home built for one, that was the way he'd imagine a woman would see him. Not Mr. Rebound, but *him*. Garrett Reid. And if Garrett Reid got involved in a relationship, things went to shit.

Mr. Rebound kept things clinical.

Garrett Reid got his heart involved and hurt the girl, then hurt himself.

He had to lean into the necessary thirty-five percent "no" and dial things back and not fall for her as hard as she maybe was starting to for him. Their contract was only halfway complete. He had to. For both their sakes, he had to.

Or he could do something else.

He moved as though on wires. Cupped her cheek in his free hand. As he pressed his lips to hers in a kiss as passionate as it was hungry, deep in those profound gut-punch places where he made his living, the truth of cutting this off after six dates nearly choked him. It would be among the most difficult things he'd ever have to accept in his life.

"I'd like to take you out again," he admitted, after parting his lips from hers.

"Of course." She spoke from behind closed eyes and slow, panting breaths. "Of course."

They kissed again. And again. And again, and he lost himself in the wonder of her lips, not caring in the slightest who saw, or what time it was, or if the earth had only ten seconds before it exploded. Her hands were just starting to clutch at the hem of his shirt as he broke back, clearing his throat.

"Lunch." He bit back delighted laughter. "I believe we are here for lunch."

She beamed at him and slid out of her car with a pained grace, striding around the front and opening his passenger door as though he were the belle of the deli ball. "Need a hand?" she said. She had the good manners to look sheepish as her gaze flickered to his leg.

He shook his head, planting a hand on the roof of the car for leverage as he hauled himself up. "Do you normally cripple guys on the third date?"

"Nah. Just the ones I *really* like." She smirked, taking his arm as they walked. "First, I buy them a swimsuit, then I cripple them. Next is circumcision."

"Too late." He couldn't suppress a cheeky grin and a nod in deference to Ari's foiled comedic plans.

She snorted, shaking her head. "TMI, but good to know. No surprises. You don't have three testicles, do you?"

He pretended to think it over. "If it helps, the third one isn't mine."

She doubled over laughing as they made it to the counter. The burst of melodic joy in each syllable rang in his ears and spread delight through his every feature. The cashier, bemused, tapped at his screen while Garrett placed his order for a sandwich. He rubbed the space between her shoulder blades, coaxing her back to the brink of intelligible glee—at least enough for her to order a sandwich.

Sure, maybe there was no such thing as instant soulmates. He'd given her the unfiltered truth. But if "becoming" soulmates was real...

She looked at him and smiled, and he smiled back, and something solidified in him. Their sandwiches were delivered in a moment, wrapped in glossy to-go paper, and he held the door for her. Together, they half-hobbled back out into the afternoon sun in the deserted parking lot.

Her gaze traced him over, an odd look in them. Something

powerful kindled behind her hazel gaze. "Hey, Garrett," she said, speaking around a mouthful of Italian meat. "Take off your pants."

The gasp he sucked in left him choking on a chunk of rye and ham. He doubled over, spluttering and coughing in a frenzy. By the time he wiped his mouth with the back of his hand and straightened up, she'd produced a glossy, heavy-looking black camera from the driver's seat.

He blinked the tears away from his eyes and stared at her. "Wha—right here? Right now?"

She grinned. "Yeah."

Two single syllable words tried to burst out of him at the same time. The "no" lost out to the question. "*Why?*"

Her grin widened. "Because I didn't get a shot of you on fire, or covered in dead grandma, and I am an *artiste*. A candid pic of where I shot you needs to mark this occasion."

He just stared.

She rolled her eyes, shaking her head in mild disbelief. "Come on, you pussy. Drop 'em."

"*We are in the middle of a parking lot in broad daylight.*"

"So? Nobody's around, and nobody who might see would give a shit. Sit in the seat with the door open if you need privacy."

He sniffed, crossing his arms and taking care not to let even a single morsel spill from his sandwich. "You sure this isn't you just trying to coax me into a dick pic?"

Ari snorted. "I've had enough of those unsolicited that I wouldn't want them even if I did solicit them." Her gaze was unwavering. Unchallenged. "Look, you can take a shot of my ass bruises in return, if it makes you feel better."

At that, laughter finally did burst from his chest. The air was warm and still, and yet he felt like he stood downwind of a tornado. While this wasn't exactly the craziest thing he'd ever done during the big one, pantsless parking lot pictures was making his top five for sure.

Before he could lose his nerve, he'd wrapped his sandwich, placed it atop the car roof, and opened both driver's side door and rear passenger door as makeshift "changing room" curtains. Then he planted his rump sideways in the driver's seat and yanked down his jeans.

His boxer briefs were a classy black. The bruise on his thigh had shifted from a bright red welt to some freakish red-purple blur halfway between a tire track in a strawberry patch and lipstick in an oil slick. His pants bunched around his knees, and he grimaced at the camera.

Her breath hissed once at the sight before she took cover behind the black instrument of mortification. The shutter clicked as she worked the controls, snapping picture after picture.

He tried not to shiver—or worse, get aroused. A hell of a lot easier said than done. "Can I pull my pants back up?"

"Sure thing." Her fingers were slow, motions tentative, as she worked at the digital screen. "I've got some great material here."

"Yeah?" Wincing with every inch the denim claimed over his bruise, he managed to reclaim his clothed status and stand up. "How do I look?"

"Like the perfect subject. Awkward, vulnerable, and cute as hell." She was still scrolling through the photos with a critical eye when he held out his hand.

"Your turn," he said. "Drop 'em."

"I'm not taking my pants off in public." She lifted an eyebrow with the sort of finality that one took when resorting to double standards of the most potently bullshit. "Nice try, buddy."

He scoffed once before swiping her sandwich from its resting place in the car and chomping an enormous bite out of it.

Her eyes widened as she lunged for her lunch. "Hey!"

"No photos of ass-bruises, no food." He shrugged as he held the sandwich in the car, twisted at an angle she couldn't reach. "I don't make the rules."

"I drove us here!" She struggled against him, her longer arm trying to bend at an awkward angle.

"I paid for lunch." Garrett leaned further over, practically in the passenger's seat, determined to win the impromptu game of keep-away, no matter what softness he felt against his chest, his shoulder, his arm. No matter how he felt about it. This was about principle, not the twitching in his boxer-briefs.

"I won the paintball match." Her face was close enough to feel the heat from her skin. Close enough to count every freckle. She locked eyes with him, holding in place, pressed against him, over him, daring him to come up with a better excuse.

He smirked. "I kissed you last."

She swooped down before he could stop her, planting her lips on his in a fearsome, fierce token of affection. Parting as quick as she'd attacked, she practically had fangs peeking out as she grinned.

"You're going to have to put my sandwich down if you want to take the photos." She offered the black camera, cradled in both hands as though it were a newborn. "Just be careful with Big K. He's delicate and *expensive*, and I cannot afford to replace him."

With a roll of his eyes, he set her sandwich aside before scooping the camera from her hands. "Big K?"

"It's a Kodak," she explained. "I'm not the most inventive

namer. Sue me."

"Tell that to 'Karma.'" He snorted.

She turned away from him, slipping her fingers into the waistband of her camouflage-patterned pants.

He placed it to his eyes, peering through the viewfinder and its artificial target reticule as she peeled the tight-fitting fabric away—

—exposing her utterly delicious ass, with two perfectly round bruises, juxtaposed over pale skin like sins on an angel…along with the distracting print of her underwear.

His finger froze on the shutter. "Ari?"

In a move as unhelpful as it was hypnotic, she swayed her hips in a sinuous motion. "I know. I have an amazing ass. Now take the photos."

"No—I mean, yes, dear *God*, but—" His mouth was already dry.

"But?" There was enough of a laugh hanging onto her question to coax him into action.

He forced himself to take the photo. Several photos. Maybe more than were necessary. "Where did you get, and why did you feel it was necessary to wear, a camo-patterned thong to paintball?"

She waited several more seconds before easing her pants back up. "Because everything else I was wearing was camo, and you never know."

They shared a smile before they both burst out laughing.

Maybe, for once, he didn't just have to provide the batting cage.

Maybe, for once, he could step inside it with her.

Chapter Seventeen

Garrett sighed through gritted teeth. The office of Mr. Rebound, Inc., was his prison for the next twenty minutes, at least. "David—"

"You pay me to do this. I'm doing this. I am yanking the leash." His voice hardened into something like an incensed father, pulling on authority given to him by Garrett.

"Come on, man. Don't do this." It was authority Garrett now deeply regretted ever giving.

"Sit," said his friend, his partner in crime and man behind the curtain. David's hands clamped down on the plush leather on either side of Mr. Rebound's head. "Now, since you seem to have forgotten what happened the *last* time someone found out you are paid to date people for a living, I am going to remind you."

Garrett groaned and clenched his eyes shut. "Can we not?"

"No. No, we can't 'not,'" said David. "You've talked non-stop about Ari, and you have yet to say a single negative thing about her."

He leaned back, staring up awkwardly over the back of the chair at his right-hand man, squinting in offense. "It's my *job* to talk about her."

"You were gushing, Garrett. You are downright fricking twitterpated. So, you are going to sit there and have a big fat dose of Vitamin C until you sober the hell up and get your head on straight." Like a medieval executioner, David snatched up the projector remote and clicked it on.

With a cold unwillingness, Garrett opened his eyes and stared at the screen. An Instagram page dripping with hashtags and comments was splayed on the wall with the sadistic grace of Hannibal Lecter butterflying a security guard across cell bars. Blown up to vulgar size, smiling at the camera, were Garrett Reid and Courtney Hazleroth. She model-pouted to the best of her ability. He wore a smile that was too tight at the corners.

"I've seen enough," said Garrett, truthfully.

"You need to be reminded of what happens when a girl finds out that your job is the reason you met." David's voice turned biting. "That's never going to be a great story to share around a Christmas turkey. 'How did you two meet? Oh, I was paid to date her after all her crappy exes left her a bitter shell.' No woman wants to spill that out in front of Great-Grandma Ida."

He let his soul shrink in him, deliberately lowering defenses to feel the sting of his every word. This *was* part of why he'd hired David.

"Fine, okay? Fine." He sunk back into his chair, swearing he could feel invisible chains binding him down.

"Good," said David. He patted the chair by Garrett's head with a dull *thump-thump*. "Take your medicine, man."

The next picture was of a pasta massacre in a cracked ceramic pan with enormous pieces missing from the sides. Tomato sauce and chunks of blackened meat were splattered apart. The center was a horrid, acrid, scarred black, so melted it appeared neither food nor object, but some strange insect carapace from the abyss that lurked in an Eldritch god's armpit.

"The lasagna," intoned David.

Garrett thrust both his hands at the image. "Oh, come on!"

"Look at the lasagna, *Gare-bear*." With a rapid-fire clicking of the projector remote, David zoomed in on the horror, forcing it closer in a macabre reminder of the past.

He cringed in the chair. "Low. Low blow."

David bristled. "No, a 'low blow' is when she took an electronic device with a lithium-ion battery and stuck it in an oven at four hundred degrees Fahrenheit."

"To be fair, I don't think she was intelligent enough to realize it would explode." He tried on an apologetic smile.

"But she was diabolical enough to still try and serve it to you," said David. "Tell me, how did that taste, again?"

Garrett fumed, staring at the photographic evidence held in front of his face with the same displeasure as a werewolf at a silver pawn shop. Slowly, he shook his head, frustration growing in the face of his inevitable choice. "It's not the same, Dave. Ari's smarter. Softer. Kinder. It's just buried, is all."

"You had to take out a cease and desist on Courtney. If you fall for Ari, then you're going to wind up telling her the truth. We already know she has a taser, and she has used it—repeatedly—and she named it '*Karma.*'" David spun the chair around on the spot, the room whirling in Garrett's vision until he was staring at his bespectacled friend. "Are we going to need to start calling a 'Code A' as well as a 'Code C?'"

"Courtney was a failed cause from the start!" protested Garrett. "She bounced through all the types like a friggin' coked-up pinball!"

"You were still hired to rebound her, Garrett. Her friend, Kim—remember Kim? She signed it. She paid for us to rebound Courtney."

"And she was impossible to rebound! I know she was our first failure, but not all women are the same. I tried everything—a jerkass-switch-up, a friendzoning, an incompatibility sequence, a conflict of interest, even a religious cockblock." Desperation leaked into Garrett's voice, threatening to change it from a legitimate protest to a feeble whine before he could finish. "I panicked, all right? We'd gone way over on the contract being fulfilled, but she wouldn't—I—you were there, dude. I stopped opening doors. Didn't pick up checks. Criticized her clothes, her friend, her diet, her family. For God's sake, I hit on her mom *in front of her*, and that *still* didn't do it. I could've been crowned Asshole-For-Life for the way I treated her—but she wouldn't let go."

His throat bobbed. He'd drawn from his well. Caved. Invested in his own feelings, and hurt her, and now she was hurting him. He'd created the Frankenstein's monster of rebounds. "Telling her I was paid to take her out was literally the only thing I could think of to get her to break it off other than framing her for a felony."

David, finally, relented. "I know. I know. We run a tight ship, but it's not foolproof. But when I catch you grinning at her photos on your phone like you're on Vicodin… it means you're falling for Arianne Reynolds, Garrett, and if you're thinking of telling her that you're paid to date her…" He sighed, rubbing his face down with one hand. "I don't want to see you get hurt."

Garrett gave him a pained, through appreciative, clap on the shoulder. "Thanks, man. I know you care about me."

"I meant physically," corrected David. "I don't want to see you in the hospital looking like you pissed in a power socket."

Garrett sniffed and swung his chair, reluctance tainting his movements, back toward his dose of Vitamin C. David was right. He had to take his medicine.

But as David clicked to the next post of a disemboweled Valentine's teddy bear, Garrett's mind slid back to Ari. The way she'd torn down the walls and opened up to him in the car. The photos. The embarrassment and the vulnerability and the acceptance.

Their kiss.

"David," he said, interrupting his friend's tirade. "You were going to lose Lauren, once upon a time."

A silence fell through the office as he steered their tight ship into cold, dangerous waters.

"Yeah, I was," said David.

Garrett stared in sympathy, but still with enough determination for one man to singlehandedly capsize an entire vessel. "You didn't. You got your head on straight, and you came back, and you stuck it out, and now you two are one of the happiest couples I've ever seen in my life," he said. "You've got a kid together. You're a family. You love each other."

"Garrett..." David's voice carried an unmistakable note of warning. "Where are you going with this?"

"I'm saying..." He rose from the chair, crossing the office. David made no move to stop him. Garrett stood before the whiteboard, swiped the marker from the tray, then jabbed it at the grave marker of an 'x' at the end of Ari's timeline. "This is the point where I'm going to lose Ari, and I don't want to get there. Maybe—maybe my head hasn't been on straight this entire time. All these past clients, all these women...I mean, sure, they were for a good cause, and I've done right by them, but...maybe falling for her is me getting my head on straight for once. Even if I have to tell her the truth."

"Look, you want to find a nice girl and make Sunday morning pancakes together?" David's eyes narrowed. "Fine. That's your prerogative. As a fan of Sunday morning pancakes, I can understand why. But never—repeat after me—never fall for a client. You can't keep them. Catch-and-release fishing only."

Prickles ran beneath Garrett's skin as though caterpillars had found their way into his veins. Maybe this was the feeling of making a titanic mistake.

Or, maybe—as he preferred to think—this was the feeling of being alive for once, instead of going through the motions.

"Hey, Garrett? Tell me about your friends from college," said David, his voice flat.

Garrett blinked. "What?"

"Everyone else you know who graduated with a Bachelor's in Theatre Arts. What are they doing?" He raised his eyebrows, gesturing in an "any time now" sort of motion as the damning silence crept around them.

Garrett clamped his mouth shut.

David sniffed. "Yeah, that's what I thought. You work maybe ten hours a *week* and get paid enough to afford your car and your swanky little bachelor pad and whatever else you want. Meanwhile, everyone else with your degree is working fifty-hour weeks teaching middle school or waiting three tables to keep the lights on."

He narrowed his eyes in return. "Dave, where are you going with this?"

"Right for where it counts, dude," he said, and the edges of his voice were as sharp and trembling as the razor that had severed a chunk from Garrett's moustache not two dates ago. "I'm trying to get you to understand that if you try and throw away the entirety of Mr. Rebound, Inc., all for this one girl in a long, *long* string of girls, that you will be doing a very stupid thing."

It doesn't matter if it's stupid if it's right. "You're worried about me getting hurt. You said th—"

"It's not about getting hurt, it's about you getting fired," snapped David. "I'm not trying to appeal to your emotional sense of self-worth or whatever. That's not why you hired me. I'm appealing to your *wallet.* If, by some miracle, Arianne Reynolds doesn't tase you into next year if you tell her about the contract, and if by some even *bigger* miracle, you two actually wind up becoming a couple...it'll mean the end of Mr. Rebound, Inc. There is no way on God's green earth that she will let you keep doing this. Not if she loves you."

Garrett's throat had sealed itself.

"That's what I'm trying to say, man." David's voice swirled with sympathy like the thickest, most syrupy poison. Like the waxy coating over the top of Snow White's apple. "You go falling for her, you're in a permanent lose-lose situation. Either you lose the girl and you're a broken-hearted mess, or you *get* the girl, and you lose your job. Car insurance. Groceries. Utilities. Rent. All the adulting bills will keep coming, and you'll be up a creek. Barista Creek, most likely, where the tips jingle instead of rustle. Any other girls out there who need the help of Mr. Rebound will have to sink or swim."

A tiny, breathless laugh kicked out of Garrett. Girls had survived asshole guys dumping them for generations before he came along and started trying to change the game. They'd still survive after he was gone, even if the thought of hanging them out to dry sent a corkscrew spiralling through his gut. He knew—he'd always known, deep down—that this could never have been a lifetime career. But it had just sort of...happened, and it helped people and paid bills, and he'd never come up with an exit strategy.

"You're right," was all he could say.

David pinched the bridge of his nose. "Just—promise me one thing, okay?"

"That strongly depends on what it is." He stared down his co-worker and companion.

"If you're really going to go through with this insane fricking plan, even though I am going on the record to say you *absolutely should not do it*—then take her to the sixth date first, okay? At least fulfil the premium contract we have with Penny. Otherwise, she'll have a case for breach of contract." With a disgusted flick of his wrist, David clicked off the projector and tossed the remote to the desk. "You don't need a lawsuit on top of potential unemployment."

Garrett heaved a sigh. "Deal." He crossed the room, and they wrapped each other in what was universally known as the "bro hug."

When they parted, Garrett couldn't keep back a groan. "Man... how am I going to figure this out?" He rubbed his hands over the back of his neck.

"Quit being so squirrely and get your crush in check, that's how. Get drunk, look at yourself in the bathroom mirror, and point out all her flaws." David's expression crumpled darkly. "Speaking from experience on that one. Do that and hope there isn't another you out there to pull you out of the spiral."

Garrett grimaced at the memory before opening the office door, officially breaching the inner sanctum and allowing public access. It was as good a sign as any that their meeting was over—and, like that, all the tension in the room slipped out on the open breeze.

"You want to stay for dinner?" David offered.

Garrett's stomach rumbled in response. "What did Lauren make?"

"Lasagna."

"Again?" he recoiled. "How much of that shit do you guys *eat?*"

"No, seriously." David laughed. "She made lasagna. Put some kind of German variety of sausage in there instead of Italian. It's going to be an experience. I know you're kind of put off, but you should really try and hop back on the horse."

He snorted. "Thanks, but no thanks. I'll get drive-thru." He paused by the door, casting a single, furtive glance back at the whiteboard with its blood-red line terminating in an ugly 'x.' "I've got some stuff to figure out."

~ * ~

The air outside was muggy and slick, threatening to zap a godawful frizz right through Courtney Hazleroth's hair. The second she emerged from the air conditioning of her faithful pink stallion, she practically gagged. The store—well, no, she couldn't call it that. Labeling Eternal Bride Photography as a "store" was an insult to the good name of stores everywhere. This place didn't even have valet parking. It was part of a bunch of other little projects all glued together like they couldn't afford the rent. This was a "shop" at best; a "hole" at its core. Window decals instead of signs. Crummy décor. Middle-class part of town; after all, it was in Whitestone. In *Queens*.

She sniffed. Well, this settled it, more than anything. The locker number at the beach hadn't been a cry for help. It hadn't been a coded message to reference their first date. If her Gare-bear really had been looking up wedding photographers because he'd been planning to propose, he never would have come to this trash heap. The idea that he would—that he could possibly think this was what she was worth—stung almost as much as being stood up at the Luna Park Ferris wheel three nights ago.

The stares she'd gotten as the night had worn on and no Gare-bear had come.

The ten *million* times she'd had to decline not getting in line, all smiles and hair flick and saying she was waiting for someone.

The dress from Ophelia's that had taken Courtney from "beauty" to "vision"—and, as the hours had worn on, less "vision" and more "flashing neon sign for people to shoot her confused or pitying looks."

How the lights and music of the Ferris wheel had finally clicked off, late at night, and how she'd been frantic—desperate—enough so that she'd nearly clawed out the eyes of the attendant when he'd closed the ride.

She'd been so naïve.

Gare-bear couldn't have been planning to propose to her. He was too twisted up between other girls' legs. He needed her help, her guidance, before he could love her the way she loved him. And if that meant she had to leave her faithful pink stallion in some dingy middle-class parking lot and walk through swampy city air into a hole for him, she'd do it. True love meant sacrifice.

Besides, if she could find this "Arianne Reynolds" and mace her for being the latest one to corrupt Gare-bear, maybe it'd be the high point to her so far spectacularly crummy week.

She exhaled, staring at the dull metal handle on the shop door. Not even polished. And there were Windex streaks on the glass. Pursing her lips, she dug in her purse for a facial tissue—with eucalyptus extracts, thank you very much—and wrapped it around the handle. It almost wasn't worth the tissue. But then, true love and sacrifice and everything.

Tiny grunts eked out of her as she tugged, then *heaved* with both arms. Her shoulders felt like they'd pop out of their sockets. Her heels crunched against the asphalt as she gasped with every slow inch of clearance. Who the hell made front doors this heavy? Was it magnetized? Hurricane-proof?

"Let me get that for you," came a woman's voice from inside.

The door slipped free from her aching fingers and swung inwards as smoothly as Clooney, leaving Courtney standing in the entryway with a stinging conscience.

Oh.

Push, not pull.

"Thanks," she said, before she could stop herself. The interior was cheaply chill. Cheap carpet. Cheap chairs. Out-of-date magazines that only people over fifty read. Cheap front desk that had to be home assembled. Walmart or Target. Not an actual furniture store.

The door dinged shut behind her as she stared at the front door attendant with the radiant smile.

This had to be the bitch who was stealing Garrett.

"Hi," The blonde extended a hand to shake. "I'm Zoey, the receptionist. You must be Rachel Salazar, right? Here for the four o'clock?"

"Uh—yeah," lied Courtney, faking a smile as she shook Zoey's outstretched hand. French tip nails. Gentle grip. *Ugh.* "Sorry I'm late. Traffic."

"No problem. You're not even late. You're, like, half an hour early. But it's okay!" gushed Zoey. "Right this way."

It wasn't even that fake professional brown-nosing kind of gush, either. She really did mean it.

What a bitch.

Courtney followed, eyeing off the framed examples of happy weddings, bouquet tosses. A couple posing for prom. A hot military guy kissing his pregnant bride's belly. Clear, crisp photos, one and all. Whoever took them knew what they were doing, even if they weren't really all that artsy.

Zoey glanced back at her, fidgeting. "Uh—you are the four o'clock appointment, right?"

Courtney lifted a pale hand and flicked her perfect blonde hair back over her shoulder before crossing her arms under her perfectly augmented C-cup bust. "What's that supposed to mean?"

Zoey's throat bobbed as she paled under her cheap rouge. "I-I just—um—I meant—your parents are supposed to be with you, right? For your modeling headshot photos?"

Courtney threw a hitch into her voice, bowing her head as if struggling under the weight of some phantom grief. "I-it's just been really hard, okay?" A hyperventilating breath for added effect. "Mom and Dad have been fighting again, and I just lost my aunt, and—"

"Oh, sweetie, no." Zoey swept her into a soft, smothering hug. Courtney managed a fake sniffle against her cheap poly-blend blouse and bit back on a groan. Because of *course*, her hugs were amazing. "I didn't mean—"

"Something wrong?"

Another woman's voice.

Courtney fake-sniffled again to sell it before peeking over Zoey's shoulder at the newcomer. Dark, wavy hair. Tan skin. Freaking gorgeous facial features. She blinked, confused. What in the name of fashion was somebody that hot doing in a dump like this? Then again, Courtney was there herself. Adding one last sniffle for dramatic effect, she wiped her eyes—surprising even herself when she actually did catch a tear on her finger—and gave her a weak smile.

"Hi," she said. "I'm Co—" Just in time, she covered her blunder with a fake cough. "Rachel. Rachel Salazar. I'm here for my headshots." *Nailed it.*

"Sierra," said the girl. Healthy hair. Decent manicure. "Right through here."

Courtney walked through a plywood door that was an unmistakable sign that this godawful hole was still under construction. It wasn't even *painted*. Behind it lay a makeshift studio with a blotchy backdrop. Shutters and lights and oversized lampshades and black electrical cables spilled around the place. It felt *dirty*. Did they shoot porn here? Share the office space with a porn company? Something to do with porn?

"All right, take a seat and face forward?" Sierra's words ended in the polite sort of upward tick that made it sound like there was a question where there wasn't one.

Gingerly, Courtney did as she was told, posing and pouting in all the ways that came naturally. The camera was her closest friend, after all. You were yourself around your closest friend. "So, tell me about yourself, Sierra," she said, trying to make herself sound airy and casual as her best friend praised her with the sound of a flickering shutter. "Are you single?"

"Happily married. Turn to the right?" Another impersonal flurry of camera clicks cut off any additional question Courtney might have asked in the moment.

She fumed. It didn't show. It certainly wasn't going to be seen by the camera. She was a model of self-restraint, in her opinion. Cool, calm, collected Courtney Hazleroth. "What about Zoey? Or, uh… 'Ari Reynolds?'" She kept her expression coy, following Sierra's every instruction. "I thought she was the photographer?"

"She is," said Sierra. "She's on her way back from a wedding shoot in Chicago. I'm her assistant. Just as capable, trust me." There was something wry in her laugh. Courtney wasn't sure she liked it. Click. Click. Click.

"So, like…they're both single?" she pressed.

"Uh-huh," grunted the photographer, non-committal. The camera clicked a few more times. "Shoulders back, hon. Open up your chest."

"O*kay*, but like…" Courtney tossed her hair, adjusting position on the hard stupid stool as she followed instruction effortlessly. "Are they *seeing* anyone?"

"I just said they were single." Another flurry of clicks from Sierra.

"You know what I mean." Courtney had been trained to let her frustration waterfall through her gaze instead of her whole expression, and she gave the black lens that was supposed to be her friend the best Niagra-Falls-ing she could manage.

Sierra grunted, noncommittal. "Not really."

Whether that meant "not really" as in "they aren't really seeing anyone" or "not really" as in "I don't really know what you mean" was beyond Courtney's reckoning. She didn't even have time to open her mouth to ask any follow-ups before a final machine-gun burst of clicks from the camera sounded and Sierra straightened up. "And…done."

In a flash, Courtney found herself swept up and ushered back out into the front room. Her teeth were set, her fingers were itching—*both* of these women were just—just—the *worst*. Women were supposed to support women, and neither of these were being even remotely supportive of what she clearly needed.

"So, like—what does Arianne look like?" She turned on her heels, staring them both down. Rapid-fire lies concocted in her brain, mixing like a perfect peppermint mojito before dripping from between her Rosé Dreams strawberries-and-cream lip gloss. "Because, like—my best friend's older stepsister is, like, totally remarrying, and she's been looking for a good photographer, but she's all, like 'she better be worth her shit but also, she better not be hotter than me because I won't be getting upstaged at my own rehearsal, never mind the wedding.'" She leaned in, lowering her voice. "Her last fiancée ran off with the last one. It was this total disaster."

The best part was that was actually a true story.

Zoey gave her a sweet, naïve smile, fumbling with the small tray of business cards. "We'd love to be able to help. Ari's an *amazing* wedding photographer. Never a bad review." With a delighted flick of her wrist, she handed Courtney a business card. Just like the one in Gare-bear's wallet. Maybe it was her who was corrupting him. Maybe Little

Miss "Happily-Married" Sierra. Nobody said they were "happily" married unless they were trying to hide something.

"Thanks." Courtney spoke through tight lips, slipping the card into her purse and making a mental note to burn it later.

"Tell your best friend's older stepsister not to worry. It's okay." Sierra's smirk slipped into something like a friend telling a secret. Bitch. They weren't friends. "Ari's like seven feet tall and kind of a bitch when she's working. Most guys aren't into that."

"She's six-six, Sierra, not seven feet," corrected Zoey, her eyes wide. "Don't go adding inches where there aren't any. That's a guy's job."

Sierra burst into loud, flat cackles that grated on Courtney's ears.

"Hm." She narrowed her eyes. Gare-bear had gone after girls uglier than her before. Overweight. Terrible fashion choices. Blotchy complexion. He wasn't shallow. That was partly why he was such a perfect guy. But dating some harsh, bitchy woman... that felt like a stretch, even for him. Probably not. It had to be either the plus-size behind the desk with—even she had to admit—the radiant smile, or else it was the Latina bombshell. Though, obviously, Courtney was still hotter.

Goddammit, *which one was it?* Her skin was crawling as her gaze darted between the two. He wasn't—maybe he was being paid to date them *both at once.* No. No way. Even Gare-bear wouldn't stoop that low.

"How much do I owe you?" she said before shaking her head. "No. You know what? Here." She fished out three hundred dollars and dropped it on the counter. Probably enough for them to hire someone to make their dingy little hole a little less dingy. "Keep the change."

"Wait—" said one of them.

She didn't care. Didn't listen. Just stomped away, shoving open the stupid Windex-streaked door and getting her hands oily on the stupid dirty metal handle and leaving the hole behind and choking back on a scream. She had to get out of there. She had to go and update her Board of Garrett then sit outside his house and figure out what to do, and also either burn or return the dress she'd bought from Ophelia's because now it was nothing but bad luck and God knew she couldn't wear the *same* engagement outfit *twice.*

Slamming the door of her stallion, she clenched the steering wheel and fumed, nostrils flaring, teeth clenched, as some stupid family with a teenage girl drove up and—

Oh. Shit. That had to be them.

She threw her stallion into gear and squealed out of the parking lot. "I'm coming, Gare-bear…"

~ * ~

Arianne had never been much for road trips, and this had been murder on the soul and on her ass. Twenty-seven hours, all totaled up, stuck in her damn car all the way to Chicago and back. The wedding was standard fare—up until the speeches. It was normal to have one or two that went off the rails. Certainly nothing she hadn't seen before. This had been an entity unto itself.

On the bride's side of the family, there had been an uncle who bore a shocking resemblance to Mick Jagger who gave one of the more memorable drunken speeches Arianne had heard at a wedding—and declared with slurring words that he'd gone to third base with the groom's mother in a coat closet two hours ago.

The groom's mother nailed him in the temple from three tables away with a champagne flute before screeching that she only let him get that far because she'd taken one look at his micro-dick and felt sorry for him.

The groom's father then announced his divorce.

The Mick-Jagger-like uncle got back up and threw the bowl of Jordan mints at the groom's father, only to hit the father of the bride by accident.

Somewhere in the chaos, food started flying, an errant elbow or fist struck the wrong person at the wrong time—and Arianne was left at the back of the hall, watching unrestrained pandemonium as the wedding erupted into an all-out brawl.

She'd documented every last bit of it.

But, somehow, even better than the father of the bride tackling the uncle into the three-tier white-chocolate-strawberry-filling wedding cake, was telling Garrett on the phone every last insane, sordid detail on her drive back. Somehow, sharing it with him etched the entire thing in liquid gold, preserving and beautifying it in her mind. Like she couldn't truly appreciate how batshit the entire thing had been until he'd exploded into laughter on the other side of the phone.

That said, even though she had to pick chunks out of her hair and wipe about an inch-thick layer of frosting from off her collarbone, the cake was pretty good too.

They'd talked about the wedding. The drive. Favorite music. Foods. The kind of simple, silly stuff that people never really remembered talking about; just that the bases were covered, and they meandered from topic to topic with the casual freedom of gods adrift in a universe of possibility.

More than that—when she'd pulled over for rest stops, she'd felt the pulsing in the back of her mind that hadn't been there since college. Before she knew it, she was photographing whatever she wanted. Not like she ever had. Subtle ways. Different ways. Playing with light and shadow. Who cared if they were slightly blurred, or if the light obscured things a little, or the angle didn't sit quite right? They were deliberate mistakes.

Something in her life was hooking a car battery up to her muse, and she had to admit, she liked it.

With a sweet, heavy sigh that breathed relief through every inch of her and finally acknowledged the ache in her backside and legs from being in the car for twelve damn hours, she trundled into the driveway of her apartment and parked. Hauling her bags up was a happy burn through tired limbs.

"I'm back!" She stuffed herself through the front door.

No voice responded.

She frowned, wandering the hallway, until she spotted her roommate in her bedroom. Her half-waterfall of blonde hair spilled, upside-down, over the edge of her bed. The rhythmic *thump-thwack* of a stress ball bouncing off the ceiling and slapping into her hand as she caught it was an immediate sign—Penny had been the victim of yet another shitty day.

Well, Arianne would just have to give her some of the good vibes she was bursting with. "C'mere, pintsize." She descended, arms open, and wrapped them around her in an awkward, upside-down, but enthusiastic embrace. Penny made a muffled noise against her ribs as her monstrous bust pillowed against Penny's own.

"You have a good shoot?" She wheezed, her tone muted and British as ever, as Arianne squeezed her tight.

"*Amazing.*" She laughed and straightened back up, ignoring the twinge in the small of her back. "Plus, I spent pretty much the entire drive up and back on the phone with Garrett. I don't know where you dug him up, but he's kind of fricking awesome. Blown what I had with Lucas out of the water."

"I'm glad," said Penny.

Arianne had spun on the spot and almost made it to the door before Penny spoke again.

"Because I'm the one he cheated with. It was me."

Chapter Eighteen

There was a ritual to his actions.

Garrett cupped warm water and splashed it up his cheeks as the sound of Genesis echoed around his bathroom. Shirtless, breathing evenly, trickles of warm water fingered down his neck and over his chest as he squirted shaving cream into one hand. The tools of his preparation laid across the sink with care and deliberation. The sculptor cared for his chisels. The samurai cared for his katana and dou. Mr. Rebound cared for his shaving equipment and personal hygiene.

True, he also couldn't sing all that well, but that was half the point of singing in the bathroom without a roommate. It wasn't like Phil Collins and Peter Gabriel were there to judge him. Phil Collins and Peter Gabriel hadn't been in the same room for forty years, and they wouldn't be getting the band back together just to judge his karaoke skills in his bathroom.

The subtle scraping sound of stubble against the edge of his straight razor was discordant against the synthesizers. He was going to be careful, this time. *Not* lose focus. His goatee was coming back in, and this would not be a repeat of the pre-game second date shaving fiasco.

The fourth date had been scheduled the night before, but he'd wanted to give Ari at least one decent night's sleep in the homestead after she drove back from Chicago. They'd spent so long on the phone together—talking, laughing, joking—that, to be honest, a night apart was as necessary for him as for her. The logical part of his brain had warned him that he might literally run out of things to talk about.

Of course, his heart said otherwise, but that was beside the point.

Under normal circumstances, the fourth date was where he would build on the sixty-five percent of a 'yes' that had been established in the third date. Certain differences would come into play that would drive the wedge a bit deeper between them. Not in a bad way, per se, just one that left the client a little unsatisfied.

He likened it to eating flame-broiled salmon with ketchup. It wasn't a bad pairing. In fact, it could be downright palatable. But then, when one had the chance to eat flame-broiled salmon with tartar sauce instead, the difference was unmistakable. Salmon went with tartar sauce. Not ketchup.

Mr. Rebound, on the fourth date, would establish himself as ketchup, and if there was a fifth date, he would get only ketchupier.

Garrett coaxed the razor down the final stroke over his jawline and washed the stubble away. Perfect shave. Smooth. Crisp. Aftershave applied. Tonight was going to be a turning point. Maybe even more so than the third date.

Tonight, no matter what David urged… Garrett was not going to be ketchup. He was going to be tartar sauce.

Ari was unlike any other girl he'd ever dated. Even before he'd given himself the title and made his career out of it. None of the rebound rules seemed to work with her. There couldn't be any lines delivered. Just…him.

So, he was going to be tartar sauce on the fourth date, and the fifth, and the sixth.

If he had his way, he was going to be tartar sauce for her for dates uncountable.

He toweled off his face as the music mixed with his voice about as well as topsoil in a coffee grinder before the song suddenly cut out, replaced by a heavy porcelain vibration. He grimaced. Phone call. Mood-killer. He dried his hands, letting his phone rattle in place for a moment before lifting it.

A frown tugged at the edges of his lips.

He thumbed the green telephone icon.

"Hey, Mom," he said. His voice was echoey in the small bathroom. "What's up?"

"Garrett, baby," was all she got through before his good mood shattered like a mirror.

Her voice was hoarse. Clogged with grief. The heavy, pain-and-sorrow-laden kind of tone that ripped the floor out from under a son and set off all the nonsensical alarm bells. Someone was dead. She was hurt. Robbed blind. The house burned down. Terrorists. Strapped to an explosive with a timer in an underground warehouse like Rachel Dawes in The Dark Knight. Maybe they didn't talk often or see each other outside holidays—and maybe even those times were stiffly cordial at best and bitter at worst—but no son wanted to hear their mother talk with that kind of voice.

"Mom?" He tried to keep his voice calm. "What is it? What

happened?"

A shaky breath on the other side of the line, more static than sound. "I-it's…it's your dad."

Someone had poured frozen mercury into his guts. "What?"

"Baby… a f-few weeks ago…" She sniffled hard on the other side of the line. Her words were bubbles, thick and slimy. "A scuba diver was out…a-and they found some bones. The police just finished identifying the dental records. Sweetheart…it's him."

He licked his lips.

"Huh."

One long, slow breath in.

One long, slow breath out.

Don't draw from your well.

"I'm so sorry, Mom," he said. His voice was calm. Even. No trace of pain. Yet. "How're you holding up?"

"I-it's a shock." Still thick. Sniffling hard in a rush of deep static. "I kept right on expecting him to walk back through that door, even thirteen years later. Now—n-now that'll really never happen."

"Unlucky thirteen, right?" He chuckled, breathless. It sounded hollow and fraudulent, even to his ears. "Do you need me over, or…?"

"Uh… probably better if you don't," she admitted. "I, um…I'm halfway through my first box of Zinfandel, and I'm not exactly planning on stopping tonight."

Yeah, that tracks. He couldn't help the cynical twinge. *Surprised she's only on her first box.* "Keep me posted, okay?"

"There's a viewing tomorrow." She gulped for air. It was like the grief was squeezing her in a vise. "Half past one. I'll text you the address for the morgue, okay? And don't—don't worry about your sister. She already knows. The, uh—there's some mix-up with the Peace Corps paperwork for family leave, so she's stuck in Fiji, but she sends her love."

"Makes sense. Love you, Mom." The words felt obligatory. Accurate, in their own way, but obligatory. The world was fuzzy beyond the hard press of his phone to his ear.

"Love you too, sweetie. I'm so—" The words didn't make it all the way out before a fresh sob exploded down the phone. "I'm so sorry."

I didn't need this. "Me too, Mom."

Quiet, he lowered the phone from his ear and thumbed the red telephone icon. Lifted the towel from the rack and dried his face, just one more time. Styled his hair. Crossed out of the bathroom, wordless, and into his bedroom, where the tools of his trade were laid out across the bed.

Dressed.

Walked back out and stopped at his living room wall. The framed photo of a blonde woman, a teenage girl, a young boy, and an older man stared back at him. His reflection was faint in the glass.

A tiny, breathless scoff kicked out of him.

Deliberate, delicate, he lifted the picture from the wall.

Then he hurled it across the living room, into the dining room. It slammed into the plastic trash can, the unmistakable high-pitched crash of smashing glass filling the void of sound like a blasphemy. The force tipped the entire can over, spilling glittering shards across his pristine hardwood floor alongside the wrappers and detritus that made up his trash.

He didn't have time to clean it up. He didn't have time for any of it.

He was on the job.

~ * ~

A cold wind scratched at the nape of his neck. Garrett bristled, tugging the collar of his jacket tighter and knocking on the apartment door without any form of flair or finesse. His knuckles stung from the impact. Secreting his hands in his pockets helped. He had to get his head on straight. This was all from the head. It was safer to be in his head than in his heart.

He was on the job.

The door creaked open to reveal Ari Reynolds, trying out a smile that didn't reach her eyes. The fire behind her deep hazel gaze had dampened, as though dust had blown over the coals and flames were trying to eke their way through the offending earth.

"What, are you trying to bang the door down?" She gave a few hesitant chuckles, stepping aside to expose the entrance. "You want to come in for a sec?"

"We should get going," he said with a slight shake of his head. "Reservation's at eight. We don't want to be late."

"Sheesh, okay," huffed Ari. She locked the door before stalking past him, lengthy strides accentuated by a familiar pair of heels. She was aiming for the seven-foot mark again. Deliberate distance between them. *Goody.* "Brisk as hell out here. Cold weather making you grumpy?"

"Something like that." The words were spiky on his tongue. He winced as she brushed past. He didn't need to see her to know the look she was giving him. Still, he made a show of opening the passenger door for her.

He had to wake up. He had to do better than this.

He was on the job.

Shaking himself, he strode around the front of the car and climbed in. "Music, or—" he tried.

"Let's not." She folded her arms, staring out the side window as streetlights washed over her, caressing her in ways he dreamed about but couldn't experience. Her breaths hissed. Fingers clutched tight at her own sleeves. Finally, a blood-red light fell over her as they stopped at an intersection. This couldn't continue if he was to do what he had to.

His foot eased on the brake as he steered into the first parking lot he found. A strip mall filled with corner offices and independent businesses greeted them; security lights and empty parking spaces abounded. He shoved the gear selector into "Park."

"Ari," he said. His voice seemed feeble, hoarse to his ears. Every word was an effort. *Focus up. This isn't about you. This is about her. Focus on her so you can forget about your own shit.* "Is something wrong?"

An incredulous scoff burst from her. "Is something—are you—" Her expression contorted, fury beginning to morph it into something frightening, until—all of a sudden—it collapsed on itself. Her shoulders sagged, and she slumped in her seat, staring at her skirted lap. "I found out who Lucas cheated on me with," she said. The lines on her forehead inverted, blurring from anger to hurt. "It was Penny." She held his gaze, as if she were waiting to see if he'd flinch.

He stared back with the immutability of a tombstone.

"Penny...your roommate, Penny?" He struggled to put the right level of incredulity into his voice. It was just easier to shut down than to act. Safer. Shutting down meant avoiding the pain. "'Penny-who-set-us-up-in-the-first-place' Penny?"

"That's her." Ari's head bobbed in a sad shake, back and forth.

"Uh-huh." He worked his face into a sympathetic expression. *She's hurting. Be there for her.* "And are you okay?"

"Do I look okay?" She turned to him, bitterness bleeding from her gaze as she searched his face once more.

He tried—he really did try—to look shocked.

Her breaths came in scoffs and slander. "You don't even care, do you? You want to—I can see it—but you don't. You just don't."

"Ari—" He forced himself to pull on his reserves. She was about to melt down. *Shut down. Focus on her. Don't feel.* Don't *feel. Remember what David said. Be Mr. Rebound. You aren't Garrett. Not now. Play the role.*

He was on the job.

"Let me out here. I'll walk back." Her hand clutched the door handle and worked it in vain. A second later, her fingers shoved the lock open. "I can't do this tonight."

"Well, I guess that makes two of us, doesn't it, Arianne?" Bitterness and selfishness clung to every word that spurted out of him, and he cursed every escaped syllable.

"You don't get to call me that." She whirled on the spot. "Only family and friends—my *real* friends—get to call me that. Not Penny. Not you. You haven't earned it." Her hazel eyes were wide. Glistening with pain. Glistening with tears she was free to shed. Tears she was brave enough to let herself shed.

He was supposed to be on the job.

"They found my dad." His throat closed, almost cutting the last word off before he could vomit it out. His eyes burned. Prickles ripped over his skin as he broke out in the burning heat that heralded a hard sweat. He hadn't said it aloud since he'd been told. As if saying it would make it real, would ground it in reality.

Funny how one phone call could ruin a person.

Ari froze, one leg hanging out of his car. "What?" Her voice was small.

Garrett couldn't unclench his teeth. Couldn't look at her. If he did, everything would spill out. His chest heaved, flooding him with oxygen until the parking lot swam in his vision and his grip on the steering wheel alone kept him anchored.

"Some rookie scuba diver stumbled across him by sheer happenstance. It took them a while to identify the bones, but they got...they got dental records, or a match, or something, but...it's him." His voice cracked. "Mom called me. Few hours ago."

Clenching his eyes shut didn't stop the traitorous wetness leaking from between his eyelashes. Every attempt to step back and think, every time he tried to remove himself and think of how to use this for good, how to redirect, how to spin it for betterment, it kept pulling him back under.

As if from a forgotten dream, the car door clicked shut. "Garrett...I'm so sorry."

"'s fine," he slurred. He palmed at his face, struggling to keep some semblance of composure. "Really. Thought I'd moved past it. You know. Scars don't hurt until you think too hard about them and everything."

"You always hoped, huh." Even from the fog of grief deafening him, she sounded faint. "Now it's gone."

He took a breath that left his head spinning and managed to nod without fainting. "I'm sorry. I'm—we—yeah. Anyway." He clutched at the gear selector. With a jerk, he threw it back into "Drive" and eased his car forward, crawling back toward the road. Driving was good. Driving required concentration, and purpose. Driving took him out of his own head.

"I'll take you home. I'm sorry." He chuckled, derisive, shaking his head in self-pity. "We'll reschedule our date for later. I'm afraid I won't be very good company."

Ari's reply was instant. "Tell me about your dad."

He blinked, his shoulders sinking. "Wha—why?"

"Because." She drifted toward him, as though hoisted on invisible strings. "I have to know what kind of man he was to make you who you were." Her hand rested on his leg, coaxing and warm.

His mouth worked, his bottom lip quivering with the weight of the truth. What sort of a man had Arnold Reid been?

"He didn't make me who I am." Garrett's voice was soft. They'd always sworn, in one sense or another, that they'd never give up hope until they knew for sure. Now they did. Now, there would have to be a grave because there was finally a body to fill it. Now, there would be a period of waiting, and grieving, and all the messy re-closing of a wound that was supposed to have scarred over already. Breathing came as a challenge. "I am who I am because I saw the kinds of men who came trying to replace him once he disappeared. Guys who didn't care, or who couldn't hang on. Mom never found anything better than Dad."

Ari's coaxing nod was more perceived than seen, a shifting of shadowy brown hair in his peripherals. "Because your dad was so good?"

"No," spat Garrett. "Because *Mom* never thought she could do better. She'd go to all this effort, and he'd just ignore it. Never compliment her. Never appreciate her. Then, once he was gone, she acted like whatever came out of a bottle was everything he never gave her. Like she was trying to be like him."

Regret seared across his mind like a branding iron.

"I mean—they weren't—like, he wasn't—he wasn't a *bad* Dad," he said, his voice stumbling and hurried, desperate to fill the metaphysical wound he'd opened. "Shitty husband, I guess, but—but not a bad *Dad*. He cared. I just—I could never tell what was on his mind. I could never tell him what was on *my* mind. He was distant. You can't be distant with your kids." He cleared his throat in a rough, harsh burst of sound. "He was there, but he wasn't. He knew more about the bottom of a bottle than he ever did about me."

"Garrett," she said. Her brows drew together. Sympathy bled from her every pore, her every look.

He couldn't stop talking. "I lost him at fifteen, Ari—but I could have lost him when I was five and it wouldn't have made a difference.

Somewhere out there is a *library* of the things he never said to me. He never taught me how to treat a woman. How to drive. How to—shit, I don't even know. Change the oil in a car? Whatever it is dads are supposed to teach. I don't even know that." A laugh kicked out of him, derision jutting in the single syllable like thorns into a thumb. "And you know what? Even if he hadn't gone out on that boat and drunk himself to death, even if he'd been around for me and Mom, I don't have a doubt in my mind" —he hiccoughed, his cheeks burning as he managed to park the car back outside Ari's apartment— "that I still would have done all of that *without him*."

"Garrett..." She squeezed his leg, a reminder she was there, that she was with him. Or she was trying to rein him in. He couldn't tell. Couldn't think. Everything was bursting out of him, hot and messy and repressed and ugly, and he couldn't have held it back for the world.

"No." He shook his head, dogged by his own insistency. "No. You wanted to know how I became who I am, Ari? It's because I looked at all the *boys* Mom brought home trying to replace something she never had, and I promised myself I would be better than that. I saw every hole Dad made in our lives and I swore I would be the kind of man who could fill them, because there wasn't a goddamn thing he could teach me about how to talk to the people I love!"

Silence rang through the car like the absence of sound after a tornado, leaving Garrett's ragged, heaving breaths as he hung his head and clung to the steering wheel. Ari's hand rested in the space between his shoulder blades. The touch was tender, the weight grounding, drawing him back from the pit he'd poured out in both of their ears.

Her voice bled strength back into him. The words were fuzzy. Distant.

He lifted his head, dazed. "You say something, Ari?"

"Arianne." Her hand lifted to his cheek. "I said 'come inside.' Just...tell me one more thing before you do, okay?"

He coughed, blinking with the slow fatigue that seeped through every part of him and drove his cheek deeper against her palm. "You've got me talking. What do you want to know?"

Her gaze held him steady. "Have you told anyone else?"

A tiny wry smile lifted one corner of his mouth. "I almost didn't tell *you*."

Their kiss tasted of salt and unrestrained vulnerability. Tangled in each other's arms, they fell up the stairs, clutching hands so tight their knuckles turned white and their joints ached. His matched hers, hunger for hunger, strength for strength, screaming for an anchor in something soft and true. She kicked the door shut behind them, and they were alone in the half-light of the apartment. Ambient dimness bled through the gaps in curtains and blinds and the introverted glow of appliance screens.

He dug his fingers under the hem of her blouse, craving the feel of her bare sides. Her hands slid their way up under his shirt, over his back, her nails digging in as though she might peel him apart, layer by layer, until there was nothing left but his essence, his core, the parts that made him who he was and who he could be. One breathy whimper in his ear promised she felt the same, every piece and particle.

Until, finally, her voice sounded in his ear, loaded with the pain of bitter restraint.

"Stop," she breathed, her chest heaving against him. Her head bowed under the weight of the word, her hand clutching the nape of his neck for support. "Stop. This... it's not right."

Silence possessed his tongue as he waited, even as he glutted himself on the feel of her skin.

"You're grieving," she said, and every traitorous word drew them out of their shadowy half-world and back into reality, back into pain and responsibility. "I'm messed up from this Penny shit, and you're grieving, and...we need time. Sleep. Drinks. Something. I don't—I don't know." Her hands regressed from his skin, her brow lifting from his. "I can't rush this. Not with you."

Shaking, he swallowed his grief. "Yeah. Yeah... drinks."

Her departure left him mourning the empty air in the hallway, even as he drifted like a ghost after her footsteps and into the abrasive light of the fridge. She stood for moments, staring at the bottle she'd withdrawn, before the fridge door swung shut. He hung at the threshold, watching, until a loud *pop* broke the silence and the reverence. The light, sharp smell of alcohol wafted into the air as Arianne broke out two large glasses and poured.

"Here." She lifted a glass of bubbling gold liquid. "First toast is on you, Garrett."

He took the glass and stared into its depths. In one way, at least, he and his father could share this—they both would rather turn to the great amber painkiller than face harsh truths about themselves. He raised the gift, the curse, and stared into Arianne's eyes.

"To Arnold Reid, and his memory," he intoned. "The best half-assed father a guy could want."

She clinked her glass against his.

With a sigh, Garrett drank, and drank deeply, as the bubbles raced across his tongue, spinning his sense of place sideways like a bottle rocket gone awry.

"Is this..." He paused, sniffing the glass, confused. "...Arianne, is this *champagne*?"

She snorted once. "It's Penny's. We've got like eight of them in the fridge. We were saving them for her bachelorette party. Like hell does she deserve it after what she did to me. To her fiancé."

"Screw Penny, right?" he said, tacking on an asterisk to his elegiac toast.

Arianne clinked her glass against his for a second time. "Screw Penny."

He surrendered and burst out laughing. Arianne joined him, one hand resting on his shoulder for support as they doubled over with hilarity borne of grief and pressure crammed into a time span too short.

The champagne drained between them as they stood in the dark, sloshing the last of the drink between them, until the heavy bottle thumped in the recycling bin, and they opened a second.

"How much of this are we going to drink?" Garrett toasted again, the familiar *cling* of crystal flutes sounding in the darkness like a distant buoy bell.

"As much as we need to." Arianne threw her head back and downed it as though it were a shot. "More than we probably should. Less than we deserve."

Garrett poured a fresh glass. He didn't remember drinking the last one. His lips were sticky with sweetness as bubbles tickled his throat once more. "I've heard it said that by the time we get what we deserve, we don't want it anymore."

He stared at the tiny puddle of gold at the base of his flute, trying to imagine an even tinier speedboat capsizing in it. The S.S. Mr. Rebound, pride of the relationship ocean, lost in waves and trying to prove to the world that there was still a good man in it, when all he had to guide him was a map of what not to do.

"If that's true, then nobody really gets what they deserve, and that…that just sucks."

A third bottle popped open. "I call bullshit." The glass glinted in the light as it rose to her lips and emptied just as quick. "We deserve good things, and we're getting them. We've got drinks. We've got each other. We're good things, right?"

His heart beat harder. "I don't know about good, overall…" He drank again. Again. His stomach was full, and yet he couldn't find relief, no matter how his head swam or how the bubbles burned the back of his nose. "…maybe we're just good enough."

Good enough. Maybe I don't have to be good for everyone. Maybe I can just be good enough. A fourth bottle opened. Time seeped past in bubbles and mumbled understanding. "We're good enough for each other," he reiterated. "And we're here."

"Damn straight." She was close to him. He didn't know when she'd come so close. Her breath was hot, her words soft and floating on a rush of alcoholic air. "Good things—good *enough* things—come to those who wait...and I'm sick of waiting."

Desire burst like a grenade in his chest. "So am I." He barely got the words out before his glass clattered into the sink, and he found her lips again.

Her mouth claimed his in return, her hands bunching his shirt, and he parted for air before sweeping his lips over Arianne's neck, each kiss a promise that he was there, that he was hers. She tugged at the fabric prison, half-dragging him from the kitchen as he moved with her, fumbling at the buttons with slow fingers. Her mouth was a dream. The strength in her grip was a riptide he could have drowned in. She was devouring ocean and lifeboat salvation all in one.

His shirt fell by the wayside as she shoved open her bedroom door with a sweep of her hip, moving in awkward crab-step into the dark before they tumbled to the mattress. The plush fabric of her comforter was a poor imitation of her skin.

As he drew in a breath, he tasted her. As he exhaled, he lost himself in a world of closeness and wordless caresses. Her own shirt was flung aside in a cascade of long brown hair and wide, dark eyes. A pale smile spread like the moon across her face. She craned her neck to steal a kiss, long and slow, that sucked out the toxin of grief and breathed in life as his fingers laced with hers.

Even in the darkness, he found her eyes. Searched them, slow and deliberate, for any sign of hesitation. "Are we doing this?"

Her gaze was tender, her fingertips drawing a stroke between his shoulder blades that sent a ripple through him.

"I'm not going anywhere," she whispered.

She could not have given a more perfect answer if he'd imagined it.

Hunger built in his chest, and he lowered himself to her as his hands grasped her anew. He savoured the hitch of her breath in her throat, every motion of her body as she fumbled behind her and unclasped her bra, casting it off.

Moving with the intimacy of a dream, he gave himself to his desires, speaking in brushing fingertips and caressing tongue. Her ecstatic whimpers and delighted gasps brought solace as pleasure became catharsis, and the night faded to the senses.

Chapter Nineteen

Really, this entire stupid cat-and-mouse thing was his fault. Courtney huffed, shoving her pink stallion into parking gear.

She could admit she had maybe a little bit of a hand in it—maybe sticking his stupid laptop in a lasagna and cooking it was a teensy bit overboard—but if he hadn't turned into such a complete stinking jerk, maybe she wouldn't have lashed out at him. They'd been dating, and she'd fallen so hard she may as well have been a nuclear bomb of love, and he'd started lashing out. Trying to flee. He'd been scared of emotional availability and commitment. All guys were.

Well, she was taking the next step for him.

Her car door closed with a hearty *fwump*. Her high heels clacked against his driveway—when she froze.

No car was in the driveway... and he didn't have a garage.

He hadn't come home last night. Which could only mean he'd spent it with—

No. Nope. It wasn't an option.

But if it was, then whichever of those sluts at Eternal Bride Photography had stolen whatever little shred of his innocence remained was going to pay through the freaking *nose*. After Courtney broke it.

It was exactly nine AM as she strode up to his front door. She'd been up since five-thirty, doing her daily regimen—CrossFit regime, shower, Korean skincare regimen, breakfast—and then she'd come straight here. Well, almost. There had been one very, very important stop she'd made on the way first.

Just in case, she pounded on his door, listening. Waiting. Hoping. Praying.

Damn.

With a sigh, she slipped her hands into her awkwardly sagging skirt and withdrew the heavier items that bumped against her thighs. She could have just carried them in her hands, but she didn't even need to.

Her skirt had pockets. It was amazing.

She placed two nails between her perfect pink lips, just like she saw those hot construction D.I.Y home guys do it. The hammer was incredibly heavy. Her wrist hurt as she tried to hold it steady. The third and final nail was held up to the door, with the intended target sandwiched between her hand and the wood.

She tapped the nail a few times with the hammer, feeling the vibrations shake her entire arm.

The fabric fell to the doorstep.

With an aggravated sigh, she stooped and hefted the lot and reset everything. Her teeth clenched as she aimed the hammer and took a deep breath. Fine. If the nail didn't want to go in with a few taps, she'd whack the living—

"*Shit!*" She howled, dropping and clutching her injured fingers, doubling over to sandwich them between her thighs. She tried not to burst into tears as burning white-hot horrible godawful *agony* rocketed through her fingers and up her hand and through her arm and shoulder and neck and clear to the top of her head.

Dear God, why couldn't this stupid hardware stuff be easier?

Whimpering, hyperventilating, she chanced a look at her thumb. She was picturing crushed raspberries. Mangled. Destroyed.

It was bright red and throbbing, and her nail polish had cracked like a broken mirror, but otherwise… it was intact.

Sniffling, hating everything, she stooped and picked everything back up. Yet another stupid mistake to blame on him. But this had to be done. It had to. It was the next step.

Tap. Tap. Tap. Tap.

Then the nail was staying, and she could let go, and bang it in, and—well, honestly, that part was kind of fun. Maybe the hot D.I.Y guys knew something she didn't.

The second and third nails went smoothly enough, and by the end, her thumb didn't even really hurt all that much anymore. Her hands were tingling and vibrating from the impacts, and she was breathing hard, but it was done.

Her engagement outfit hung from three crooked nails on his front door. The cyan number from Ophelia's was now an acrid black and old-parchment brown, suspended in burned tatters against the wood. On each of the three nails was a single impaled sticky note.

'WE NEED TO TALK!!!!!!!'

'Call me! =D ^_^ <33'

'- Your sweet little C <3'

Along with her phone number and a perfectly shaped lipstick

kiss, she considered this a message he literally could not possibly miss.

Sticking the hammer back in her skirt pocket at a jaunty, construction-girl-chic angle, she about-faced and waltzed back to her faithful pink stallion. This called for a hand massage. And a manicure. And a new outfit.

He'd call.

She was sure of it.

If he didn't, well… she had more dresses, and cigarette lighters weren't exactly expensive.

"Cease and desist…" She huffed, turning on the engine. "Like, my *ass*."

~ * ~

The sunlight seared through the gap in the curtains that hadn't been properly closed the night before. It had to be nearly ten AM, judging by the scale of pain bursting in Garrett's eyeballs at the sight. His head throbbed. Cotton-mouth abounded. His stomach roiled.

He'd never been good at holding his alcohol.

Sighing, he closed his eyes and listened to the metronome *thump* of his pulse in his temples, trying to concentrate on other senses to clue in where he was. A breeze across his face and one arm. The ceiling offered a calming current of air. The sheets were smooth and sleek against his skin—against *all* of his skin, he discovered, as he shifted. Then, as heaven brushed against his side, soft and plump, he realized his skin wasn't alone.

Daring to open his eyes a slit, he focused his bleary vision on the vision of loveliness beside him. Arianne Reynolds was out cold, her shoulders rising and falling as she slumbered on her side. Her hair tumbled in an explosion of tangled ringlets over her neck and pillow. The bare, shapely canvas of her back was exposed, the sheets tossed awkwardly over them both. Her legs stretched clear to the end of the bed, her feet slipping over the edge.

The memories of the night before crept through the fog of hangover to stroke against his mind. Not so much the physical aspects— though those were far, far beyond anything he could have imagined— but the way they'd spoken to each other. Through touch. Through breath.

Favoring himself with a private smile, he creaked his eyes open wider, wincing at the bright light, and simply watched her as she slept.

Whatever last reserve he'd held had collapsed somewhere in the midnight hours. Here, now, it was like some internal ceiling had given way, opening up to a world as startling as it was electric. He didn't need to say it. Not yet, at least. But he couldn't go back on it. Not now, not ever. The ecstatic terror that rippled through him was more than confirmation enough.

He was in love with Arianne Reynolds.

Dizzy with reality, he drank in the shape of her figure, at once protective, at best admiring...at least until she erupted in a snore that practically rattled the bed. She shifted, mumbling nonsense, and hugged an armful of covers to herself as she resumed her slumber.

Keeping his affectionate chuckling on the inside, he slipped from the other side of the bed and left her sleeping as surely as any pleasant dream—until his feet hit the carpet and the floor lurched under him. His stomach churned as he fought not to keel backward, swallowing dry until he could tiptoe over to his pants and pull them on. The apartment was dead silent. No murmur of television. No sounds of movement. Nothing. He zipped up his fly with extreme care. There was no harm in going commando. For all he knew, they'd go at it again after she awakened.

He closed her door with painstaking care, creeping out to the kitchen where they'd last toasted his departed father. He could see them, as though shadows in the mist, left only by the impressions in the air and the debris of their drinking.

Penny's champagne.

Penny.

He crept through the apartment, examining every door with the silence and stealth of a hungover assassin. Her room was an explosion of laundry, and a bass guitar stood vigil in the corner, but otherwise, it was abandoned. Either she'd come home late and left obscenely early, or she hadn't come home at all.

His mouth stiffened as he strode to the kitchen and assembled ingredients on the counter. He'd promised her a heads-up if he and Arianne were going to make love. He'd sworn he'd give Penny a digital sock-on-the-doorknob. He had not come through. Though, apparently, neither had she.

For once, he struggled to care. More than that—he didn't even *want* to care. For once, he'd acted on his own heart, and he'd found love with a girl who had given it and given it again.

The frying pan hissed as he beat eggs into a scrambled mix, dousing them with pepper and a splash of Tabasco sauce. Penny and Arianne were on the outs. They would be even worse off, he knew, if Penny found out they'd downed a half-dozen bottles of the champagne for her bachelorette party between them the night before.

She could get over it. He'd been grieving.

He scowled at the eggs as he scooped them into a flour tortilla, adding salsa and a side of reheated ground beef from the fridge. Arnold

Reid was dead. It was confirmed. Now would come all the family responsibilities. Comforting his mom. Arranging for an actual funeral. Showing up. Doing eulogies. The truth grated against Garrett's conscience, drawing blood from his battered old Jiminy Cricket.

The cold reality was that Arnold Reid had been of better service to his son when he'd been missing.

Pouring a glass of orange juice, Garrett kept any dismissive shaking of his head on the inside. He would need a solid hangover cure himself. Sure, this breakfast was a variation of the "orange juice and egg" hangover cure, but it didn't look the most appetizing at that moment.

Either way, he thought, brushing open Arianne's bedroom door, *I hope she appreciates breakfast in bed.*

Swallowing against the next unwelcome heave from his stomach, he exhaled through his nose and fought not to throw up. It was coming. He just needed to keep it down until she could have something to settle her stomach first...and maybe for him to appreciate the whole of her goddess-like form in the daylight. Stealing a second from the ticking time-bomb of his stomach, he made sure to paint her expression into his memory. Mouth half-open, strand of brown hair velcroed to the corner of her lips, utterly vacant. Not exactly a Disney princess sleeper. Something in his heart lightened at the sight.

Quiet, he set the breakfast on her bedside table and threaded his fingers through her hair. "Good morning."

Arianne made a sound like a contented cat, her nostrils twitching as she snuggled deeper into her pillow. "Good sex," she purred. Her eyes fluttered open, spying the food. "Wha... you made me breakfast in bed?"

He couldn't repress a happy sigh as he continued stroking her hair. "I thought you could use it, since technically we never actually had dinner last night."

"Debatable." She grinned, shifting to sit up, bunching the sheets under her armpits in a toga-style wrap.

"We didn't have a *real* dinner." He rolled his eyes and laughed.

Arianne seized the plate and breakfast burrito, pausing halfway toward her first bite. The burrito bobbed in mid-air, betraying her hesitation as she fumbled for words. "Nobody's made me breakfast in bed since I was seven." Her gaze lifted to him. "You're something else, Garrett."

He offered a humble shrug in defense.

She shook her head, her insistence mounting as her stomach growled under the sheets. "I'm starting to wonder what you're doing with me." Her morning-after-vibe melted as the salsa juice dripped from the corner of the burrito to splash on the plate. "I mean...okay, I know

I'm good in bed, but…what do I bring to the table that's even keeping you here? I feel like you could have any woman you wanted, the way you treat me."

He swallowed. The truth was he had experience aplenty with women of every sort and knew the difference between a little ego-stroking and exposing a soul. This wasn't her fishing for compliments. She needed the truth—she was *telling* the truth. It wasn't just on him to tell it back to her…it would be his pleasure.

If there was one rule, at all—it was lies had no place in love.

His gaze traced over the glistening streams of grease on her fingers. This was a mistake. She was vulnerable. The Arianne he knew—laughing, walled-up, keeping-him-completely-off-guard-in-every-word-and-action Arianne—didn't ask questions like this. She deserved his honesty. His attention. But all he could do was focus on the translucent smear of burrito grease on the plate as she held the breakfast he'd made.

His stomach lurched again. "I…don't feel too good." A tide of burning hot and sour rose in his throat and nudged his gag reflex.

Her eyes narrowed, one cheek bulging with breakfast burrito. "Well, sorry if my question came at a bad time." She huffed. "And here I thought I'd—"

He didn't hear the end as he shoved his way toward the door—and knew, in the space of three steps, that it was too far. An ocean of acidic heat rocketed up his throat. In a rush of color, he spotted a wastebasket.

Dropped to his knees.

Over the sound of his emptying stomach splattering against paper, Arianne groaned in sympathy.

He coughed. Spat. Shook his head. "Gorgeous," he wheezed.

A disbelieving laugh sounded from her, back on the bed. "Not quite the way it sounds from here, but you do you, buddy."

"I meant you, Arianne." He gasped for breath against the hot pokers of his insides. Nothing—*nothing*—was going to stop him telling the truth. "You're funny. You're spontaneous."

"What on earth are you talking about?" Her voice rang clearer. She must have swallowed the mouthful she had. "Not complaining about the compliments, but what're you—"

"I'm answering your freaking question." His voice was hoarse. The words were heavy. His tongue felt thick and slimy, rasping against a throat that burned and eyes that stung—but he was getting them out. He clutched the basket with an iron grip. "It seems like nothing rattles you. Super artistic. You teach me stuff I didn't know before."

Her confused silence rang over the storm in his stomach before she spoke again. "Are you seriously still complimenting me while you're—"

He plunged his head into the basket again and heaved.

"O-okay. Apparently, yes, you are." Over the tinny echoes of his gasping and spitting, he made out her incredulous, nervous laughter. "You are officially the first guy to ever compliment me mid-puke."

"What can I say?" His voice was ragged, his breath sour, as he sat back in a heap of limbs. "I can be myself around you." Wiping sweat from his brow, he caught her gaze from over the crest of the bed. The way her forehead creased. The smile, half sympathetic, half-self-conscious, that drew her lips up.

"Toothbrushes are in the bathroom," she said, still smiling. "Spares are under the sink."

It might as well have been an "I love you" in return.

Nodding, feeble, he wiped his mouth with the back of one hand and staggered into the bathroom...in time to feel his guts lurch again.

~ * ~

He could be "himself" around her. And he'd up and darted into her en suite bathroom before she could summon up the guts to tell him the same thing.

With a quiet, contented sigh, Arianne reveled in the feeling of a full heart. He'd wrung himself out rotten trying to break down her walls. It was all she could do not to burst out into a giddy, unabashedly *validated* laugh and bounce on the spot.

Instead, she shoveled the rest of the breakfast-in-bed into her mouth and kicked the covers aside. The whole affair served to remind her how *starving* she was. He was right. They really hadn't had dinner last night. From the way the burrito ceased to exist once it passed her lips, she would need more than one. Sure, maybe it wasn't the best idea to have a huge breakfast on a day where she felt like doing nothing but lounging around in a post-coital bliss with the best man who had ever walked into her life, but who cared if she put on a few pounds? Garrett didn't mind that she was half a foot taller than him. He probably wouldn't care if she went up a pants size either.

Forgoing clothing, she tugged the liner from the wastebasket, wrinkling her nose at the smell, before she knotted it shut and loped out to the kitchen. Disposing of it in the larger trash can—and washing her hands, to be on the safe side—she set about fixing another helping of breakfast burrito as the sound of retching echoed, yet again, from the far recesses of the apartment. She winced. *Poor bastard.* With pursed lips, she seized a bottle from the countertop, dumping two tablets of Alka Seltzer into a glass of water. She wasn't feeling the greatest either, but she was used to the dull thump in her temples from a morning hangover.

There was no fear of waking up anyone else. She knew Penny wasn't home. If she had been, she would have been awake, already home from the red-eye shift at Starbucks and freshening up before she ran to her internship.

Arianne's head tilted to the side, musing as the Alka Seltzer dissolved in the water. On the one hand, Penny had stabbed her in the back in the worst way a friend could. Worse still, she'd lied about it every day since. Even if she'd set her up with Garrett, there was no way she could have known they'd hit it off anywhere near as well as they had.

No, Arianne decided. Fixing her up was a pathetic attempt at an apology. Trying to get her to date some random guy who could have turned out to be an absolute creep instead of even confessing what had happened. It was classic Penny, trying to distract, or divert attention, and leave without taking responsibility for her actions.

Not this time.

Arianne winced at her date. The poor guy was pale as porcelain, shaking, preceded by his spearmint-tinted breath as he staggered around into her kitchen. His gaze swept over her bare form before he chuckled, his voice reed-thin and wry.

"Exhibitionist, huh?" he said.

She waggled her eyebrows and smirked. "Only for you. Plus, Penny's not home, so who gives a shit?" She seized the glass and burrito—which had been her second helping, but he so clearly needed it more—and presented it to him with a peck on the forehead. "And as soon as she is, I'm booting her out."

He blinked, stumbling over to collapse into a chair at the dining room table. Arianne waited just long enough to recreate a second helping for herself before she sat down, a shiver rippling through her as her bare ass hit the cool wood. Without hesitation, she set about devouring the sumptuous breakfast. The eggs were watery, and it could have done with a side of hash browns, but for a girl whose breakfast consisted of four packets of instant oatmeal and maybe a cinnamon toaster-waffle on a fancy day, this was a delicacy.

"Really?" His word was clipped as he clamped his mouth shut to stifle a belch, the Alka Seltzer already taking effect. He groaned, his eyes clenched shut as he swayed in his seat, but—trooper that he was—he pressed forward. "You're going to...kick her out?"

"She can stay at a hotel. Other friends. Family. Gutter. Lucas. Keith. I don't care." Arianne shrugged, a bravado filling her as surely as breakfast. She chugged her glass of orange juice before slamming it on the table. The heavy thump echoed off the walls.

Garrett cringed, one hand cradling his temple.

She winced in sympathy pain. "Sorry."

"'s fine," he grunted.

She scarfed another bite as she struggled to put her thoughts in order. "I mean…" The words came in impressions and intent, as though she were feeling her way across the axis on which her life was turning at that precise moment. "I feel…new, you know? Better. I think it's about time I started cutting out things in my life which are dragging me down and replacing them with better things."

He stayed quiet. She finished her second burrito and leaned across the table, her bare breasts brushing the surface, before planting a kiss on his cheek, which was just scratchy enough to tingle her lips.

"You're included in that list of 'better things,' by the way," she said.

"Good to know." He was clever enough he should have known in a heartbeat, but he also looked like a seasick cat thrown in a tumble dryer. He did manage a smile through the silhouette of his goatee.

Which reminded her.

"I've got something for you." A tingle danced its way through her as she strode across the living room, plucking a manila folder from her artist's station. It didn't matter if he wouldn't be able to fully appreciate them. What mattered was that he would have something into which she had infused herself. Her throat tightened as she placed the folder before him.

Maybe she'd already given more of herself than she was willing to admit.

He stared for a moment before lifting the flap, reverent in his movements. Laid before him, were several eight-by-ten photos. Different colors and filters. Artistic. Intimate. Unlike anything she'd shot before, where every detail was stock-photo perfect. Pictures of Garrett, sitting in her car with his pants around his knees, a vulnerable smile and a gigantic bruise. Pictures of herself, pants tugged down, camo-patterned thong and twin paintball-souvenirs peeking out.

Best of all, his face changed when he saw them. His gaze darted back and forth. The corners of his mouth tugging up in awe, even despite his condition.

There it was. The reason she loved photography.

It wasn't about what was in the photos. It was about how people felt when they saw the photos. When they saw her photos. When they saw *her*.

"Do you like them?" she asked. Her voice was meek. A supplication before a higher power. Last night had been truly intimate, but this… somehow, this was almost deeper.

He blinked once, slowly, before exhaling. "Magnificent," was all he managed, before clambering himself to his feet, folder in hand. He came around the table and lifted himself to his tiptoes, and he left a kiss on her cheek.

Confetti explosions of giddiness fluttered through her insides.

Somewhere out there, in the great unknowable scheme of things—or maybe somewhere deep inside her—something clicked into place.

"They're all yours," she said. A heavy gulp punctuated the last word. Her chest heaved as she tried on a brave new smile. The world spun.

He nodded, once, before a melancholy settled over his face where once a hangover had been. "I have to go."

"What, so soon?"

"Yeah," he said. "I'm supposed to meet my mom this afternoon at the morgue."

"Oh. Shit. Um." She fumbled with the tortilla shells as reality wormed its fingers back into her. Through the pink and amber fog of last night came the black remembrance of why it had happened in the first place. "Do you need…? I can come with, if you need me?"

He paused at the entryway to the hallway, one hand bracing on the wall. His thoughts were reflected in the weight on his shoulders.

"No," he said at last.

Disappointment poked through the wall in her heart, even as selfish relief patched up the hole.

He turned back to her. "It should be a family thing." He swallowed hard. "But… I… if it's not too much trouble, um… I think I'm going to need you at the funeral. If we have one. I don't know if— we haven't—" His throat closed.

She strode through the rooms and had him in her arms in an instant. "You're not your dad," she said. Why, she couldn't tell. It was worlds away more intimate and unusual for her. True, in art, sometimes she had to chase the strange urges to see what happened, but this wasn't art—it was love.

It just felt like something that maybe he needed to hear.

Her skin was on needles as she waited for his reaction, until finally, his arms curled around her bare waist and a few unmistakable warm drops spilled onto her shoulder. She stroked the back of his head, her breathing slowing as his did. The yoke of responsibility was settling across her. For once, it felt as natural as picking up a camera. He needed her, and she *wanted* to be strong enough to fill it.

"Arianne," he said suddenly. "What's your favorite movie?"

She frowned for a moment, her hand pausing mid-stroke. He could have been going anywhere with this. Maybe it was a simple distraction. It had to be. Something to take his mind off the fire walk of grief facing him a few hours away.

"I have several," she said with a frown. It was true. Nobody could be expected to pick just one. Still, she sucked her teeth and hemmed and hawed until a decision came to mind. "I mean, if you put a gun to my head... I guess *Field of Dreams*."

He stared at her with a strangled look.

She blinked. "Have you ever seen it? It's good. Baseball movie. We could, uh... we could watch it, afterward. If you're up to it."

He rose against her and kissed her, long and slow.

"I'll take that as a yes," she said, her voice drawn from her as his lips departed.

His hands rested on her upper arms and a tiny exhale punctuated the upward tug at the corners of his mouth. "Hey, Arianne...um—"

"Yeah?" The interruption kicked out of her.

He shrugged one shoulder, somehow innocent and genuine in a way that had her fighting not to bury her lips against his all over again. "I mean, we haven't said it in clear terms or whatever, but...I think it's safe to say we're pretty much there." The corners of his mouth tugged higher, shoving away the weight of the grief in his eyes. "So, now that we're all 'official,' let me take you out to dinner. A real date. Pull out all the stops."

Her eyebrows shot up. "Who says we're official?"

He pointed to the all-consuming blush burning through her cheeks. "Your freckles."

Her cheeks ached from the intensity of her sudden smile. She drew her tongue across her lips, trying to at least play at hemming and hawing, even if her insides felt like warm chocolate chip cookie dough. "Well, I mean...if you really need something to look forward to, and all...I guess, since I don't have anything better to do...oh, fine."

He grinned in that stupid, incorrigible, confident way that guys did. Not the douchey overcompensating ones, but the ones for whom the impossible was a matter of habit. Even if it was weary at the edges. "A week from tonight. I'll make the reservations. Dress to kill."

Her eyes slipped shut as he stole a kiss from her. Unwilling to let him escape, she slid her arms around his ribs as her toes curled against the floor. Their affection stretched until every thought of what she'd said, or what had happened, or any lick of embarrassment had faded into pink fog, and when he parted with a tenderness matched only by their last night, she burst into a creamy giggle.

They were a couple now.

"I'll be in touch, okay?" he said.

She kissed him again, softer, tasting the spearmint toothpaste and tremulous strength on his breath. "I'll be waiting."

Chapter Twenty

Arianne wiped a light layer of sweat from her forehead with the back of her wrist, folding a pair of pants laughably too small for her into a neat square and placing it in a cardboard box with the rest of the clothes. Some people might have said this was on the extreme end of the spectrum. If anyone asked her, she would have responded that this was an incredible moment of personal growth. Normally, she would have had Karma in one hand and possibly a Louisville slugger in the other.

Tugging loose a piece of tape from the roll, she taped the box shut. She even scribbled "clothes" on it in black Sharpie. That was that, then. The bed was next.

The framed photos were gone from Penny's desk. The portraits from the walls left only hollow spaces of static colour. The dresser drawers were half ajar, their contents boxed.

Arianne stood the mattress and box spring up against the wall and had just finished collapsing the last part of the bedframe when she heard the unmistakable sound of a key in the front door.

Showtime.

Lips pursed, prim, unswayed, she kept going about her business.

Penny's voice echoed from the entryway. "Arianne?"

"Ari," she corrected. "I'm in here." Her tone was calm. Even. There was no venom. This was simply the way things were.

"So, uh… why is there a U-Haul truck parked out in front of our apartment?" Penny's voice was hesitant. Confused.

Arianne's back remained to the doorway, but she could feel the shock like a vibration through the air as her roommate froze in place. Arianne glanced up, taking in her handiwork as she knelt in the middle of the massacre of organization.

"Sorry." She glanced over her shoulder to Penny. "I didn't think you'd be home yet, or I'd be further along. Thought I'd help out."

Penny staggered in as though pulled on a leash. "I beg your

pardon, but I seem to be misunderstanding something. Help out with… what, exactly?"

"You don't live here anymore." She kept her voice light. Casual. Matter of fact. Behind it, her insides shook.

Penny's jaw fell open. "Don't I get some kind of say in this?" She gazed at the naked expanses of her walls. "I mean… my name is on the lease."

"No, you don't. You were my friend. That's why I'm being careful with your things and packing them for you instead of dumping them on the sidewalk. See?" She hefted a framed photo wrapped in clear plastic, waggling it as evidence before carefully replacing it in a box. "Even bubble-wrapped them for you."

"Bubble-wrapped…" Penny echoed, trailing off.

Seeing her there, gaping at the walls, had Arianne dancing on the head of a pin. She didn't want to respond with rage. That wasn't her anymore. She'd be like she'd told Garrett—she was cutting out the negative in her life. "You're done here, Penny."

Penny's upper lip quivered as she stayed rooted to the spot.

Arianne placed the last of the bed frame to the side and stood. Blood rushed through her legs, her knees aching from kneeling, her lower back twinging. She'd forgotten how much of a toll on the back it took to pack boxes.

"I'll let you finish up." She rolled her shoulders until they popped. "You've got until six to get the hell out."

"There's got to be—"

"Got to be *what*, Penny?" At last, the rage bled into her words. Fists formed at her sides. "A way to talk this out? A way for you to stay here? After you ruined my love life then tried to apologize by setting me up on a blind date?"

"What happened?" demanded Penny. The indignation in her voice stoked the coals of Arianne's own anger. "Did Garrett do something last night? Because you haven't said a word about this, Ari."

Something flared inside her, burning and dangerous and violent. A flashpoint had been hit that she didn't know she had.

"Garrett has been the best thing to happen to me in a long, long time," snapped Arianne. "He's the one good thing you've done, but he doesn't make up for you stabbing me in the back. Worse—what about Keith, Penny? You didn't just cheat on me, you cheated on him too."

"I—" she blustered, but her words were hollow. "I haven't told him, okay? I'm going to, but I haven't."

Arianne tried to hold it back, but something exploded inside her. An untapped well of venom erupted, sickly and black and acidic, and the more she looked at her petite British roommate, the more her stomach churned. Visions of her and Lucas sucking each other's faces. Pawing at each other's bodies. Flinging away clothes. Laying right in the space where she now stood. Breaking everyone's hearts and stabbing everyone in the back.

All while Arianne was asleep.

All while Keith, Penny's fiancé, was asleep.

Arianne had to say it.

"I don't know why he'd want you," she spat. "You're a snake."

Penny lifted her chin. "And you're a mess."

She blinked. "Ex*cuse* me?"

"You heard me." Penny stared up. Icicles could have formed on her glare, every bit as cold as Arianne's was burning. "You act like I was the single factor, the greatest bloody reason that your love life imploded. Do you want to know why Lucas and I did what we did? Why we've *kept* doing it several times since he cut you loose?"

It was finally happening.

Arianne scoffed, shaking her head in disbelief. So, Penny and Lucas were still cheating together. Fine. Whatever. And there Penny was, dangling some twisted kind of resolution to the whole thing like a rotted peach pit on a hook.

Part of Arianne hated that she wanted to know. Another part—a bigger part—didn't care anymore. But that stupid shitty niggling doubt won out. "Oh, do enlighten me," she grumbled.

"We cheated together because you drove him away, Arianne."

Her mouth contorted. "You don't get to call me that anymore, Penny."

"*Arianne,*" snapped the British girl. "Lucas couldn't talk to you about anything. You were impatient, you were short, you were dismissive, and you were about as easy for him to open up to as a bloody Easter Island statue. You were so bloody *competitive all the time.* I gave him a listening ear, and he gave me one in return, and *that's* why we made love that night."

Arianne paced around the enclosure of what had been Penny's bedroom. Her footsteps were heavy, slowed, ensnared by the net of the truth that Penny had cast across Arianne, and as they both seethed at each other, she could see it. Penny knew she was right.

That *bitch*.

"That doesn't change what you did," she growled.

Penny nodded, her mouth a flat line. "I know. And maybe you're right. I probably shouldn't live here anymore." Her words were thin, and she crossed her arms as she chose to stare at the walls instead of at her.

"But throwing me out on the street won't change the past."

Their friendship dangled on the same strand of hair that held the sword of Damocles. All that mattered now was who sat in the throne.

Arianne sucked her teeth, staring a hole through the dresser. This wasn't how it was supposed to go. She was supposed to be the victor here. Penny wasn't supposed to be blindsiding her with this unforeseen truth shit and exposing her own flaws. *She* was the one who had cheated. *She* was the one who had impaled Arianne's love life and then covered it up with a blind date.

Well, nobody said cutting negative things out of her life was going to be a clean or surgical procedure.

"Just… pack your shit and get out." Arianne blew past like a train, leaving Penny standing in her denuded room as the door closed behind her. "You owe me for this month's rent. And the security deposit."

"Sod off, you condescending bitch," came the caustic reply.

It took everything she had not to give Penny a big fat taste of Karma.

Garrett would have been proud.

~ * ~

The thing nobody explained to Garrett about funeral homes was how normal everything looked. The funeral home was about as unobtrusive as could be—a simple, white-bricked building with a single glass door. A modest sign out front. A humble parking lot that could have belonged to any family dentist's practice. The sun was bright, the weather pleasant, and the entire state of affairs was obnoxious to a fault.

A middle-aged man with a paunch who exuded sympathy led Garrett into a waiting room devoid of any stimuli. No faint radio stations playing over discreet overhead speakers. No religious iconography to ease faithful grievers. Carpet, comfy cushioned chairs, a coffee table. His mother occupied the one furthest away, folded in half, staring at the off-taupe carpet with her hands clenched between her knees. She didn't look up until he made a point of closing the door, just so there could be something to disturb the ungodly stillness.

"Hey, Mom," His voice was tinny, artificial against the empty walls.

His mom was on her feet in a flash, wrapping her arms around him and smoothing down the hair on the back of his head. It took a moment to remember how to lift his arms and hug her back.

"Hey, baby," she said, her voice thick. She guided his face into the crook of her neck. "How're you holding up?"

He managed a shrug in her embrace, closing his eyes. "'m all right. Dunno. It's still too soon to tell, I guess."

It was honest enough, in its own way. He lifted his head and drifted back, just enough to size her up and see if she needed the comfort more than he did. Her eyes were red-rimmed, the bags under them swollen and obscuring. Her cheeks were blotchy. Either she'd neglected to put on makeup, or she'd already cried it all off. The scent of wine still clung to her, sharp and thick all at once, and he steeled his insides. He could blame her for regularly drinking on any day ending in "y," but not there. Not that day. Not for those reasons.

She gave him a watery smile, stroking her fingers through his hair and hiccoughing a little laugh.

"Your hair is getting long. It needs a trim."

He blinked. "Oh. Yeah. I'll, uh—I'll get it cut next week. I'm kind of scheduled out through the rest of the week."

She sniffled, nodding. "There's a new place that opened up on 107th. It has those fancy massage chairs. You should try there. It's more of a salon, but—"

"Mom." He fought back a relieved scoff. Better the polite mother-to-adult-son bickering than having to deal with the reason behind their meeting.

The door creaked open again, revealing the same middle-aged paunchy man who had escorted Garrett. He took pains to close the door as quietly as he could, holding a clipboard with a blank sheet of glossy paper. His movements were polite. Smooth. The picture of authority and restraint.

"I'm Mr. Rodriguez," he said. He smiled wistfully beneath a moustache that closely resembled a salt and pepper comb over his lip. "You would be Garrett Reid and Susan Reid, correct?"

"Susan Kidman," she corrected.

Garrett's neck popped at the speed with which he spun to look at her. "You went back to your maiden name? You never told me."

"You never asked." She sniffed.

A muscle pulsed alongside his jaw as he worked it. She was right. He hadn't asked. It would only have dug up old wounds, old information for him to stress and grumble over. Nor should he have cared, in his mind. If she wanted to go back to her maiden name before they knew the truth—if she wanted to give up early—that was her prerogative. Even if he'd given up as well, there was something to be said for loyalty. Maybe it was hypocritical of him, but—valid or not—it was one emotional burr to stick in his side, and they hadn't even finished the greetings yet.

Mr. Rodriguez didn't seem to notice. "And Emily Reid will not be joining us, correct?"

"Not here, no," said Susan. "She's overseas at the moment. We don't know if she'll be able to get back. Peace Corps. Paperwork and passports and—and whatnot." She nodded, as if trying to convince herself it was okay.

Mr. Rodriguez grimaced. "I'm going to give you a breakdown of how this will go, so there won't be any surprises at all, okay? This is family. We'll take this as slowly as you need, so if you have to take half an hour between each step, that's all right. After we're done, we can refer you to licensed grief counselors if necessary."

Garrett retreated into his memories, listening to Mr. Rodriguez insofar as he had to. Apparently, due to ocean currents and natural biological processes, the remains of Arnold Reid consisted of only bone, and only what they could salvage from where they had been spotted, and therefore not everything would be present. It felt fitting, in his view. His father had only been partially there in his life in one sense or another. Of course, he would only be partially there in death. It had been easier when he hadn't been there at all.

Easier for Garrett to form his own opinions, easier to slip on the twenty-twenty prescription glasses of hindsight, easier for him to live according to who he felt he ought to be. Now, thanks to some dumbass scuba novice, he had to confront everything that should have scarred over.

Arnold Reid had been a provider, but he'd never been a dad.

Garrett glanced at his mom, who was clenching her jaw to stop her lower lip from trembling.

Mr. Rodriguez stood with his hand at the ready, holding the cover sheet to the clipboard.

Garrett looked back and forth between the two. "Did I miss something?"

"We're waiting on you," said his mom, in that kind of mom-like sympathy that hamstrung his confidence and made him feel fifteen again. "Are you ready, sweetie?"

He sucked his teeth and nodded.

Mr. Rodriguez slid the cover sheet back and placed the clipboard on the coffee table. A photo gleamed, bright and glossy in the overhead lighting, the glare forcing Garrett to lean forward to view it properly. On a silver examining table, lit with white light, was a yellowed skull, several vertebrae from a spine, shoulders, what looked like half of one forearm, exactly three finger bones between both hands, and a femur.

His mother clutched at her mouth and clenched her eyes shut, collapsing in on herself. A choked sob pushed between the gaps in her fingers. Her sorrow ebbed from her like radioactivity, threatening to spread into him with its cancerous aura and canker him from the inside out.

Swallowing, he fought against the urge to respond with anger in the face of grief. Instead, the cloak of responsibility settled over him, clothing him in protection as he placed an arm around his mother's shoulders in support. Whether they were on good terms or not, whether they didn't see each other more than twice a year or not, she needed him.

Still, he scoffed, quiet and to himself, as he stared at the bones.

It wasn't his father.

Not really, anyway. Not in his mind. This was… this was a heap of bones, indistinguishable from any screenshot of any of a hundred generic police procedural TV shows. This was a pithy attempt at a body, a half-assed excuse by a half-present father to try and butt into his life one last time and send him off-kilter. If there was one truth Garrett could attest to beyond his budding new love for Arianne Reynolds, it was that Arnold Reid did not deserve to reopen a wound fifteen years in the closing.

Squeezing her tight, Garrett murmured platitudes as her trembling fought to pass into him and failed. His own feelings didn't matter. Not now, not this time. His mother had always held more of a candle for Arnold's return than him—her dating and drinking notwithstanding—and now he could be strong for her. No longer was he the fifteen-year-old boy sitting in his room, dizzy with grief and lost.

"It's okay, Mom," he said, and he simply held her as she cried.

As time calmed Susan Kidman's sobs to sniffles, to eventual brave mumbles of "I'm okay" and "I'm fine," he left her standing for just long enough to cross the room and knock on the door.

It swung open. Mr. Rodriguez stood vigil, gazing on with patience and understanding, as though he were a statue of an aged Catholic saint atop a high peak of a cathedral. "Will you be in need of grief counseling?"

Garrett noted the heavyset man did not make a pre-emptive motion for a pen or flipping paper back on the clipboard. He was skilled. A veteran in guiding people through loss. Garrett nodded in respect, before realizing what he was nodding to and changing to a firm, deliberate headshake.

"No. No, uh, I won't. I'm fine." He glanced down to the photograph on the table once more. "That's not my father. That's just what's left. It doesn't make much difference to me."

His mom heaved a sigh. The woman practically had a doctorate in putting on a brave face with a minor in internalization. "I think we'll be all right." She glanced up to Mr. Rodriguez. "Thank you for the offer."

The mustached man flipped over pages. "In that case, if you're ready to talk about it, I have a few different options for the internment of your husband; traditional casket burial, in-ground, above-ground, so on. I also have the number of several…"

Garrett tuned out, his gaze wandering over the naked walls. His involvement with his father would have an awkward hiccup or two in the future, as far as familial necessity dictated. Beyond that, he could close this ugly reprise and move on to the next chapter of his life.

What was more, his ears twitched as his mother selected the worst possible choice for a funeral. "Cremation."

A titanic laugh sprinted up his throat. The leash of sheer social necessity choked it back, causing Garrett to burst out in a strangled squawk and double over, staring at his shoes as his shoulders shook. His mother's hand rested on his back, sympathy dripping from her every word as her own grief threatened to overcome her again.

"Oh, honey, I know, it seems inhumane, but…it just doesn't feel right to put him in a casket." She stooped, trying to catch his eye. "Do you—I mean, if you don't want him cremated, we can—"

"No, no." He gasped, wiping tears of mirth from his eyes. *Bye, Grandma Perkins.* His mother's face contorted in his blurry vision, empathy trembling her lips again at his supposed breakdown. "It's fine. Really. Cremation works fine."

His mother rubbed small circles between his shoulder blades. "Are you sure?"

"Yeah." At least that way he wouldn't have to bury the leftovers himself. Or shower them off. Or get them in his mouth, or in his swim trunks, or other places where the sun didn't shine.

His mother gave him a hesitant look but turned back to Mr. Rodriguez as he continued with his job.

Garrett sighed as he took stock of his mother. She was a strong woman. Like Olivia. Like Arianne. She would make it through this. He'd make it through, all the same. A new chapter for all of them.

All that remained now was to figure out how to come clean to Arianne Reynolds without driving her away forever.

Chapter Twenty-One

In her bedroom that resembled a pink Faberge egg thrown into a Forever 21 outlet store, Courtney stood before a corkboard and blew a strand of hair out of her face. Colored yarn stretched from photo to photo to email printout to text message screencap, coordinated by date and time and viability of legitimate lead. In the center was the cutest selfie she'd ever taken. The golden hour made her hair look like liquid honey. Garebear had said so, right before he'd planted a kiss on her cheek with the grace of a Disney prince, and she'd immortalized the moment in four thousand pixel ultra-high-def.

She sighed, her heart cracking as she spread her arms and flopped backward onto her poster bed, staring at the fabric ceiling. This was all wrong. She was chasing, and chasing, and she was getting closer—she could *taste* it—but sometimes, every now and then, she kind of had the occasional teensy-weensy doubt that she might be going too far. Specifically, going too far for a guy who maybe possibly didn't quite feel for her the same way she did for him.

She never liked those doubts. They made her stomach feel like she'd eaten too much gluten. But they cropped up all the same.

"Am I crazy?" she asked the ceiling. A tiny whimper followed with the same tenacity as she followed him. "I just wish he'd stop being so *stupid*. I mean… sure, it's the past, but don't I deserve a guy who'll treat me like he did?" Huffing, she hitched herself up onto her elbows, staring at her handiwork. "Is it bad that I'm talking to myself about this?"

"Of course it is, Courtney," she said, answering herself as she carried on both sides of the conversation, raking her gaze over thumbtack and thread. "None of your friends could be bothered listening to you, and Kim's been on your Bitch List since she turned everyone against you at her stupid album launch at Pomona Beach, so you're just doing their job for them and talking to yourself. You're a great sounding board, anyway."

She gave a resigned giggle, more amused at her own antics before she heaved another sigh and sat up on the edge of the bed. She felt creases worm across her forehead as she drew her knees to her chest and hugged them in lieu of any stuffed animal within arm's reach.

Sometimes, it was just so terribly *lonely.*

Idly, almost unconsciously, she tapped at her phone and positioned the camera by her face, trying to give herself the best set of puppy dog eyes she could, swiping through filters with the apathy of someone half-hungry at a buffet, before discarding her phone entirely. It was a cold day in hell when a well-lit selfie couldn't cheer her up, and there she was, starting to shiver.

At least, until her phone rang. The caller ID listed an unknown number.

She blinked through full, Katy-Perry-envious eyelashes, taking the call. "Hello?"

"Is this Courtney Hazleroth?" A man's voice. Unfamiliar. Not all that bad to listen to, but she'd been cold-called enough to already be dreading the sales pitch that *had* to be coming next.

That didn't mean she couldn't be polite. "Speaking."

"My name is Lucas Thompson. I got your number from Kim at her album launch party. She's still pretty mad, by the way." He snorted once, a rush of static over the phone. "Told me to tell you a bunch of stuff I'd rather not say."

Courtney made a disgusted sound in the back of her throat. "Look, if Kim's making you call me to chew me out after I already told her I couldn't make it, then you can tell her *I* said to go fu—"

"I understand you're looking for a guy named Garrett Reid." His interruption was as sharp as her eyes were wide. "I know how to find him."

Her squeal nearly cracked the vanity mirror on her desk.

~ * ~

A heavy bead of sweat rolled down Garrett's temple. His insides were melted butter, and he swore every pace across the asphalt left more of himself behind. His spine was mush. His hands wouldn't stop shaking. The image of the burned and tattered rags seemed stamped onto his eyeballs.

She'd *nailed* it to his *door.*

He'd almost called the cops on the spot...but the problem was, he didn't have any actual *proof.* Beyond filing a cease-and-desist letter—which technically carried all the legal weight and worth as the sheet of paper it was printed on—he wasn't sure he had it in him to take any personal steps. Victor Frankenstein hadn't been able to kill his own creation, after all, and Garrett certainly related to the man after seeing what his own actions had wrought. Courtney may have been a handful before he'd been hired, but everything since…it was his fault.

Maybe he needed to call the police. Maybe he needed to finally take it further. Maybe. A hundred maybes, and none of them mattered as he crossed the parking lot. He didn't have the time. She would have to go on as a wild card for a little longer. Too many pieces of his life were in motion.

It wasn't every day a man committed employment suicide.

Garrett thumbed at his phone as he strode toward the intricate brown brick building. A moment later, he'd fired off a text to one of his most important contacts—Louis Herriot, manager and special contact at *Le Filou*. French dining and a shot to complete the real first date—but with a proper, deliberate, Arianne-styled twist.

Garrett could only hope it wouldn't set her on fire like it had him.

3:25 PM Louis! I need a favor. Reservation for two, next Saturday, 6:30 PM? Bonaparte dining room?

3:25 PM Garrett! The Bonaparte has been booked already, but I can get you both in the Louis XIV without a problem. The view over the balcony is better anyway.

3:26 PM You are a miracle worker. Think you can pull off a dining specialty for me?

3:27 PM The chefs owe me a big one. Whatever you need, my friend, I can do it.

Garrett pushed open the glass door, and the little brass bell dinged in announcement. The last time he'd been in a wedding dress shop had been two years, now. Eliza, if he recalled. Or Lizzie. One of the Elizabeth's. This one wasn't any different. The most current styles dripped from featureless dummies in the front window, the carpet flooring was plush and cream, and additional mannequins dotted on oval displays around the store displayed the larger, flashier gowns. The inside smelled of filtered air conditioning and wisps of a generic "ocean breeze" sort of smell that he supposed was intended to conjure mental images of "freshness."

An attendant was on him in a heartbeat, leading him past rack after rack and around a corner. Another attendant stood on a small stage, wrapping a measuring tape around the waist of the bride-to-be. The groom-to-be stood to the side, his arms folded as he scrutinised them both.

Well, then. Not only had she cheated on her fiancé, but there she was, having the groom seeing her in her wedding dress. Garrett snorted to himself. There was hedging one's bets, and then there was deliberate self-sabotage.

"The fabric's kind of bunching, sweetheart." The groom-to-be frowned. "Have you been skipping meals again?"

"A little?" Her accent was clipped with stress as she smoothed down the front of her dress. "I haven't had exactly the smoothest time of things lately. That's why I moved in with you, remember? So what if I've dropped a few pounds? Can't we just…I don't know, pin it, or something?"

"Hello, Penny," said Garrett.

Two sets of eyes jolted up to stare at him. The attendant remained focused on her tape measure as she continued her job with the insulated focus of expertise.

Garrett put on a charming smile. Even after the morning he had, the motion came as second nature. He was chameleon smooth. Just because he was giving up his career didn't mean the skills that came with it vanished alongside. "Hi. You must be Keith?" he said, offering a hand. "I'm a co-worker of Penny's. I've heard a lot about you."

"Oh yeah?" Keith smiled as he took Garrett's hand. Firm, confident grip. Open stance. Head up. Casual clothes, easy-going posture. Garrett shook it and released as Keith glanced back between fiancée and newcomer. "She's never mentioned you," he added. "Are you from Starbucks or Hell?"

Garrett scoffed. "I see she's regaled you with the sordid details of the law firm."

"No kidding." Keith glanced to the attendant, who was rolling up the measuring tape and standing from where she'd been measuring along Penny's armpit.

She crossed to Keith, tapping his arm. "I'm almost done. If you'd like, we can go over some of the payment options for alterations."

Keith nodded, then crossed the store to follow the attendant who had him by the financial balls.

Garrett waited until Keith was out of earshot before tugging a folded piece of paper and a pen from his pocket.

"You look good," Garrett said, by way of introduction.

"Piss off," Penny said, by way of goodbye.

He rolled his eyes. "Relax. I came for business."

"I know, I haven't wired you the last date payment." She eyed her reflection in the half-dozen mirrors spread at every angle in a semicircle in front of her. "You haven't given me the bill yet, so how am I supposed to—"

"I'm invoking Article Eighteen of the contract." He handed her the pen.

Her gaze darted back and forth over the paper, devouring words like wildfire, disdain hardening her gaze with every paragraph. "'Immediate termination of all services?'" she snapped, looking up at him. "What the hell do you mean by that?"

"I mean, I'm done."

She blinked rapidly, even if she continued to squint in suspicion. "So—hang on a moment. Are you telling me you failed? You're refunding me the eighty percent?"

He snorted. "Not a chance in hell. Even if I did fail, I wouldn't return the money. You don't deserve it."

Her mouth fell open.

He ploughed ahead regardless. "I'm saying, she's rebounded. Our contract has been fulfilled earlier than expected, and I hereby consider the case closed and terminate all connection and financial obligation with the undersigned—that's you—effective right this second." He shoved the pen at her. "Sign it, and you'll never have to pay me a cent again."

She glared at him, snatching the pen and scowling at the offending document as though it were a criminal. "Does this mean we're through?"

"Almost. The NDA you signed has a two-year expiration. Just because the contract is fulfilled doesn't mean you can go telling Arianne I was paid to rebound her," he explained. "If you do, I'll hold you liable for breach of contract, and it's right into court." He fought not to wipe his palms on the sides of his pants.

If she told Arianne before he was ready—before everything was in place—he would be in for so much worse than a mere drawn out, bloodsucking legal battle. He would lose his best shot with a girl with whom he could be himself—not one of a million masks he had to stitch on every time he signed a contract.

Penny didn't waste a moment scribbling her signature at the bottom before shoving the pen and paper back into his chest.

He smiled in satisfaction as he reviewed the information. "Oh, and put the date here, please." He gestured to the empty space beside her scrawled name.

Her throat bobbed as though she were about to hock a particularly thick loogie into his face, but she only growled before scribbling the date as bidden. "I told her the truth, you know." Condescension dripped from her expression. "I told her I was the reason she and Lucas broke up."

"Yeah, I know. She covered everything." He folded the contract, stuffing it into his back pocket. "The truth is, Penny, if you really do care... I'm not rebounding Arianne. I'm dating her."

Penny stared at him. "I...don't get it. That's what you do to rebound someone. Date them. Isn't it?"

"No," he said, patience working through the single syllable. "I'm *dating* her." He took the time to meet her gaze. His shoulders squared. He smiled wide, irrepressible; one that he knew Penny recognized. Anyone who'd felt what he felt knew that smile. "I think I'm...well, I'm in love with her."

Penny just stared.

He glanced behind him to ensure their privacy. "I'm giving up being Mr. Rebound. I'm gonna date Arianne, and I'm gonna make a go of this, because I think—if I'm very, very lucky—she might feel the same way about me."

Penny kept staring, and he stared right back.

"You've gotta know what that's like." He slipped his hands into his pockets. "Keith is in the other room. He's the love of your life. That's why you're marrying him and not Lucas, isn't it?"

Her nostrils flared as her gaze darted across the store to her fiancé, leaning on his elbows at the register counter as an attendant tapped at a tablet with a stylus. "Don't be an asshole, Garrett."

"Take care, Penny. And, from the bottom of my heart, thank you for hiring me. Taking Arianne on as a client is the best decision I've ever made in my life." He turned his back on the British pimple, smiling to himself for a myriad of reasons.

Passing Keith in transit, Garrett bid the man with the happy eyes a delighted goodbye, then tugged open the door. Below the sound of the dingling brass bell, he heard Penny's voice, faint, from the other end of the store.

"Keith? We need to talk."

~ * ~

The sun could never be in the right place when she needed it to be.

Courtney squinted through her aviator sunglasses, pouting as she tried to scoot around and angle herself to get the perfect lighting without losing sight of the cute kale-and-spinach salad with the organic goat cheese and raspberry vinaigrette on the plate in front of her. How was she supposed to *#ketolifestyle* and *#allnatural* with the sun constantly in the wrong place? Let alone being able to *#nofilter*. That was her *thing*. Worst of all, the boy across from her, with his elbows on the table like a total Neanderthal, was judging the hell out of her when she'd invited him out to the table in Central Park in the first place. *Rude.*

"Do you mind?" said Lucas. He stared at her with all the expression of one of those faceless clay statue things she'd seen at the art museum. The ones without limbs that were supposed to be majestic art instead of unfinished crap. Or maybe they'd lost a fight with a chainsaw.

"Do you?" She huffed, pouting and taking the photo anyway. A swift apology about the lighting was added with plenty of sad face emojis. Maybe her fans would play it off as being "real" or "accessible" or whatever. Courtney Hazleroth had bad lighting days too.

She placed her phone down on the table, careful not to scratch the bedazzled case, and stabbed at the salad with a fork. "Besides, you haven't, like, been even remotely useful since we came here. I'm still waiting for this big fancy revelation of yours about my Gare-bear. You know, the one I put off going to hot yoga for? Because you just *had* to talk about this in person instead of over the phone or whatever?"

Honestly, it was insulting. But, as with all things remotely related to Garrett Reid, it required her utmost attention. For both their sakes.

Lucas didn't say anything. He just sipped his chai latte—with actual regular two-percent milk, like he was *trying* to bloat himself—and sighed.

Courtney stuffed a bite of salad into her mouth and chased it with her much healthier almond milk Americano, waiting until every last morsel was gone, before she picked up the conversation from where he hadn't touched it.

"So, why are you helping me, again?" She squinted at him.

He stared at her like her fourth-grade teacher used to, all squinty-eyed and frowning, like she wasn't quite right. "Let me spell it out for you," he said. "The girl who's dating your guy is named Ari Reynolds."

"Yeah, I know that part." Courtney rolled her eyes. "Thanks for the mansplaining."

His jaw moved like he was trying to crush gravel between his teeth. "She's also my ex. However, Ari's roommate, Penny, is the love of my life, and I'm the man of her dreams. Problem is, Penny is engaged to some domestic-type suit-and-tie bastard. I dumped Ari to get to Penny. Penny, in turn, was with me and promised she'd dump her square of a fiancé."

Courtney sucked her teeth and nodded. "So, you're a total piece of shit, is what you're saying."

Lucas glared. "I don't recall asking for your opinion."

"Nobody ever does. The best things in life are free." She mimed dropping a microphone.

A beat of irritated silence passed between them. "When Ari found out, she threw my girl onto the street," he said at last. "Now, instead of being with me, she's shacking up with the fiancé she promised she'd dump."

Courtney blinked several times. "I still don't see what this has to do with me."

"Tit for tat." He sipped his chai latte. "Ari drove the woman I love right into the arms of the worst possible person for her. So, now I'm going to do the same thing to her and drive the man *she* loves into the arms of the worst possible person for *him*."

Her jaw dropped. "I'm not the worst possible person for him."

"Do you want my help breaking them up or not?" His latte cup hit the table. Lucas might as well have pounded a fist on it for the effect it had.

She stuck out her bottom lip, glancing down and away. Like it or not, she hadn't been able to pin Garrett down and talk to him on her own merits. "Fine. Hashtag-deal-with-the-devil." She stabbed at a single piece of goat cheese and examined it for imaginary flaws before popping it past her bubblegum-pink lips. "And you know where to find this bitch, right?"

"I know where she lives, which means I know where he'll be eventually." He frowned as he shook his head. "But I don't know how to get her and him in the same place at the same time shy of stalking them day and night."

Courtney giggled, a shaky smile lifting one corner of her mouth. "And—and that'd be *crazy*, right? Like, nobody would actually *do* that, right?"

Lucas frowned deeper. "No?"

"Right. 'No.'" She gestured to him in a "duh" sort of way, hands out flat, hating every verbal hiccup that came out of her. "Because that'd be crazy."

Her phone pinged. It was in her hand in a heartbeat. Tossing her bangs out of her eyes, she swiped at her screen and sorted through the new messages. Garbage, nothing, notifications of people liking, commenting, etc, etc. All clear.

"Sorry, what were we talking about?" She placed the phone back on the table.

He stared at her like she was a fly on a muffin. "Crashing a date between Ari Reynolds and Garrett Reid and ripping them apart so I can get her back for what she did to my girl, and you can get your 'Garebear' back."

"Right? Ugh, I cannot *wait*. Like, I've been so close for ages."

She chewed on another bite of salad as her phone pinged again. Once more, her manicured nails tapped at the screen with the alacrity of an Irish dancer.

Lucas fumed out of the corner of her eye. "Do you mind maybe not answ—"

She held up a single finger to silence the Neanderthal, pausing as she stared at the screen. A message from someone on the top tier of her Patreon; one of the faithfuls who occasionally earned a steamier picture from the greatness that was Courtney Hazleroth. Her gaze rolled over the screenshot, then the message that followed. She reread it. She drank in it. She *devoured* the message with glee.

Lucas's indignation had melted to suspicion as he jerked his chin at her phone. "What's going on?"

Courtney waggled her smart phone in front of his face. "Ever heard of *Le Filou?*"

Chapter Twenty-Two

The evening air was brisk as Garrett made his way through the meandering, well-dressed patrons entering and exiting the restaurant. Olivia had rescued him from a pre-date panic attack, tires a-screeching and husband in tow. Between the three of them, they'd calmed him and dressed him, advised him and coached him, and—as Garrett glanced at his reflection in the restaurant window—they'd worked a miracle. Navy blue suit, pressed shirt, cornflower blue tie to bring out his eyes to an almost luminescent degree and give his neatly trimmed, though still shorter, goatee a darker hue.

Heaving a long, deep breath, he checked his watch, then his phone, and waited. No word from Arianne yet. At least, not until someone wolf whistled from halfway down the block and chills raced across the nape of his neck.

Laughter was on his lips as he spun around, just in time to see her lowering her fingers from her mouth and striding up with a cheeky grin.

A sleek, satin black cocktail dress hugged her figure like a sleeve, the hem dancing above her knees and the bust line just coy enough, even on her endowed frame, to expose freckled curves. Black lace sleeves swirled over her arms, linked to a fabric choker. Her hair fell over the front of one shoulder and behind the other. She swept up the sidewalk with the unrivalled grace and stature of some seven-foot Amazonian demigoddess, the light clicks of her six-inch pumps deigning to acknowledge she was walking on mortal ground rather than floating through the air.

She was going for attention, again—but this time, the purpose was different, and he knew it. The six-inch high-fashion stilts she was styling weren't a metaphorical middle finger to him, or a challenge to see if he could handle her, as it had been on their first date. Here, now, they were a beacon. She wanted people to see her, so they could see her with him. They told anyone who saw them that there was a man who let her wear whatever she wanted, body type be damned. The shoes, her whole outfit, were a tribute.

She stood before him, beaming down.

His eyes were level to the creamy surface of her neck, as though he were the world's luckiest vampire, and as he lifted his gaze heavenward, he searched her hazel depths and found a better cocktail than anything a restaurant bar could offer—an intoxicating mix of attraction, nervousness, and delight.

"You look amazing." They spoke in unison, voices layered accidentally over the top of each other, before laughing together.

He offered his arm, head high and peacock proud.

She took it, adding an awkward mock curtsy.

"May I help you both?" said the hostess. To her credit, she only sort of gaped at them.

"We have a reservation for the Louis XIV dining balcony," said Garrett.

The hostess tapped at a tablet for a moment before nodding. "Right this way."

He squeezed Arianne's arm in his as they mounted the ballroom-style stairs, past quiet couples and candlelight, to their own circular table. Their destination sat secreted in a cozy nook of a balcony overlooking the restaurant as a whole, just past a single hip-high bronze railing. Below them, the burbling chatter and tinkling silverware churned like an underground river. He made a point of drawing out Arianne's chair and taking a mental snapshot of her expression as she deliberately sat and scooted in with him.

"This is probably the fanciest place I've ever had dinner at." She offered him a smile that was tight at the corners. "I know this was our first date and all, but you recall how that went, right?"

He cocked his head. "You set me on fire."

"Technically, Lindsey set you on fire." Arianne smirked. "But my point is, I know I look damn good in a cocktail dress, but you should also recall this really isn't my scene."

"I know." He nodded. "And yes. You do. Actually, you're underselling it. You look *divine* in that dress."

She rolled her eyes, even if her smirk softened into an actual soft smile. "Cheesy."

His eyes widened, blinking in pure innocence. "We're in a French restaurant. It's only appropriate. They're very particular about their cheese."

She blinked and groaned as the weight of his pun crashed down on her.

He maintained a grin and sipped at the ice water brought by their waitress, who also placed menus on their table and departed without a word. He didn't pick his copy up. Louis had already confirmed their arrangement.

Arianne frowned, squinting at the flowing script and the prices without dollar signs. "Okay, Mr. Polyglot. Mind translating this for me?"

"There's no need," he said simply. "Just pick whichever wine you want. I've got dinner covered."

Her eyebrows quirked. "Really? You're gonna order for me?"

"Yup."

"Bold move." She leaned forward on her elbows. "Think it'll pay off?"

"Mr. Reid?" said a too-familiar voice to their side, light and bubbly. "Your dinner will be right out. The chefs have prepared it according to your specifications."

"Thank y—" Garrett choked on the words as he turned to the waitress.

The waitress who stood at precisely five-foot-one, with blonde hair tied up in a neat bun, bubblegum-pink lips, and a voice like a harpy. The white button-down shirt and black apron was a new look. The manic, possessive look in her eyes was not.

His eye twitched as his heart froze. Below his breath streamed a steady river of cursing as a cold, cold sweat broke across the nape of his neck.

"Not a problem!" Courtney beamed, whisking away like Tinkerbell with a switchblade.

His throat seized shut. This was impossible. This couldn't be happening. She never could have known he was taking Arianne here. The cease-and-desist letter was supposed to be in place, for all the good it did.

"Garrett?" said Arianne, her forehead creasing. "You okay? You look freaked." She twisted in her chair, frowning deeper as she peered after the blonde she-devil. "Did you know her?"

There was no choice. No chance for finesse, or for a slow warming up to the truth. This was the worst-case scenario. He clenched his eyes shut for precious moments before clutching his glass in both hands and chugging the water down to the clinking ice.

"Wha—o-kay, I'm gonna guess that's a 'yes,'" said Arianne. "Who is she?"

He didn't need to see her to know the wide-eyed expression on her face as he bowed his head and gasped for air. "Remember on the beach," he started. "On our second date?"

"Uh-huh," said Arianne. "Elizabeth. Crazy stalker ex. Is—is that seriously her?"

He swallowed and fought to keep his voice from retreating down his throat to his yellow guts. Time to unveil the first lie of the night. "Not 'Elizabeth.' Her name is Courtney."

Arianne sucked her teeth as her eyes clouded, mulling over the first bite of the truth. "Okay. So, a few questions. First, why did you try to bring me to the restaurant where she works—*twice*?"

"Because she doesn't work here." His cheeks flushed. The cold sweat seared against his skin as it rocketed through the temperature to a burning soak that dampened the armpits of his shirt. "I don't know what she's doing here."

Arianne nodded, her mouth hardening. "Okay. Second question. Why did you lie to me?"

He took a shaky breath. "Because it was only the second date, and I'd heard from Penny that you had a penchant for using your taser. If something happened—something literally like this—I didn't want to risk you tracking her down and leaving her twitching and foaming at the mouth when she's my problem."

Her eyes narrowed as she pointed a dagger-like finger at him. "That's—" She paused, frowning, before lowering the digit. "—a fair point. Okay. Fine. Is there anything else you've been lying to me about? Your name's still Garrett, right?" She laughed at her own joke before freezing mid-"ha." "It *is* Garrett, isn't it?"

"Yeah. Yeah, it is." He craned his neck, peeking past her. No sign of the harpy yet. "My name is Garrett Tiberius Reid."

She choked on a fresh round of laughter. "'Tiberius?' You're kidding."

"Named after my grandpa." His words came as rapid-fire as he could speak. "I haven't lied about anything else." *Not true.* "Well, not, like—not to your *face*. Not—I mean, sure, there's things I haven't *told* you, exactly, but—I mean, there's a *lot* I haven't—but—" He couldn't help but feel he was drowning on dry land. "To be fair, I don't know everything about you, either, and—"

Arianne put up both hands, patting at the air between them in universal "whoa, Nelly" sign language. Sympathy curved her eyebrows upward and tugged sideways at her mouth. "Slow down, Garrett. If we need to go somewhere else, we can. I don't want to have a dinner served by your crazy stalker any more than you do."

A voice sounded beside them. Not the shrill, saccharine warble of the miniature blonde creature. A man's voice. "Sorry about the wait.

Dinner will be out in a moment."

Garrett had never seen him before.

Arianne, however, jerked so viciously she was in danger of toppling both the chair and table. Her voice dripped pain and confusion and fury. "Lucas?"

Garrett's heart fell into his stomach as his hands shook and dampened his pant legs.

"Ari." Lucas turned to look at him. "I can only assume you're this 'Gare-bear.'"

"Garrett Reid," he said, automatically. The words eked past his lips as he fell back on the one thing he could think of—his natural, charismatic, professional façade. "Nice to meet you."

Arianne shook in her chair. "What the hell are you doing here? I made it clear I never wanted to see you again. I *excised* you from my life. You're a cancer."

"Oh, I'm aware." Lucas's fists clenched at his sides. "This is revenge for throwing Penny out."

"How did you know about that?" she snapped. "Did she send you?"

"She didn't send shit." Condescension pulled his face into an ugly sneer. "But you drove her away. Drove her right into the arms of her fiancé. Right where none of us want her to be. So, now I get to screw you one last time."

"Oh, burn in hell." She lunged for her sleek black purse, rummaging with the single-minded fervor of a woman with homicide in her eyes. "You've got until I find Karma before you get an even bigger taste than I gave you last time."

"Arianne—" Garrett put his hands out to try and sway her from her destructive path. He may as well have tried to stop a hurricane by shouting at it.

Worse, striding up beside him was the blonde bane of his existence, eyebrow quirked, as though she'd been vomited out of the digital screen of one of her thousands of selfies. And then she had to open her mouth. "Has Garrett ever told you what he does for a living?"

The rummaging in the purse stopped. A makeup case and a packet of tissues fell to the desk from Arianne's slender fingers as she froze. She gazed from Lucas to Courtney and back.

He trembled in his chair. "Arianne, I'm—"

"He's paid to date other women." Courtney pouted, crossing her arms over her chest. "He's literally hired by a girl's best friend, and they pay him per date. They call him 'Mr. Rebound.'"

Garrett's eyes burned in shame. He couldn't breathe. Couldn't speak. Every word was a nail in his coffin, a lash across his back. He sat, helpless, as the incarnations of every lie he'd ever told ripped apart his covers and his actions, his best-laid plans, and exposed the blackened beating heart of the matter—he hadn't dated Arianne because he'd been into her.

Except that he absolutely, completely *was*.

"Penny paid for him," Lucas said.

Arianne scoffed, incredulous, disbelieving. For a brief second, there was a bell ringing over his grave. Garrett sucked a ghost of a breath only for it to expire as her expression morphed through the five stages of realization. First denial, then anger, then—then she just stayed at anger. "Bullshit!"

Lucas snorted, shaking his head in mocking pity. "This is why we never worked, Ari. You never wrap your head around simple, basic shit. You try and keep everyone at arm's length—Penny and I included—then when Penny literally *pays for a guy for you to keep at arm's length,* you try and bring *him* closer? You don't *think,* you caustic bitch!"

He slapped her.

Before the sound echoed across the second floor, Garrett was on his feet, legs jolting the table and clattering the silverware. Courtney blocked his path. In a fraction of a glance, he spotted her expression. Slack-jawed, afraid, shrinking back, yet in his path she remained. Awkward, he staggered, caught in mid-momentum and tangled up in the blonde obstacle. By the time he'd sidestepped and pushed past her, Arianne was lunging with one hand.

The crackle of electricity was audible even over Lucas's cry as he spasmed and collapsed like a damp sock. Her eyes were ablaze, slamming Karma into his arm, his side, three straight times, until she tossed her hair back and sucked in a shuddering breath as her nostrils flared.

"Hit me again." She seethed, glaring down at the twitching mess. "Come on. You wanna try it? I'm right here. Get your weak ass up and try it again! Let's go for round two!"

"Arianne," said Garrett, his voice small.

Her gaze rocketed to him.

His shoulders sagged.

Her throat bobbed.

For seconds, neither of them spoke.

"I need to hear it from you," she said, at last. "Tell me you weren't paid to date me. Tell me you weren't hired like I was a goddamn rescue case and tell me it wasn't the worst friend I ever had who paid you to do it."

He couldn't stop shaking. "I...wish I could."

The words came as though gunshots. He saw every impact, every force of destruction on her as she collapsed inward. Her eyelashes fluttered as she blinked. Her jaw worked. She swallowed. Finally, she swept the spilled innards of her purse back into their black hole, shaking her head as though the action alone would keep the world standing.

"I have to get out of here." Arianne, despite her words, didn't move. She clutched the edge of the table, her knuckles white. Her chest heaved. "I have to go."

Lucas groaned from the floor.

"I forgave him," said Courtney.

Garrett blinked in shock. He had to be in a coma. She wasn't— she wasn't *helping*?

"That's why we're soulmates," she said. "Because I forgave him for taking money to go around dating sluts like you. That's why we belong together. You don't deserve him."

Against his survival instincts, he buried his face in his hands. This couldn't be happening. "Courtney—" A rage fueled by pain and panic ignited both syllables. "Do you—"

He was cut off by a roar from the floor. "You want round two?" Lucas grunted as he jerked himself up from the carpet. "Fine!"

Beyond him, a frantic waiter in a white dinner jacket pointed toward the staircase, where a police officer was trucking up the red-carpet stairwell.

Garrett moved on instinct. Lucas had struck the love of his life once already. Once was a million times too many. Garrett's fist clenched. He lunged.

Before his fist made contact, his torso collided yet again with a pixie-sized blonde mass. His legs tangled with hers. Tripped. Stumbled. "Courtney—*move out of*—"

Lucas's blow cracked Garrett across the temple. His head jerked to the side as he stumbled, off-balance. Stars burst in his eyes. Something caught him across the small of the back, hard and flat and vertical. A wall swept at his legs as his torso dangled in the air. He had a single thought.

The second-floor balcony.

The world spun. Somebody screamed. There was a crash.

The wind exploded from his lungs. Something had collapsed under him in an explosion of snapping wood and shattering glass and flurrying tablecloth. Two shapes staggered back from him. Voices were muffled as his lips worked. No air would come.

His head swam. His vision blurred.

From the edges of a nightmare, he thought he heard Courtney's voice going "Holy *shit*, you're tall—" before everything he cared about, and everything around him, blinked out.

~ * ~

Eighteen hours later…

The world was spinning too fast for Courtney Hazleroth to keep track. In the last day or so, she'd been through more than she ever thought she would. Seen things no girl ought to have to see. Been treated like some interchangeable, generic faceless *thing* passed around a police station and here and there and back again before she'd made it home.

Now, she was dabbing cucumber moisturizer over the bags under her eyes as she went back to the same crummy, germ-filled hospital she'd already been thrown out from.

But this time, *everything was different*.

Her Gare-bear had come to his senses. She'd thought her phone had been glitching when she saw his number and heard Katy Perry's "Unconditionally"—Courtney's ringtone assigned just for him. But no. His voice, scratchy but so incredibly *him*, had come beating down the line and asked to see her. No, he wasn't joking. Not that she asked, of course—she wasn't going to jinx it—but she could hear it in his voice.

She paused at her reflection in the windows outside, combing her gorgeous blonde tresses with her fingers and trying to straighten herself up and look like she hadn't come out of a tumble dryer. She wasn't quite a hot mess. More like a lukewarm, needs-another-two-minutes-in-the-microwave mess. It would work. When they would Instagram their first selfie together, she'd look tired but happy; sweet, cute, but kind of scraggly, as though she'd gone through the same harrowing journey he had.

She totally had too. Arguably even more so, come to think of it. She'd been chasing him for *way* longer.

The pompous security guard with the gut straining his Batman-pouch-belt-thing scowled at her and made a point to start waddling her way.

She held up her phone like it were a cross before a vampire, strutting up to the unimpressed front desk receptionist. "I'm here to see—"

"Yeah, I know," said the receptionist. "He called down. Room six-two-one."

Courtney already knew this, of course, but she graced the rude overweight thing in scrubs with a perky smile nonetheless. About-facing, she paused, staring up at Security Guard McFatAss.

"Courtney Hazleroth?" His voice was a deep wheezy croak, like if a gnarled oak tree had a voice.

She scoffed. "I have permission to visit him, okay? He already called down, so the stupid letter thing doesn't matter anymore. Talk to the front desk lady. She can tell you."

His dust-bunny eyebrows scrunched together with his eyes as he held back a groan. "I know. I'm escorting you up."

It was like he was speaking Greek to her. "Huh?"

He spoke slowly. "You're a security risk. I'm a security guard. I'm escorting you up."

Her cheeks bulged like a volcano about to erupt. Her nostrils flared. This hairy, thick-fingered behemoth was seriously going to ruin her big reunion moment? *Seriously*? She choked on her vehemence, managing to push it back down and buckle it back into its seat. Fine. It was fine. He could come with. What mattered was that she and her Gare-bear would finally have their moment in the sun.

The elevator played stupid dingly-dingly music and the hallways smelled like lemon-scented dish soap and sick people. Doors flew by in a blur until she skidded to a halt before the heavy wooden door with the simple black plaque reading "621."

The flat steel door handle lay before her.

She stared at it, and it stared right back. Goosebumps crept up her arms as she peeked back at the brawny man standing there, huffing, his arms folded across his flabby chest. She blinked several times at the door, her shoulders sinking as she chewed at her bottom lip. Her gaze slid back to the man as she swallowed and pinched the waistband of her hip-huggers between two fingernails.

"I, um," she mumbled. Her lie was barely audible over the ambient sounds of the hallway. "I…don't like hospitals."

He responded with a hissing breath out his hairy nostrils.

Her hands trembled as she seized the door handle and pushed it open, inch by inch, peeking around the corner. The foot of a hospital bed hung in the way, with lengthy bulges under the covers that had to be Garrett's feet. The plain path of linoleum stretched past the bathroom door and into his room. Her shoes seemed to have sunk into the ground.

Suddenly, the door swung wider as the security guard pushed it the rest of the way open and violated the moment.

Cringing, she scurried forward, pausing at the foot of the bed as she looked up to the man she'd dreamed about for exactly one year, three months, two weeks, and six days. His hair was greasy, limp. Dark circles hung under his eyes. The crappy hospital gown flowed over him like a king size bed sheet over a queen mattress. A clear plastic tube led from a bag of medicine over to a mess of white surgical tape around his elbow.

"Courtney," he said. His voice was hollow, dull, like the echo of a gavel.

She gulped. "Gare-bear." Her gaze crawled over him. Words wouldn't come. She'd fantasized about it more times than she could count—hospital fantasies could be some of the sexiest things, all sweet and hurt-comfort and loving—but this… Everything was wrong. She wet her lips. "You wanted to see me?"

"Yeah," he said. "We need to talk."

She stayed quiet, rooted to the spot. The repeated message from her sticky-notes wasn't lost on her, but somehow it just made everything worse. Her knees ached, locked in place, until she tore her gaze away from him and searched the room. "Can I sit?"

He nodded.

She dragged a cushioned chair built for one closer to his bed, nestling herself in and drawing her knees to her chest, egg-like. Her arms wrapped around her ankles. He wasn't talking. He was just staring at her like the world had dropped onto his shoulders. Maybe it was the drugs. Maybe he was waiting for her to speak.

Then he opened his mouth. "I'm sorry, Courtney." Weariness infused every word. "I'm sorry about how I treated you. I'm sorry I lied to you. I'm sorry I manipulated you, and I'm sorry for being an asshole to you, and I'm sorry I had sex with you when I didn't feel anything for you."

It was the apology she'd dreamed of—almost—since they'd first gone on a break. Since they'd first…split. A tear smudged her mascara as she blinked it away. Her chin bounced against her knees as she shook her head, once. "Gare-b… Garrett." She took a shaking breath. She couldn't do this—not while she was looking at him, broken and tired and wrung out in a hospital bed she'd help put him in. "You shouldn't have to apologize."

Her eyes clenched shut as she reached inside herself with trembling hands and scooped up the mess of the truth she tried to keep behind every mental lock and key she could. "I'm…kind of crazy. I know. And—and I get it, okay?" Her throat bobbed as she peeked over her knees. Her voice peeped out of her, tiny, echoing in the cavernous hall of his hospital room. "You had every reason to run from me and keep running. Just…nobody's ever been as nice to me as you have, and… I didn't want to let go."

He didn't speak.

The words wouldn't stop kicking out of her. "You might not realize this," she said, sniffing bitterly as she fished in her purse for a tissue, "but I'm not exactly Ms. Self-Confidence, okay? I don't get to have guys like you. I get the hot guys who are great in bed. The ones with muscles who drive Jeeps and buy you things and don't listen when you talk. Those are my guys. Then suddenly you walk in, and you're like this perfect mesh of all the good aspects of these guys and none of the bad, and—and I panicked, okay?"

She hated herself. Her mouth was motoring at ninety miles a minute. For all she knew, she'd wake up in the space of a blink and be at home in her bed, surrounded by her throw pillows and stuffed animals, and this would have been a hallucination. She dabbed at her eyes with the tissue, her voice hoarse. "I didn't think I was good enough for you, so I tried to do everything to keep you and I just drove you away, and it was the biggest regret of my life."

"Courtney." His voice was quiet. Sincere. The tone of voice that made her insides quiver. "I was out to dinner with Arianne because I was going to tell her what I did for a living."

The words hit Courtney like a frying pan to the face. She could even hear the ringing in her ears. "Wait," she said. Her mouth twitched and tightened. "You were trying to push her away?"

"No." His gaze never wavered, not even once. "I was going to tell her the truth because I love her. I was going to give up being Mr. Rebound. For her."

If gravity had ceased to exist right at that moment, she still would not have been more surprised. What was worse was that she could see the honesty of it, right there in those big, tired baby-blues of his. That kind of pain didn't come without it. He was heartbroken, and it was her fault.

Well, hers and Lucas's, but splitting hairs on blame wasn't going to fix anything.

Her throat bobbed as she sucked in deep breaths and tried to wrap her head around it. Her Gare-bear didn't love her. She wanted to be shocked—really, with everything in her, she did—but she couldn't help but swallow the medicine. There hadn't ever been any doubt. Just a fool's hope. "But…she's taller than you," she pointed out, as though it were reason enough to render his words untrue.

He gave a minute shrug.

She chewed her bottom lip until it felt like her teeth would permanently imprint on it. Maybe it was stupid to even ask. But if there was anything—any doubt, any inkling—maybe… "A-are you sure?" she mumbled. "Like…are you maybe, like…falling in love with the idea of a relationship with her? Not just her? Because, like…you could maybe have a relationship with someone else and have it be just as fulfilling?"

Even now, eighteen hours after she'd surrendered her dignity, hearing the words come out of her mouth like that stung in a way all too brutal.

One corner of his mouth lifted, regretful. It was the kind of smile someone gave who couldn't help telling the truth. "It's not an idea I'm in love with," he said. "It's her."

Her throat constricted. "I broke you two up, didn't I?" Her bottom lip trembled. "I... Gare-...Garrett, I..." She buried her head in her hands and sucked in breath after breath, fighting against the urge to hyperventilate.

"Courtney, I'm sorry," he repeated. "I wish I hadn't had to take out the cease-and-desist against you, but everything you were doing...it was inappropriate, to say the least. I can—" She could hear him clenching his teeth as he spoke. "I can even forgive what you did to me and Arianne. But Courtney...don't you think, maybe, you might want to talk to someone about these issues?"

She sniffled, shaking her head. "I would have talked to you if you'd let me." After a moment, she dared to lift her gaze. She must have looked a nightmare, mascara running and puffy bloodshot eyes.

He met her stare, his face contorted in tiredness and sympathy. "Maybe someone who's certified to listen and counsel?"

There it was. Her shoulders sank. Wordless, she nodded.

Everything was sprawled out between them. Every uncomfortable truth, every screaming feeling in her mind had all been addressed...almost. The words flooded out at the last hiccup on her conscience. "I-I didn't know he'd hit her." Her eyes stung at the memory. "I-I didn't know—Garrett, please believe me, I—"

"Lucas is in jail." His voice remained as weary as ever. "Olivia told me when I first woke up. He's facing an eighteen-month sentence for something like five separate misdemeanors. Arianne got off on a self-defense plea."

Courtney's gaze fell to the dirty linoleum floor. "They gave me a fine." It wasn't remotely the worst thing about the situation.

"They also banned me for life from the restaurant, so...there's that." Garrett dropped his open hands in an "oh well" sort of gesture.

She sniffed. "Trust me, you're not missing out."

A moment—a single, shiny moment—of laughter rippled between the two of them like a sun-warmed spot in a lake.

He gave her a battered smile as he slumped back in his reclined hospital bed.

Courtney slipped her legs away from her chest and opened back up. The air between them didn't stink of hospital and betrayal anymore. He'd laid everything on the line, and so had she, and even if they would never see each other again…this was one of those moments where everything would change.

He'd apologized. He'd made it right. Now she had to do the same for him.

"I'm gonna fix this." She launched to her feet.

He raised his head, eyes wide. "You're what?"

"I'll make it right." Something inside her had caught fire. A spark racing across dry tinder and igniting into perfect purpose. Her Gare-bear didn't belong to her anymore. He'd chosen someone else. She'd come between them. Now she had to make him happy, since he'd made her whole—well, not *whole*, but he'd put her on the right path. "If I can't make you happy by being with you, then I want to at least fix what I did wrong."

"Courtney…" Doubt filled his voice. His head might have begun to shake. It didn't matter.

She beamed at him, patting his arm. "You get your rest, Gare-bear. Courtney Hazleroth is on the job."

Her phone was already in her hand as she strode past Security Guard McFatAss. First things first—tracking down the busty behemoth woman he'd fallen in love with.

Color returned to his cheeks once more. It was a better look for him. "Courtney, wait—"

"I got this!" She shot him one last smile before she darted for the elevator.

Chapter Twenty-Three

The office chair squeaked as Arianne Reynolds flopped into it and stared in mute, dry boredom at the camera on her desk. Today was the day. There hadn't been enough clientele over the last few weeks, and technically, while they did have to remain open for business hours… she would be locking the doors on Eternal Bride Photography for the last time in about an hour. They'd come back at the end of the week with a U-Haul and the truck Zoey promised her brother would loan her and move the desk and bigger items out of the office space.

The business—*her* business—had failed.

Her mouth twitched. She shook her head, blurred and bitter. She was fine. Really.

A knock sounded at her office door.

She jerked, scrubbing at the burning in her eyes as she huffed a breath into her hands. The sharp scent was unmistakable, but only if someone knew to look for it. She could get away with it. Nobody had to know. The heavy glass bottle was still under her desk.

"Come in." She fought to keep the slur out of her voice.

The door creaked open, showing Zoey's plump features and sympathetic expression. "Hey," she said, in the tone of voice reserved for mothers addressing sniffling children with broken bicycles and skinned knees. "You okay?"

Arianne seized the camera from her desk as an excuse to pretend to be occupied. "Fine. Anyone walk in? Call-ins?"

"No." Zoey still spoke in that same dripping tone. More, she had the gall to walk farther into Arianne's office. To approach the desk.

The closer she came, the sharper Arianne focused on the digital screen as she scrolled through the memories of photo shoots past. The camera was heavy in her grip, but responsive to even her slightest touch. She did have those magic fingers, as she'd bragged once upon a first date. Her breath shortened as Zoey dragged a chair over to her desk.

"Sweetie…" She lowered her head, trying to catch Arianne's eye.

"Don't wanna talk about it, Zoey," Arianne growled, swiping through photos. She didn't want to talk about her pending unemployment, let alone poke at the carcass of her love life. There would be no attempted emotional autopsy. She was sealing the leftovers in a concrete casket.

It was easier, this way. Safer. All she had to do was acknowledge, once and for all, that this was the way things were and would always be. If you put up enough walls, you could forget there was ever anything else. Every time she pulled them down, there came a reason—sometimes a good reason, sometimes a weak one, but *always* a reason—to go building them right the hell back up and adding watchtowers at the top for extra measure. Garrett had proved that, no matter how much she wanted it to be wrong.

No matter how much.

"Ari… c'mon. He'll call." In Arianne's peripherals, Zoey was trying to smile. A soft, encouraging, "chin up" token of friendship.

"Who's 'he?'" Her voice was as thin as cheese wire. Photos were a blur before her fingers as Arianne jabbed at the screen.

"Garr—"

The camera hit the desk.

Vodka was heavy on her breath as she rounded on her wide-eyed intern, who reeled back in her chair. Arianne didn't say a word. She just stared her down, fighting to keep the trembling to her hands and keep the anger in her gaze from melting into pained tears.

"S-sorry…" Zoey stammered, wilting beneath the yoke of her fury.

"Okay, I've seen enough," said an accented voice at the office door.

Arianne jerked her head over, brown hair flopping like snakes, at the altogether-too-pretty Sierra standing in the doorway with her arms crossed and a no-nonsense look that spoke of more trouble than Arianne was willing to deal with.

"Come on. Both of you." Sierra jerked her head behind her. "We're closing up shop early, going out, getting cheesecake, and you are going to deal with your shit."

"I'm dealing with it." Arianne planted her elbows on the desk and picked up the camera once more.

Sierra stalked forward and dipped out of sight in a flash of midnight hair before she re-emerged, dragging an empty bottle of vodka out from under the desk. She stared at the bottle for seconds of silence.

Arianne gazed back, sullen and surly, her mouth curled in a sour snarl.

"By getting trashed at work? Yeah. Real professional," said Sierra.

Arianne smacked her lips. "Fine. Y'r fired."

Sierra scoffed. "Uh-huh. C'mon, *cadela*. Get your ass out of that chair. We're going home."

"Nope." Arianne shook her head until the office swam in her vision and the world tilted under her.

The camera clattered to the desk once more as she half-slumped across it, bracing herself with one arm and knocking a small calendar over.

Sucking deep breaths, she slowed her shaking, but maintained the action with fervor. "I'm dealing with it. My way. And I'm fine. So, shush."

"Girl, you'd better—"

"I'd better *what*, Sierra?" Her head snapped up so fiercely her neck popped. Tears, unbidden, flooded Arianne's vision. "I'd better 'deal with it?' I'd better spill out all the gushy shit and get all emotional? Like Zoey? Or like *him*? I won't do it. It's bullshit. Dating, guys, going out on a goddamn limb—it's *bullshit,* all right? I never should have tried it. I never should have trusted him. I just—if I'm into someone, and they're into me, then I'm just gonna bed 'em and kick 'em out. Scratch an itch. That's all I need." She hiccupped, shaking her head as she clawed at her eyes and tore away the unbidden weaknesses dripping down her cheeks. "'s all I'll ever need."

Someone placed a hand on her upper arm. She couldn't see through the haze and her blurry vision, but Sierra's voice sounded by her ear. "C'mon, just…talk it out, okay? You're already doing it. Venting is good for the soul. We're here for you." Every platitude from her was a dynamite blast to the walls Arianne cowered behind. This was what friends did. "C'mon. Open up. I know it hurts."

"I don't wanna." She whimpered. "It's—it's total…it's crap, okay? I mean, I finally think that maybe I've fallen in l—" The word gagged her.

She stared straight ahead, caught in a fugue state. She never said that. Not like that. Sure, the word would slip out every now and then, in certain cases. When she was excited, and a friend surprised her. When she had the kind of sex that left her hair an explosion and her toes curled and fingers gripping the mattress. Those weren't this. She didn't say that word like that.

But she knew, as soon as she breathed, it had been said without speaking. Her realization had been an admission, recorded in the universe and ringing through every tense vibration in the air, forever and irreversibly permanent. Even if she never saw him again, even if she scrubbed every instance of their interaction from her life and she drank herself comatose, the fact would remain and would always remain.

She, once upon a time, was in love with Garrett Reid, professional rebound dater.

She swallowed against the pain and wiped her nose with the back of one hand. Her shoulders shook, and she stared at the ceiling in a wordless prayer.

Zoey, to her relief, gave her the kind of selfless, supportive smile that spoke of true friendship, beyond the fear of professional obligation or castigation.

In the doorway, Sierra's voice was surprised, but firm. "Now's not a good time. We're closed."

Arianne blinked, looking through the open door.

Her assistant blocked the entrance to someone short and blonde.

Then the voice came through. "Let me in, okay? Like, I have to talk with her."

Arianne's train of thought didn't derail so much as it skidded across tracks made of plastic explosive while carrying eighty tons of nitroglycerin and pin-less hand grenades.

Sierra stepped aside, and the miniature blonde bitch who had single-handedly ruined Arianne's life stood in the doorway.

Her mouth flapped, wordless. Courtney was...there. After teaming up with the worst man in her life and ripping away the best thing she had going for her. As if Courtney didn't expect to have her head put through a window. In those big blue eyes was a possessive, manic energy. That part was familiar. That look was burned into Arianne's mind. Behind it, though, was something else. Something different. Hope. Pain. Maybe just the unexpected fact there was actual depth, no matter how shallow.

"What would it take," said Courtney, exhaling through her as-yet-unbroken button nose, "for you to forgive him?"

Arianne's jaw dropped. "Did he send you?" Her breath came in short, incredulous gasps. "Are you serious right now?"

"A hundred and ten percent." Courtney wasn't smiling. "For real. What would it take for you to forgive him?"

"I... Shit, like I have any idea?" she blustered. "He was *paid* to *date me*. Everything he'd said, everything he'd done, all of it was a lie! You don't forgive guys like that. You dump them in the ditch and move on with your life." She looked to Zoey, to Sierra, desperate for concurring opinions.

Courtney crossed her arms. "He did the same thing to me, okay? My best friend paid him." Her lips drew together into a sour pout. "He was sweet. Charming. Treated me like a total princess. Everything he said was, like, totally smooth. Like, I thought I was dating a Disney prince in real life. He probably did the same thing to you, right?"

Arianne blinked. Rooster Jim's tavern came to mind. How he'd smiled. The ease with which he'd had an answer to her every barb. The look on his face when she shot down the lines with pinpoint accuracy because she'd known they were exactly that—lines. The look on his face when he answered again, truthfully, and skewered her expectations. Every time she'd caught him off-guard. Their laughter. Their chaos. Their messy, stupid, crazy, genuine experiences.

Courtney huffed in the face of her silence. "I came on too strong, okay? He was a good guy, and I didn't wanna let him go, and eventually he had to, like, *tear* himself away from me. Like…I got a teensy-weensy bit crazy." Her gaze slid to the side as she brushed her bangs aside, shielding her face at whatever phantom jury was pointing in condemnation. "I didn't wanna let go even when I found out he was being paid to date me, and he only told me that because he was *trying* to push me away."

Arianne's eyebrows shot up. "So he was trying to push me away?"

"No, dumbass." Courtney practically had to hop to slap Arianne's arm.

She stared down in frozen fury. First an insult, then a physical strike. It was like stealing someone's wedding dress then wearing it in front of them as they walked down the aisle—the sheer audacity of the act alone was the very factor ensuring its survival.

Regardless of the danger, Courtney continued flapping her bubblegum-pink lips. "He was going to tell you the truth because he loves you."

Arianne snorted. "I've heard enough." She grunted, grabbing the camera from her desk. Summoning looks were given to her co-workers and to Sierra in particular. "C'mon. We're still okay for cheesecake, right?" She took a step forward and nearly bowled over the yapping blonde chihuahua, who had—impressively—held her ground. Her voice was shrill, thumping against the growing ache between Arianne's temples.

"Garrett Reid is the best king of a man someone like you could ever hope to get, okay? And I am not gonna let you walk away and hurt him like this!"

Wordless, Arianne Reynolds reached down with one hand, gathered a handful of whatever tree-ring melange of brand name layers Courtney wore, and hefted the harpy off her feet. Her shoulder burned. Her arm ached. But she lifted the woman a foot into the air and stared her down. "Shut. Up."

Courtney's feet dangled as her hands clutched at Arianne's wrist. Her manicured nails dug into the skin. Her nostrils flared as she gasped for breath. "Do you mind, you Amazon bitch? This is cashmere! You'll stretch it!"

"Ari." Sierra deliberately stepped around and into her view, a grave look on her face. "After the *legalities* of *the past week*, I really don't think you want to add an assault charge, do you?"

The truth tasted like ash and ass.

Finally, she dropped the pint-sized headache to the carpet. "Doesn't much matter now, does it? Since we're officially out of business and shit." She stood by the door, gesturing with fanged and bureaucratic manner. "Sorry that you're too late for your big day and all. This is...*was*...a wedding photography studio, after all. Unfortunately, we've had to close down, but I'm sure you and Garrett will find someone else just as capable and shitty to capture your memories."

Courtney brushed down her front before flipping her salon dye job. "What do you mean?" Her tone was unnervingly professional. It nearly made Arianne neglect the threat of an assault charge.

"I mean, we went under," she snapped. "We're closed. *Finito*. You wanna rub it in some more? We're out of jobs because people don't need wedding photographers because they aren't getting married. Love is dead and life is pointless. Congratulations. Now get the hell out." She gave her the most acidic glare she could muster, fists clenched at her sides. Maybe it was ruined because she was swaying on the spot from the heavy buzz she had going. Alcohol and rage did not subtlety make.

The little blonde nightmare crossed her arms under her chest. Worse, she was *still standing there*. "What if I bought it?"

"You mean died?" Arianne scoffed, deliberately misinterpreting her words. "Go for it. I hear huffing oven fumes is the classic way to go."

"Like, first of all—poor taste, bitch." Courtney glared up at her. "Second of all, I meant..." She trailed off, frowning, before fishing in her oversized purse. Out came an eyesore of a familiar business card. "...Eternal Bride Photography. What if I, like, bought out the company from you? Kept you going. Paid for you. Like, same jobs, same salary, everything. I totally wouldn't change a thing."

Arianne blinked as though her words were a strobe light held six inches from her face. "What?" She squinted at her. Frowned. Her mind churned behind the vodka fog. "Why?"

"Because you mean everything to him, okay?" Courtney snapped. "And if buying your stupid company and helping you keep your job will make him happy, then, like, I'm gonna buy your stupid company. I gotta make it up to him."

Arianne could finally see the wires in Courtney's perky brain short-circuiting. "Can you even afford it?" She thought back on the loan that had taken a hammer to her financial kneecaps.

Courtney responded by preening her hair back and lifting a single eyebrow. "Like, do you even have to *ask*?"

Arianne seethed. She'd never understood where people like that ever got their obscene amounts of money, but it always pissed her off on principle. "Okay. I'm gonna break this down using very small words." She snarled, taking a single, threatening step forward. "a.) I don't like wedding photography. It's cheap. It's stupid. There's no art to it. I only started this business to pay my bills and because I thought the market demand would hold up for it. And, most importantly, b.) I will never work for you, you goddamn psycho bitch."

The silence pulsated in the room like a gestating demon. When it broke, it knocked the wind out of Arianne's lungs like she'd crashed into a brick wall.

"I will," said Sierra.

Every set of eyes turned to look at her.

Sierra shrugged, but the look in her eyes was pure Machiavellian pragmatism. "The job market is awful, Ari. I've been your assistant for ages. I know how to take wedding photos. If you don't want to sell to her, then sell to me. Zoey and I will run the business. You can work for me, if that's what it takes." She gave her a half-smile, regret tinging every inch. "Like you said…you never liked doing it anyway."

Courtney nodded, a satisfied look crossing her Barbie-doll features as she glanced back to her. "See?"

"Sierra…" Arianne's throat bobbed. Her head was swimming. She was sixty miles underwater and had no conceivable clue which way was up. She hated her for saying it, but she couldn't blame her. The fact that Sierra was even offering to carry on the biggest legacy she'd ever had in her art, in some way, was a miracle—or, it would have been, if it didn't involve Arianne hating Sierra for kowtowing to the woman who had nuked her life. All she could manage was a feeble "Are you sure?"

Her assistant chuckled. "No. But whoever is with these things?"

Arianne turned to the one who'd been silent throughout the entire exchange. "Zoey?"

The intern buried her gaze and fumbled with her hands. She

mumbled something, too quiet and indecipherable to make out. Arianne could tell, deep in her gut, that whatever she was mumbling wasn't going to amount to a "no."

"Guess the only one out of a job today is me," she said, and the sigh that accompanied her words carried a fatigue that myths could be written on.

Digging into the pocket of her jeans, she tossed the keys to the office onto her desk. The clatter they made, to her ears, was heaven-shattering. Hell-breaking. She was stranded, alone, in every sense, with the world entire before her. No chance of going up. Too stubborn to go down. She was just…stranded.

"I'll have my lawyer-people come around and draw up a business contract or whatever it is they do." Courtney waved a hand dismissively. "But, like, I'm glad—"

"Courtney, just…" started Arianne, before she turned away. "…have a nice life."

There was no point telling Courtney to get out. This was her place now. If she wanted to buy Eternal Bride Photography because she thought it'd make Garrett happy, well, that was her prerogative. It didn't matter to Arianne anymore. The office, the past pictures she'd taken of happy couples in black and white…they were pieces of a sandy, salty hermit crab shell she was casting off.

She had outgrown it.

Wordless, she walked out and closed the door behind her.

There was no point looking back.

Chapter Twenty-Four

Garrett Reid had been out of the hospital for thirty days and had yet to smile once.

He'd called Arianne more times than he could count. Texted. E-mailed. When the radio silence had been too much, he'd knocked at her apartment door when she was most likely to be there. Stopped by her studio, only to be sharply—pitifully, but sharply—turned away by Sierra, because apparently it wasn't her studio anymore. It was Sierra's. And, somehow, for some bizarre reason, also Courtney's studio. He hadn't even tried to untangle the "how" and "why" behind that mess, even as he fought not to compare his desperation in trying to contact the love of his life to Courtney's insanity toward him.

There was a difference, dammit.

For God's sake, even the singing telegram hadn't worked. The girl had come back with electrified hair, a filthy scowl, and he'd lost his security deposit—a deposit he'd struggled to afford. Mr. Rebound, Inc. had collapsed. He'd killed it. David had spared him the tongue-lashing after he'd shown up at the front door in a neck brace but had still given him a solid "I told you so." Garrett had begged him for a lifeline. As such, he was due to start as David's assistant at CyberTek Industries the following Monday.

True, Garrett didn't know a damn thing about cyber security, but he was a fast learner.

He sure as hell couldn't go back to acting. He'd been paid to act for the last five years, and it had left him as empty and alone as an old beer bottle on an unmanned boat.

Which led him to the last reason why he hadn't smiled in a month. Of all the places he could have been—doorstep, photography studio, apartment, car, hospital—a crematorium was dead last.

Furthermore, even though the black marble floor beneath his shoes and bone-cream walls were functional over formal, he couldn't help but add a mental grumble. For a place where the dead were laid to rest, they could have spruced the place up a *little*. A warmer color palette, at least. Maybe some flowers or wreaths or some crap besides the single bouquet his sister, Emily, had ordered online. White roses, white lilies, plenty of greenery, all placed in a simple glass vase. It was the most present she could be, according to his mother.

Apparently, in order to ship out with the Peace Corps, they had to list Arnold Reid as deceased because "missing" wasn't an option, which then meant there was a paperwork hang-up to approve bereavement leave so she could fly home, and state law required the signatures of every family member to approve of cremation, and the Fiji office had been closed because of a tropical storm, and on and on and on, and somehow it seemed typical of the Reid family. Always making excuses. Always never quite good enough in the way people hoped.

Or, he supposed, staring at the burnished silver kiln wherein his father's bones would enter and where his father's ashes would be dumped out, *maybe this is good enough as it is*.

His mother's arm was around his shoulders. His arm was numb but remained dutifully in place around her side.

On the steel rollers before them laid what was essentially a cardboard box with clear tape around the seams. A simple end for a simple man.

The priest stood by, hands clasped. "Are there any words you wish to say prior to the cremation?" he offered.

Garrett waited for his mom to speak. Instead, he felt a pressure around his shoulders. Her arm. Her gaze, expectant, as she nodded a prompt at him.

He sucked his teeth as he regarded the last of his father.

"Well... bye, Dad," he said, his voice as hollow as the box. "Y'know... again."

It was a terrible example of an impromptu eulogy, and the memory of one only slightly better brought tears to his eyes. At least there, he'd been on a beach. At least here, though, he still had the privilege to be alongside a spectacular woman whom he loved. Just in a different way. It wasn't a perfect metaphor. But then, he wasn't a perfect person, so it fit.

"I remember when Arnold and I were dating," said Susan Kidman. "This was in the early eighties, you understand. He had the most spectacular mullet you'd ever seen. He was so proud of that thing. I'm pretty sure he used more hairspray on it than I used on my perm." Her smile was grim. Fond. "He swore he'd have it for the rest of his life. I used to joke that he'd never love else anything as much. The next time I saw him, he was bald as an egg. He hadn't only taken clippers to it, he'd coated his whole head in shaving cream and shaved it. You could see your reflection in his scalp. I laughed until I fell over. I couldn't see. Just—just tears, for days. Then, next thing I know, he's down on one knee, like he's going to propose."

She blinked fiercely, her expression wilting toward the wistful. "He had a black briefcase across his leg, and he tells me to open it. Inside, instead of fabric or plastic or whatever they'd use, he's lined the entire briefcase with his own mullet shavings…and on top was a little velvet box with a ring in it."

Garrett stared at her.

"He told me he needed me in his life more than any mullet, and he would give up anything and everything he had to for it to come true." She stared at the ceiling, laughing even as glittering trails made their way down her cheeks. "Your father was the cheesiest man I ever had the pleasure of falling in love with."

He gazed away, to the cardboard box resting on the steel rollers. A tiny scoff pulsed from his lips. "He made you happy, didn't he?"

"Well, not always," relented his mother, as she nodded in matronly wisdom. "But that's not how love works. It's an anxious state of concern about the other's well-being, and that was your father's life for both of us."

"Sounds depressing," he said. "Shouldn't love be happier than that?"

"It is, at times," she said. "You get the honeymoon phase, but then you get these little nuggets here and there that remind you that life with him—even the ugly parts, the lonely parts—they're all so, so much better than life without him."

Garrett heaved a sigh, regarding the box. Inside was his progenitor. More importantly, inside was the man his mother had loved through thick and thin. Separated by a thin wall of cardboard and fifteen years underwater was all that remained of the person to whom she had devoted her heart and her life.

"When was the last time he told you he loved you?" he asked, glancing over to his mother.

She blinked, taken aback, but a watery smile soon tugged across her features. "Right before he took his boat out for the last time. He said it every time he went out on the water. Never missed it, not once. Not when we fought. Not any time."

He chuckled, shaking his head. "Can't believe he proposed with his own mullet."

She bobbed her eyebrows, her smile tinging toward the cheeky.

"Honey, you should have seen the tattoo I was going to get before he made me a respectable woman."

"*Mom*." He cringed like he was fifteen again as they laughed together. It was a teary, awkward, hushed kind of laughter that bowed their heads together. They stood there, in each other's arms, before she sorted through the purse resting against her hip and plucked tissues for them both.

"Are you ready, kiddo?"

He sighed. "Yeah. I'm ready, Mom."

The priest nodded and pressed a single button on a sleek chrome console. The hatch in the wall slid open as the steel rollers turned in somber duty, carrying their cargo into the kiln before the hatch closed and a soft electric hum signaled the beginning of the end. Arnold Reid was gone, and in his place stood Garrett Reid, who could only swallow and swear by every iota of who he was that he wouldn't drop the ball as hard as his father. He'd sworn it before, but it had been entirely for the cause of Mr. Rebound and the string of healed hearts he'd left in his romantic wake.

Now, he swore it for the sake of Garrett Reid and his own happiness.

"Mom." He turned to his mother and laid out the words, tremulous and tender, and for the first time in thirty days, he couldn't keep a smile off his face—bittersweet, pained, and afraid, but a smile. "I've met a girl."

She blinked the tears away, looking up at him in confusion. "You have?"

He took a deep breath. "I'm…I'm in love, Mom. And I think she might feel the same way back, but… I screwed up. Bad. Now I have no idea what to do to fix it. She won't talk to me."

To his shock, his mother embraced him on the spot. Her voice was strong in his ear. "Forgive yourself, first. Then do everything you can to show her how you feel and wait."

His arms dropped to his sides. "It's not that simple, surely?"

She scoffed, holding him at arms' length and eyeing him with the affectionate-yet-critical kind of gaze only mothers could do. As if finding the biggest problem in his approach, she combed his bangs with her fingers, smoothing his hair into a fashion appropriate in her expert opinion.

"Forgiveness is a highly underrated phenomenon, but it's all you can do for someone you love," she said. "When we realized your father wasn't coming home, I forgave him that same night. I think it took you a lot longer."

His mouth closed as he fought the urge to look back at the door to the kiln.

Her lips folded inward, wan and wise, as she squeezed his shoulders between both hands and released him.

"Father Inneman?" She spoke to the priest, who lifted a wizened head in attention. "Can you show me the area where the ashes will be collected? I, um—I'd like to confirm the model of urn." She flashed Garrett a dripping wink.

He knew what she was doing.

"Of course, Mrs. Kidman," said the priest, gesturing to a heavy white door at the end of the room.

Their footsteps marked their silence as Garrett stood by the irreverent conveyor belt, staring at the wall wherein his father was combusting at eight hundred degrees. Something inside him quivered, and welled up, and drained out from beneath every emotional and mental scar he'd kept covered.

"I forgive you, Dad." The words had never felt so foreign and yet so natural. He had to try again. He had to take the next step. "I…" Air filling his lungs in stark contrast to the water that had filled his father's. "I love you, Dad." Again, the soft feeling of truth closed over his heart like a glove.

He stood there, staring at the door to the kiln, until Father Inneman and his mother returned. She met Garrett's eyes with an expectant question. When he smiled back, free and light, she beamed in pride and wrapped her arms around him.

"Go get her," she whispered in his ear.

He shook his head. "You and Dad need me here."

She waved a hand in dismissal. "Dad's going into a vase then next to his fishing trophies. I'm fine. You go get that girl. Then, when everything's dandy, you bring her home to meet me, you understand me? No more of this 'holidays and anniversaries' crap. A real family dinner." Behind the glistening eyes was a fire he hadn't seen in his mother in years.

He had to admit, it sounded nice. "When she's ready."

"That's my boy." She chuckled, nodding to the exit behind him. "Go on. Go."

He squared his shoulders. Even despite everything, he had one last try in him. "Already gone."

Chapter Twenty-Five

The lighting in the Cheesecake Factory was a perfect slap in the face to Arianne's eyes, but the promise of future taste-bud-orgasms in the form of a solid slice of Godiva chocolate cheesecake was too good to pass up. It wasn't like she was watching her figure anymore anyway. Even if her leggings did cling too tightly lately, or if her chest stretched her shirts more than usual. At least she'd stopped getting blackout drunk. Constantly fending off the attention of the man who had shattered her, for thirty days straight, tended to drive a girl to the bottle.

Besides, today was supposed to be celebratory.

Her soul was splayed out in black and white and digital print across the tabletop, glossy pictures exposed to the eyes of the man who represented everything she wanted. Rick Miller of Eyeshot Photography was a bony man with fingers like spider legs, a ginger ponytail tugged back, and the sort of wispy beard-attempts that looked more like face pubes than an actual beard. Clearly, he couldn't grow a good goatee. But there was a sharp, burning intelligence behind his red-rimmed eyes, as he poured over her portfolio one last time.

"Glad you applied," he said. He seemed to speak only in sentence fragments, as if he were dissatisfied with words as a whole. "Deserved this win. Shots like these… I'm excited to see what you can do."

Her cheeks burned. Garrett said it brought out her freckles. It was true. "Thank you for the chance." The bustle and clatter of other customers around fought to steal her attention. "I, uh… I never thought I'd actually win."

"Talent shines through." He grunted as he perused her portfolio once more. "You were the best candidate. End of story."

The photography residency offered by Eyeshot Photography was a dream. A five-year commitment with an annual living allowance of forty-grand, plus another five-grand as a material grant—all to do what she'd always wanted to do. All to be able to pour herself out through a camera lens. It had been weeks of work to prepare and submit the portfolio. As much as she hated to admit it, she did owe her success—in a small, grit-her-teeth-and-hate-the-words kind of way—to Courtney. Selling her ownership of Eternal Bride Photography had given Arianne a shockingly large financial cushion to cry into. Enough to support her for months. Enough to give her peace of mind, so she could put on her big-girl panties and swing for the fence. Now, here she was, rounding the bases and heading for a bright, shiny home plate.

She couldn't keep a bitter smile off her face. *If you build it, they will come.*

"I'm a fan of this shot." He spun a print around by his fingertips and slid it toward her. "Tell me what inspired you here."

She knew it immediately. A grayscale photo of a turkey vulture flying low near a child's playground. Her heart pounded. Somehow, she was launched back in time. A different place. A photo that wasn't hers. A grayscale crack in the sidewalk, enlarged and on display in a gallery, titled *Belief.* She hadn't attached a title to hers. None of them had titles.

"It, uh…" She swallowed. Her time to shine. "I took this on a road trip. It was at a rest stop. I'd come from the most insane wedding reception I'd ever been to, and I'd just gotten off the phone with this guy I—"

Her throat closed. She cleared it, harsh, coughing into her elbow. "Sorry."

"Take your time." He laced his fingers.

She stared down at the print. Maybe it had been an omen at the time, even if she knew she never would have heeded it. "I felt inspired. Thinking about life, love, death. The future. All those big things. And I saw the shot, and—I had to take it."

He kept watching her. "Do you care what people see in your photos?"

She shook her head. Firm. Adamant. "No." She'd never cared what people had seen when they looked. They'd see what they wanted to see, regardless of what she presented. "I care about how they feel when they see them. How my photos make them feel."

Rick smiled, thin-lipped. "Knew I made the right choice." His gaze fell to the portfolio again, selecting another photo. "And this? It's a bit different."

The filter was acidic. Smoky. Like polluted neon fog. She'd spent three days fiddling with the digital filters on this shot alone, but she was damn proud of how it had turned out. Her skin was electric, paled to luminescence. The camo pattern of her thong was deep, vibrant.

The bruise on each ass cheek was a familiar miasma of ugly colors.

"Who was the model?" he asked.

She raised a hand.

He grunted. Examined the shot again. "Make-up or actual bruises?"

"They're real, trust me." She resisted the urge to shift in her seat. "I was sore for days. Paintball."

"Important to suffer for your art." He chuckled. "Good composition. Fantastic lighting."

With a nod of satisfaction, he withdrew the print and placed it back in the manila folder. "You start tomorrow." He handed her a small printout. "This address. Bring all your gear. Start with paperwork, stuff like that. Fill out forms. Get your accounts set up. Nine AM, sharp."

Her phone buzzed. A curse of a distraction. One new email. She could have ignored it "Sorry," she mumbled. "One sec."

"Not a problem." His voice was just monotone enough for her to doubt whether it was true. Quick. She'd be quick. It was probably nothing.

Her gaze swept over the screen, taking in the words with the manic energy of an addict seizing a fix after a drought. Her insides quivered. Her throat bobbed.

Arianne,

This is my last email to you. I won't say I'm sorry for trying to get in touch with you so many times over the last month. I will apologize, however, for the singing telegram. You didn't have to tase her, but I know Karma is a bitch, and I know I vicariously had it coming. It's clear now that you don't want anything to do with me, and as much as it sucks, I will respect that. It's going to hurt, because I... well, we both know how I feel about you, and I'm pretty sure you feel the same. Or maybe you did, once, but it's changed by now. Either way, I'll respect your boundaries, and I will miss you terribly.

I hope I haven't hurt you beyond repair. Regardless, I know I did hurt you, and I will never stop being sorry.
Yours,
Garrett

She stared at the screen as the words clicked into place. That…was it. He was done. She'd closed the door on them both, and he'd pounded his knuckles bloody, but here, now, he was the one to lock it. Here, now, was the proof he was walking away without looking back.

The email was the nail in the coffin. She wasn't losing him. She'd *lost* him.

"Son of a bitch…" she breathed. Her soul was in a vise.

"Something the matter?" Rick's voice cut in through the panic, an auditory yank on the leash to pull her back.

"Huh?" She stuffed her phone back into her purse. "No, no. Everything's—" Her tongue seized.

The email meant nothing.

It meant *nothing*.

Without pausing, Rick rose, buttoning the single remaining button on his corduroy jacket. She stood, shaking his hand. His grip was brittle. Weak. Her hand swallowed his.

"One last question," he said, mid-shake. "What's your muse?" His eyes glinted. She couldn't read him for the life of her. Not like she could with Garrett.

She blinked. "Sorry?"

"Your muse. Where do you get your inspiration? A state of mind? Food? Drink? Person? Something more abstract?" A hint of something unreadable tugged at his lips. "Curious."

Her portfolio flashed across her mind's eye. Shots of laughter. Feelings rushing and coalescing and churning, and suddenly everything was obvious. How her art had changed. Why it had. Who had triggered it.

Her words failed her.

He grunted. "Don't wanna jinx it? That's cool. However you need. This isn't an easy residency. You'll want to keep your muse on hand."

Rick left her standing, alone, in the hustle and bustle of the Cheesecake Factory. The world was still spinning and her muse was unmasked, and she couldn't think and she couldn't breathe, and she wanted it—she wanted *him*—more than she wanted air. She wanted the man who would smile at her without lying.

The man who could give her a single glance through those piercing blue eyes and see past all her cocky defensive bullshit and love her anyway.

The man who would say "no" to her because he wanted the best, purest outcome, not because he was playing a game neither of them could win.

The man who hadn't once, not *once*, said a single goddamn thing about the fact that she was taller than him.

The man she could laugh with.

The man she could be herself with.

She shook her head. With every second came a yearning, building and capitalizing and exploding upon itself, exponentially at a time, as the jarring truth ripped through every last piece and particle of her and obliterated the cracked and shuddering walls she'd put up. She was exposed, and raw, and she couldn't stand to be anywhere else but the one place she needed to be.

If that meant going elbow-deep in shit for a phone call, then she'd do it.

She had to find Garrett Tiberius Reid and tell him the truth.

~ * ~

Arianne Reynolds jerked her car into parking gear outside a modest bachelor pad she'd never seen before and stared at the front door. The car in the driveway was immediately familiar. So was the man dressed to the nines and strolling toward the driver's seat, keys in one hand and looking at her car in confusion.

Here went nothing.

The car door closing behind her was the suburban equivalent of a fight bell ringing out the beginning of the bout as she took a step forward and promptly tripped over the curb.

"*Shit*—" She gasped and staggered across the grass, struggling to stay upright. Clearing her throat, she tossed her hair back out of her face and smoothed down her front.

"Garrett," she said, too loud, before suddenly she was standing before him.

His eyes were level to her lips. He stared, for just a touch too long, and she saw the effort it took him to lift his gaze to hers. The confusion. The awkwardness. The shock.

The pain.

"Arianne?" He scrambled for a response. "Um—geez, it's— what brings you out here? You look like you just got out of an interview."

She gulped the cool night air as her gaze devoured every inch of his face. He was refined. Trimmed. His goatee had come back in.

"I could say the same thing of you." She crossed her arms. "You're awfully dressed up."

His mouth twisted into something resembling a grimace. "Well, Arianne, if you must know...I'm meeting someone."

The words hit like hammers.

Arianne nodded, numb reactions to the revelation as she fought to keep her composure. She'd come to him. She'd sought him out. In the face of all the chances he'd taken on her, she was taking the chance this time.

All she needed was for him to return the favor.

"Stand her up."

His head tilted to the side. "Pardon?"

"You heard me." Her hands trembled at her sides. He was steady as a rock, unmoving and immutable, and it took everything she had not to cling to him to stop the earthquake that was liquefying her insides. "I don't know who she is but stand her up."

She saw the flicker in his eyes. The flashes of confusion, burning their way toward indignation and hardening into resentment.

"You don't really have a right to ask me to do that," he said. "You show up in my driveway after giving me the coldest shoulder this side of the goddamn *Arctic,* and expect me to just…just what? Go out on a limb?"

"Yes." The rising lump in her throat almost cut off her words. "Because that's exactly what I'm doing by being here. Because you're already so goddamn *good* at it, and because it is really, *really* scary dangling out here on the edge of this metaphorical tree branch on my own, okay?"

A sort of gut-wrenching, ecstatic terror erupted in his face. She knew it well. The same feeling was sending liquid lightning through her veins.

He opened his mouth. "Arianne, I can't—"

Screw it all.

She pressed her lips, her body, her soul and all that she had to offer—hopes, dreams, chocolate-cheesecake-breath, insecurities, all of it—into the kiss. Her eyes closed. The light scratchy feeling of his goatee tingled against her mouth. Her hands trembled as they cupped his cheeks. The kiss stretched out, and in, between them and beyond them, until her foot floated upward in the universally known "pop" sign, and she fought against a giddy smile until her cheeks ached.

Ruing every particle of air between them, she relaxed her lips from his until they stood again as separate people. She dared to open her eyes.

His chest heaved, sucking gulps of air as though he were drowning on the spot. He wouldn't look away from her. "Arianne, I'm sorry," he said. The words kicked out of him in bursts, in gasps. "I'm sorry I was paid to date you. I never—God, I never imagined doing what I do. I mean—this—all of this—" He gestured to himself. "All this 'Mr. Rebound' bullshit—that's all it's been. All it's ever been. I've been a walking talking relationship placebo for women for years, and I can't take it anymore, and I'm sorry I took money to date you."

It took everything she had to keep her mouth shut. Everything she had to bite back on the words.

He trembled, head to toe, looking as terrified as she felt. "Arianne—there's something I have to tell you."

"I love you," she said. The words burst out, ignoring her best efforts, trembling and meek and truthful in the way she'd never been able to be with anyone else.

All at once, his shoulders slumped. "How'd you know?" he asked with a light scoff. "Kind of takes the 'oomph' out of the big reveal."

She exhaled. "No, dumbass," she said. "*I love you.*"

It took her several seconds before his own words—and the sentiment between the lines—finally registered. His hand covered hers. His eyes widened. A smile that could have stood as its own separate sun in their dark corner of the driveway burned across his face. "Wait," he stammered. "You—"

"Yeah..." She nodded faster as he lit up. It wasn't just her. It was them. They were an "us." "I—and you—"

"Love you too." He nodded as a manic energy swept between them both. "Yeah. Yes!"

To her giddy delight, he wrapped his arms around her hips and heaved her off the ground, twirling on the spot with her legs dangling in the air. She yelped in panic and delight, bracing her hands on his shoulders as she fought to keep her balance and the world spun in a dizzying array of streetlights and happiness. She staggered when her feet hit the pavement once more, and she swallowed hard, willing the alcohol and dessert to stay down.

"For the record," she giggled, poking his chest with a long finger. "I am aware I have been drinking tonight. Not a lot, but I have. But that does not mean"— she drilled him with her gaze, pressing her forehead to his in affection, drinking in the touch of his skin— "that anything I have said is untrue. I had to get rid of my inhibitions to be this honest. Also, Courtney told me where you lived."

He laughed. "Geez...you went to *her* to get my address? You really *do* love me."

"Damn straight." Arianne smiled at the sight of Garrett's forehead melting into an array of delighted, almost pained lines as something spread inside her. She didn't need her walls up anymore. This was good. They were good. She jabbed at his chest again. "What took you so long to say it to me, punk?"

He responded with an eye roll. "Oh, come on. The guy always says it first. What, do you expect me to adhere to *every* convention?"

She shook her head in disbelief and swooped down for another kiss, only to collide lip first with Garrett's finger as he pulled his vibrating cell phone from his pocket.

"One sec," he said, tapping at the phone. "Hey. You're on speaker."

"Garrett?" said a woman's voice. "Where are you? Nathan and I are waiting. You should've been here by now. We're gonna cut the cake without you, I swear."

"Sorry, Olivia," he said. Arianne gave him a look of strangled patience which he defied with a giddy, lovestruck smile. "I know you wanna celebrate getting pregnant with your first and all, but I've got someone in my driveway who needs my attention." He covered the mouthpiece to the phone and mouthed the words "best friend."

Arianne lifted an eyebrow before Garrett pointed to his finger and mimed "married."

That was enough invitation for her.

"Hey, Olivia." She leaned down to the mouthpiece with a devilish grin. "This is Arianne. Garrett's probably told you about me. If he hasn't, I need to kick his ass."

The squeal from the phone was answer enough, even if Olivia's wild "go go go" and sudden termination of the call hadn't sufficed.

He pocketed his phone and snickered. "Sorry. Had to."

"You're frigging ridiculous," Arianne said.

"You're one to talk," He swept a finger up and down through the air, marking her appearance. "Declaring your love to me in my driveway in a well-cut secretary get-up? I didn't realize I was dreaming."

Arianne laughed, a loud, delighted, unrestrained sound that rang down the street and announced to every empty car and every star in the cloudless sky that tonight was the best night of her entire life. "Well, mission accomplished." She placed a hand on his chest, curling herself down to hold, with the effort of a goddess, an inch from her lips. "You were paid to rebound me. I think you did it."

"Good...because I am officially retired," he murmured. Gentle, he brushed her hair back over her ear. "I'm done. I'm yours. No more Mr. Rebound. Deal?"

She pursed her lips, pretending to mull it over. "Only if I'm yours."

He didn't hesitate. "Deal."

They laughed before closing the gap once more in a kiss that sent every thought from her head and her toes curling in her shoes.

"And, before you say anything," he said. His kisses drifted south, claiming the area at the base of her throat. "I am not out of a job just because I'm not Mr. Rebound anymore. I've got a holdover for the moment, and, well…I'm going back to school." He glanced up at her. "I'm gonna get a second degree. Become a marriage counselor. I think it's an appropriate redirection of skill."

She raised an eyebrow.

He laughed, and she closed her eyes as he continued to caress her neck, her collarbone, with his lips. "You won't have to carry me financially. I can support myself."

"I mean…" She struggled to get words out between the tingles erupting over her skin. "You could—ooh…"

Clearing her throat, she twisted away, loathe to relinquish an inch but doing so for sheer pragmatism. "You could do that, but school loans are kind of a monster bitch…so…maybe you blog?"

He blinked. "Blog?"

"Yeah." She shrugged. "Blog, or YouTube, or whatever. I mean…you gotta admit, 'Ask Mr. Rebound' is kind of an awesome idea. Monetize it, and you'd have a golden opportunity."

She swooped down, pecking his cheek. He was willing to put himself back through the hell of college so she wouldn't have to support him financially. More, he'd literally given up his job to be with her. A weird, gross, insane job, but still.

If she was the rough, he was the diamond in her.

"Maybe," he mused. "Maybe."

She nuzzled his neck, tracing the shape of his arm with her hand until, with a sudden tug and the sound of metallic jingling, she swiped the keys from him.

"Hey!" he blustered.

She sorted through them until she found what had to be a house key, holding it up for the dim golden streetlight to shine on. She smiled. "Come inside." There was no question in her voice.

Instead, he smiled right back, stealing a kiss from her neck as well as the keys from her grip. "I believe that's my line."

Acknowledgements

This story wouldn't exist without so many people, all helping out in ways I can't even begin to fathom. First and foremost, my absolutely spectacular wife. You've been there for me every step of the way, challenging me, talking me through plot holes and character blocks, laughing and encouraging and loving me all the way through it. I never could have done this without you (literally, you're the reason I switched to writing romance). I love you, darling of my heart.

Next, my family. Mum, Dad, Ashley, Adam—I'm where I am today because you taught me the importance of sticking to my guns. You recognized the talent in me and encouraged me to cultivate it and never doubted me. You cheered every success, no matter how small, and always followed up. Thank you all.

Jana, my agent—thank you so, so, so much for believing in me and this book and for remembering it from the first time around. This journey has been infinitely easier with you in my corner. Thank you from the bottom my heart.

Michelle and Katie, I cannot thank you both enough for believing in me and in this book enough to choose me as your mentee for Pitch Wars. The lessons you guys taught me and the encouragement you gave have stayed with me and will for the rest of my writing life.

I can't go without thanking my mentors and friends and peers at the DFW Writer's Workshop. You guys stuck a turbo engine on the butt of my writing career, stripped the brakes, and sent me hurtling forward light years when I would have been muddling around in the mire on my lonesome. Thank you to Dana, Alex, Brooke, Russell, Larry, Leslie, Stacey, Allen, Melissa, Rosemary, Candice, Kat, Brian, and Tex.

A special thanks also to everyone who cheered me on, checked in with me, praised me, encouraged me, critiqued me, or spurred me to follow my dreams. My friends, my co-writers, the ones who saw the first rough shapes of these characters and inspired me to push forward. Abby, for being my ultimate alpha reader and whose reactions give me life and being my literal lifetime friend and pseudo-sister. Wolfie and Candace for helping me craft Ari in the first place, way back in the WATWD days. Jesse, for being the best writing bro a bro could ask for and one of the best friends a guy could ever hope to find. KT, KC, Crane, the whole Earth Infinity crew for cheering me on.

Finally, thank you, the reader, for taking this trip with me. I hope I see you again soon.

About the Author

Taylor Koleber grew up in a forgotten corner of the world in Tasmania, Australia. A hopeless romantic with a goofy side, his stories often involve cute banter, wholesome romance, comedic shenanigans, and women finding their voices with emotionally intelligent men to support them. Newly married, one may blame his wife for the romance novels he now reads and writes voraciously. He and his family reside in Texas.

Taylor loves to hear from his readers. You can find and connect with him at the links below.

Facebook: https://www.facebook.com/taylor.koleber/
Instagram: https://www.instagram.com/austayk/
Twitter: https://twitter.com/AusTayK

~ * ~

Thank you for taking the time to read *Mr. Rebound* and hope you enjoyed it as much as we loved bringing it to you. If the story brought you pleasure, please tell your friends, and leave a review. Reviews support authors and ensure they continue to bring readers books to love and appreciate.

Now turn the page for a peek into *The Reluctant Princess*, the first book of a sexy contemporary romance series by M.C. Vaughan.

He's everything she needs in a muse—killer body, fun, adventure, and…a dad?

Nothing's more important to twenty-five-year-old goth girl Zara Kissette than making her bones in the art world. When a fire destroys her paintings, she needs two things to fulfill the art gallery's contract for multiple masterpieces—a quick hit of cash for supplies, and a way to rekindle her creativity. Otherwise, she can kiss her career-making gallery spot good-bye. So she reluctantly returns to a lucrative gig as a fantasy princess/face painter, where she meets a hot, divorced dad who could bring a spark to her life…or ruin everything.

Brendan Stewart is doing all he can to keep the world a soft and stable place for his beloved little girl. While his ex breezes in and out of their daughter's life, he's determined be her rock. The last thing he needs is another relationship to balance with the rest of his life. That is, until a gorgeous princess shows up to paint faces at his daughter's birthday party. Zara's open heart and distracting curves tempt him to lower his defenses, despite having been burned before.

Their romance is all cake and bubbles—and lots of steamy sex—until Zara betrays Brendan's trust for her shot at the gallery, and Brendan takes her career into his hands and, well, screws it up. If they can't make peace with each other's mistakes, they risk losing the one person who loves them for who they truly are.

Chapter One

February snow swirled around Zara Kissette as she hoofed it to her day-job in midtown Baltimore. She was happy. Well, happy*ish,* which was why she should have known the universe was about to punch her square in the lady junk.

That was the kind of relationship she had with the universe, after all.

As she approached the corner of Eager and Cathedral Streets, the crossing signal switched to red. Traffic whipped past as she sipped her frothy coffee from Zeke's. A total splurge, but she was rewarding herself for her recent Grade-A adulting.

She'd paid her bills, restocked her art supplies, and acted like a consummate professional during yesterday's meeting with the gallery owner. Honestly, it had gone *way* better than she expected. Afterward, she'd tucked her portfolio in her studio, avoided eye contact with intimidating blank canvas on her easel, and proceeded to check her email every five minutes for the notification about the show.

Her belly flipped. If she landed a coveted slot in the Schwarz Gallery's showcase, *that*, right there, would be her career's turning point. She'd have proof she was more than a disciplined hobbyist. Even better, gallery sales would mean she'd be able to honor the deal she'd made with her parents.

She stuck out her tongue to catch a fluffy snowflake. Her painter's block would melt away with a vote of confidence like that. Wouldn't it?

Her cell buzzed in her coat pocket. She fished it out and peered at its paint-speckled screen.

Eleanor.

Zara sighed and accepted the call. "Hey, listen, if this is about studio rent, I sent the check."

Not *quite* a lie. She'd slipped the late payment into a mailbox fifteen minutes ago.

"No, dear." Eleanor sighed. "There's been a fire."

Zara dropped her coffee and ran.

~ * ~

Fifteen minutes later, she trembled in her combat boots as she stood on the threshold of her studio. Acrid, plastic, smoky odors tightened her throat. In the far corner, Eleanor scribbled notes on a pad on a clipboard. The older woman's untamed silver hair strained away from her head in stark relief against the blackened walls.

"Eleanor," Zara said, "what happened?"

Her mentor lowered her clipboard. "I'm sorry, dear."

Zara stomped into what had been her beautiful, curated space. She turned like a lathe and drank in the destruction. Drenched watercolors peeled from the walls. A sketchbook, smeared and bloated, drowned in a puddle. Her palette bled colors across the worktable. Even the big blank canvas, now covered in soggy soot, was ruined.

The coffee she'd drunk threatened to back up on her, and she clapped a hand over her mouth. If she'd eaten breakfast, for sure she would have lost it too. "Was it the radiator? I told you it kicks out an obnoxious amount of heat."

"No." Eleanor pointed to the ceiling with the nib of her pen. "The marshal said it was an electrical fire that started there and burned through this corner. You can see where they punched additional holes to confirm nothing is smoldering. We're lucky the sprinkler system kept it contained."

"Lucky?" Zara's gaze focused on the charred mountain next to Eleanor. It had been the stack of the paintings she'd shown John Schwarz and her tidy collection of brushes, paints, and paper stock. A compact, 'eggs-in-one-basket' location.

"Poor choice of words on my part, Zara." Eleanor's glasses' chain swooped against her cheek as she cocked her head. "I meant it could have been worse."

"Nobody was hurt, right?"

Eleanor shook her head.

"Good." Zara shuffled through a puddle toward the remnants of her portfolio. She lifted the scorched corner of an abstract entitled *Gut Punch*. It broke off like a wilted petal.

Her heart crumpled.

Eleanor slipped her glasses from her nose and dropped them to her chest. "You've had a shock, but, as the building manager, I need to talk business for a moment. To inform you of the next steps."

Zara thumbed a rebellious lock of dark hair behind her ear. "Go for it. I'm already numb."

Eleanor nodded and sidled next to her. Zara sensed her mentor wanted to throw a hug around her, but she didn't want hugs. Hugs would squeeze tears from her, and she was determined to keep them sandbagged deep, deep down. Crying was pointless. It never restored what you loved.

Zara shifted away from Eleanor, who cleared her throat.

"Per the lease agreement, the Tower will coordinate and pay for repairs to the wiring, the wall, and the floor." Eleanor slapped the clipboard against her thigh. "I'll contact our insurers today to get the process started and hound them to rush it through so you're back in your space as soon as possible. You'll also need to file a claim through your business insurance provider to get a check to replace your materials."

"Got it." Zara sucked air between her teeth.

File a claim against the policy she'd allowed to lapse, because food had been more important than insurance.

Maybe her roommates could help lighten her mood. If not, they'd at least commiserate. She held her phone at arm's length and clicked off a few pictures texting them to her roommates along with the message, "*This is *my* day. #FML.*"

"Are those for your insurance company?"

"I guess?" Zara groaned. The reality of her financial situation was pretty grim. "It'll cost me at least a thousand dollars to replace my stuff."

A cacophony of text tones burst from her phone, signaling her roommates' replies hurtling back: a camera shutter click for Grier, a violin scale for Brooke, and applause for Melinda.

Zara glanced at the screen.

Wait!

An e-mail alert was mixed in with the emoji-riddled texts. Zara brought the phone closer to her face. The message was from John Schwarz, the gallery owner she'd met with yesterday.

She launched the e-mail, trying to scan the whole message at once, unable to read the words fast enough. Before her vision blurred and her breath hitched, she'd read good words like *invite*, and *participate*, and *contract*. She'd also caught bad words like *weeks*.

Her vision grayed at the edges, and she couldn't get enough air. Zara crouched and put her head between her knees before she fainted.

Eleanor pressed a broad hand to Zara's back. "Oh, Zara, it'll be okay. The fire is unfortunate, but you could use this. Make lemonade—"

Zara waved her phone over her head. "No pep talks. Will you read this e-mail to me?"

"Of course, dear." She plucked it from her Zara's grip and read aloud. "Dear Zara, thank you for coming to my gallery yesterday." Eleanor lowered the phone. "You met with John? Why didn't you tell me?"

Zara laced her fingers behind her head. "I didn't want to jinx it."

"I'm surprised he didn't mention it to me either, since I'd put in a good word about you." Eleanor raised an eyebrow and continued reading.

"I wish you hadn't done that. I want to earn this on my own."

"Don't be silly. My word may open a door, but it's your work that would earn you a place at the table. Now, shall I continue?"

No point in arguing with Eleanor. "Yes please."

"I liked what you had to say with respect to your vision and process. You could be a good fit for the gallery. We'd originally spoken about the New Artist Showcase in June, but it's your lucky day, kiddo, because an artist dropped out of our 'Phoenix' exhibition. We're hanging in five weeks—"

Zara barked a noise halfway between a sob and a laugh. A laub?

A saugh? Whatever it was, it hurt her throat.

"I'd love to include you. I'd need three pieces for the exhibit." Eleanor squatted next to Zara and nudged her. "What wonderful news! This will be your first gallery show, won't it?"

"It would be." She closed her eyes against her wrecked studio. "If my paintings weren't pulpy cinders."

Eleanor rubbed a small circle on the flat spot between Zara's shoulder blades. "You can't pass this up. You simply can't. It'll open dozens of industry doors for you."

"I know." She rose and raked her fingers through her hair. Deep breaths, like her Gramma had taught her when she had low-key panic attacks. This wasn't an open-ended invitation. If she turned it down, there was no guarantee Schwarz would extend it to a future show. She needed this for all kinds of reasons, but mostly to satisfy the deal she'd made with her parents.

"The fire was fate," Eleanor said. "The show is named 'Phoenix,' after all."

Canvas, stretchers, paint, and brushes—she'd have to replace it all, but her credit was wrecked. How would she earn enough money to replace her materials and paint three pieces in five weeks? Pieces worthy of a prestigious show?

Well, there's always...

A plan surfaced. A plan so perfect, so nauseating, it must be right.

No. Not that. Anything *but that.*

She sucked in a chest-bursting bucket of air.

Oh, God. Do I still have the dress?

There was one speedy way she could make the bundle of cash needed to replace her art supplies.

Chapter Two

Brendan Stewart rolled his neck. He was certain this meant surrendering his man card. Didn't matter. A dad's gotta do what a dad's gotta do.

"Okay, Pinterest, let's see what you've got."

He keyed in his daughter's favorite cartoon princess, "Ravenna from *Rising*" and "party ideas," hit return, and boom. His browser loaded with a billion different ways to make his daughter's fifth birthday party epic.

He slogged through the pictures. Elaborate cupcakes, costumes, party favors—all of which appeared to be homemade. What kind of free time must these people have? Even if he didn't have a monster deadline in a month, he'd refuse to spend hours of his free time on stuff like this. His days with Emma were already cut in half.

Nah, he'd buy as much as he could, stock up on the best Party City had to offer, and maybe go overboard on the balloons. Emma loved balloons almost as much as she loved candy.

Now, what the hell would a dozen little girls do during the festivities?

He scratched his neck and yawned.

Kid parties were the worst. There's the party for the kids, but the parents have to hang out because they happen to have kids the same age. Most of the parties Emma'd been invited to this year involved the same conversations—*Are you Emma's older brother? You're her father? You look so young!*

Because he was young. Most of these parents had a good ten years on him.

Maybe he'd hire some entertainment to take the strain off parental small talk. Like a magician maybe? Or a clown? He shivered. No. Definitely not a clown.

He opened another browser tab and searched up children's party entertainers in Baltimore. Hmmm…a face painter could be fun. The third link was for one who dressed like a princess. Bingo. As soon as the site loaded, Brendan widened his eyes. The face painter, Zara, could be Ravenna's twin. Authentic black-and-purple hair, glacier-blue eyes, porcelain skin, and Ravenna's signature scowl. Her austere website could use an overhaul, but never mind the site's design. This girl was *perfect*.

He had to hire her.

After he clicked the 'Contact' button, Brendan typed the details of the party and shot the note off into the ether. Not a bad night's work—he'd ordered the food, decided on the decorations, and had feelers out for the entertainment. Time for a beer.

Eh, who was he kidding? Time to get back to coding. Those queries weren't going to write themselves.

Before he could move from the couch to his workstation, his e-mail alert chimed. Zara had gotten back to him.

Hi there—

Got your note. I'm available. The charge is $200 for 90 minutes and includes a gallery of photos after. If you want to book me, Venmo a 50% deposit to the account below, and Ravenna will be there.

—Z

No hesitation. He paid the deposit and texted the link to her site to Jess.

Adorable! Jess wrote a few minutes later. *I'll kick in half.*

Huh. That was unexpectedly generous of his ex.

Thx, but I've got this.

When is it, again?

Sighing, he texted back. *2 weeks—Sunday, 2/11 @ 1:00 p.m.*

Jess notoriously double and triple-booked herself. But come on. This was her daughter's birthday. Unlike last year, for the sake of Emma, they'd agreed to co-host one party instead of separate events. They'd chosen this date *weeks* ago.

Pulsing dots. They disappeared, and reappeared. Aw, hell. This was no good. Whenever Jess started and stopped texts, she was about to drop a bomb on him.

Oh no! I thought it was the next weekend since that's closest to her actual birthday. I'm away for her party. ☹ Booked a sponsored blog post for a spa.

He clutched his phone and ground his teeth together. A fucking *spa?*

Jess, you *have* to come.

It kills me, but I can't. Signed a contract. Her private school's expensive, Brendan. I have to pay for it somehow.

His hurled his phone across the room, and it crashed into wall. Good. He wouldn't have to deal with the follow-up texts she'd shoot his way throughout the night.

Have to pay for it somehow...

What a load of horseshit. They split the cost fifty-fifty. Besides, she pulled down ten grand a month in ad revenues alone. He should know—he'd developed her site. This trip was probably a freebie rendezvous with her selfie-happy boyfriend. Couple of pictures of their feet on the boardwalk, hints she was dating someone new. Lather, rinse, repeat. This kind of nonsense was all Jess seemed to publish since Brendan put the legal clamp down on posts about their daughter.

He stood, shoved the chair away, then paced toward the stairs of his Federal Hill townhouse. He had to burn off some of this irritated energy. Damn, *Jess's me-first* attitude picked at every scab he had about their relationship.

Splitting up and disentangling from the fat cash cow her blog had become had meant sacrificing control over the work he chose to do. He'd given up independent contract work and had settled into a salaried job with benefits. Emma's EpiPens alone were a nightmare without decent insurance. He'd get back to freelancing someday, but for now, he needed a guaranteed flow of money to keep things steady for his daughter.

In his bedroom, he tackled the enormous jumble of laundry he'd meant to put away for the past week. He yanked a Ravenna towel free, almost toppling the whole pile of clean clothes to the floor. As he folded the towel in thirds, and in thirds again, he wished with everything he had that the princess would help Emma have a happy birthday.

Chapter Three

The cherry red Mercedes ferried Zara through the streets of Federal Hill, the centuries-old residential neighborhood hugging Baltimore's Inner Harbor. The car purred to a halt in front of the townhouse bearing the address of her gig.

"That," Zara said and jerked her thumb over her shoulder, "is a shit-ton of balloons with my face on it."

Grier cut the engine and peered through her roommate's foggy window. In the front garden, a vast bouquet of silvery orbs strained against their tethers. One more, and they'd probably uproot the black iron address plaque to which they were tied.

"Oh my God." Grier snickered. "It is. You resemble her even more in this new wave of party merchandise. Especially now you've streaked your hair with purple again. It's pretty amazing."

"What's amazing is how lucrative it is to be a dead ringer for Princess Ravenna of Everly."

"At least she's the most gothicky princess. Jewel tones suit you. Think about it—her costume could have been pastel pink."

Zara shivered. "Bite your tongue."

"What I enjoy most about shooting these parties," Grier said as she checked her chirping cell phone, "is your unparalleled acting skill. If I didn't know better, I'd say you actually like kids."

"I don't *not* like kids." Zara flipped the passenger sun visor down and checked her makeup in the mirror. "At worst, I'd say I'm neutral. They're fine when they aren't manic balls of soul-sucking neediness. It's the parents who get to me. I can't deal with the ooey-gooey 'kids are special snowflakes' mentality most of them have."

"Yes. Parents should tolerate their children, not celebrate them."

"That's not quite—"

"Oh." Grier glanced up from her phone. "Andrew texted to ask if I can help him with a wedding next weekend. I need more nuptials to round out my portfolio. Do we have any more kid parties, or is this the last gig before you re-hang up the face paints?"

"Yes, thank the sweet baby Jesus." Zara dabbed a tissue at the overdone eyeliner on her lower lids. "Five done, one to go. Two hellacious weekends, but a girl's gotta make that paper."

"I can't believe your parents wouldn't lend you money." Grier shoved her phone into her coat pocket.

"I didn't ask. They'd use it as an opportunity to highlight how stupid and chancy my career is. Except they'd call it a hobby and enroll me in community college business classes so I can help them run their inn when I retreat home."

"Solid vote of confidence there."

"Right?" Zara reapplied the dark berry stain on her lips. "Can I borrow your Bluetooth speaker thingamajig? I broke mine last weekend."

"Yep." Grier snatched the sleek blue amplifier from the depths of her backseat. "Gimme your phone so I can sync it up."

Zara handed her crackled black device to Grier.

"OMG, Zara, you can't have nice things." Grier poked icons until she found the Bluetooth settings. "What did you do? Use your phone as a hammer?"

"I walked into a spider web. Fear happened. Arms flailed and phones flew."

"One hundred percent correct reaction. So, do you want the normal play list?" Grier scrolled through the music on Zara's phone. "Or a different one?"

She squinted at the screen.

"Wait, why do you have Britney Spears's 'Work Bitch'? I thought you didn't listen to music recorded after 1997."

"It gets me pumped at the studio." Zara clunked open the passenger door. "Come on. I have to hurry and sneak in before the birthday girl arrives."

"I'm judging you so hard right now."

"Yeah, yeah." Zara butterflied her hand at Grier. "I've seen your Top 25. Abba, much?"

"Abba is crazy good. You're not sophisticated enough to appreciate their music."

Zara unfolded herself from the car and dropped the train of her jade gown to the ground. She twisted and tugged her leather breastplate down a few inches. The damned thing had shifted position on the way over and mashed her chest flat.

The costume must have been designed for a B-cup Ravenna, at

best. While Zara's cups runneth over. Still, she was grateful for the corset-like piece of armor. It did double-duty, desexualizing her a little, and providing a much-needed shield in the chilly February air. Stiff nipples at a children's party was *not* the look.

"Oh, much better." She sighed once she seated the breastplate where it belonged. "I bet I have bruises."

"What about me? I am such a pack mule whenever we do these parties." Grier wheeled a crate stuffed with Zara's face-painting supplies behind her. The speaker was in her other hand, and a chunky camera hung around her neck.

"I'd offer to help, but princesses don't hump huge crates around." The rear car door creaked when Zara popped it open.

She lifted Ravenna's double-sworded belt from the backseat and buckled it around her hips. Once the belt was in place, she sheathed the gleaming, thin-bladed prop replica swords.

"I would think swords are a bad idea at children's parties." Grier snapped a photo. "For obvious reasons."

"I'm a stickler for authenticity. If Princess Ravenna of Everly carries swords, then so must this humble impersonator."

"I worry you'll chop a kid's arm off if she tries to hug you."

"I wouldn't. Probably." Zara arched an eyebrow. "But I might spank a kid with the flat of the sword."

"Hey, do you have plans after dinner tonight?" Grier trailed Zara as they made their way along the tidy fieldstone path to the front door.

"Yeah." She yawned. "My studio's usable again. I'm hitting Pla-Za tonight to buy canvases and oil paints."

"Oils?"

"Yep. Didn't I tell you? I'm not feeling the watercolors anymore. They seem weak, and if I have learned anything, it's to…" Zara ticked off her fingers, "…one, get business insurance, and two, use more durable materials. I'd fucking sculpt in steel if I could weld."

"If you change your mind, Melinda and I are watching a bunch of movies that pass the Bechdel test."

"Thanks." Zara gathered her skirts before climbing the steps to the glossy red door. "But I need to concentrate on work."

Before she could ring the doorbell, the front door swung inward. A heart-stopping heap of dimpled handsome filled the doorway.

~ * ~

As soon as Brendan Stewart clapped eyes on the princess on his stoop, the iceberg of tension in his chest melted. It had drifted into place two weeks ago when his *OMG-so-busy-traveling-meetings-meetings-meetings* ex-wife, Jess, bailed on the party for Emma.

He'd gone overboard with the party prep to compensate, and a real, live Ravenna had become his Hail Mary. Now that she was here? He wanted to go back in time and buy himself a beer.

Ravenna had migrated from the two-dimensional cartoon world and landed on his front stoop. Man oh man, he loved her in 3D. How had he not noticed those pouty lips in her pictures online? The woman in front of him blinked, and the thick fringe of her eyelashes kissed her creamy cheeks.

They stared at each other. *Did Ravenna always give off a sexy vibe?*

Something low and primal tightened in his groin, and he began a silent mantra: *Focus on her eyes...focus on her eyes...focus on her eyes...*

"Um..." The princess raised a thick black eyebrow. "Is Mr. Stewart home?"

"Right here." He smiled and tapped his chest. "I'm Brendan. Come on in."

He pressed himself to the side to allow her room to enter the house. As the face painter princess crossed the threshold and passed him, her skirts caressed the floor. *Don't stare at her ass, don't stare at her ass, don't stare at her ass.*

"Wow. You...really resemble Ravenna."

"That's kind of the idea." She swished around and stuck out her hand. "I'm Zara Kissette, children's entertainer by day, starving artist by night."

He grabbed hold. Her fingers were long, tapered, and calloused, and her grip was firm. She eyeballed his stubble and rumpled plaid shirt. Might've been a good idea to shave and iron.

"Hi, I'm Grier." The second woman clumped into the house, towing a stubborn plastic crate behind her. He hadn't noticed her behind Zara on the porch. "I'm the photographer and party grunt."

"Can I help?" Brendan released Zara and stood aside to give Grier and the crate room to pass.

"What a gentleman," she answered. "Thank you, I've got it. But I'll be happy to give you my coat."

She shrugged off her red trench and stuffed her gloves into one of its sleeves. He took it from her and hung it in the foyer closet. Cold clung to the material. The princess, Zara, hadn't been wearing a coat. She must be freezing. Should he offer her coffee or tea to warm up?

When he turned back around, the two women were whispering to each other.

"You look familiar," Grier said. "Do we know each other?"

"I don't think so." He forced himself to keep eye contact with Grier. She was cute, but Zara was in a different league. A dark-haired, edgy league.

"I'm sure we've met at least once. I have a memory for faces. Professional hazard, but I won't torture you with twenty questions. The princess and I have a job to do, after all."

Zara narrowed her eyes at her friend, then asked Brendan, "Is the birthday girl here?"

He almost didn't hear her question over his silent *don't stare* mantra.

"She's out with my mom." He glanced at his watch. "They're due home in ten minutes." He dipped his gaze to her cleavage. *Whoops.*

"What about your wife?" Zara crossed her arms over her breasts and tilted her head.

"Ex, actually." He stuffed his hands into his pockets. "She's not coming."

"Oh, that's…hmm." She untangled her arms and darted her gaze around the house. "So, where do you want me?"

Where don't I? He riffled his hair. *Christ, Stewart, get it together.* "Follow me."

Hopefully she couldn't tell she'd flustered him. He wasn't normally this goofy about attractive women, but he hadn't mentally prepared for this scenario. He was in dad mode. All the other women who'd be here today were either relatives or married moms.

Not exactly potential flirting opportunities.

Probably didn't help he hadn't been with anyone since the divorce. Who had time? Dadding, work, and the gym absorbed his undivided attention. Or it *had*, right up until five minutes ago when this scorching woman entered his house.

Now, he could barely focus on anything besides the princess.

He had to squash that, and quick. Today was about his kid and making her feel special. Besides, the princess was here to do a job. He'd bet the last thing she wanted was a dad hitting on her at work. One thing was for sure—it would be nice to run into Zara out in the city sometime.

"So," Brendan said as he approached the end of the hallway. "I went nuts with the decorations."

He'd strewn hundreds of Ravennas on every surface in the family room. Banners, balloons, streamers, tablecloths, plates, cupcakes, and even a Ravenna pull-string piñata.

"Nah. This is rad. Your daughter will love it. Is that me, over there?" She pointed to a breakaway table in the corner, next to a picture window that overlooked a manicured yard.

"Yeah. Is it okay?"

"It's spiffy. Thanks." She maneuvered the table around a bit. "I like to create a flow where a line of kids can wait, hop into the chair to be painted, then exit without bumping into another kid right away."

Grier rolled the crate over, and Zara bent forward to free the lid.

Brendan replayed his mantra and stared at a cluster of balloons in the upper corner of the room. He had to, otherwise his gaze would slip to wildly inappropriate geographical highlights on Zara's body.

"Any predictions for which face paint design your daughter will want?" Grier unfurled a banner then taped it to the front of the table. Twenty portraits of face-painted children dotted its surface.

Brendan knelt in front of the table and peered at the pictures. "I'd bet the house on Ravenna." To Zara, he said, "These are cool. Are these your designs?"

"I'm taking light readings," Grier said to no one in particular and went as far into the opposite corner of the room as she could.

"Yes." Zara spilled her brushes on the table. "Grier gets the credit for the photos, but the designs are mine. Some are more inspired than others, and I always mix in non-*Rising* characters. A few girls are over it and want Wonder Woman or Maleficent. I'm dying for a girl to choose Frida Kahlo, but no takers as of yet. The boys always want Spider-Man or Ninja Turtles. Not much for the little dudes in *Rising*."

"I wouldn't say that." He thumbed the cleft in his chin. "I liked it. The message about loving yourself and not hiding what makes you unique is pretty powerful for kids."

"I thought the message was that marriage can be great, but shouldn't be everyone's end-goal."

"Both, when you think about it." He rose from his crouched position. Her quick, efficient hands organized the table in the blink of an eye. Watching people who were good at their gigs fascinated him, as did the gleam of her black nail polish, another perfect copy of the Ravenna look.

"I'm sure a Ph.D. candidate has written a thesis on it by now." Zara pointed a brush at him. "By the way, if I create a masterpiece on your daughter today, can I add her to my catalog?"

She smiled. The brightness of it blinded him. He wanted to get a smile from her again.

"Definitely. Anything I can help you with?"

Eagle-level boy scouting, Stewart. If he stayed busy, maybe he could clamp down on his urge to hit on the princess. This was not the time or the place. His five-year-old was about to skip through the door. Yet, here he was, laser-focused on Zara's perfect plum of a bottom lip.

This woman shut off the controlled, logical part of his brain.

"Um…" Her gaze flitted around her table. She snatched up a plastic container and held it out to him with a paint-splotched hand. "Could you fill this with water?"

"Sure." He took the cup and forced himself to ratchet his pace down to a mosey into the kitchen. The struggle to appear relaxed was real.

Zara called after him. "Are you a gamer? Or an evil genius plotting to take over the world?"

"What?" He glanced over his shoulder to see what prompted the question. Ah. She was staring at his workstation. It took over what had once been a breakfast nook. His heart swelled with pride at his home HQ.

Four enormous monitors formed a concave command-center, and several devices dotted the desk. Sleek bundles of cables dripped toward a computer tower below the desk. He'd taped a dozen of Emma's colorful butterfly, flower, and Ravenna drawings to the wall around the set-up.

"I game, but that's my office. I'm a software developer."

"Impressive." Zara lined her brushes up and arranged her paints in rainbow order. "By the way, do you have party music planned? I can play the *Rising* soundtrack. Unless you're sick of it by now."

"It's perfect—Emma loves it," Brendan called over the water rushing from the kitchen spigot.

"*Rising* on repeat, then."

"I'll try not to sing along." He returned to her station and held out the container. The moment stretched and slowed as her cool fingers grazed his. He knew it. The cold temperatures had gotten to her. He wanted to take her hands between his to warm them, to warm her.

Instead, he let the moment pass.

"Thanks." She settled the water among her paints, her eyelashes a thousand tiny whips on the curve of her cheeks. "What happened to your hand?"

He glanced at his raw knuckles. "I, uh…got into a fight with a wall."

Why the fuck did I admit that?

"Ah." She laughed. "Who won?"

"The wall. The wall always wins." He took stock of her table. "Need anything else?"

"Nope." She placed her hands on her hips. "I'm ready to paint facial masterpieces."

A zillion conversation topics slipped through his mind, but they were all ridiculous and inadequate. Because all he really wanted to ask this princess if she wanted to get a drink, get a meal, or get naked upstairs.

Jesus, did he need a cold shower? Yeah, it'd been three forevers since he'd been anywhere close to alone with a woman, but now was *not* the time for lust. A dozen kids and his family were seconds away from arriving.

On cue, a staccato honk sounded outside. His mom. They'd prearranged the weirdo honk as a signal.

"That's the birthday girl." Brendan glanced toward the hallway. "Can you make a big deal out of meeting her?"

"It'd be my pleasure."

The way her mouth shaped the word *pleasure* was almost too much. He hightailed it away from her, scrubbing the impure thoughts from his brain, and slapped on his dad cap on tight.

~ * ~

Zara picked up her skirts and minced to the middle of the family room, ready to play her part in his little girl's fantasy. Pinned to this spot, she drank in the way Brendan's rangy form loped down the hallway, like invisible rope was tied to his hips, drawing him forward.

Grier's digital SLR camera *thunked* next to Zara's ear.

"*Those* shots are for my personal collection." Grier held the camera aside and craned her neck. "Can you believe that guy's a dad? With that ass? If you can tell it's a fine ass through cargo shorts, you know it's a piece of art."

"He's okay." Zara ramrodded her spine to mimic the regal bearing of Princess Ravenna of Everly.

"Okay, huh?" Grier trained her lens on Zara. "Then why do you act like you want to lick him?"

"Shut up." She tucked a twist of raven-purple hair behind her ear. She'd admit nothing. And clean-cut dads in cargo shorts and polo shirts were not her type. Terse guys with arm cuffs were her normal speed. "Why are you so chatty with him, anyway?"

"Chatty? This is my gracious socialite training. I am full of etiquette, whereas you normally utter four words to the dads at these parties. Methinks you have a tiny crush."

"Don't be ridiculous."

"So, why'd you ask Hot Daddy if I could take a picture of his daughter for your poster?"

"Brendan. His name's Brendan."

"I don't care. He's still Hot Daddy. This is your last party, right? You've earned what you need to replenish your palette. Why would you need more face painting pics?"

"It slipped out." Zara gulped a lungful of sweet air. The whole house tasted of sugar. "Now, zip it. Here they come."

"Emma Bear." Brendan's voice, rumbly and rich, flowed from front door. "Close your eyes. I have a surprise for you, sweetheart."

Sweetheart. An endearment wrapped around an anchor. Her mother had sprinkled it throughout the conversation they had earlier this month, when Zara phoned to share the happy news about the Schwarz Gallery invitation.

That's nice, sweetheart, but I don't think it'll matter, will it? The year's almost up, and it's time for you to start paying back the tuition we loaned you. We're expecting you to move home and work it off at the Inn. Your bed's waiting for you...I don't understand why you're fussing, anyway. You can still paint in your free time here. The Beach Gallery always shows local artists' seascapes.

Zara clasped her hands and pointed rigid elbows out to the side. Yes, this was Ravenna's pose, but it helped stop her from dry heaving at the thought of painting imaginary seagulls swooping across a rosy sunset.

"What is it, Daddy?" a small voice asked.

"You'll see, Em."

Brendan reappeared, arm flexed around a sprite whose eyes were squeezed shut. The little girl was cute, but it was hard not to stare at how his blue shirt strained to contain his bicep. He pressed a finger to his full, kissable lips and winked at Zara.

Grier steadied her camera and snapped away.

A woman with a honey-colored bob—the grandmother, Zara guessed—captured the moment with her phone.

Brendan knelt and deposited three feet, nine inches of girl in front of Zara's skirts. From what she could observe, Emma was made of sugar, spice, and forty pounds of wild, curly, waist-length hair. Not to mention amazing style—the kid wore a tie-dyed, long-sleeve shirt, a purple tutu, and black mini-combat boots.

"Can I open my eyes, Daddy?" She clutched a Princess Ravenna of Everly action figure.

He made the "okay" signal with his thumb and forefinger. For a second, they locked gazes, and Zara couldn't breathe. She and Brendan were in cahoots on a delightful surprise, and the fizzy joy it caused shocked her to her core. Almost to the point where she'd forgotten her cue.

Whoops.

"You may indeed, Emma Stewart of Federal Hill," Zara said.

Emma blinked big moon eyes.

Zara held her breath and prepped for the weepy shrieking these encounters produced.

"Hi." The girl fluttered her tiny sausage fingers. "I'm Emma."

"Greetings, Emma." Zara peered down her nose, maintaining her royal stance. Kids normally lost their minds at this point, but Brendan's daughter furrowed a brow and planted a fist on her waist.

"Are you for real?" the little girl asked.

Zara folded herself with a dancer's grace until she stared into brown eyes flecked with green and gold. The same color as Brendan's. "Of course. Why would you doubt it, little one?"

Emma inspected Zara's face. She gasped when she glimpsed Princess Ravenna's delicate port-wine seashell birthmark, the Mark of Everly. Before each performance, Zara used her finest sable brush to paint this tiny, intricate symbol on the tender spot between her left cheekbone and her ear.

Emma's eyes went wide, and she dropped her Ravenna doll. "Eep!" The strangled noise escaped the little girl.

"You appear to be quite excited, Emma."

Emma bounced on her toes and her curls jangled like yo-yos on elastic strings. To settle her, Zara clasped the girl's shoulders and rubbed her thumbs along Emma's avian bones.

"I'm excited to meet you too."

Emma threw her arms around Zara's neck and squished her cheek next to hers. "I love you."

As Zara's heart melted a few degrees for the kid, Emma coughed. Right onto Zara's face. A small puff of air. Nothing liquid, or phlegmy about it. Obviously, the kid had just infected Zara with Hantavirus.

"Sorry, sorry, sorry." Emma squeaked and covered her mouth.

"Don't let it trouble you, little one." She kept the Ravenna veneer buckled on tight, but she yearned to dunk her face in antibacterial gel. It would suck hard if she got sick. She'd have to skip teaching at the retirement home for a week because she couldn't risk infecting the residents, which meant her grocery money would be down the drain.

No sense worrying about it now. Time to concentrate on today's job.

"Emma, may I paint your face?" She led Emma to the poster with the design options.

"Brend?" The grandmother said. "I'll set up the snacks in the kitchen."

"Thanks, Mom."

She smiled at Zara. "Nice to meet you, by the way. I'm Robin."

"Princess Ravenna, at your service." Zara bowed. To Brendan, she said, "I'm sure you want a design as well. Maybe a lion? Or a bear?"

He laughed. "No thanks."

"I want this, please." Emma jabbed at the Ravenna design.

"Excellent choice." Zara helped Emma into the chair. "Now, do you promise to hold still?"

Emma nodded and folded her hands in her lap. "You're pretty."

"Why thank you." Zara smiled. She surveyed Emma's face, identifying the perfect place to start. "Ready? Here we go."

Zara lifted a brush, and her shoulders relaxed.

The brush brought peace.

Lost in the paint, she dipped the brush into the deep purple pot, slanted Emma's face a fraction to the side, and went to work. This was always the best part of these parties. No matter what medium she chose, the act of creating, of making an interesting image, satisfied her like nothing else could.

She rested the tip of the brush at the bridge of Emma's nose and swept upward in confident strokes. A seashell unfurled over the expanse of Emma's forehead, followed soon by ribbons of color curling across her temples. Zara swapped the brush for another tipped in silver shimmer, and then another covered in black, layering highlights and shadows to give depth to the design.

Behind her, Grier clicked and clunked to document the transformation.

In three minutes flat, Zara painted a masterpiece on her wriggly canvas. Time for the finishing touches… She fixed a series of adhesive gemstones across Emma's cheekbones and a final, larger one above the bridge of her nose.

"Here you are, little one." Zara picked up an elaborate hand mirror from her array of party props and showed Emma the results.

"I'm handsome." She nudged the emerald on the apple of her cheek.

"You sure are, sweetheart." Brendan's voice came from close behind Zara, low, intimate, as if he'd whispered in her ear. Heat collected at the nape of her neck and oozed, thick and languorous, down her spine.

She stiffened.

"Sorry." He placed a steady hand on the naked patch of her back, right above the band of the breastplate. "Did I startle you? I didn't mean to sneak up on you. I wanted a closer peek at Emma."

Sparks erupted into fire where his palm pressed against her exposed skin, and the fire spread along Zara's neck and to her cheeks. Her ears must be melting from her head.

She cleared her throat and glanced at him with her peripheral vision. "It's fine. I'm fine."

She was not fine. She was about a million degrees hotter than fine.

He dropped his hand, but didn't leave. Zara willed him to go away to give her a chance to tranquilize the reaction her body had to him. With him right here, her body temperature couldn't cool. Grumble. Why wouldn't he go away?

"Em, be sure to sit still to let it dry," he warned.

Zara busied herself by cleaning her brushes. She swirled the purple-tipped brush in the water, clouding the clear liquid.

The doorbell chimed.

"My friends are here!" Emma scrambled from the chair and sprinted toward the front door.

"Be right back." He jogged after Emma.

"Zara." Grier snapped a few pictures. "You're blushing."

"Fuck off." Zara stabbed the wet paintbrush into a thick pile of paper towels.

"Well, well, well." Grier laughed. "I've hit a nerve. You *do* have a crush on Hot Daddy."

"Fuck off twice." She glared at the camera lens, imagining Grier's unblinking eye on the other side.

"You should ask him out."

Murmured greetings and high-pitched giggles swirled down the hall.

"I'm titling these shots *Besotted*." Grier snapped more pictures of Zara.

"Can you act like a professional, please?" She clasped her hands and resumed a majestic pose. The partygoers would tumble into the family room at any moment.

"I will. As soon as I am a professional."

Emma reappeared. She spread her arms wide. "Guys, look! It's Ravenna!"

The passel of little girls following Emma squealed like teakettles. The energy of it blew Zara back a pace. It had taken her a dozen parties to understand that this moment was the kid equivalent of meeting a squee-worthy collage of your favorite actress, athlete, and president.

"Welcome," Zara announced in a voice an octave deeper than normal, "to Emma's fifth birthday party. To celebrate, you may choose a face-paint design."

Slightly terrified by the number of children popping up around her, Zara gestured to the poster in front of the table. Wide-eyed girls clustered around it, each shouting their choice of design.

The doorbell rang, and a few seconds later two young boys and their pixie of a mother joined the party. Brendan greeted Pixie with an ursine hug and an enormous smile.

What was this twist in Zara's gut all about?

Someone small tugged on her skirt. A girl with a fine curtain of bright blonde hair lisped, "Can I be Ravenna?"

"Of course, little one." Zara patted the seat of the chair. "Hop up here."

Over the next half-hour, she cycled through the children and produced four Ravennas, Wonder Woman, a butterfly, a puppy, and two Teenage Mutant Ninja Turtles.

She was impressed she hadn't screwed any of them up, considering the constant furtive glances she shot toward Brendan and Pixie.

As Zara cleaned her brushes, the opening strains of the *Rising* anthem trickled from the speaker. The girls mimed Ravenna's blocking from the famous questing scene, extending their arms on the same lyric, pretending to throw shadows and darkness at their enemies. Emma caught her father's shirttail and dragged him into the fray, and he didn't hesitate. In fact, it appeared as though he might be leading the little girls through the choreography.

Zara chuckled at the sight of this grown man enthusiastically dancing with a gaggle of tiny children. His ease with them made her heart happy. Most of the dads at these parties tended to busy themselves with the practical set-up stuff, and then hang back in the corner on their phones.

He flicked a glance her way, and crap, he'd caught her staring at him. As the song came to a close, he eased next to her. The warmth from his body skimmed her skin.

"You did a nice job," he said.

"Thanks." She dabbed a brush against a paper towel. "I'll knight Emma next, and then we'll take pictures."

"Gotcha." He scratched the back of his neck, showing off his triceps. "Do you want me to do anything?"

Zara's flesh prickled.

Yeah. I want you to kiss me until I can't think straight.

What the hell? Where had *that* come from?

"No." She cleared her throat. "Thanks though. Whoops, there's the end of the song." She killed the music app on her phone and emerged from behind the worktable. "Children," she said, "gather 'round. We're here to celebrate Emma's birthday."

"Yeah." Emma pumped her tiny fists in the air. "I'm five."

The kids collected in a wiggly group in front of her. Zara glanced at Brendan. With his arms crossed over his chest, his biceps, triceps, and Jesus Christ, *all* of him bulged against his sleeves.

The soft-bellied models she'd sketched during freshman year's The Human Body class were nothing like him. If those guys had resembled the man in front of her now, she would've gone to class more often.

She shifted her attention to Emma and unsheathed a sword.

"Can I hold your sword?" Emma asked.

"No." Zara shook her head and tapped the little girl's shoulders with the blunt blade. "I dub thee Lady Emma. Lady Emma, I call you to my service. Will you be brave?"

"Yes," she shouted. "Can I hold your sword now?"

"Nope." Zara knelt next to Emma and winced when the breastplate's stiff leather dug into her hips. "We will, however, pose for a photo."

"Okay." Emma threw herself at Zara like she expected to be caught. Which she was, but still, that was weirdly trusting of the little girl. As they cuddled for the pictures, Zara caught the scent of strawberries from Emma's untamed ringlets.

Grier snapped a few shots, then called over the other children and arranged them so their painted faces were visible.

"Now," she shouted over the restless children, "on the count of three, yell, 'monkey feet.'"

Half of the giggling children did as they were told. Grier's flash fired a few times, and she reviewed the pictures on the camera's display. "Got it."

"Okay, kids, who's ready for a game of pin-the-tail on Kilda?" Emma's grandmother asked. Kilda was Ravenna's horse.

"Me!" the kids yelled and scattered.

"Emma." Zara held the little girl's shoulder. "I must take my leave now."

"Why do you have to go?" Emma's lower lip puffed out. "I don't want you to."

"Everly needs me. I will always carry you in my heart." She smoothed a curl from Emma's face. "It has been a pleasure to attend your party."

Emma wrapped her arms around Zara's neck and squeezed. Whoa, this tiny girl was refreshingly free with her affection and zero percent shy. For a second, she let herself sink into the embrace.

"Thank you for coming to my party, Ravenna."

"You're welcome, little one."

Emma let go and scurried toward the basement to join her friends. Zara rose, brushed her skirts, then started toward the table to tidy up.

"Hang on, Princess." Grier touched Zara's sleeve.

She did not trust the impish expression on Grier's face. The first time she'd worn it, they'd crashed a senior's rooftop party and gotten footless drunk on Jungle Juice, a deadly strong grain alcohol and fruit punch cocktail. Lucky for them, Melinda had abstained and had gotten them home safe. Zara darted her gaze around the room. Lots of fruit punch, definitely no booze. What was Grier up to?

"Emma's Dad?" she called across the room. "Let's get a shot of you and Ravenna."

He raked his hand through his hair. "Okay."

"You're such an asshole," Zara said from the corner of her mouth.

Grier winked.

He stood next to Zara. "Like this?"

"Closer." Grier held the camera in front of her face. "Now, Princess, hook your arm around his."

If Zara could transform into Ravenna and command the princess's magical powers, she would, without question, throw shadow daggers at Grier's head.

Instead, she wrapped her arm around Brendan's. Oh. Was he smuggling bowling balls under his sleeves? He gazed at her and smiled, and the heat pooling in her belly all afternoon rushed everywhere. No way he'd miss the stupid exuberant blushes now.

"This is like a prom photo, isn't it?" he asked.

"I didn't go to prom." She glared at Grier and mouthed, "I'll kill you."

"Smile, Princess," Grier said.

The flashbulb blinded her.

"Nice." Grier reviewed the picture on the back of her camera, shoulders quaking. "Total keeper. I'll start packing up."

Zara let out a long, measured breath and unwound from Brendan, hyperconscious of the way the polo's cotton buffed the palm of her hand. Besides Grier, the two of them were alone in the family room.

"That's pretty much it for the whimsy, except for this," she said, fished around in her skirt pocket.

Aha, there it was. She held her fist out to him, palm up.

"What is it?" he asked.

"A miniature. Here." She opened her fingers. The tiny portrait she painted of Emma as part of the standard party package lay in the center of her palm. "It's a keepsake for Emma. Or you, I guess."

"Wow." His fingertips kissed her palm as he took the portrait. He shifted the tiny likeness, inspecting its intricacies. "Did you paint this?"

She tipped her lips up into a smile. "I did. I based it on the picture you sent when you booked me."

"I didn't expect this." He glanced at her and flashed the dimples. "You must hear this all the time, but you have a gift. How did you capture Emma's personality without even meeting her?"

Wow, those dimples. There goes the swoony. Is it hot in here? Stupid eleven million layers of dress and leather are making me sweat.

Zara plucked at the linen peeping above her leather breastplate to encourage a breeze to cool her heaving chest. "You like it, then?"

God, would the flush in her cheeks stop? She must look like she has scarlet fever.

"I love it." He nestled the portrait among the photos on the mantelpiece.

Whomever, whatever sculpted his ass deserved first place in the show.

"Uh, rad," she muttered. She shifted her gaze to his rounded shoulders. Nope. Didn't help. The way his muscles strained the stitches of his shirt made her blood pound faster.

She redirected her view toward the safe, non-Brendan direction of the kitchen. The bobbed mom mafia hovered near the veggie tray. One of them, Pixie, clutched a carrot stick and beamed at them like she'd stumbled across a double rainbow.

"So, Zara…" He scratched the nape of his neck.

Pixie's smile grew wider. Was she elbowing his mother to get her attention? Ugh, what was it with her? Why were they staring? Whatever. Zara had to escape this foreign land stuffed with sugar and kindness.

"Time to go. While the kids are downstairs, it's time to pull my Cinderella routine and disappear. We'll get our stuff and catch our carriage home."

"Hang on." He touched her elbow, setting off the glitter bomb on her insides. "I wanted to ask you something."

Out Now!

What's next on your reading list?

Champagne Book Group promises to bring to readers fiction at its finest.

Discover your next
fine read!
http://www.champagnebooks.com/

We are delighted to invite you to receive exclusive rewards. Join our Facebook group for VIP savings, bonus content, early access to new ideas we've cooked up, learn about special events for our readers, and sneak peeks at our fabulous titles.

Join now.
https://www.facebook.com/groups/ChampagneBookClub/

www.ingramcontent.com/pod-product-compliance
Lightning Source LLC
Chambersburg PA
CBHW030105260626
47156CB00008B/2527